Eileen knew she should not be focusing on Simon's charming smile.

"I've always heard one should be cautious when dealing with a woman who insists on having the last word." Simon shook his head with an exaggeratedly solemn expression that was belied by the twinkle in his eyes.

"As you should be. Most women with that trait tend to have a quick mind and a sharp wit."

He chuckled. "I'll keep that in mind." And with a wave, he turned and sauntered away.

Had they actually been flirting? Eileen shook her head to clear it. Time to concentrate her efforts on something productive, like the mending that sat in her sewing basket.

Strange, though, how difficult it had become to complete even the simplest of tasks. Surely it was due to nothing more than the presence of so many houseguests.

As she accidentally jabbed the needle into her thumb, she acknowledged that perhaps there just might be something more specific tugging at her focus.

Winnie Griggs
and
Karen Kirst

Her Holiday Family
&
The Sheriff's
Christmas Twins

LOVE INSPIRED
INSPIRATIONAL ROMANCE

LOVE INSPIRED®

INSPIRATIONAL ROMANCE

Recycling programs
for this product may
not exist in your area.

ISBN-13: 978-1-335-45674-8

Her Holiday Family and The Sheriff's Christmas Twins

Copyright © 2021 by Harlequin Books S.A.

Her Holiday Family
First published in 2014. This edition published in 2021.
Copyright © 2014 by Winnie Griggs

The Sheriff's Christmas Twins
First published in 2016. This edition published in 2021.
Copyright © 2016 by Karen Vyskocil

This edition published by arrangement with Harlequin Books S.A.

For questions and comments about the quality of this book, please contact us
at CustomerService@Harlequin.com.

Love Inspired
22 Adelaide St. West, 40th Floor
Toronto, Ontario M5H 4E3, Canada
www.LoveInspired.com

Printed in U.S.A.

CONTENTS

Winnie Griggs is a multipublished, award-winning author of historical—and occasionally contemporary—romances that focus on small towns, big hearts and amazing grace. She is also a list maker and a lover of dragonflies, and holds an advanced degree in the art of procrastination. Winnie loves to hear from readers—you can connect with her on Facebook at Facebook.com/winniegriggs.author or email her at winnie@winniegriggs.com.

Books by Winnie Griggs

Love Inspired Historical

Texas Grooms

Visit the Author Profile page
at LoveInspired.com for more titles.

HER HOLIDAY FAMILY

Winnie Griggs

If anyone among you thinks he is religious, and does not bridle his tongue but deceives his own heart, this one's religion is useless. Pure and undefiled religion before God our Father is this: to visit orphans and widows in their trouble, and to keep oneself unspotted from the world.

—*James 1:26–27*

To my marvelous Starbucks writing buddies, Connie and Amy, who helped me smooth over rough spots and figure out what direction to take my characters when I lost my way. And to my wonderful editor, Melissa Endlich, who always helps me tweak my stories and nudges me to take my writing to the next level.

Chapter One

Simon stood at the front of the church with hat in hand, trying very hard not to look as rattled as he felt. Ten orphan kids—TEN!—all looking to him to turn this disaster around and set their world to rights again. What in blue blazes did a bachelor like him know about taking care of kids, especially so many of them?

When he'd agreed to this venture he sure hadn't counted on ending up as the sole caretaker of these kids. But they *were* his responsibility now, and he'd have to see it through.

Sending up a silent "Lord help me" prayer, Simon made himself smile in what he hoped was a relaxed, neighborly fashion as he watched the members of the small-town congregation file into the hastily called emergency meeting. He and the kids were strangers here—didn't know a soul—and he had no idea what to expect from these people. If they didn't help him, he wasn't sure what in the world he was going to do.

The children stood lined up in front of him, and they edged closer together as the church began to fill. Some of them held hands, as if trying to draw strength from each other. He could do with a bit of that himself, but unfortunately he was on his own—just like always.

Fern, a much-too-serious thirteen-year-old, was looking out for the youngest, as usual. Three-year-old Molly and four-year-old Joey stood on either side of her, holding on to her hand. He quickly checked over the rest of them, feeling a little kick of relief at the way they held themselves. He knew they were worried and scared, but not one of them uttered a word, and all the tears had been dried before they left the confusion of the train depot. Miss Fredrick had taught them well.

He glanced over their heads, studying these strangers who held his and the children's fate in their hands—at least for the next few days. He disliked the idea of begging for handouts, but for the sake of his charges he would swallow his pride.

If there was ever a time he needed help, it was now. Hopefully there was a motherly sort out there who would know what to do and would be willing to take care of his charges.

At least he wasn't facing these folks entirely alone. The town's minister, Reverend Harper, stood at his side with his wife and daughter nearby. Thank goodness someone had had the presence of mind to call the clergyman in when they'd arrived. The reverend had assured him that the folks in his congregation were generous, warmhearted people who would help in any way they could.

As the people settled into the pews, he noted their expressions were a mix of curiosity and sympathy. Most offered encouraging smiles to the children. How many had already learned of their situation?

When it appeared the last person had taken a seat, Reverend Harper stepped forward. "Thank you all for responding to the bells and joining us here on such short notice." He motioned toward Simon. "This gentleman is Mr. Simon Tucker and he'd like to introduce these fine children to you."

Ready or not, he was up. How best to personalize these children for the congregation? Considering he'd only gotten to know them himself over this past week or so, it wouldn't be easy.

He laid his hand lightly on Fern's shoulder. "This young lady is Fern. She's thirteen and the oldest of the children. She's very responsible and is always looking out for the younger ones."

He moved his hand to the shoulder of the boy on her right. "This little man here is Joey. Joey is four and loves animals." Joey had told him more than once that Miss Fredrick had promised him he could have a dog when they reached Hatcherville, and it was as if she'd promised him the moon.

Simon shifted to the child on Fern's left. "And this little sweet pea is Molly. She's three and the youngest of our group." Molly slipped her thumb in her mouth, and Simon couldn't find it in his heart to blame her.

Next he moved on to the children he had the closest ties to. "These two are Audrey and Albert. They're seven years old and twins." They were also his niece and nephew.

He quickly went down the row, introducing the rest of the children—Rose, Lily, Tessa, Harry and Russell—trying to mention something positive about each of them. His gut told him it was important that these folks feel sympathy for the children.

When he was done, Reverend Harper spoke up again. "Thank you, Mr. Tucker." He signaled his wife and daughter. "Now, while we grown-ups talk, Mrs. Harper and Constance will escort the children over to Daisy's Restaurant, where Abigail is planning to serve them up a nice hot meal."

Several of the children looked to Simon for reassurance. It once again drove home how dependent they now were on him. Scary thought. But he smiled and nodded.

Mrs. Harper took Lily's hand while her daughter Constance took the hands of the twins. Together the whole lot of them filed out.

Simon resisted the urge to rake his hand through his hair. He needed to make a proper impression on these people.

When the little troupe had made their exit, Reverend Harper spoke up again, placing a hand on Simon's shoulder. "Mr. Tucker finds himself in need of our assistance, and I've assured him that the people of Turnabout are up to the challenge. As some of you may already know, there was an emergency on the train when it pulled into town this morning that required Dr. Pratt's services. It turned out to be very serious indeed. I'll let Mr. Tucker tell you more about what's happening."

Simon nodded to the clergyman. "Thank you, Reverend Harper." Then he turned to the people seated in the pews. "The lady who is now in Dr. Pratt's care, Miss Georgina Fredrick, is the guardian of the children you just met. I was escorting her and the children to a new home that's waiting for them in Hatcherville. But just before we pulled into the station here, she had an attack of some sort. Your Dr. Pratt tells me she suffered a stroke. And her outlook isn't good."

He was encouraged by the sympathetic looks focused his way. But would it translate to action? "First, let me tell you a little about this dear lady. Miss Fredrick is a warm, generous and caring person. For the past nine years she's opened her home to children who had nowhere else to go. Over that time, all of those children you just met have been left in her care and have found not only a safe home but have formed a family bond as strong as any blood kin." His admiration for the woman knew no bounds. To his way of thinking there was no higher calling than to care for children.

He let his gaze roam across the people seated before him, briefly holding a gaze here and there before moving on. "Recently Miss Fredrick decided that her existing home in St. Louis could no longer accommodate her stretched-to-its-limits household. So I helped her find a new place. That's where we were headed. I'm here because she asked me to provide an escort for her and the children, and to help them get settled in."

He slid the brim of his hat through his fingers. "We obviously can't move on until she's recovered enough to travel." *Please God, see that she* does *recover.* "So what I'm asking you folks for is a place for me and the kids to stay while we await that outcome." Had he said too much? Not enough? He prayed he'd touched their hearts in some way. Simon drew back his shoulders. "I figure you all might have some questions for me before you respond, so feel free to fire away."

A plump woman in the second row stood. "May I ask what your actual relationship is to Miss Fredrick and these children?"

"My sister Sally was Miss Fredrick's housekeeper for a number of years and helped her care for the children." He felt his chest constrict as he remembered his feisty younger sister. "Sally passed away three months ago, and Miss Fredrick continued to give her two children a home when I could not." He would be forever grateful to the woman for taking in Audrey and Albert—goodness knows she was able to give them a better home than he ever could.

A tall bearded man near the back of the church stood. "Have these children been given a Christian upbringing?"

"Absolutely. Miss Fredrick sees that they attend church services regularly and reading from the Bible is part of their daily routine." He gave what he hoped was a reassuring smile. "And just so you know, they've also been taught proper manners and behavior."

Apparently satisfied, the man sat back down. After a short silence, Reverend Harper stepped forward. "If there are no other questions for Mr. Tucker, we need to discuss his request for temporary lodgings for himself and the children. Is there anyone willing to step up and answer this call?"

To Simon's relief, a number of hands went up. At least he'd be able to lay *that* worry aside.

"I can take three or four of them in."

"I can take two."

"I can take one."

"I can take three."

As the offers came in Simon's optimism faded. He held up his hand to halt the offers. "That's mighty generous of you folks, but I'm afraid there's been a little misunderstanding. I need to keep them all together right now." The idea of splitting them up brought back unpleasant memories of how he and his sisters had been farmed out all those years ago. But it was more than that. "It's not that I don't appreciate your very kind offers, but since these children are in my sole care right now, I need to be able to keep an eye on all of them. And separating them when they're already feeling so anxious about their foster mother is just going to upset them more."

That announcement was greeted with an uncomfortable silence. What was he going to do if they couldn't make this work? He'd promised he wouldn't separate them—he personally knew how wrenching that could be. Even if they all had to sleep on pallets on the floor, it would be preferable to scattering them, especially now when they needed each other.

He tried again. "It's not as if they each need their own room. They're used to sharing tight quarters."

Reverend Harper cleared his throat. "I think we all understand and sympathize with your reasoning, Mr. Tucker, but what you're asking is a mighty tall order to fill. There are eleven of you, after all."

The reverend said that as if Simon weren't already painfully aware of the situation.

But before he could respond, the man continued. "You may have to accept the need to separate them for a few days. We can likely find accommodations for two large groups, but there's not many households large enough to accept eleven guests for an overnight—"

He paused as if he'd just had an idea, and Simon immediately felt his hope rise. Had the man come up with a solution? Simon was ready to grasp at any straw.

Reverend Harper had looked to the pews on the

right-hand side of the church as if seeking someone out. "Unless... Ah, there you are, Mrs. Pierce. Perhaps you would allow us to impose on *your* generosity?"

Simon followed the minister's gaze, trying to figure out who he was looking at. Then a slender, blonde woman, dressed in the purple and gray of half mourning, stood. There was something arresting about her. She was taller than the average woman and held herself with an elegant grace, but it was more than that. Aloof, cool, distant—she seemed not so much a part of this gathering as a disinterested observer. Her face seemed expressionless, but her thickly lashed brown eyes seemed to miss nothing.

And yet he sensed something vulnerable about her, a just-below-the-surface fragility that tugged at him.

While her expression gave nothing away, he had the distinct impression this ice queen was not going to go along with the reverend's verbal arm-twisting happily.

Which didn't bode well for just how "motherly" she would be toward the children.

As all eyes in the church turned her way expectantly, Eileen Pierce hid her surprise, maintaining the composed, disinterested pose that was second nature to her.

She had just been thinking how shocked her neighbors, who had ignored or outright snubbed her for the past two years, would be if she volunteered her home. The idea had amused her, almost to the point that she'd been tempted to do it just to see the scandalized looks on their faces.

Almost. Because she hadn't had any real intention of doing so.

God had seen fit not to give her any children of her

own, and she'd come to accept that there was a reason for that—she wasn't the kind of woman who was cut out to be a mother. She wouldn't know what to do with one child, much less ten.

But she wasn't truly surprised that Reverend Harper had turned to her, even though she was persona non grata in Turnabout. After all, she owned the largest house in town, one that could easily accommodate these stranded visitors. But as satisfying as it would be to dispense a bit of noblesse oblige, it wasn't worth the risk. Opening her doors to so many outsiders would mean exposing how far she'd actually fallen from her days as the wife of the town's wealthiest and most prominent businessman.

For just a moment, however, she was disconcerted by the way Mr. Tucker looked at her, as if she were his lifeline. She could feel the impact of his intently focused blue eyes from all the way across the room. It had been some time since she'd felt herself the object of such interest. She finally recognized the emotion—he *needed* her. She couldn't remember a time when anyone truly needed her. And she wasn't certain how she felt about it now.

Eileen gave her head a mental shake, refocusing on the current situation. She couldn't let herself be distracted by such frivolous emotions. Or by a winning smile from a man with intriguing blue eyes and hair the color of rich, loamy soil.

Still trying to figure out how to extricate herself, she gave a nonanswer. "I assume by that question you are asking me to open my home to the entire group."

Before Reverend Harper or the stranger could speak up, Eunice Ortolon, the town's most notorious busybody, stood. "Excuse me, Reverend, but while Mrs. Pierce's home is large enough, surely that shouldn't be the only consideration." The woman drew her shoulders back. "While I understand Mr. Tucker not wanting to separate the children, perhaps it would be best to house them in two or three homes with families that are more—" she cut a quick look Eileen's way "—let us say, accustomed to dealing with children."

Eileen stiffened. Eunice might as well have used the word *suitable*—it was so obviously there in her tone.

Ivy Parker, the only other person sharing Eileen's pew, and the closest thing she had to a friend here, stood up immediately. "As a former boarder of Eileen's, I can attest to the fact that her home would be the perfect place to house these children—her home is both roomy and welcoming." She gave Eileen an encouraging smile. "That is, if she feels so led to make the offer."

Eileen appreciated that Ivy had come to her defense, but now was not the time for everyone to suddenly approve of her. Unfortunately she could see several folks giving her tentative smiles of encouragement.

The urge to give in to her frustration was strong, and Eileen maintained her impassive expression by sheer force of will. She wanted so much to be accepted by the community again, but this was not the way.

Of course there were still those, like Mrs. Ortolon, who looked either hesitant or disapproving.

How in the world could she extricate herself without sounding selfish and uncaring?

And why was she so oddly reluctant to disappoint Mr. Tucker?

Chapter Two

Eileen decided to buy herself some time with a question. "How long do you suppose you and the children would need a place to stay, Mr. Tucker?"

He didn't seem to take offense at her question. "I wish I could tell you, ma'am, but to be honest, I can't really say. We're completely dependent on when Miss Fredrick recovers enough to travel again. And Dr. Pratt couldn't give me any indication of when that might be."

It was the answer she'd expected. "You have my sympathies, sir. But you must understand, boarding so many individuals for an extended length of time is quite a challenge, regardless of the size of one's home. Especially on such short notice."

"As I said," Mrs. Ortolon declared in a self-righteous tone, "the children will be better off if we send them to smaller but more suitable homes."

The words and the tone they were delivered in got Eileen's back up again, though she refused to show it. It was the stab of disappointment and frustration that she saw in Mr. Tucker's eyes, however, that prodded her next words. "I didn't say I *wouldn't* invite them in, Eunice, merely that it would be a challenge."

"You *do* have the space to house us all, though?" Mr. Tucker pressed.

At her nod, he continued. "I wouldn't ask this if it wasn't important, ma'am. The children need the comfort of each other's company right now. I'd be mighty grateful to you if you could see your way to providing that for them. If you'd find it in your heart to provide them with a place to stay, I promise to do my best to keep them out of your way. I assure you they are well behaved." Then he flashed her a disarmingly self-deprecating smile. "Or as well behaved as kids their age can be expected to be."

She nodded again, entranced by the friendly warmth of his manner. "Of course."

"Does that mean you'll do it?" His expression held a guarded hopefulness that she couldn't bear to disappoint.

"I suppose I will."

No sooner had she uttered the words than she came to her senses. Why had she said that? This was a disaster. There was no way she could keep her state of affairs hidden in the face of such an invasion.

But before she could find a way to take it back, she found herself being thanked and applauded by various members of the congregation.

Ivy stood. "Since you're providing the housing, I believe I speak for all the members of the Ladies Auxiliary in saying we will do our part to help in other ways." She looked around the church, where she received a number of nods, then back at Eileen. "We can provide meals and anything else you might need to help accommodate your new guests."

Eileen wasn't particularly pleased by the offer. After all, she was *not* a charity case to be accepting handouts. If she was going to do this, then she would do it in a manner befitting her position. "I appreciate the offer but there is no need." She kept her tone polite. It would stretch the limits of her pantry if the group stayed with her more than three or four days, but she would manage somehow. Better to go hungry later than have folks think she was unable to provide for her guests.

Ivy gave her an uncomfortably perceptive look, then spoke again. "It's very commendable of you to do this, Eileen," she said in a gentle tone, "but you're already opening your home to our visitors. Surely you won't rob the rest of us of the joy that comes with sharing our blessings."

Bless Ivy for coming up with the perfect way to help her save face. "Of course not." Eileen waved a hand in gracious surrender. "Since you feel so strongly about this, I will defer to the Ladies Auxiliary to provide the meals."

"Excellent." Reverend Harper beamed approval at his flock, then turned back to Eileen. "Mrs. Pierce, your generosity does you great credit."

His words made her feel like a fraud, so she held her tongue.

But the reverend seemed not to expect a response. Instead he clapped Mr. Tucker on the back. "I told you these people would rise to the occasion."

"Thank you folks." Mr. Tucker executed a short bow in her direction. "And you especially, Mrs. Pierce." He left the preacher's side and approached her with a broad smile on his face.

Ivy stepped out of their shared pew to allow him to step in.

"You have no idea what a wonderful thing you've done for the children," he said, stepping past Ivy.

Goodness, was the man planning to join her in the pew? She should have followed Ivy into the aisle.

Keeping her features carefully schooled, Eileen nodded. The whole congregation was watching them and the pew suddenly seemed crowded. The impact of his warm smile and deep blue eyes was even more arresting up close. And he was a good half foot taller than her.

It didn't help her equanimity that her feelings of being a fraud had deepened. "There is no need for thank-yous," she said stiffly. "One does what one can to help those in need."

There was a flicker of something she couldn't quite read in his eyes, then his smile returned. "Nevertheless, you have my gratitude. I don't have much money to offer you, but I'm a handyman and cabinetmaker by trade. I'd certainly be willing to repay you by taking care of any repairs or other work around your place that needs attending to."

There were certainly a number of things that could use a handyman's touch around her place. Eileen allowed a small smile to escape her lips. "Thank you, Mr. Tucker. We shall see." Then she took a mental step back again. "I will, of course, need time to get everything prepared for your stay."

He spread his hands. "Understood. Will a couple of hours be sufficient?"

She'd like to have more time, but she supposed she

couldn't ask him to keep ten children standing around indefinitely. And besides, more time would not make her sold-off furnishings magically reappear. "I shall see that it is."

His smile grew warmer. "Again, thank you. And please don't go to a lot of trouble. All we really need is a place for everyone to sleep."

If he only knew—she was going to have trouble providing very much more than the bare necessities.

"I don't want you to feel like you're in this alone." Ivy's words brought her back to the here and now. "Tell us what you think you'll need, besides help with the meals."

Eileen considered that a moment. She supposed she shouldn't let the children suffer for her pride. "Some extra bedding would be helpful."

"Of course. I'll work with the Ladies Auxiliary to round some up for you."

Eve Dawson approached them with a smile for Mr. Tucker. "After the children finish their meals at the restaurant, bring them down to the sweet shop and I'll treat them to some candy."

Mr. Tucker turned his smile her way, and Eileen felt an unaccountable stab of jealousy that it wasn't still directed at her.

"That's going to really perk up their spirits," he said. "Thank you."

Eileen took herself in hand. That little prickle of jealousy was a clear indication she'd let her guard down much too far. That wouldn't do at all.

The meeting broke up, and folks were chatting in clusters or slowly filing out. He had his back to her now, releasing her from the strain of keeping her expression neutral under his gaze. Instead she had a view of the back of his head. His hair was worn shorter than what was usual for the men around here. But she decided it suited him.

Then she straightened. What in the world was she doing thinking of such things, especially about a stranger? Just because the man had looked kindly at her was no reason to get moon-eyed over him.

Mr. Tucker's hand was being shaken and encouraging words said to him, giving Eileen time to gather her wits. A quick glance toward the front of the church revealed several members of the Ladies Auxiliary were already gathering.

She mentally winced. At one time she'd been head of the Ladies Auxiliary and now, despite the face-saving efforts of Ivy, guests in her home had become the object of their charitable efforts, and by extension, she had, as well. What a long way she'd fallen since her husband's ignominious death two years ago. If her mother were still alive today she would be mortified, but probably not surprised, by her daughter's loss of status in the community.

Time to get some air. "If you will excuse me, I should return home and prepare the house to receive guests."

Mr. Tucker stepped out into the aisle to let her pass. "Please allow me to escort you home."

She again felt that tingle at his friendly, dare she say approving, smile. And again she strove to ignore it. "Thank you, but it's only a few blocks away and I'm sure you want to get back to the children."

But Mr. Tucker didn't take her hint. He raised a brow with a teasing look. "I insist. The kids are in good hands for the moment. Besides, not only will this allow me the pleasure of your company, but accompanying you will let me know where your place is so I can escort the children there when it's time."

Before she could protest again, he turned serious. "And there are probably a few things we should talk about before I bring the children around."

There was no polite way to refuse such a request. "In that case, I accept." Again she'd acted against her better judgment.

She would definitely have to watch her step with this one.

Simon allowed his soon-to-be-hostess to precede him from the church building. She had returned to the cool, aloof individual she'd been when she first stood up in the meeting. Usually he had no use for pretentiousness and haughty airs. He'd seen too much of that in the home of his Uncle Corbitt, the man who'd taken him in when his folks died.

But for a few minutes he'd seen behind the mask she wore to a warmer, more vibrant woman. And that intrigued him, made him think that perhaps she was a person worth getting to know better. And she had, after all, opened her home to him and the kids. He could forgive her a lot for that.

But which one was the real Mrs. Pierce—the ice queen or the vulnerable, warmhearted lady? It would be interesting to find out.

He'd sensed some uneasy undercurrents between this woman and the rest of the townsfolk, and that, too, intrigued him. Not that the situation was any of his business. Besides, he preferred to form his own opinions about folks rather than pay attention to hearsay and gossip.

And the fact that she wasn't exactly enthusiastic about having them as guests—that just made it doubly generous of her to have done so as far as he was concerned.

As for that standoffishness she wore like armor—he was just going to have to go into this arrangement knowing he couldn't count on the kids to get any warm motherly attention from her. But perhaps there was a housekeeper or someone else in her household who could supply that. And if not, then at least they would all be together.

Still, there was something about Mrs. Pierce that made him want to look deeper, to find out what was at the heart of this woman.

Then Simon took himself to task. What *really* mattered right now was how much help she'd be with the kids.

"You said we had something to discuss?"

Her dry words and tone brought him back to the present. Truth to tell, he hadn't had anything specific in mind when he said that—it had just been a way of getting around her protests. But there *were* a few things he was curious about. "Do you live alone?"

"I have one boarder, Miss Dovie Jacobs."

Boarder—not family. Interesting. "Is Miss Jacobs likely to be bothered when we all descend on your home this afternoon?"

"I don't believe so. Miss Jacobs is a very motherly sort of woman. In fact, she is much like your Miss Fredrick, though on a smaller scale. She once took in and raised an orphaned child. If I'm wrong, however, she can always retreat to her own room."

"That's a relief—that our presence won't bother her, I mean." At least there'd be one person in the house who knew how to deal with children. Assuming she was willing to lend a hand.

If this Miss Jacobs was the only other person in her household, however, that would mean…"Forgive the personal question, but you were addressed as *Mrs.* Pierce. Is there no Mr. Pierce?"

"My husband has been deceased a little over two years now."

There was no change in her expression and she didn't expand. "My condolences."

"Thank you."

Again there was no emotion. Mrs. Pierce was obviously a very private person. Which made him all the more curious to learn more about her. And was it wrong that he was just the tiniest bit pleased that she was single?

Before he could ask about household staff, she halted next to a small wrought iron gate and waved a hand toward the place the gate guarded. "This is my home," she said simply.

He studied the three-story house with interest. He could see why Reverend Harper had thought this would be the answer to his need. Not only was the structure impressively grand, it was also set on a large piece of property with plenty of room for rambunctious kids to run around. It was also one of the few brick buildings he'd seen in this town. From the front porch that was supported by imposing columns, to the rounded, turretlike section that jutted from the right side of the structure, to the dormered roofline edged in stately woodwork, this place spoke of wealth and elegance, much as the woman herself did.

It seemed a waste that Mrs. Pierce and her boarder were the only residents—the place practically cried out for a large family to inhabit it.

A closer look at the structure, however, showed that it wasn't quite as well maintained as it seemed at first glance. Some of the woodwork was in need of painting and at least a few of the shingles on the roof were loose. The yard needed raking and trimming. And that was just what he could see from here. One thing was certain; he'd definitely be able to make himself useful while he was here.

A profusion of well-manicured plants fronted the structure—the garden hadn't suffered from the same neglect as the house. A woman with a pair of garden shears in her gloved hands knelt among the plants lining the front walk.

A gardener perhaps? It stood to reason that a woman such as Mrs. Pierce, with an impressive house like this one, would have servants.

The woman stood as soon as she saw them, and Simon was surprised by how tiny she was. She couldn't be any taller than four foot six or seven. And she looked old enough to be his companion's mother.

"Well, hello." The woman tugged off her gardening gloves, her eyes alight with friendly curiosity.

Mrs. Pierce gestured toward the smiling gardener. "Miss Jacobs, this is Mr. Simon Tucker. Mr. Tucker, this is Miss Dovie Jacobs, the boarder I mentioned."

He touched the brim of his hat. "Pleased to meet you, ma'am."

She acknowledged his greeting with a friendly nod. "Did you two just come from the town meeting?" She absently brushed the leaves and dirt from her skirt. "I'll admit I've been nigh on bursting with curiosity."

Simon wondered why she hadn't gone to the meeting herself. But it wouldn't be polite to ask. "We did," he said as he opened the gate. "And it so happens *I* was the subject. I find myself stranded here in town with ten children and their guardian who has taken seriously ill." He nodded deferentially to his companion. "Mrs. Pierce has generously agreed to open her home to us while we await the outcome of our friend's illness." He gave her what he hoped was a winning smile. "I hope that won't inconvenience you any."

"Not at all. And I'm sure enough sorry about your friend. I'll pray she recovers quickly."

Then she turned to Mrs. Pierce and gave her an approving smile. "Good for you. I've thought this place was crying out for a big family ever since I moved in. And ten children, bless my soul—that will certainly keep us on our toes."

From Miss Jacobs's tone, the two women's relationship seemed more friendly than the businesslike face Mrs. Pierce had put on it. Good to know that the tension he'd sensed at the meeting didn't extend to her household.

Miss Jacobs turned back to him. "You can count on me to help with the little ones in any way that I can."

He was glad to hear it. He could already sense she would be one who balanced doting and discipline the way Miss Fredrick had seemed to. "Thank you, ma'am. From what I've seen of them on this trip, these are a mostly well-behaved lot, but they *are* children."

"Don't you worry none, young man, between me and Eileen here we'll manage nicely."

Mrs. Pierce didn't respond to that. Instead she gave him a puzzled look. "So you don't know these children well?"

He shook his head. "Up until a short time ago, I knew Miss Fredrick and her charges mainly through my sister's letters. I popped in and out over the years to visit Sally and her children, of course, but that was all." He straightened. "Make no mistake, though, these children *are* my responsibility until I get them to where they're going."

"Of course." One delicate brow rose a fraction of an inch. "Was there anything else we needed to discuss right now?"

"No ma'am, unless you have questions for me."

She gave him a "you're dismissed" look. "I thank you for walking me home, but if you will excuse me, there are many preparations to be made."

Simon touched the brim of his hat again. "Then I'll be on my way. Thank you again for your hospitality, and I'll bring the kids over in a couple of hours."

Then he paused. "Can you direct me to the restaurant?"

With a nod, she turned to face the way they'd come. "Go back as far as Second Street, then turn right. The restaurant will be a block and a half on your left." She faced him again and the movement brought them unexpectedly closer together.

Her eyes widened and for a moment her aloof exterior cracked the tiniest bit. Her breathing seemed to hitch for just a heartbeat and her fingertips fluttered to her throat as if seeking a pulse there. Oh, yes, beneath that ice-queen exterior, an ember glowed. An ember he'd like to see burn brighter.

She recovered quickly, though, dropping her hand and schooling her expression. "The sign in front of the building reads Daisy's Restaurant," she said coolly. "You can't miss it."

With a thank-you for Mrs. Pierce and a tip of his hat for Miss Jacobs, Simon took his leave.

Meeting Miss Jacobs had relieved at least one of his concerns. The woman seemed willing and able to provide whatever mothering the children would need these next few days.

But his wayward mind was more interested in Mrs. Pierce than her boarder. That little close encounter they'd just had had obviously rattled her. And he wouldn't deny he'd felt something, as well. It was nothing more than mere curiosity, though—he couldn't let it be anything more. He had no time in his life right now for anything but meeting the kids' needs. Still, there was nothing to say he couldn't enjoy getting to know his hostess better while he was stuck here.

Would she be able to maintain that ice-queen demeanor once the children invaded her home? Or would that other, less confident but much more interesting Mrs. Pierce show through?

Well, if anything could strip the standoffish tendencies from a person, it was dealing with a houseful of kids. And he was rather pleased he'd be around to watch it happen.

Chapter Three

Eileen watched Mr. Tucker walk away, studying the casual confidence of his demeanor, still confused by her own reaction to him. There was nothing sophisticated or polished about the man. He'd called himself a handyman and cabinetmaker, which to her translated into a common laborer with some carpentry skills. His hands had been callused and even had a couple of rough-looking scars.

Not at all the kind of man she should be attracted to.

So what was it about him that drew her? There was the confidence in his bearing and his earnestness. And then there was his warm smile that reached all the way to his cornflower eyes that just drew a person in.

"That Mr. Tucker seems like a nice young man."

Eileen started, as if she'd been caught mooning over some imaginary beau. She turned and stepped through the gate, ignoring Dovie's knowing smile. "I suppose."

She returned to a businesslike manner, dismissing her wayward and totally inappropriate thoughts. Better to focus on the trouble that was about to descend on her. Ten children—what had she been thinking? She had no idea how to deal with children of any age, much less a horde of them.

But she *could* handle this. After all, she had been trained to be ready to rise to any sort of social emergency with grace and confidence. How much worse could this be than handling household servants or an unruly party guest or even a last-minute menu disaster? As for the matter of her financial straits being discovered, she'd have to put a good face on that as best she could. Surely it was only a matter of remaining unruffled and not allowing her guests to get overly familiar.

She turned to Dovie with returning confidence. "As the person in town with the biggest home, I felt it was my duty to offer shelter to these poor stranded children." Not entirely true—she hadn't volunteered so much as been cornered, but in the end she *had* agreed to help.

Dovie eyed her approvingly. "Opening your home to them was a generous, Christian gesture, especially being as you're such a private kind of person. And don't you worry, like I told that young man, I'll pitch in and help where I can."

Thank goodness Dovie liked to keep busy. This new situation would certainly afford her boarder plenty of opportunities for that. "I appreciate your offer." She unbent slightly. "I'll admit, I don't have experience dealing with children." No, that was one lady-of-the-manor skill she had never been taught.

"Don't you worry about that none. The only thing you have to know is that what children need most is love, patience and discipline. And of course a grounding in the Good Book. Give them that and the rest will work itself out."

Eileen didn't have a response for that, so she moved

on to something else. "The members of the Ladies Auxiliary have agreed to help with the meals."

Dovie fell into step with her as they moved to the house. "It's always good when a whole community comes together to help those in need." She gave Eileen a sideways look. "So when are the children supposed to get here?"

"In about two hours."

"Then we'd best get to work."

Eileen took a deep breath. Since her husband's death, she'd found herself overwhelmed by the debt he'd left behind. She'd been reduced to selling many of her prized furnishings, as furtively as possible, of course, and had had to do some creative rearranging of the remaining pieces to try to cover it up.

The result was that many of the unused rooms were stripped to the bare essentials and had been closed off from view, even from her boarder. Not that she had many visitors these days.

But now she was going to be forced to open those rooms up for her guests' use and there would be no hiding anything. It would be best to prepare Dovie for the reality she would soon see. "You should know that the furnishings are rather sparse in most of the extra rooms."

Dovie seemed to see nothing wrong with that. "As long as your guests have a bed to rest in, I don't imagine they'll be doing any complaining."

"There are six girls and four boys to accommodate besides Mr. Tucker." It was just hitting her that the man who'd thrown her so off balance today would be residing here, as well. She would really have to keep her guard up for the next few days. But, strangely, she was more energized than irritated by the challenge.

Not that Mr. Tucker was of any more import than the children. "There are five extra bedchambers on the second floor and four on the third." She frowned. "But I don't think it necessary to give each child his or her own room."

"Oh, my, no. In fact, they'll probably be happier if they have someone to share with. Why don't we put the girls in three of the second-floor rooms and Mr. Tucker and the boys in three of the rooms on the third?"

Eileen nodded, relieved that Dovie agreed. That would mean fewer rooms to prepare and fewer bed linens to deal with. "That sounds like an acceptable approach."

The two women had barely started when the doorbell sounded. Eileen left Dovie to finish opening the windows and stripping the beds while she went to see who was at the door. Surely Mr. Tucker hadn't returned already?

When she opened the door, however, it was Ivy Parker, and right behind her was her husband, Mitch, and a couple of young boys. All four of them were loaded down with armfuls of linens.

"Hello," Ivy said cheerily. "Where would you like us to set these?"

Eileen stepped aside. "Please come in." She waved to the open doorway on the left. "You can set it all on the table in the dining room."

As they trooped into her home, Ivy chattered away. "The members of the Ladies Auxiliary all contributed something. You'll find sheets and coverlets enough for eight beds. If you need more, let us know. We also figured you'd need some extra towels so we brought a stack of those, as well."

Extra towels—of course. She should have thought of that. What else hadn't she taken into consideration? And the thought of ten children needing baths was enough to send a shiver up her spine.

But it would never do to show a lack of confidence— she was the lady of the house. It was her duty to make all of her guests feel at home. "Thank you. I'm sure we will be able to put all of this to good use."

Once everything was safely deposited on the table, Ivy shooed her husband and the youths away, then turned to Eileen. "Now, what can I do to help you get ready for the invasion?"

"That's really not necessary. Dovie is assisting and between the two of us—"

Ivy interrupted with a wave of her hand. "Fiddle-sticks. I don't mind a bit, and it'll give me a chance to visit with Nana Dovie."

Ivy had been orphaned as an infant and Dovie had been the one to raise her. They were very much like mother and daughter even though there was no blood tie between them. Eileen supposed, more than anyone else in town, these two women could truly relate to these children and their situation.

Without waiting for a response, Ivy headed for the stairs. "By the way, Reggie volunteered to take care of the evening meal for you all today so there's no need to worry about that."

Regina Barr was Eileen's nearest neighbor and the current head of the Ladies Auxiliary.

Ivy looked back over her shoulder without slowing.

"And there's a list forming of volunteers to handle the meals for the next several days."

At least that was one worry off her shoulders. The food she'd put up from her garden this past summer and what she had left to harvest from her fall planting was supposed to take her through the winter. She could ill afford to feed an army of children solely from her own stores for more than a few days without adversely affecting her future menus.

With a start she realized Ivy was already headed up the stairs. Since Ivy had boarded here for a while before she married the schoolteacher, she knew where everything was.

Managing to catch up to her without breaking into a hoydenish rush, Eileen decided it would do no good to argue—she'd learned Ivy usually went her own way.

Ivy rolled up her sleeves and set to work as soon as she reached the second floor. As far as Eileen could tell, her former boarder seemed to see nothing amiss with the stark furnishings and lack of fancy drapes and coverlets in the spare bedchambers. She supposed, if anyone in town had to see her true state of affairs, then Ivy and Dovie would be the most sympathetic to her situation. Neither had known her before her fall from grace or had witnessed the lavish way she'd conducted her life back then. For that matter, nor did any of the visitors who would be here for the next few days. So there were no unflattering comparisons for them to make, no unpleasant history for them to remember.

As for Mr. Tucker, the admiration she'd seen in his eyes had been very disconcerting. No one had looked at her like that in a very long time. And she was honest enough to admit, just for a moment, she'd wanted to bask in it.

Perhaps it was worth all this bother just for that small, precious gift.

She just had to make certain she didn't get used to it.

Because it wasn't likely to come from anyone else anytime soon.

When Simon checked in at the restaurant to see how the kids were faring, the women there assured him they had everything under control. He'd been surprised to see that one end of the restaurant housed a library. He hadn't expected such niceties in this small-town community.

The reverend's daughter, who looked to be about sixteen or seventeen, was reading a book to several of the younger children, while some of the older ones were browsing the shelves and thumbing through books on their own. Mrs. Harper pulled him aside to assure him they would keep an eye on the children for as long as he needed them to.

Satisfied they were in good hands, Simon headed to Dr. Pratt's clinic to check on Miss Fredrick.

He was thankful they'd landed in the midst of such good people. On his own he'd have been totally inadequate to the task of looking after the children. After all, what did a thirty-year-old bachelor like him know about taking care of kids, especially little girls. And while Mrs. Pierce might not be the maternal type, her boarder, Miss Jacobs, would know how to deal with the needs of the children. Surely between the three of them, they could manage whatever was required over the next few days.

And hopefully they wouldn't be here in Turnabout longer than that. He had to keep believing Miss Fredrick would recover soon and they could be on their way once more. Surely God wouldn't allow for any other outcome.

That thought made him wince. He of all people should know that bad things *did* happen to good people, even innocent children, and God alone knew the reasons.

Unbidden, his thoughts turned to when he was nine years old and his own parents had died. He and his sisters had been farmed out to different relatives and rarely got to see each other again. In fact, his youngest sister, Imogene, had passed away the following year without him even knowing until the funeral was over and done with.

Just one more sign of what Uncle Corbitt's opinion of "that side of the family" had been.

Simon determinedly pushed those thoughts away and entered the doctor's office trying to maintain a hopeful outlook. "How's Miss Fredrick doing?"

The somberness in the spare, white-haired doctor's demeanor wasn't encouraging. "I wish I had better news for you, but she's not showing any signs of improvement."

"But she *is* going to get better, isn't she?" He couldn't quite mask the hint of desperation in his voice.

The doctor came around his desk and leaned back against it as he faced Simon sympathetically. "I'm afraid you need to face facts. There's a very real possibility she might never regain consciousness. If there's anyone to be notified, I would do it now."

Simon raked his hand through his hair, not wanting to accept what the doctor was saying. "She has a brother—his name is Wilbur I believe—but they had a falling-out. Other than the children, she doesn't have anyone else that I'm aware of."

"Notify her brother." The doctor's tone was firm. "I find most people put their differences aside at a time like this."

"Of course. But it *is* possible she'll recover, isn't it?"

The doctor looked at him with sympathy. "Anything is possible, son. But it's very much in God's hands now."

Before Simon could respond, one of the side doors opened and a woman dressed in black with a crisp white bibbed apron stepped out. The doctor straightened. "Mr. Tucker, allow me to introduce my niece, Verity Leggett."

Simon tipped his hat. "Pleased to meet you, ma'am."

"She and her daughter have recently moved in with us," the doctor continued. "Verity is helping here at the clinic. Between her, my wife and me, someone will be with Miss Fredrick at all times."

"Thank you. I appreciate all you're doing for Miss Fredrick." He scrubbed his jaw, trying to collect his thoughts. "The kids have been asking after her. Would it be okay if they came around to see her?"

The doctor hesitated before replying. "As long as they are prepared for what they will see. Unless something changes, she'll be unconscious and unable to move or speak."

"Mr. Tucker." Mrs. Leggett's tone was sympathetic but firm. "I hope you don't mind my interference, but as a mother myself, I feel it would be unwise to bring the children here just yet. It would only serve to upset them further."

Simon nodded. "I appreciate your advice, ma'am."

He thanked them both again, then asked the where-abouts of the telegraph office and took his leave.

What was he going to do if Miss Fredrick didn't make it? More to the point, what would become of the children? He'd given Miss Fredrick his word that he'd do everything in his power to get them all safely to their new home. But what was the use of getting them to Hatcherville if Miss Fredrick wasn't there to look out for them? He certainly couldn't step into that role himself, not alone at any rate. He'd take in his niece and nephew, Audrey and Albert, if there was no other choice but to separate the children. But he'd scour heaven and earth to keep them all together if he could.

Almighty God, please let this dear woman live. She's doing Your work here and it doesn't seem right to not let her finish it, especially now when she is in reach of her dream of giving these kids a new and better life. They need her—they have nowhere else to go, no one else to look out for them.

And I certainly didn't sign on to become their full-time guardian. You, who know all things, know that I wouldn't be the kind of caretaker they need—they need a mother's touch.

Simon rubbed the back of his neck, remembering his own mother, aching a little that she'd been taken from him so young. Uncle Corbitt's housekeeper had been a poor substitute. He didn't intend to let that happen to these children.

Exactly two hours from the time he'd left the church, Simon led a parade of children to the front gate of Mrs. Pierce's home. He was doing his best to keep up a cheer-ful facade, trying to paint this as an adventure, a temporary stopover on their journey to their new home, rather than a tragedy.

They'd just come from the sweet shop, which was located in the same space as a toy store, so the children had been chattering happily when they set out. But now they had quieted, and he sensed nervousness and some anxiety in the group.

Understandable. He'd tried to give them a hopeful report on Miss Fredrick's condition, but he hadn't wanted to lie, so he was sure the older ones, at least, had read between the lines. And now they were approaching a strange place, owned by a person they'd never met, to reside there for an unspecified amount of time. It would be a nerve-racking situation for many adults to walk into—how much more so for children?

"It's a castle." Molly's eyes were wide as she stared at Mrs. Pierce's home. "Just like in a fairy tale. Does a queen live here?"

Simon smiled down at her. "Not a queen, but a couple of very nice ladies."

Molly stuck her thumb back in her mouth, appearing unconvinced.

With a mental sigh, Simon climbed the wide stone steps onto the porch and twisted the ornate brass doorbell. The ring echoed from inside the house. Then the silence stretched out for what seemed forever. Behind him the children shuffled restlessly. And he had a sudden stab of fear that Mrs. Pierce might have changed her mind. After all, it had been obvious she wasn't thrilled with the idea of housing them.

He was just contemplating whether or not to give the bell another twist, when the door finally opened.

Chapter Four

Simon was almost embarrassed by the wave of relief that flooded through him. He hoped he did a good job of hiding it. Then he saw who'd opened the door and had to hide his reaction all over again.

Why was Mrs. Pierce answering her own door? Didn't she have a housekeeper? Surely the elegant widow didn't care for this huge house herself? Perhaps her servant was otherwise occupied at the moment.

Mrs. Pierce stepped aside to let them enter. "Forgive me for keeping you waiting. Miss Jacobs and I were just finishing preparing the rooms for you."

Again, no mention of a servant. It was beginning to look as if there truly were no servants after all. If that was true, then he was doubly in her debt for agreeing to take them in. And it made him rethink a few things about her, as well.

As he ushered his charges inside, Miss Jacobs bustled down the hall toward them. "Hello, Mr. Tucker. And here are the children. Welcome, welcome. I've been looking forward to meeting you ever since I heard you were coming."

Simon wondered how two such different women could get along under the same roof. Miss Jacobs seemed as approachable as Mrs. Pierce was aloof.

As the last of the children entered, he stepped forward to make the introductions. "Kids, this is Mrs. Pierce, the nice lady who has opened her home to us. And this is her friend, Miss Jacobs, who also lives here."

They all nodded and there were a few mumbled hellos. Simon quickly went down the line, introducing the children one by one.

When he was done, Mrs. Pierce gave them a reserved smile. "I'm pleased to meet you all. Welcome to my home."

"Are you a queen?" Molly asked.

To give her credit, their hostess didn't so much as bat an eyelash. "No, I'm not," was her only response.

Joey, apparently emboldened by Molly's question, turned to Miss Jacobs. "Why are you so short?" he asked.

"Joey!" Simon was caught off guard by the boy's artlessly uttered and much-too-personal question. Would Miss Jacobs be insulted?

But the woman merely smiled at the young boy. "I reckon God made me this way because He knew how much I love being around young'uns. It makes me feel closer to kids than to grown-ups."

Miss Jacobs shifted her gaze to include all the children in her next comment. "And I'd be right grateful if you children would call me Nana Dovie while you're here. It's what my own daughter calls me."

Yep, these were definitely two very different women.

Joey wasn't done with his questions, though. He turned to Mrs. Pierce. "Do you have a dog?"

This time the widow frowned slightly. "I do not." There was definitely a tone of "and I don't want one" in her voice. And there was also no offer to let the kids call her by an endearing name.

"When we get to Hatcherville," the boy said proudly, "Gee-Gee says I can get a dog."

"Gee-Gee?" Mrs. Pierce cast him a questioning glance.

"It's what the children call Miss Fredrick," Simon explained. "Her first name is Georgina."

Mrs. Pierce nodded, then turned to Joey. "I'm sure that will be very nice." Then she turned back to Simon. "The rooms are ready for you and your charges. I hope the children won't mind doubling up."

"They're used to sharing," Simon assured her. "Their former home wasn't nearly as grand as this one and they had much tighter sleeping arrangements." He'd seen their bedrooms, crowded with bunk beds like a cramped dormitory. It was one of the reasons Miss Fredrick planned this move. "Do you have a specific way you'd like to assign the rooms or are you leaving it up to us?"

"I have put you and the boys in three rooms on the third floor," the widow responded. "The girls will be in three rooms on the second floor with me and Miss Jacobs."

He nodded. "An excellent arrangement. If you'll show us the way, we'll get everyone settled in." He paused. "By the way, I asked the young man over at the train depot to have our bags delivered here so they should be arriving soon." Most of the kids' belongings, along with all the household items, had been sent on ahead to Hatcherville, but luckily Miss Fredrick had seen that they each had a change of clothing packed for the trip. At least clothing wouldn't be a problem for the next few days.

He wished the same were true about everything else to do with this setback.

Eileen led the way up the stairs, trying her best to remain composed. Seeing all those children up close was more than a little overwhelming. The questions the two youngest had asked had bordered on impertinence. They were little more than toddlers, of course, but her mother and instructors had always insisted one was never too young to learn good manners.

She certainly hoped Mr. Tucker had told the truth when he said they were well behaved. Of course, the conditional that he'd tagged on about their age hadn't inspired her with much confidence.

These visitors seemed impressed with her home, but they were about to see how starkly furnished their rooms were. What would they think? Of course, one could hardly expect children to be discriminating in such matters. But Mr. Tucker was a different matter. And she found his opinion did matter.

When they reached the second floor, she turned to Dovie. "Would you please help the girls get settled in while I show Mr. Tucker and the boys to the third floor?"

"Of course." Dovie smiled at the girls. "I'll let you all decide how you want to pair up and then we'll pick out rooms for everyone."

Eileen led the way up the stairs to the third floor. A part of her envied Dovie's easy manner with the children. It might not be dignified, but the children seemed better able to relate to her. Then she mentally took herself to task. As her mother had often drilled into her, Paylors *always* maintained their dignity and composure, no matter what.

As they stepped onto the landing she felt the need to apologize. "These rooms haven't seen any use in the past two years. Miss Jacobs and I aired them out but they may still be a bit musty."

"I'm sure it'll be just fine." Mr. Tucker looked around and she watched him closely for signs of judgment. To her relief, he seemed to see nothing amiss.

"Do you have a preference for who gets which room?" he asked.

Good—they were going to keep things businesslike. "The three on this end have been made ready—you may assign them however you wish."

With a nod he turned to the boys. "Harry and Russ, you two take the far room. Albert, you and Joey can have the middle one. And I'll take the one nearest the stairs."

The doorbell sounded and Mr. Tucker turned back to her with a smile. "That's probably our bags." He waved to the two older boys. "Harry, Russell, come help me get everything carted upstairs."

"We're coming, too," the one he'd called Albert said.

"Yeah, we're coming, too," Joey said with a great deal of bravado.

To Eileen's surprise, Mr. Tucker merely grinned at this bit of assertiveness. "All right, men, the more hands, the lighter the load I always say."

By the time they made it to the first floor, Dovie had already opened the door to their caller. As Mr. Tucker had predicted, it was Lionel from the train depot.

As soon as Lionel saw Mr. Tucker over Dovie's shoulder he straightened. "I brought your things, Mr. Tucker, just like you asked. It's all on the wagon—I'll get it unloaded in a snap." He reached into his pocket. "And I brought this telegram that came for you, too."

Eileen stiffened slightly. Mr. Tucker was already getting telegrams here? It certainly hadn't taken him long to make himself at home.

She watched as he sent the four boys to help Lionel unload the cart, and then unfolded the piece of paper.

Whatever the news, he didn't appear to like it. Had he received more bad news on top of today's events?

Simon stared at the very terse telegram he'd received in response to the one he'd sent Miss Fredrick's brother.

KEEP ME APPRISED
W. FREDRICK

Apparently Wilbur Fredrick didn't intend to rush to his sister's bedside. Simon didn't understand that—he would have given anything to have had that opportunity with Imogene, to have been able to have a few last words with her before she passed on.

He refolded the paper and shoved it into his pocket. Perhaps this was his fault. Maybe he hadn't made it clear just how serious Miss Fredrick's condition was. Should he send another telegram?

He glanced up and caught Mrs. Pierce watching him, a hint of sympathy in her expression. But she immediately turned away, her demeanor once more aloof, and he wondered if he'd merely imagined it.

Lionel and the boys deposited the first load of baggage just then and went back for more. Before he could join them, the girls were trooping downstairs to investigate what was going on. So Simon pushed aside thoughts of Wilbur Fredrick, and Mrs. Pierce's show of concern, to ponder at a quieter time.

He joined the "menfolk" unloading the wagon and they managed to get the remaining items in one more load.

Once everything was deposited in the entry hall, he dismissed Lionel with a coin and his thanks. When he turned back, the children were already digging into the pile with noisy enthusiasm as well as a bit of good-natured shoving, each looking for their own items. Mrs. Pierce cringed and drew back into herself. Was it the noise level or the overall chaos that bothered her more?

Then she straightened. "Children, please." Her voice, while not loud or strident, carried the ring of authority, and the children closest to her paused in their scrambling to look her way.

"Quiet, please." This time her voice carried to the rest of the children, and everyone turned to stare at her in surprise.

"There is no need for this unruly behavior. You are all old enough to know how to conduct yourselves in a more orderly fashion."

Simon frowned. This might be her home, but she couldn't expect the children to act like miniature versions of herself. "Mrs. Pierce, I believe what you are seeing is enthusiasm rather than unruly behavior."

"One can be excited and show decorum at the same time." She turned to the children. "Now, starting with the oldest and the youngest, step forward and find your things. Then take them up to your room."

Fern stepped forward stiffly. "Yes, ma'am." She held out a hand. "Come on, Molly, I'll help you find your things."

To Simon's surprise, the children followed her instructions, and two by two, with one of the older children helping one of the younger ones, they each collected their things and headed up the stairs. There was no more horseplay and very little chatter, and the task was accomplished in short order.

Okay, so maybe her way was effective, but it certainly hadn't done anything to make the children feel more at ease here.

He glanced Miss Jacobs's way. She was observing in silence. Did she agree with Mrs. Pierce's approach? Or was she just hesitant to disagree with the woman who was, after all, her landlady?

When the last of the children had headed upstairs, Mrs. Pierce turned to him. Was that a glint of triumph peeking out from her serene expression?

"I realize this is your home," he said before she could comment, "but I would appreciate it if you would give the children a bit of latitude. They've been through quite a bit."

She appeared unmoved. "They have my sympathy, of course, and I understand they are anxious. But I believe maintaining discipline is for their good as well as that of those around them. It gives them a sense of order that can be a comfort when the rest of their world appears to be falling apart around them."

Did she truly believe that? "They also need the chance to work off some of their pent-up energy."

"Within the proper parameters." Then she waved a hand. "Are these last few bags yours?"

He swallowed his response and accepted her change of subject. "That brown duffel is mine and the trunk contains my tools. The smaller trunk belongs to Miss Fredrick." He furrowed his brow thoughtfully. "It seems pointless to cart the heavy tool trunk up two flights of stairs, especially since I'll need most of the tools down here if I'm going to do some work on your place while I'm here. Is there somewhere down here where I could store it?"

She hesitated a long moment—so long that he thought about withdrawing his request.

But then she drew her shoulders back and nodded. "Of course. Follow me."

He couldn't quite pinpoint what it was, but something in her demeanor made him wonder if there was more going through her mind than simply finding him some storage space.

Without a word, she led him down the hall and around a corner. They went down another shorter hallway until she finally stopped in front of a closed door. Taking a deep breath, she threw the door open and indicated he should precede her inside.

He stepped into a darkened room that, from the musty smell, hadn't seen use in some time. It had a definite masculine feel to it and was dominated by a massive desk.

She crossed the room and pulled open the curtains, letting in some much-needed light. It was only then that he noticed that the *only* piece of furniture in the room was that desk, which he could now see was finely crafted and graced with some fine parquetry work.

The walls were bare, although there were indications that several large paintings had hung in here at one time.

The built-in bookcases that flanked the fireplace were also empty. And there was a thin layer of dust over everything. But the paneling and richly carved woodwork spoke of bygone elegance.

"This was my husband's study," she said, "but as you can see, it is no longer in use." She folded her hands lightly in front of her, and he thought he detected a slight tremble, though it might have been only his imagination. "You may store your things in here for as long as you are in residence."

It seemed a bit grand to be used as a storage room, but it wasn't his place to question her choice. "Thank you. I'll get one of the boys to help me carry the trunk in here later." He could also store Miss Fredrick's things here.

She looked around. "I apologize for the state you find it in."

Other than a bit of a musty feel, he didn't see anything that required an apology. "No need. And I certainly don't expect you to go to any trouble on my account."

She nodded and continued to stare at the room as if picturing it differently. Was she remembering her husband seated in here? Did she still mourn him? The temptation to move to her side to comfort her was strong. He'd actually taken a step forward when she suddenly straightened.

"If that is all," she said, "I have a few matters to attend to."

Not sure if he was more relieved or bothered that she'd unknowingly forestalled his impulse, he gave a short bow. "Of course. I'll get the last of the baggage cleared from your entryway." As they shut the door behind them, he added. "I'll encourage the children to either nap or entertain themselves quietly in their rooms for the next hour so you shouldn't be interrupted by any of them."

She gave another of her regal nods and they retraced their steps in silence. When they arrived back at the foot of the stairway she excused herself and headed into the parlor. Was she still thinking of her deceased husband?

Simon watched her go—elegant posture, graceful movements, unhurried pace. He should have told Molly that yes indeed, a queen *did* live in this palace-of-a-home.

But he had the feeling that Eileen Pierce was a very sad and lonely ruler of her faltering domain. The question was, did she realize it, and if so, did she want to change things?

Chapter Five

Eileen sat in the parlor, working on a bit of embroidery. Stepping into Thomas's study had conjured up memories not only of her husband but also of all her past sins. How could she have been so blissfully blind to what she'd been doing to him, of how much her extravagances had cost him, not just in money, but in his integrity and sense of honor? He had paid with his life. Her justly deserved penance was to have been brought low.

The house had grown quiet at last—there'd been no sounds from upstairs for the past ten minutes and even Mr. Tucker and Dovie had disappeared into their own rooms.

So far, things appeared to be working out moderately well. It had been hectic for a while but the children had responded appropriately to her authority. Now that she'd set the proper tone, perhaps the worst was behind them. As long as Dovie and Mr. Tucker took most of the responsibility for actually dealing with the children, and she was left to just play hostess, she was certain they could get through these next few days just fine.

She stilled. What was that noise? Had Mr. Tucker

decided to come back down? This unexpected zing of anticipation she felt whenever he was near, or she even believed he was approaching, was new to her. And it was affecting her ability to maintain her impassive facade.

Then she heard the sound again and she realized it had to be one of the children. Ignoring the little stab of disappointment, she set her sewing aside. She couldn't have the children roaming around her home unattended. Then again, what if the child needed something? Would she be up to handling whatever it was on her own?

But she was the lady of the house and she had responsibilities to her guests. Rising, Eileen moved into the hall and stopped when she saw the youngest child—Molly, was it?—coming down the stairs. The little girl was dragging her doll forlornly behind her and had her right hand on the banister.

As soon as she saw Eileen, she stilled.

Eileen stared at her uncertainly. "Shouldn't you be taking a nap?" she asked.

Molly pulled her doll forward and hugged it tightly. "Gee-Gee always rocks me before I go to sleep."

Why did the child think it important to tell her this?

"But Gee-Gee is sick," the little girl added in a mournful tone.

Eileen felt her heart soften. "That's right. And I'm certain, when she gets better, Gee-Gee will be happy to rock you again."

The little girl studied her with disconcerting intensity. "Will *you* rock me?"

Eileen was both touched and thrown off-kilter by the child's request. What did she know about such motherly activities? But something inside her ached to try.

Then common sense reasserted itself. "I'm sorry, but I don't have a rocking chair," she told the child. "Why don't you just go on back up to your room and lie down. I'm sure—"

"I want to be rocked." The little girl's mouth was now set in a stubborn line.

Eileen looked around. Where were Dovie and Mr. Tucker? They were so much better equipped than she to handle an obstinate child. "I told you, I don't have a rocking chair. But—"

"I want to be rocked." There was almost a wail in Molly's voice this time and she rubbed her eyes with her fist.

Gracious, was she about to *cry?* That just would not do. Then Eileen remembered the porch swing. It wasn't a rocking chair but it might serve to calm her down.

"All right," she said quickly. "I think I have a suitable compromise."

The little girl's expression changed from pouty displeasure to uncertainty. "What's a com-prize?"

"Com*pro*mise," Eileen corrected. "It means I don't have a rocker but I have something I think will work just as well." She nodded toward the front door. "But we'll have to go outside."

"Okay." Molly, now all smiles, came down the last three stairs and held out her hand.

Surprised by the trusting gesture, Eileen hesitated for just a moment, then accepted the girl's small, pudgy hand into her own. Together they exited the house and Eileen led her to the porch swing.

When Molly saw it, she giggled in delight. "A big rocker swing. I like your com-prize."

"Compromise," Eileen corrected again, but more

gently this time. She sat down on the swing and the little girl scrambled up into her lap.

As Eileen set the swing gently into motion, Molly snuggled down more comfortably in her lap, leaned her head against Eileen's chest and stuck her thumb in her mouth again. A happy sigh escaped her as she cuddled her rag doll.

Placing her arms around the child, Eileen felt something deep inside her stir to life.

"This is my fault. I shouldn't have fallen asleep." Fern's eyes were wide, her tone bordering on hysteria.

"You were tired." Simon kept his tone matter-of-fact, trying to keep her from panicking. "And I'm sure Molly hasn't gone far."

"That Mrs. Pierce lady scared her. I don't think she even wants us here." Fern was obviously looking for someone to blame. "Maybe we should find someplace else to stay."

He was surprised by how strongly the urge to defend Mrs. Pierce kicked in. "Fern, this is Mrs. Pierce's home, which means she's allowed to make the rules. She's just not accustomed to being around children, especially as large a group as we have. Give her time to get used to you all and she'll come around. Besides there *is* no other place, unless you want everyone to be split up."

Simon ushered the agitated girl out of the bedchamber and toward the stairs. He'd checked in on all the kids a few moments ago, just to assure himself they were settling in okay, when he'd discovered Molly's bed was empty.

He'd crossed the room to see if Molly was hiding somewhere. Unfortunately Fern, who was the toddler's roommate, had awakened. And now she was blaming herself. Truth was, Simon knew this was his fault. He should have made certain they all knew to stay in their rooms until the clock chimed the hour.

"Maybe we should just call out for her," Fern suggested. "Sometimes she likes to hide."

Simon shook his head. "Not yet. I don't want to wake the others and get them worried unless we need to. I'm sure she hasn't gone far. Let's just look around a bit first."

He and Fern checked the corners and niches on the second floor then headed downstairs. "Can you think of something she likes to do or someplace she likes to go that would give us a clue where to look?" Simon asked. Regrettably, he didn't know enough about Molly or any of these kids to figure it out for himself.

"She might try to find the kitchen if she was thirsty." Fern's tone was doubtful.

"All right. You check the kitchen—down that way I believe—and I'll see if Mrs. Pierce is still in the parlor to find out if she's seen her."

Fern nodded and took off at a sprint.

He'd already turned in the opposite direction, How would the widow feel about the interruption? Would she help in the search or lecture them on discipline? Not that he minded squaring off with her under less troubling circumstances—getting a rise out of her was actually quite entertaining.

When he looked in the parlor he found it disappointingly empty. He even checked behind the sofa and softly called Molly's name to make sure the little girl wasn't hiding.

When he stepped back out in the hallway he noticed

the front door was slightly ajar. Molly was too small, of course, to open the heavy wooden door. But if someone else had left it open...

He quickly crossed to the entryway, pushed open the screen door and stepped out on the porch. He could see the front gate was closed, which eased one worry at least. Perhaps she—

A movement he'd caught from the corner of his eye grabbed his attention.

There, on a porch swing that he hadn't even noticed when they arrived earlier, sat Mrs. Pierce with a sleeping Molly cuddled on her lap. And the widow had the sweetest, gentlest smile on her face, for all the world as if Molly were her own beloved child. The soft expression transformed her, turned her from an ice queen to an achingly sweet image of maternal devotion.

Then Fern came up behind him and he heard her quick intake of breath. Before he could stop her, the girl gave vent to her feelings.

"What are you doing with Molly?" There was outrage and accusation in the girl's tone.

Mrs. Pierce stiffened and the softness disappeared from her expression. In its place a cooler, more impersonal facade settled in. Simon felt a physical sense of loss at the transformation.

"The child insisted on being rocked." Her tone was dispassionate. "It was this or let her wake the house with her crying."

"You should have called me." Fern marched forward. "I know how to take care of her."

Simon knew Fern was still rattled by Molly's unexpected disappearance, but rudeness was never a proper response. "Apologize for taking that tone with Mrs. Pierce," he said quietly but firmly.

Fern threw him a defiant look, but he kept his gaze locked to hers and his expression firm. After a moment she turned back to Mrs. Pierce. "I'm sorry." But her tone was anything but contrite. She stiffly bent down to take Molly from Mrs. Pierce's arms.

"As you wish." Mrs. Pierce smoothed her skirt across her now-empty lap, then stood. "If you'll excuse me, I'll return to my needlework."

Simon wanted to let her know that he appreciated her tenderness with the toddler, that Fern hadn't really meant what she'd said. But the kids had to be his first concern right now. So he settled for giving her a quick thank-you.

She acknowledged it with a frosty nod, barely pausing as she stepped past him into the house. The ice queen had returned with a vengeance.

He turned back to Fern, careful to keep his irritation out of his voice. "Where do you think you're going?"

"I'm going to put Molly to bed." That touch of defiance had returned.

He stepped in front of her. "Give her to me." When she balked, he gave an exasperated shake of his head. "She's too heavy for you to carry up the stairs. Once I've got her in bed, you can tuck her in and fuss over her all you want."

With a reluctant nod, Fern handed a still-slumbering Molly over. The three-year-old was definitely a sound sleeper. Simon crossed the foyer to the staircase, noting that Mrs. Pierce had returned to the parlor and had her head bent over her sewing. She was as composed as if nothing had just happened. If Fern's tone had upset her there was no sign of it.

Simon quickly carried the little girl up the stairs and placed her in her bed. Then he left Fern to tend to her while he headed back downstairs to see the widow.

He had some fence-mending to do on Fern's behalf.

Chapter Six

Eileen stabbed the needle through the fabric, trying to keep her hands from trembling.

She had gotten used to being something of a social outcast in Turnabout these past two years. But to have that same distrust and dislike focused on her from the eyes of this newcomer, a child no less, was altogether unnerving. It had stung more than she cared to admit.

And all the more so because she'd let her guard down with Molly. She would need to remember these people were just temporary guests in her home. Getting attached to any of them was not to be allowed.

As for Mr. Tucker, she hadn't been able to tell what he thought. He'd wrested an apology from Fern, but other than that, he'd shown no sign of what he was thinking.

She tried to tell herself it didn't matter, but knew that to be a lie.

She looked up when she heard a tap at the parlor door frame. Mr. Tucker stood there watching her. Had he just walked up or had he been there awhile? It bothered her that he might have been watching her without her realizing it.

"May I come in for a moment?" he asked.

Was he here to take her to task as Fern had? Well, she was prepared now; she would not be caught unawares a second time.

Placing her sewing in her lap, Eileen nodded permission.

He smiled diffidently as he moved farther into the room. "I wanted to apologize on Fern's behalf. I'm sorry if she seemed rude—she was just worried about Molly."

Some of her tension eased at his obvious sincerity. But it seemed to her that Fern should do her own apologizing. "I was not harming the child." Had she managed to keep the hurt from her voice?

"Of course not. In fact, I appreciate the attention you were giving her. Molly seemed quite comfortable there with you."

And she had been surprisingly comfortable holding the child. It was the first time she'd been in that position, and it had left her aching more than ever from the knowledge that she would never have a child of her own. "Molly was insistent that she be rocked before she could sleep—humoring her was a simple enough thing. As for Fern, she should know better than to take such a tone with an adult. It appears your Miss Fredrick was not big on teaching the children manners."

"It's been a rough day for them, and they're only children." He'd frowned at her words, but his tone remained calm. "One can't expect them to react with the control of an adult."

"I disagree." Her teachers had gone to great lengths to school her on the correct behavior for a young lady of breeding. It was only when she had proven that she could conduct herself with proper decorum that she had been allowed to dine with adults or join them in the parlor, and then only on special occasions.

"Still and all," he said, interrupting her thoughts, "it was very good of you to comfort Molly."

Eileen deliberately pushed away thoughts of the little girl's snuggling presence in her lap. She might not have the makings of a good mother, but that didn't mean she didn't have maternal longings. "One does what is needed."

To her relief, the doorbell sounded, putting an end to their current discussion. She rose from her seat, setting the sewing aside. "If you'll excuse me, I need to see who is at the door. And I'm sure you have matters of your own to see to, as well."

He stepped back as she exited the parlor, but rather than following her pointed hint, he trailed along behind her. Was he just curious? Or was he expecting someone?

When she opened the door, Regina Barr and her housekeeper, Mrs. Peavy, stood there holding cloth-covered baskets. It seemed the Ladies Auxiliary had put their promises into action.

She greeted them, then stepped aside. "Please come in."

"The Ladies Auxiliary worked out a schedule for meals and I made sure we were first up," Regina said with a smile. "I wanted to get this food to you early so it would be ready whenever the children got hungry."

"Thank you, that was most considerate." What time did the children normally eat? She supposed it would be up to her to set the schedule now.

Mr. Tucker stepped forward. "Good afternoon, ladies." He reached for the baskets. "Let me help you with those."

"Oh, hello. I'm Reggie Barr, one of Eileen's neighbors." Regina waved to her companion. "And this is my friend, Mrs. Peavy."

Mr. Tucker gave a short bow, then reached for her basket, but she resisted with a smile. "These aren't heavy." She waved a hand toward the open door. "But if you'll help my son Jack with the rest, I'd be most obliged."

Eileen glanced outside to see Jack standing at the foot of the porch with a small wagon containing two large hampers.

As Mr. Tucker stepped outside, Eileen turned to the women. "You can set your baskets down on the dining room table."

But Regina shook her head. "Nonsense, we can carry these to the kitchen for you."

Mr. Tucker returned with the two hampers, and Jack was right behind him with a smaller basket. Eileen didn't have any choice but to lead the small procession to the kitchen. At least that room was not expected to be lavishly furnished, so perhaps they'd see nothing amiss.

As they walked, Regina described the contents of the baskets. "We have a sliced ham, some squash, butter beans, fresh-baked bread and two pecan pies." She grinned. "I figured with ten kids and three adults to feed, you'd be needing a goodly quantity."

"That will make a fine meal," Eileen said. Actually, it sounded a veritable feast. She couldn't remember the last time she'd had ham.

"Tomorrow," Regina continued, "Hortense Peters promises to deliver a basket of fresh eggs in the morning along with a generous length of summer sausage. And Eunice is going to bring over a roast with some vegetables that should be enough to take care of your noon and evening meals."

Eileen nodded. Eunice Ortolon might be a gossipy busybody but there was no denying she was a great cook. "I'm certain the children will be quite grateful for your generosity." It seemed as long as the children were under her roof she would be eating well. An unexpected benefit.

Mr. Tucker set his things down, brushing closely past her. Had he done that on purpose?

He made a short bow in Regina's direction. "Absolutely, ma'am. I can't begin to tell you how grateful we are to have fallen among such kind and generous folk."

Regina smiled, obviously not immune to the warmth of his tone, either. Then she turned to include Eileen in her comments. "And don't you worry. We have folks lined up to take care of your meals for as many days as you need us to."

Eileen was getting hungry just smelling the tempting aromas coming from the hampers. She hadn't eaten such fine fare in some time—meat was a rare treat indeed.

Regina sent a subtle signal to Mrs. Peavy, and the older woman made her exit, taking Jack with her. Then she turned to Mr. Tucker. "Thank you so much for your assistance getting these inside. I'll just help Eileen get everything put away before I go."

This time Mr. Tucker took the not-very-subtle hint. "If you'll excuse me, then, I'll leave you ladies to it. I think I'll check in on Molly to make sure she stays put this time." He gave Regina another of those warm smiles. "Thanks again for the food, ma'am."

Once he'd gone, Eileen turned to Regina. "It's really not necessary for you to stay and help me. You've done enough already." She really wasn't comfortable having people poking around in her cupboards and closets.

Regina opened one of the hampers. "I don't mind. And there's something else I wanted to say."

Eileen steeled herself. Was Regina, like Miss Ortolon, concerned with her suitability to house young children? Was this to be some sort of advice or condition set down for her?

But there was no hint of censure in Regina's expression. "Daisy and I discussed how children can be hard on dishes, and it didn't seem right that you should bear the brunt of that. So she sent over some of the plates from her restaurant that have seen a bit too much wear and that she was ready to take out of service. I hope you don't mind. They have some small chips and cracks but are still serviceable."

Regina seemed to sense her hesitation. "If you'd rather not use them, that's okay, too. But Daisy wanted me to assure you that either way she doesn't need them back—she was ready to replace them anyway."

Had these women suspected her true circumstances and decided to offer her charity? That was a lowering thought, but Eileen couldn't afford to turn down the offer. She hadn't given much thought to place settings, but she'd be hard-pressed to set a table for the ten children, much less the full complement of thirteen now residing here.

First towels, now dishes. Was she forgetting anything else?

At least Regina had worded the offer in a way that left Eileen with some of her dignity intact. She nodded matter-of-factly. "I had not considered the added wear and tear these children could have on my things. I will have to thank Daisy when next I see her."

Regina touched her arm lightly. "I know you were put on the spot earlier. And given all that's occurred the past couple of years, it was mighty generous of you to open your home to these folks. If you need any help at all in the coming days, you know where I live. Don't hesitate to fetch me."

Eileen was surprised by the genuine warmness of the gesture. Was this the start of a thawing of the community toward her? Or would the friendly overtures disappear as soon as her houseguests departed?

Once Regina took her leave, Eileen made quick work of unloading the various baskets and hampers. Dovie joined her just as she emptied the last one.

"Goodness, but isn't this all a welcome sight. I don't mind saying I'm not a bit sorry we won't need to rustle up supper from scratch for all these folks."

Eileen folded her hands in front of her. "I'll admit I don't know how much children eat, but there seems to be enough here to feed us all."

Dovie peered inside the various bowls and pots. "I agree—this should be more than enough. There might even be some ham left over to serve with breakfast in the morning. I'll get the stove stoked. We can set these things on the warming rack so it'll all be heated through when we're ready for it."

Eileen glanced up toward the ceiling. "How much longer do you think the children will nap?"

"I imagine some of them are awake already, if they slept at all. It's been an emotional day for them and different children will react differently to that."

Emotional—Eileen didn't like the sounds of that. Orderly and obedient—that's how children should behave.

But Dovie was still speaking. "As to your question, Mr. Tucker instructed them to stay in their rooms for at least an hour." She grinned. "I imagine it was as much to give you a reprieve as to let the children rest."

Eileen relaxed, pleased that he might have indeed been thinking of her feelings. And it seemed there was an expectation that the children were at least able to quietly amuse themselves. Good. "That being the case, I don't suppose they'll have the energy for much activity the rest of the day."

Dovie shook her head sympathetically. "You really don't know much about children, do you, dear?"

Eileen didn't like the condescending tone. "I remember my own childhood quite well."

The older woman gave her a long, considering look, and it was all Eileen could do not to fidget under that gaze.

"Don't you remember how hard it was to sit still for long periods?" Dovie finally asked. "You can't expect them to stay in their rooms all afternoon. An hour or two, yes, but no more. Children need activity to keep them from getting restless."

Eileen disagreed. It was merely a matter of training and discipline. Most of her childhood, at least that part after her father's death when she was five, had been spent with boarding school teachers in quiet, educational pursuits. Those teachers had believed in the adage that children should be seen and not heard, and they had vigorously drilled their students on matters of etiquette, deportment and other matters of social acceptance.

But if indeed these children had *not* been trained properly, she would have to find other solutions. If she hadn't had to sell her pianoforte or stereopticon she could have entertained them in a decorous, proper style. She'd also sold most of her books and her husband's finely carved chess set. There was nothing even remotely appropriate for entertaining company of any age left in her home.

Dovie startled her by patting her hand. "Don't worry," the woman said. "Children are easily entertained. Just leave it to me."

"And so I shall. In the meantime, I should take care of organizing our meal."

Just as Dovie had predicted, thirty minutes later there were sounds of stirring from the upstairs rooms. When Eileen stepped into the hallway a few minutes later, she saw Dovie leading the entire group of children into the parlor. Curious as to what the woman was planning, Eileen followed, as well.

Dovie knelt down next to the low table in front of the sofa and signaled the children to gather around. "I want to show you a game my mother used to play with me." She untied the cloth and spread it open with all the flair of a pirate revealing his treasure. The children all pressed closer to get better looks.

Eileen couldn't resist taking a step forward herself. Peering over the children's heads, she identified a thimble, coin, needle, spoon, button, pumpkin seed, pecan, twig, two rocks, a hairpin, hat pin, chalk, a bit of ribbon, a candle stub, a feather and a spool.

"Now, I want everyone to study all these items very

closely," Dovie said solemnly. "In a moment you're going to turn around, and I'll mix them up and take one away. Then we'll see who can be first to figure out what's missing."

The children immediately leaned in closer to study the contents intently.

Eileen was amazed. Dovie had managed to capture their attention with very little effort. And with such a simple device.

"It looks like she's in her element, doesn't it?"

Eileen turned to find Mr. Tucker at her side, his gaze on Dovie and the children.

"Very much so," she agreed.

He turned to her. "If you don't mind, perhaps we can step into the hall to talk for a moment?"

"Of course." What did he want to discuss? Had she done something he didn't approve of?

"I want you to know that I meant what I said about taking care of any maintenance or repair work that needs tending to while I'm here."

Some of her tension eased as she settled back into her lady-of-the-manor role. "As it happens, there are a few things that could use some attention."

"Good. If you'll let me know what you think are the most pressing tasks, I'll start figuring out how to best tackle them."

Eileen didn't have to think about it. "The gutters require a good cleaning and there are a few loose rails on the back porch."

He nodded. "That shouldn't be a problem. Is there anything else?"

Surprised he hadn't balked, even a little, she added another item to the list. "Since we'll need to do more cooking than usual and heat more wash water and more rooms, there's the matter of firewood."

"Of course. I've split many a cord in my day."

"You may need to gather the wood as well as split it."

"Understood. Why don't you show me the porch rails you're concerned about now so I have a better idea of what's needed?"

Relieved that he didn't seem overly concerned by her requests, she nodded. "Of course. This way."

As she led the way to the back of the house and out the kitchen door, she was very aware of him walking beside her. What was wrong with her today? She'd never let herself be distracted by such feelings before. Nor even admitted that she had them.

They stepped out onto the back porch, and she immediately put some distance between them. Moving to the far end of the porch, she pointed out the loose railings. "These three spindles and a couple of the ones lining the steps, as well."

Mr. Tucker followed her and examined the rails in question more closely. "I'll need to replace at least one of these, maybe more, but it shouldn't be difficult to do. And I might as well check all the other spindles while I'm at it."

It would be such a relief to have those things taken care of. Perhaps he could even get a little ahead on the firewood so she wouldn't have to buy so much when winter set in.

He stepped down onto the lawn and looked up at the roofline, rubbing his chin. "I have my own tools with me, of course. But I'm going to need a ladder for getting up to those gutters." He glanced her way. "And an ax for chopping firewood."

She waved a hand toward a structure at the far end of her property. "I believe you'll find what you need in the carriage house. Feel free to look around in there and make use of whatever you need." The carriage had been one of the first things she'd sold off. The only thing she used the structure for these days was as a storage shed and a place to keep her gardening implements.

"I'll check it out first thing in the morning." He took a long, slow look around her property. "I could get the boys to rake up these leaves for you, too, if you'd like."

"That would be appreciated." She was beginning to feel as if she were taking advantage of him. She hadn't expected him to work for his keep.

"Good. It'll give them something to focus on besides Miss Fredrick's situation."

She wondered what he was really thinking about the state of her home and property. It had to be painfully obvious to him that she hadn't been able to take care of the place as she ought for some time now.

But his next comment indicated nothing of the sort. "It appears you have quite a garden," he said.

She felt her cheeks warm in pleasure. "It's done well this year. There's not much left to it right now, but I should still be able to harvest a few things from my fall planting until first frost."

"You take care of it yourself?"

Was that surprise in his expression? She tilted her chin up. "I do. Though Dovie helps." Truth to tell, she actually enjoyed working her garden. What had been a pleasant hobby in the past had turned into a means of survival. Many was the day the only thing she ate for her meals was what she'd harvested from her garden. And she'd learned to preserve what she didn't need for her immediate sustenance so that she could stretch her bounty even further. It was surprising, the sense of accomplishment she felt at having vegetables she'd grown and harvested herself in her pantry.

He nodded. "Miss Jacobs seems like a fine person. And I can tell she knows how to deal with children."

Unlike her—was that what he was thinking? And was he assuming Dovie did most of the gardening, as well?

She turned and moved back toward the door, feeling suddenly rattled by all these unaccustomed thoughts. Time to take control of the conversation again. "Speaking of the children, perhaps we can discuss what sort of routine they are accustomed to. And then determine what routine will work best while they are here."

She felt better already. Routines and discipline, that was what provided order and structure, the two things that were essential to a smoothly run household. And it was becoming obvious to her that these children could benefit from some training in that department.

She had a feeling, though, that she and Mr. Tucker would not see eye to eye on that point.

If so, she would just have to bring him around to her way of thinking.

Chapter Seven

Routine? Why was she asking him about that? Simon had no idea what sort of routine Miss Fredrick had set for them, or even if they had one at all. "I'm not sure I understand what exactly you're asking about—what sorts of routines?"

"I would think it would be self-explanatory. I'd like to know what they are accustomed to in the area of mealtimes, bedtimes, quiet times, bath times. What portion of their day is set aside for educational pursuits such as reading, sewing, nature studies, journaling? Are they accustomed to daily readings from the Good Book? That sort of thing."

He didn't appreciate the condescending tone she'd used, but he was determined to remain civil. "Mrs. Pierce, perhaps I didn't explain my role clearly. I had no involvement in the kids' day-to-day lives prior to our boarding the train in St. Louis. I am merely the escort, charged with seeing them safely to Hatcherville and getting them securely installed in their new home. I have no idea what their normal routines are, only what we experienced during the trip, which I imagine was anything *but* normal."

"I see. Then perhaps we shouldn't worry about what they did in the past and concentrate instead on what makes the most sense for now."

"I agree." Though he had some doubts that they would agree on just what *would* make sense.

By this time they'd stepped back inside the kitchen, and she waved a hand toward the table. "Shall we have a seat while we work it out?"

"You mean now?"

"Is there some reason we should wait?" Her expression reminded him of a severe schoolmarm who was dealing with a difficult student.

"I thought perhaps Miss Jacobs should be involved." He tried to be diplomatic. "I mean, we've both admitted to not having experience dealing with children, and she obviously has. Don't you think she could be helpful?"

Mrs. Pierce took a seat, her expression set but her copper-colored eyes flashing like a bright new penny. Was she enjoying this?

She placed her clasped hands in her lap. "For the moment I think it is more important that she continue to keep the children entertained so we can discuss this without distractions."

He tried again. "But if we don't have any point of reference to draw on—"

"Surely laying out routines and schedules has more to do with the adult's perspective than with the children's. And I am not so far removed from my own childhood that I don't remember the routines imposed on me at my boarding school." She shifted slightly, as if she'd said more than she intended.

Boarding school. So she came from money, did she? That explained a lot.

Simon moved toward the table, deciding he might as well hear her out. He took a seat across from her. "All right. I'm willing to give it a shot. Where would you like to start?"

"The first thing I think we should decide is whether everyone should take their meals together or if we should eat in shifts."

"Together," he said immediately, before she could launch into a discussion of pros and cons. "I want to maintain the feeling of family for them as much as possible."

Something flashed in her shiny-penny eyes that he couldn't quite identify, but it left him with the impression that he hadn't given her the answer she'd wanted. To do her credit, though, she nodded. "Very well, then we will need to add back the leaves to the dining room table and find three additional chairs."

"No problem. There are four perfectly fine chairs right here—we can take three of them into the dining room. And if you'll show me where you keep the table leaves, I'll take care of that, as well." Perhaps this routine-setting thing wouldn't be so bad, after all. "What's next?"

"Mealtimes. I would suggest breakfast at seven, the midday meal at noon and dinner at six, but I'm open to suggestions. However, I do feel that whatever schedule we decide on, we should make a point to adhere to it."

"I'm sure, if that's the most convenient schedule for you, it will work fine for the children."

"Good. Now let's move on to bedtimes. I believe it should be no later than eight."

"For the younger ones, perhaps, but the older ones might find that restrictive."

"I suppose, if they want to occupy themselves quietly in their rooms for the first hour then that would be acceptable."

Was she worried about them being too much of a bother for her? But they would only be here for a few days, God willing, so he supposed he could go along with her on this. "All right. What else?"

They discussed bath times, responsibilities for keeping their rooms tidy, and the level of decorum she expected them to maintain in her home.

Simon tried to keep his thoughts to himself and go along with her plans. But he had to wonder—what kind of childhood had the woman had if she thought this was an appropriate routine for youngsters? If this was how she'd spent her time at her boarding school he'd say she would have been better served staying home. "So, are we done?" He hoped his tone didn't convey any of his disdain for her plans.

"Not yet. We need to discuss the amount of time we might want them to spend learning artistic and social skills."

Enough was enough. "Mrs. Pierce, these are *children*." He didn't bother to mask his irritation. "They also need time to just *be* children, to play."

She remained unruffled. "Of course. But it is also important that they be trained while they are young so they may grow into adults who respect and value knowledge and refinement."

"What did you have in mind?" Simon reminded himself once more that this was her home and that they wouldn't be here for long. But he would draw the line quickly enough if he saw her do anything that would make the kids feel as if they didn't measure up to some arbitrary standard she might have in mind. They'd already faced enough of that in their young lives.

And quite frankly, so had he.

"I would be willing to work with them on literature, art, music and etiquette." She actually had a hint of a smile on her face, as if this was something she looked forward to. "In addition, I could work with the girls on their household skills, and perhaps you could work with the boys on whatever skills are particular to young men."

"Mrs. Pierce, I don't—"

She held up a hand to interrupt his protest. "Of course I didn't mean to imply we would address all of these things at the same time."

Thank goodness she recognized that much at least.

"Depending on the length of your stay," she continued, "we might not get around to all of it. But we could assess what skills they already possess and what they might be most interested in learning, and work up a plan from there." She gave him an "I'm right on this" look. "Because it is always good to have a plan worked out."

He chose his words carefully, not wanting to insult her. "Mrs. Pierce, while I know you mean well, a governess is the last thing these children need right now." Or maybe ever. "I think it'll be a better use of everyone's time if we just assign them their fair share of the household chores and leave it at that."

There was the merest hint of disappointment in her expression but it disappeared quickly. "I disagree. But if that is how you feel, then of course that is what we must do." The frostiness was back in her tone.

"Maybe when they get settled into their new home and begin to establish their own routines—" he figured she'd like his use of that word "—then that will be soon enough to worry about all that. But for now they just need some calm and as much normalcy as possible in their lives."

She seemed somewhat mollified. "As I said, you are their caretaker so I will defer to your wishes. If you should change your mind, however, I stand ready to do my part."

Her capitulation surprised him. Perhaps he'd read her wrong. "Thank you. And as I said, I'll expect them to do some chores around here."

"Such as?"

"Well, in addition to keeping their rooms neat and tidy, the girls can help with the dishes, sweeping, dusting, laundry—whatever housekeeping chores need tending to while we're here. The boys can help me with some of the yard work and outdoor chores."

"That seems reasonable." She raised her chin. "I assume, however, if there is time in their schedules, and if it does not unduly tax them, you'd have no objection to my introducing them to a small taste of the finer arts?"

So she hadn't really given up. Perhaps it would be best if he just came out and said what he was feeling. "So long as you don't use such lessons to make them feel inferior, then I don't see any harm in it."

She stiffened. "That would *never* be my intention, no matter what I was teaching them."

Not her intention perhaps, but it could still be the result if she went about it the wrong way. "I'm glad to hear it. But let's go easy with them for the next day or two. And who knows, we may even be able to resume our travels and let you return to your normal routine by then."

Her gaze softened ever so slightly. "If you don't mind my asking, what is the true situation with Miss Fredrick?"

Simon raked his fingers through his hair. "Dr. Pratt says it's all in God's hands now." He grimaced at his own words. "But that's always the case isn't it? Everything is in God's hands at all times." He refused to give up hope.

"Have you given any thought to what you will do if she doesn't get better?"

The widow sure didn't shy away from difficult subjects. "I think it's too early to be giving up on her."

Her expression changed back to that of a no-nonsense schoolmarm. "Planning for a less than happy outcome is *not* giving up on her, and it's definitely not too soon to be thinking of such things. One must strive to be prepared for any contingency. I would think, especially in this case, that would be true."

She was right of course, at least about facing facts. But he wasn't ready to discuss going on without the children's foster mother.

"If the time comes when that becomes necessary, I'll figure something out. Rest assured, I won't abandon these children until I've made certain they'll be well cared for."

"A commendable sentiment. But again, you aren't doing the children any favors by not planning ahead."

He knew she was right but he wasn't ready to deal with it just yet. "Is there anything else you need to discuss with me?"

"I would like to know a little more about the children."

"Such as?"

"Do you know anything of their history? For instance, how did they all come to live with Miss Fredrick? And are any of them siblings?"

"I'm not well acquainted with them personally, but my sister gave me bits and pieces of their stories in the letters she wrote me. And Miss Fredrick gave me some information when I agreed to help her find a new place to set up her household." He chose his words carefully. "There are some sets of siblings in the group and some who have no blood kin here. But they are *all* siblings now, at least in spirit."

"Of course."

Perhaps it would help her feel more of a kinship to the children if she did know some personal information about them. "Fern, Rose and Lily are sisters," he elaborated. "They were the first that Miss Fredrick took in so they've been living with her the longest. They're the children of a distant relation of Miss Fredrick's. She took them and their mother in when the woman learned she had consumption. She gave the girl's mother her word that they would always have a home with her." No need to mention that their father died in jail. "They were the first Miss Fredrick took in and that was about six years ago."

"Is that when she decided to open a children's home?"

"She didn't decide, exactly. She told me that was God's idea, not hers."

Mrs. Pierce frowned slightly. "What does that mean?"

"She made no real effort to take other children in— they just landed on her doorstep, so to speak." He marshaled his thoughts, hoping he had the details right. He had to be careful not to share any of the secrets that weren't his to share.

"Less than a year after the three girls moved in," he continued, "a neighbor who'd recently lost his wife asked Miss Fredrick to look after his kids during the day while he was at work until he could make other arrangements. Those kids were Russell, Harry and Tessa. Two weeks later, the man died. The kids didn't have anyone else step forward to claim them, so she assured the children they would have a home with her for as long as they wanted one." He didn't go into how the father died. The man took to the bottle after his wife died and got himself killed in a bar fight. He wasn't sure how much the kids knew about that sad event, but he certainly wasn't going to be the one to spread the word.

"They were fortunate to have found a place with someone so kindhearted," Mrs. Pierce said.

"That they are—all ten of 'em. In the following years, four infants were left on Miss Fredrick's doorstep—I guess folks heard that they would be welcome there. Unfortunately two of the infants didn't survive long." Many of Miss Fredrick's neighbors held the opinion that it was prostitutes who abandoned their offspring at her door. And they were likely right.

"I take it Molly and Joey were the two who did survive?"

He nodded, surprised that she remembered their names.

"So they are the ones who have no siblings among the others."

He stiffened. "Like I said, something you need to remember about these kids if you want to understand them is that in every way but blood they consider themselves siblings and Miss Fredrick as their mother. She worked very hard to instill that in them—the fact that they are truly a family, I mean. I don't intend to let anyone take that bond away from them."

"Of course." She wrinkled her nose delicately. "It sounds as if people took advantage of her kindheartedness."

"I don't think she saw it that way. In fact I think she looked on it more as an opportunity and a privilege. She truly loves these children."

A slight frown line appeared above her brow. "But I believe you haven't accounted for two of them, Audrey and Albert. You mentioned in the meeting that they are your sister's children?"

He nodded. "Their mother, my sister Sally, passed away three months ago."

"I'm sorry. Was she your only sibling?"

He felt a little kick in the gut at this reminder. The memory could still hit him that way, even after all these years. "No, I had another sister, Imogene, but she died when we were children." Both of his sisters were gone. And he hadn't been there for either of them at the end.

"I'm sorry," she repeated.

He nodded an acknowledgment of her apology, then moved on. "I knew I wasn't up to the task of raising her kids, not on my own anyway. Miss Fredrick and I discussed it and she generously offered to give them a home. That's part of the reason I helped her find a new place for her and the kids to settle down in. That, and the fact that I wanted to make sure I continued to have some involvement in Audrey's and Albert's lives."

"Such as providing this escort when Miss Fredrick decided to move."

He nodded. "But it wasn't just to provide escort—I intend to move there myself so I can be close by. As I said, I want to be a familiar part of their lives. Audrey and Albert are family and I want to be close by should they ever need me for anything." He was determined to never again be too far away to help someone who needed him.

"It's good that you want to be a part of their lives. But was it so easy to uproot yourself?"

He shrugged. "I don't really have strong ties to St. Louis. No family left there now, and I work for myself doing carpentry and occasional odd jobs here and there. Hatcherville has a brick-making facility that I could hire on with if nothing else works out." He was determined to do whatever he had to do to take care of Sally's kids.

But Mrs. Pierce wasn't finished with her questions. "Was there a particular reason Miss Fredrick decided to move so far from her established home? Surely, if her household had outgrown her current residence, there were options closer to home. One would assume she already had friends and connections there that she could call on for assistance should she need it."

"She had her reasons." Reasons he wasn't going to go into, especially with someone who seemed as strait-laced as Mrs. Pierce. These children needed a clean break from their past, and he wasn't going to do anything to jeopardize that.

To do Mrs. Pierce credit, though, she didn't press or seem unduly put off by his answer, or rather, lack of one. Instead she moved on. "Which brings us back to the question of what you will do if Miss Fredrick is no longer able to take care of the children." She said this as matter-of-factly as if saying they had run out of flour. "We will, of course, continue to pray that she recovers fully, but even so, with a stroke there is likely to be a long recovery period."

That was something he hadn't considered. If Miss Fredrick became a convalescent, would her brother put aside this bickering between them and take care of her? And the children?

But that wasn't something to discuss with his hostess. Then it struck him that she might be worried he would try to overstay his welcome. "The house in Hatcherville is already paid for and most of the furnishings from her previous house have been shipped there, so having a place for the children to live won't be an issue."

He was thinking things through as he talked. "I suppose, if the worst *does* happen, I can hire someone responsible, perhaps a married couple, to serve as the children's caretaker while I keep an eye on them as I'd originally planned."

"Then you *have* put some thought into this—good." She stood. "If you will excuse me, there are some things I should take care of before we serve the evening meal."

He stood as well, knowing a dismissal when he heard one. "Of course. And I want to check in on the kids to see if Miss Jacobs needs rescuing."

"I imagine she is in her element."

He agreed. "But still, I don't want to take advantage of her kindness."

"As you wish." She turned toward the cupboard, apparently assuming they were finished with the conversation.

Simon headed for the parlor, still trying to figure out

Eileen Pierce. The woman was much too rigid in her thinking—that much was obvious. It was also obvious she hadn't been around children much, and her ideas of how they should be treated were of the ivory-tower as opposed to the down-to-earth variety.

But to be fair, she did have some good qualities. It seemed she'd gone to the trouble of learning everyone's names. And her method of settling them when their baggage arrived had been surprisingly effective, proving that there was a place for discipline, as long as it wasn't taken to extremes.

She'd also shown both resourcefulness and concern when she'd turned her porch swing into a rocking chair to accommodate Molly. That soft expression on her face when she'd thought herself alone with the toddler had been sweetly transforming, as if she *did* have some semblance of maternal instincts.

He could forgive her her routines and other rigid nonsense if he was certain that deep down she really did have the kids' best interest at heart.

But how could he be sure?

Chapter Eight

Eileen moved to the cupboard to take stock of her place settings once more. Mr. Tucker's insistence that the entire household eat at the same time was regrettable, but she would have to make it work. To her relief she did have the right number of place settings, but only because Daisy and Regina had thought ahead and sent her some extras. Not everything would match, of course, and some of the children would be drinking from mugs rather than glasses, but there was no help for it. She cringed at setting such an unharmonious table, but she would just have to put the best face on it she could.

She momentarily considered eating separately. With Ivy and Dovie she had been able to justify keeping her distance. They were boarders and there were boundaries to be maintained. She hadn't wanted to invite familiarity, hadn't wanted to invite the kind of closeness that would make her boarders feel comfortable prying into her personal life. If that made for a lonely life, so be it— she'd had enough of being judged and found wanting.

But *these* were not boarders—Mr. Tucker and the children were guests. Which meant she had obligations as their hostess. And that included presiding over the meals. Besides, she'd told Mr. Tucker she believed the children should be trained in the proper way to behave. She had a duty to teach them, and how better than by example?

Eileen counted the dishes and silverware one more time. She hoped the children would be careful—if any of these plates were broken she had nothing to replace them with.

As she crossed the room, her thoughts shifted from the dishes to Mr. Tucker. What a strong sense of family he had. It was as admirable a quality as it was foreign to her. She had two younger half sisters, but she hadn't been raised with them, and her mother and stepfather had been distant. So this bond he was so passionate about was difficult for her to understand.

But it sounded like something she might have enjoyed.

Perhaps there was a reason these children—and Mr. Tucker—had ended up in her home. They obviously needed some order and discipline in their lives, and that was something she could definitely provide. It had taken a bit of persuasion, but Mr. Tucker seemed to have finally understood that.

And it had not escaped her notice that he hadn't spent any time thinking through his options given the situation. Of course, said situation was recent and he'd had other things to contend with in the meantime.

Still, she received the distinct impression that he wasn't the sort to do much planning. Which might be something he could get by with in the usual way, but this was hardly a usual situation. And one should always strive to do more than merely *get by*.

Eileen headed down the hall to the bathing room. She carefully took stock of her towels and the supply of firewood. She'd taken several cold baths lately to conserve the wood, but a good hostess wouldn't expect her guests to do the same. She had a vague idea that little children caught chills easily, and the last thing she needed was to have to deal with sick children.

In this room, at least, she had no need to worry about what her visitors might think of her social status. The washroom was one of the luxuries Eileen had insisted on when she'd first moved to Turnabout as a new bride, and Thomas had indulged her, lavishing on her whatever she wanted. She still felt that sense of being pampered when she walked in here. The floor was beautifully tiled; the water was piped into a receptacle that sat on a low stovelike apparatus for heating. The partially sunken tub, which she had had specially shipped in from New Orleans, was opulently large and carved from a single block of marble. It had taken a whole team of men to move it in here. It was why it was still part of her home and had not been sold off with some of her other furnishings—it would have been too difficult to remove.

She let her eyes scan the rest of the room. To one side, a beautifully carved four-panel screen stood ready to provide the bather with additional privacy. Brass hooks lined the wall for keeping one's clothing off the floor. A door on the far end led outdoors.

Then her gaze came to rest on the less indulgent aspects of the room. She'd had to make a compromise or two in the past couple of years. When her housekeeper had been let go and she had to start doing her own laundry, Eileen had brought the washtubs in here and strung a clothesline across one end of the room so that she could do her menial work in private.

Dovie and Ivy knew it was in here, but she never did her laundry while they were around. Just because she had been reduced to doing her own housework didn't mean she had to put herself on display while she played the part of washerwoman.

Of course some of that would have to change now. The sheer volume of laundry the residents in her house would generate would dictate that the clothes be hung outside to dry. She'd have to speak to Mr. Tucker about stringing an additional line for her.

And she had to stop waiting until problems fell in her lap and start planning ahead, just as she had pressed Mr. Tucker to do. What other issues related to her new houseguests was she likely to encounter?

It was time she found a quiet place and thought through the possibilities so she would be prepared.

At dinnertime, Dovie recruited the children to help set the table. Eileen no longer owned the elegant wrought iron cart that her housekeeper had once used to transport the dishes and food from the kitchen to the dining room, so it was necessary to hand carry everything. Eileen didn't take an easy breath until everything had been transported without incident.

As they prepared to take their seats, Dovie looked around the table. "The little ones will need risers on their chairs," she said thoughtfully.

Risers? Eileen looked at her chairs. Entertaining children in her dining room had never been a consideration before. What could she use to improvise?

But before she could formulate a plan, Mr. Tucker

spoke up. "I'll take care of finding or making something to serve the purpose tomorrow. For now, if you or Mrs. Pierce will hold Molly in your lap, I'll hold Joey in mine."

Apparently reading the panic in her face, Dovie quickly spoke up. "I'll be glad to hold Molly, if Eileen will allow me the honor."

Grateful for the woman's offer, Eileen gave a regal nod. "Yes, of course."

"Then that leaves you to serve everyone's plate," Mr. Tucker said, smiling her way.

Eileen hesitated, then stood. She supposed if she had to choose between server and nursemaid, she preferred the role of server. The memory of how Molly had felt snuggled up against her flitted through her mind, but she shoved it away. Such things were not for her.

As Fern no doubt agreed.

"So how shall we do this?" she asked. "Would it be better for you to pass up your plates for me to serve? Or for you to each bring me your plates to fill?"

"I would suggest they bring you their plates," Dovie answered. "Less handling and confusion that way."

She nodded, seeing the logic in that. "Very well. Children, take your plates and line up. And do take care to hold them straight so nothing slides onto the floor."

Eileen served the first two plates without incident. Then it came to the third child, Rose. She placed a generous slice of ham on the plate then ladled up some of the butter beans.

"No!"

Eileen froze, startled by the little girl's vehemence.

"Rose doesn't like for her food to touch." Fern said. The older girl's lips were pinched in disapproval, as if

Eileen had been sloppy, or worse yet, had done it on purpose.

Why did Fern seem to dislike her so much? But now was not the time to worry about that.

"My apologies." She set the plate with the offending contents aside and picked up her own. She very carefully dished up the ham, squash and butter beans so that very little liquid made it to the plate and then placed them so nothing touched.

Rose studied the plate suspiciously, then smiled, nodded with a thank-you and moved to her chair.

The next three children were served without incident, and Eileen began to breathe easier. She wasn't sure why she'd been so nervous; this was a simple task after all.

Then Harry stepped up for his portion. Just as she put the last spoonful of vegetables on his dish, it happened—Harry dropped his plate. The food splattered everywhere, including the bottom of her skirt. And the plate—one of the precious few remaining from her good china service, broke into three pieces.

Eileen stared at the mess, unable to move, horrified by the extent of the disaster. It wasn't the mess; it wasn't even the possibility that her dress was stained. That broken dish meant someone would not have a plate to eat from for this meal or any subsequent ones while her newfound guests remained in residence.

She turned her gaze on the offender, prepared to scold him for his clumsiness. Then she spotted his stricken and mortified expression and the words dried in her throat. Their eyes locked for a moment and Eileen found herself searching for the right words to defuse the situation.

She managed to drag out a smile and keep her dismay out of her tone. "No harm done."

Dovie set Molly down in the chair and bustled over. "Harry, why don't you let me help you clean up this mess while Mrs. Pierce finishes serving the others."

Grateful for Dovie's intervention, Eileen took a quick glance at the others in the room and saw expressions displaying various degrees of wariness. Were they worried there would be repercussions?

She took care to smile at the next child in line. Keeping her expression and movements calm and unruffled, she mechanically placed the food on Tessa's plate and each of the others that followed, making sure she said something to each of them. But her mind kept spinning over what she would do to replace the broken dish.

By the time she filled the last plate, the mess on the floor had been cleaned up and she handed Harry the plate she'd fixed earlier for Rose. Hopefully the boy wouldn't mind that the food touched.

And she still hadn't come up with a solution to being short by one plate.

Time to make a graceful exit—or as graceful as possible given the circumstances. "If you will excuse me, I have something to attend to. Please go on with your meal without me."

Her announcement was met with an awkward silence and some of the wary glances returned. Her gaze snagged for a heartbeat on Mr. Tucker's frown, but then she turned to make her exit. Leaving her guests to their own devices seemed preferable to making a spectacle out of her lack of a place setting.

But before she could get away, Mr. Tucker spoke up. "Mrs. Pierce, whatever it is you need to take care of, surely it can wait until after we eat." His gaze practically demanded she stay.

But she ignored both the gaze and the words. "I'm afraid it cannot." And with that, she left the room without a backward glance.

When Eileen reached the kitchen, she looked around as if a plate would appear out of thin air. The only thing that seemed remotely appropriate was the meat platter, but it was big enough to serve a full-grown turkey. Even the saucers were on the side table in the dining room, awaiting time to serve the pecan pie.

She gave a mental shrug. That was irrelevant. The fresh food was back in the dining room and she didn't plan to go back out there before the others were done eating.

Eileen moved to the sink and wet a rag. She lifted her hem and began scrubbing at the food spatters on her skirt with firm, even strokes. Too bad she hadn't been wearing the black skirt. She no longer had so much clothing that she could afford to discard something merely because it was stained.

Her stomach rumbled—she'd had a very light lunch. She supposed she could always open one of the jars of vegetables she'd put up from her garden. But after the savory meal she'd just dished up for the others, she had very little enthusiasm for such fare.

Perhaps she would just wait. Once the dishes were washed and the children were put down for the night she could come back here and snack on whatever leftovers were available.

The door opened behind her and she quickly dropped her skirt. Then she turned around with hastily mustered dignity. Mr. Tucker stood in the doorway, looking oddly diffident.

She managed a haughty look. "I will thank you, sir, to knock when entering a room with a closed door."

"My apologies, ma'am. I guess I'm just not used to knocking before entering a kitchen."

He was quite right, but she ignored both that and the hint of amusement in his tone. "And just what are you doing following me in here? Shouldn't you be keeping an eye on the children?"

"The better question is, what are *you* doing in here. After we said the blessing I told the kids I'd check on you. They all think you're angry with them, or at least with Harry."

It seemed she was failing in at least one area of her duties as a hostess. "Please put their minds at ease." She brushed at her skirt, keeping her expression politely distant. "You may assure them it is only that I prefer to take my meals in private."

"Nonsense."

She stiffened. Had he just called her a *liar?*

"You were all set to eat in the dining room before Harry's accident."

He had her there, so she held her tongue.

"Accidents happen—" his voice had taken on a more cajoling tone "—especially when children are involved. But as adults we need to be understanding and forgiving. They shouldn't be made to feel that they've been found lacking."

Time to put an end to this. She tilted up her head and gave him a direct look. "Again, I apologize if they misread my mood. Was there anything else?"

Her words only seemed to intensify his irritation.

"Reassurances from me won't help the situation—they need to see it for themselves. You can't really want to have the children think you don't care for their company."

Why couldn't the man just drop the subject and go away? "The children have you and Miss Jacobs to help build their self-esteem. My function is to provide shelter, and perhaps also provide them with instruction on matters of propriety and taste."

"And do you consider your current actions a good example for them to follow?"

She had no answer for that.

"Just put aside your own feelings for a moment and think of theirs. Surely you can do this one thing, just to put their minds at ease."

She knew he was trying to manipulate her by playing on her sympathies. But that didn't stop her from feeling a pang of guilt.

"Afterward," he continued, "if you want to eat every other meal for the rest of your life in total isolation, then I won't interfere."

His sarcasm was easier to deal with than his cajoling. "And what makes you think you have the right to interfere now?"

He threw up his hands. "Have it your way."

He pushed out of the room in a huff, and Eileen heard him mutter something that sounded suspiciously like *impossible woman*.

She sagged against the counter, feeling more than a bit sorry for herself. There were tears pressing against the back of her eyes, but she refused to let them fall. Better he think her selfish than that he learn the pitiful truth.

Without warning the door swung open again.

"I don't think you truly under—" Mr. Tucker paused midsentence, studying her face. Then he gave a short bow. "Forgive me for being such a thoughtless lout. I'm sorry if I upset you—of course you have every right to your privacy."

It was his unexpected kindness that did her in. "I don't have another plate!" She clapped a hand over her mouth. She hadn't meant to blurt that out—she *wasn't* a blurter. But at least she had the satisfaction of seeing surprise replace the sympathy on his face.

He recovered a moment later and gave her an incredulous smile. "Is that all?"

"Is that *all?*" She took a deep breath, calming herself and trying to reclaim her dignity by brute force. "Mr. Tucker, it seems to me a plate is an essential part of the meal process."

"Well, sure, but one can get creative and improvise."

Without waiting for her response, he moved to her cupboards and shifted a few things around.

She watched him, trying to figure out how to get the situation back under control after her pitiful confession. What must he think of her now?

"Ah, here we go." He turned back to her in triumph. "Two shallow bowls."

Did he really expect her to eat from a bowl while he and the others ate from plates? That would be so undignified. "Bowls are for soups and stews."

His cocky attitude didn't falter. "What I was *actually* thinking was that in the future, we can serve Molly's and Joey's food in these while the rest of us eat from the plates." His pleased-with-himself grin should have irritated her, but for some reason it didn't.

"I see." She supposed that could work. But it didn't take care of tonight's meal.

"As for today," he said as if reading her thoughts, "I can't eat my meal knowing you are back here alone and hungry. Please return to the dining room with me."

His smile was disarmingly charming, but she stiffened her resolve. "Mr. Tucker, please don't waste your time worrying over me—I am neither lonely nor unduly hungry. I have told you that I will not eat my meal from one of those bowls. And I can hardly swap dishes with one of the children now that they have already started on their meals. Feel free to make what excuses you feel necessary to relieve their anxiety." She marched to the pantry and snatched up a jar at random. "I will open this jar of—" she looked at it more closely "—speckled butter beans. It will do quite well for my dinner." Hopefully she put more enthusiasm in her voice than she truly felt for the bland fare.

Did he actually roll his eyes at her?

Chapter Nine

Simon couldn't believe Mrs. Pierce would rather go hungry than sacrifice her dignity. But he was relieved to discover that *that* was her issue rather than a selfish desire to make Harry feel bad.

If the infuriating woman would just relax and handle the situation with a touch of humor, no one would give it a second thought. But humor didn't seem to be a strength of hers—he'd have to come up with something else—something that would allow her the cold comfort of her dignity. "All right, if you won't eat from a bowl, perhaps you can claim to have a light appetite and eat from one of the saucers."

There was no thawing in her demeanor. "Those saucers are for the dessert. If I take one for my meal, then we will be short one when it comes time to serve the pie."

That was an easy fix. "Not necessarily. I'll just eat my dessert from my dinner plate. No one will think anything of it."

Still she hesitated, so he tried another approach. "If you won't do it for yourself, then do it for the children.

Right now they still think you're angry with Harry. And the longer we stay back here, the stronger that feeling will grow." He gave her a direct look. "*Are* you angry with Harry?"

"I've already told you I wasn't," she said stiffly. Then she unbent slightly. "Actually, I suppose I *was* angry at the time."

He was pleasantly surprised by her honesty. It confirmed his belief that she was a woman of integrity.

"But only for a moment," she continued. "Anger is a useless emotion that accomplishes nothing."

At least they agreed on that point. He gave her what he hoped was a persuasive smile. "I know eating from a saucer is not the most dignified way to take your meal, but I'd consider it a great favor if you'd do so just this once. Come on and rejoin us in the dining room so the children can see for themselves you're not angry."

He thought he could detect some of her resolve slipping and searched for a way to press his advantage. "You said earlier that you wanted to give the children instruction on social skills. Isn't showing grace under pressure one of those skills?"

She didn't say anything for several heartbeats. Then she nodded. "You are correct. And if it truly means that much to you and the children, I suppose I could make do, just this once."

"Thank you. Your selflessness is a wonderful example for the children."

She moved to the door, her expression composed. She either hadn't heard the teasing note in his words or chose to ignore it.

When they entered the dining room, all discussion

stopped and the children studied them with wary expressions.

"My apologies for being gone so long," Mrs. Pierce said pleasantly. "I wanted to clean my skirt before the stain set." She casually reached for one of the nearby saucers, then sat down with a graceful movement.

Simon studied her relaxed demeanor with approval. One would think her the hostess to a gathering of welcome friends rather than unanticipated houseguests, most of whom were children.

She looked around the table. "I declare, it's been more than two years since I sat with so many for a meal in here. It feels almost like a dinner party."

"I like parties," Molly said hopefully. "Me and Flossie have tea parties sometimes."

"Tea parties are quite nice," Mrs. Pierce agreed. "Perhaps we can have one while you are here."

Simon felt some of the tension ease from the room.

"I understand you had the opportunity to visit the Blue Bottle Sweet Shop this afternoon," she said to Harry. "Were you able to sample any of Mrs. Dawson's fine treats?"

"Yes, ma'am." The boy sat up straighter. "I never tasted such fine caramels in all my born days."

She smiled. "Caramels were always my favorite treat as a little girl, as well."

Then she turned to one of the other children to ask a question about their meal at Daisy's restaurant.

Throughout the meal she was a gracious hostess, making certain the conversation didn't lapse or grow stale and trying to draw everyone out. She might not have much experience with children, Simon reflected, but her social skills were excellent.

Once the meal was over, Simon stood. "All right, it's time for us to show Mrs. Pierce how much we appreciate her hospitality. Audrey and Albert, you clear the table. Rose and Lily, you take care of washing, drying and putting away the dishes."

"I'll help with that," Miss Jacobs offered as she stood.

With a nod, he turned to Fern. "If Mrs. Pierce would be so good as to show you where things are, you can help Molly and Tessa take their baths. Harry, Russell and Joey, let's bring in some firewood for the morning."

Mrs. Pierce stood, as well. "We'll also need some wood for the firebox in the bathing room."

"Then we'll take care of that first thing. Come on, boys."

Fern took Molly and Tessa by the hand. "Let's go get your nightclothes." She didn't so much as look at Mrs. Pierce.

Simon swallowed a sigh. He didn't know whether to say something to Fern or just hope things worked out on their own—he was no good at that sort of thing.

Dealing with the children's squabbles and emotions was something he'd expressly told Miss Fredrick he didn't want to get involved in. She'd assured him she was quite capable of handling that aspect of the trip herself. The possibility that she would become incapacitated had never crossed his mind.

Simon instructed his helpers on how much wood to bring inside and where to put it, then gathered up an armload to carry into the bathing room himself.

He'd realized her woodpile was nearly depleted when he'd checked it out earlier and had hiked along the nearby tree line to gather what he could find quickly.

Tomorrow he and some of the boys would do a more thorough job. If possible, he wanted to lay up enough wood to last the widow through the winter before he left.

Simon stepped into the hallway a few minutes later just as Mrs. Pierce was leading the three girls toward the washroom.

"Good," she said when she saw him. "You can follow us."

She led the way to a room at the very back of the house. When she pushed the door open and allowed the girls to precede her he heard the little gasps of pleasure from Molly and Tessa.

"It's beautiful," Molly said. "This house really *is* a castle."

When Simon entered he saw what had triggered that reaction. The surprisingly large, beautifully tiled room was the picture of opulence. The impressively large, heavy-looking carved tub must have taken an army of men to install, not to mention they had to have built the room around it. A bench, made of cypress wood, sat to one side of the tub, awaiting the bather's needs.

Even the squat, cast-iron stovelike fixture near the tub had gleaming brass fixtures and fancy enameled face plates. As he stoked the fire, he took in the large reservoir built onto the top of the firebox.

Mrs. Pierce moved to the tub and turned on the water. "We'll let a little bit of cool water in here while we wait for the water on the stove to heat." She then stepped over to the stove to turn on the faucet there, letting in the water to be heated. At the same time he finished lighting the stove and stood. The action put them in unexpectedly close proximity for the second time today.

Not that he minded.

Not even a little bit.

Eileen's breath caught in her throat as she got an unexpected close-up look at his eyes. His flashing forget-me-not blue eyes that seemed to see so much more of her than anyone had before.

Shaken by that thought, she took a hasty step back and nearly tripped over her own feet.

He shot out an arm to steady her and she actually felt a tingle at that contact. This was ridiculous. She was no starry-eyed schoolgirl and he was no knight in shining armor. But her treacherous pulse seemed to think otherwise.

Her cheeks burned as Mr. Tucker gave her a knowing smile.

Fortunately, he didn't put her on the spot. "Since there are so many baths to be had," he said instead, "I'll get another armload of firewood."

Eileen watched him leave, still feeling oddly unsettled.

She turned to see the three girls watching her curiously and quickly pulled herself together. "It's going to take a little while for the water to heat up, so let me show you where everything is while we wait."

She turned off the tap on the tub, then quickly showed the girls where the towels and soap were stored. With their help she moved the screen so that it shielded the tub from the door. She also showed them where they could hang their garments while they were bathing.

She stepped out into the hallway and leaned back against the closed door, trying to gather her thoughts.

What was wrong with her? She hadn't even known this man for a full day, yet he was affecting her in an altogether uncomfortable manner.

It had to be only because it had been so very long since anyone had paid her this kind of attention. The unapologetic interest and appreciation were a heady tonic to her flagging morale. Even when he argued with her, he did it in a manner that made it clear he had really listened to what she had to say; he just didn't happen to agree with her.

But she was honest enough with herself to realize he probably treated everyone this way. It had nothing to do with her.

It would be a huge mistake to give in to the temptation to believe otherwise.

Chapter Ten

According to the children, it was a standard practice for all of them to gather together in the parlor before bedtime and have some family discussion time.

After everyone was seated, Simon looked around. "How do you usually spend this family time?" he asked.

"Gee-Gee has us each mention something that happened during the day that we're thankful for," Russell said. "She says it's important that we go to bed thinking on blessings, not complaints. And then we say a group prayer—we each take a turn voicing it."

The more Simon learned of Miss Fredrick, the more he appreciated how special she was. He nodded to the child on his left. "Would you like to start us off Audrey?"

The seven-year-old didn't hesitate. "I'm thankful that today I got to visit a candy store that was in a toy shop."

They moved clockwise around the room. Some of the children had to think harder than others—given the day they'd had, Simon wasn't surprised.

When they reached Dovie, she didn't question whether or not she should participate. "I'm thankful to have met such fine children," she said without hesitation.

Simon wasn't sure about Mrs. Pierce, but to his relief, when her turn came up, she lifted her chin. "I am thankful for the generosity of my neighbors who provided the meal for our supper and other household items for our use."

He gave her a smile of approval before turning to the next person in their circle. Eventually they made it all the way around the room and back to him. "I'm thankful for many of the same things you all have already mentioned," he said, "but I'm also thankful that I have met these two wonderful ladies—Mrs. Pierce and Miss Jacobs."

Russell indicated it was his night to voice the evening prayer and the boy did it with a quiet poise and articulateness that surprised Simon.

After the final amens, Simon stood. "Now, it's been a long day, for all of us. I think it's time we turned in for the night."

"But we haven't had our bedtime story yet," Joey said.

Simon barely managed to suppress his grimace. "Bedtime story?" Surely they didn't expect *him* to take Miss Fredrick's place in that ritual.

"Gee-Gee *always* tells us a story before we go to bed," Molly explained.

Simon rubbed the back of his neck. "I don't think I know any bedtime stories to tell you." He turned, intending to ask Miss Jacobs for help. But before he could do so, Molly hopped up and went to stand in front of Mrs. Pierce.

"Do you know any bedtime stories to tell us?" she asked.

Mrs. Pierce looked startled, then she nodded. "When I was a little girl," she said slowly, "my father had a book of stories that had wondrous tales of adventure. I still remember some of them. I can tell you one if you like."

Molly nodded vigorously enough to make her braids dance. "Oh, yes, please."

"Very well. Take your seat."

Molly plopped down on the floor at Mrs. Pierce's feet and stared up expectantly.

Mrs. Pierce stared at the little girl a moment with one of her unreadable expressions, and he wondered for a moment if she would make the little girl move to a chair.

But she finally looked up and glanced around the room to include all the children. "Long ago in a far-away land, there was a mother duck who sat on her nest, eagerly awaiting the hatching of the six eggs resting there. She sat, and she sat, and she sat, until finally, one by one, they all hatched—all, that is, but the very largest egg."

Simon listened as she told the story of the ugly duckling who tried and tried to fit in with his hatch-mates, but never did. He was surprised at how animated she became, conveying emotion and character through her voice and gestures. It was almost as if she were a different person from the stiff, reserved woman he'd been dealing with all day.

Well, perhaps not *all* day. There'd been those two moments when they'd connected in a very personal way. There'd been nothing stiff about her then.

Whatever the case, she had the children completely

enthralled. And as he listened to the story, she had him captivated, as well. It was as if that particular story had been written for him.

Like the ugly duckling, he'd been placed in the wrong nest and didn't fit in with the others there. Orphaned at nine, he'd ended up in his uncle Corbitt's home. Uncle Corbitt's son, Arnold, was a year older than Simon and could do no wrong. The comparisons between the two boys were as inevitable as they were harsh.

In the beginning, Simon had strived to please his uncle. He gave up his love of working with wood when his uncle sneered at such an occupation. Instead, when he'd turned thirteen, he'd apprenticed alongside Arnold at his uncle's accounting firm. He'd hated it—hated being hunched over a desk indoors all day, hated working with figures and files, hated the fact that no matter how hard he worked, how painstaking his efforts, his uncle always found something lacking.

He had spent four miserable years in that office, and had watched other young men move up the ladder past him, before he came to his senses and realized that he would never be good enough to please his uncle.

He moved out, apprenticed himself to a master cabinetmaker and never looked back. Like the ugly duckling, he'd discovered who he was meant to be.

When at last the story was over, there was a moment of silence when no one spoke and no one moved.

Molly, still wide-eyed, was the first to break the spell. She let out a big, happy sigh. "Have you ever seen a swan before?" she asked.

Mrs. Pierce shook her head. "Not in person, but I've seen pictures of them and they are truly beautiful, elegant creatures."

"I'm so glad the little duckling found some friends," Tessa said dreamily.

"As am I." Mrs. Pierce stood, her control now firmly back in place. "I believe it is time for you children to go upstairs and turn in for the night."

Molly jumped up. "But first you have to rock me in your com-prize rocker."

"What's a prize rocker?" Joey looked at Molly as if he thought she was getting away with something.

Mrs. Pierce answered before Molly could. "Since I don't have a regular rocking chair, Molly and I sat out on my porch swing this afternoon."

"A swing." Joey was immediately intrigued. "Can I see?"

Molly frowned at him. "I get to sit on her lap."

Joey frowned right back. "Says who?"

Audrey and Tessa chimed in with requests to join them, as well.

Simon intervened. "I don't think that swing could hold all of you at the same time. If Mrs. Pierce is willing, those of you who want to be rocked can go two or three at a time. But only for a few minutes, mind you. We don't want to wear her out." He shot the widow a teasing grin. "Not on our first day here anyway."

She didn't acknowledge his teasing, but he thought he detected just the tiniest smile trying to slip past her controlled demeanor.

Turning away from him, she nodded toward the kids. "Of course. We'll start with the youngest since they should be tucked in first. The rest of you will sit quietly here in the parlor until it is your turn."

Yes, she was most definitely back in control of herself.

"The night air can have a bite to it this time of year," Dovie said. "Wait here and I'll get a blanket for you."

While they waited, Mrs. Pierce gathered Molly, Joey and Tessa together, and then assured Audrey, Albert and Lily that they would be next.

"Mind if I join you?" Simon wasn't sure exactly why he'd asked her that. Except that he wasn't ready to turn in just yet. And that he found her company, if not pleasant, very intriguing.

At her surprised look he hastily raised a hand to forestall her response. "Not on the swing. I meant I'd like to sit out on the bench by the door. Just thought I'd enjoy the night air and do a bit of whittling."

Miss Jacobs showed up with the blanket just then so the widow gave him a short nod as she turned to take it from her. "As you wish."

Eileen escorted the three children outside. As they headed for the swing, she was grateful for the blanket. Now that the sun was down there was a definite chill in the air.

Almost before she had settled into her seat, Molly clambered up into her lap as if it were a prized position that one of the others would try to snatch from her. Tessa and Joey took a seat on either side of her and Eileen was startled to have Tessa burrow under her arm and Joey hang on to her other one.

By the time they were all settled under the blanket, Mr. Tucker had stepped outside carrying a pocketknife and a chunky piece of wood. She watched him for a moment, admiring the strength and confidence in his movements as he freed playful curls of wood from the stodgy block of pine. It was almost hypnotic.

"Sing me a song."

Molly's sleepily uttered request broke the spell, and Eileen guiltily turned her attention back to the children, glad Mr. Tucker hadn't caught her staring.

She felt self-conscious at the thought of singing with him there, but he seemed to be focused entirely on his whittling.

After a moment, Eileen set the swing in motion, and the children let out a collective sigh of pleasure.

Not wanting to spoil this fragile peace, she dredged up the memory of a song from long ago, one her father had sung to her. She began to softly sing the strains, haltingly at first, still very aware of Mr. Tucker's presence. Then more confidently as he showed no signs of paying any attention.

Simon kept his gaze focused on his whittling, but every other part of him was acutely aware of the woman seated just a few feet away. He'd felt her stare on him like a feather on his neck. He'd heard the hesitation in her voice as she began the lullaby and known it was because of him.

Then, when she'd settled into it more comfortably, he'd felt as if she'd accepted not just his presence but *him*.

Which were all just fanciful notions, and he wasn't normally given to fancifulness.

Listening to her now, he had to admit that she had a very nice voice—soothing and something he thought of as smoky at the same time.

It was the same with the story she'd told the kids earlier. She'd had them—even the older ones—eating out of her hand. It was as if, when she lost herself in story—spoken or sung—she became someone different, someone warmer and more approachable.

It had him seeing her in a whole different light. She might not have the friendliest of demeanors, and she obviously wasn't accustomed to dealing with kids. But there was an instinctual tenderness and caring below the surface that the children were beginning to respond to.

The puzzle was, why did she try to keep those virtues so well hidden? Because she obviously put up that cool, reserved front deliberately.

She finished the little lullaby she'd been singing and flowed seamlessly into a soft humming, keeping the swing in motion. He chanced a glance her way and saw Molly had fallen asleep and Tessa and Joey were yawning. Mrs. Pierce was stroking Tessa's hair with the gentleness of a loving caress.

Her demeanor seemed dreamy, unfocused—until she glanced his way. Then her eyes widened as if she'd just remembered he was there.

Simon set his whittling aside and stood. "It's time to get this crew to bed," he said softly as he approached the swing. He reached down to take Molly and for just a heartbeat she resisted. Then she released her hold and he scooped the sleeping toddler up.

Mrs. Pierce straightened and patted Joey and Tessa's legs. "Come along, you two. Time for bed." She took each by the hand and followed Mr. Tucker into the house.

Fern met them at the foot of the stairs. "I'll take Tessa and Joey to their rooms and tuck them in."

To Simon's surprise, Mrs. Pierce didn't react to the challenge in Fern's tone. She merely surrendered the children's hands. "Thank you, Fern," she said politely.

"I'll take Audrey, Albert and Lily out to the swing while you're doing that."

Simon followed Fern and her two charges up the stairs, but his thoughts were still with their hostess. Was she unaware of Fern's puzzling hostility, or had she just chosen to ignore it?

He remembered how woebegone the widow looked when he'd returned unexpectedly to the kitchen earlier. It had made her seem more approachable, somehow, more human.

More attractive.

Still, the idea that she could remain so calm over everything else that had been thrown at her today and then fall to pieces over being short by one place setting made no sense to him.

One thing was becoming obvious though—the ice queen was beginning to thaw. If he stayed here long enough, would he see her melt completely?

Chapter Eleven

Eileen headed downstairs earlier than normal the next morning. Truth to tell, she'd had trouble getting much sleep at all last night. So much had happened in just one day. To think, this time yesterday she hadn't even heard of Mr. Tucker and his charges.

And to be perfectly honest, it was Mr. Tucker himself who'd been responsible for her restlessness. In just one short day he'd managed to put her on edge, make her question her way of looking at things and generally upset her well-ordered life.

The fact that she had taken a little extra care with her appearance this morning and that she found herself eager to see him were proof that he was not good for her equanimity.

And, to be honest, she wasn't exactly sorry the children had descended on her house, either. Despite some of the problems having so many unexpected houseguests had introduced into her life, it actually felt good to have a purpose other than just surviving day to day, and to have people around her who looked to her for help.

And perhaps, once this little interlude was over and

her guests had departed, her neighbors would look on her with a friendlier eye again.

But for right now, there was much to be done. She had convinced Mr. Tucker yesterday that they should set a routine for the children, so now she must follow through with her plans.

Her foot had barely touched the bottom stair when she heard a light knock at the front door.

Wondering who would be calling at such an early hour and why they hadn't rung the bell, Eileen headed for the door. She opened it to see Hortense Peters's oldest son halfway down the front walk.

He turned back. "Hello, Mrs. Pierce. Hope I didn't disturb you or the other folks inside. Ma told me to just leave the baskets on the front porch if no one was up and about."

Eileen looked down and sure enough two large cloth-covered baskets sat there.

"Thank you—Dwight, is it? And thank your mother for me, as well."

"Yes, ma'am." And with a nod of his head, the lanky youth turned and continued on his way.

Eileen took hold of both baskets and headed for the kitchen. She pushed the door open with her hip, then paused on the threshold. Mr. Tucker was already there, getting the stove stoked and ready

He glanced over his shoulder and gave her a broad smile. "Good morning. Looks like I'm getting your stove heated just in time."

She moved to the table to set the baskets down, determined not to let him see how much he rattled her. "I see you're an early riser." She lifted the cloth on the first one to find it contained eggs, very carefully packed. A

quick count revealed there were seventeen of them—
quite a generous gift.

"One of the best parts of the day is watching the
sun come up." Mr. Tucker stood and brushed his hands
against each other. "I've actually been up for a while—I
went over to check on Miss Fredrick first thing."

She met his gaze, trying to discern how it had gone.
"How is she?"

"No change." He nodded toward the basket. "What
do you have there?"

Eileen accepted his change of subject. "The ingredients for our breakfast." She checked inside the second
basket and found it contained a length of summer sausage and two small loaves of fresh-baked bread. There
was even a jar of what looked like pear preserves. She
met his gaze again. "There is enough here to make a
hearty breakfast for everyone."

Dovie bustled into the room just then. "Good morning, you two. I guess I'm the slugabed today."

"I believe it's more that we are up extra early." Eileen
waved toward the baskets. "I figured with so many to
cook for, it might be wise to get an early start."

"It 'pears like Mr. Tucker has spoiled us and gotten
the stove going." Dovie peered into the baskets. "Oh,
my, yes. We can whip up a fine breakfast with these
ingredients."

Dovie crossed the room to pluck an apron from a peg
by the door. "Why don't you two see about getting the
children up while I start cooking these eggs."

Get the children up? Eileen wasn't sure she liked the
sounds of that. What all was involved?

But Mr. Tucker was already nodding agreement and
holding open the kitchen door for her so she swallowed

her protest. She was very careful, though, not to brush against him as she stepped past him to make her exit.

"If you get Fern up first," he said as they moved to the stairs, "she'll help you with the others. I'll take care of the boys."

He seemed all business this morning. Which was perversely disappointing. "Very well." Eileen gave him a stern look. "But please make it clear that they should straighten their beds and put their nightclothes away neatly before they come down."

He frowned at that, but then nodded and executed a short bow. There *might* have been a touch of sarcasm in the gesture, but she chose to ignore it.

When Eileen knocked on Fern's door, she discovered the girl was already awake. Had she had trouble sleeping, as well? Eileen felt her first touch of kinship with the prickly girl.

"Miss Jacobs is cooking breakfast," she said. "Time for everyone to get up and get dressed. Do you need help with anything?"

"No." Fern's tone was stiff. "And I'll help Molly."

Fern's tone indicated she thought Eileen would argue the point with her.

But she was mistaken. "Very well." Eileen moved back to the door. "I'll check in on the others. You two can join us downstairs when you are ready. And don't forget to straighten your room."

Eileen got the other four girls moving, helping them start on their morning ablutions before she headed back down the stairs to help Dovie in the kitchen.

Breakfast went much smoother than last night's supper had. Molly and Joey were given the shallow bowls to eat from rather than plates, which meant not only were there enough plates for the rest of them there was even one to spare if it should be needed. And rather than Eileen serving the plates, Dovie filled each plate with eggs and sausage from the stove and transported them to the dining room already filled. There was only the bread and jelly to be passed around at the table itself.

Mr. Tucker offered the blessing, including a prayer for Miss Fredrick's recovery.

After the amens were said, Fern spoke up. "May we visit Gee-Gee today?"

Eileen paused in her eating, curious to hear how Mr. Tucker would handle the question.

He hesitated, then set his fork down. "I'm afraid there's not much visiting to be done. I checked in on her this morning. She hasn't awakened yet. I think it might be better to wait another day or so before you try to see her."

"But she *will* get better, won't she?" Fern pressed.

"That's for the Good Lord to decide." Mr. Tucker glanced around the table. "The best thing we can do for her is to continue to pray."

The kids sobered and began eating their breakfast in silence.

Despite the somber mood his words had evoked, Eileen admired Mr. Tucker's ability to speak honestly but with great empathy to the children.

Miss Fredrick had chosen well when she asked him to accompany her.

After breakfast, as they pushed away from the table, Simon decided to speak up before Mrs. Pierce could bring up the subject of routines. "Girls, please take care of the table and the dishes this morning. Boys, you're going to come outside with me and help with some chores I have lined up."

"What kind of chores?" Harry asked.

"There are leaves to be raked, firewood to be gathered and some repairs to be made." He turned back to the girls. "Once the table is cleared and the dishes are done, I'm sure you'll want to help with whatever household chores Mrs. Pierce or Miss Jacobs assign you. Isn't that right?"

Heads nodded and a few "yes sirs" echoed across the room. He glanced Mrs. Pierce's way, but couldn't gauge her reaction. She certainly wasn't shy about speaking up, so he was sure she would tell him if she disagreed with his approach.

He turned back to the boys. "Come along, men. Let's get to it."

When they stepped out onto the back porch, Simon rubbed his chin a moment, trying to decide where to start. Then he pointed to the carriage house. "I think the first order of business is to take a look inside there and see what kind of materials and tools we have to work with."

"Sorta like a treasure hunt," Harry said.

Simon grinned as he led the way. "Exactly. Only we're looking for useful tools and supplies rather than jewels and coins." When they reached the structure, he had the boys help him open all the doors and shutters to let in as much light as possible.

There were two windows on both the east and west side, as well as a smaller door straight ahead on the back wall. That should have been enough to provide light to the entire interior. But vines had grown up over some of the windows and the rear door would only open partway. Which meant the light from outside was only able to penetrate about two-thirds of the way in—the rest of the interior was just shadows and musty odors.

Near the entrance was a collection of gardening tools that looked well used and well cared for. It included a wheelbarrow, which he figured would definitely come in handy.

As he examined the tools, he tried to picture the reserved widow using the hoe and other implements to work the soil in her garden, but his imagination failed him. What was her story anyway?

Her bearing and manner spoke of a privileged upbringing. And this home she lived in spoke of wealth. But she had no servants, and the house showed signs of having been stripped of many of its furnishings. And he had sensed some kind of tension between her and the other townsfolk yesterday at the meeting.

Had she fallen on hard times recently? But why would that have put her at odds with the community?

"What exactly are we looking for?" Russell asked, bringing his thoughts back to the present.

"An ax, ladder, nails, paint." Simon shrugged. "Anything that might come in handy for chopping firewood or fixing up the place."

"There's an ax," Russell said as he crossed to the left wall. "And a ladder, too."

"Careful." Simon quickly followed the boy. "Better let me get the ax down."

Russell frowned. "I know how to handle an ax."

Conscious of the boy's feelings, Simon nodded. "I'm sure you do, but I need you to help the other boys get that ladder down and drag it outside. Stretch it to its full length on the ground and then check the rungs for soundness." He placed a hand on the boy's shoulder. "I'm counting on you to make a thorough check."

Appearing slightly mollified, Russell took charge of the ladder and his small team, and they had the ladder outside in short order.

Simon took the ax down and examined it closely. It needed sharpening, but that was something easily handled. Otherwise it was in good shape. And he spotted a heavy mallet and wedge, as well. Both would come in handy when splitting firewood.

He joined the boys outside and was pleased to see the ladder was in good shape, too. One of the lower rungs had a small crack in it, but he could fix that. And, once extended, it would easily reach the gutters.

He'd have Mrs. Pierce's house and yard fixed up in no time. It was the least he could do for her.

And hopefully it would gain him one of her rare smiles in the process. Something he found himself looking forward to more and more.

Midmorning Eileen stepped out on the back porch and saw Russell and Harry hard at work corralling the sodden mass of leaves and twigs that had overtaken her lawn into large piles.

There was no sign of Mr. Tucker or the other boys.

The two boys paused when they saw her, and she stepped up to the porch rail. "Miss Jacobs has made some lemonade. She thought you gentlemen might want to take a break."

"Yes, ma'am!" The leaves were immediately abandoned as both boys headed for the porch.

"Where are the others?"

Before they could answer her, Mr. Tucker and the two

younger boys appeared around the corner of the house. "Somebody looking for us?" he called out cheerfully.

"Just wondering where you'd disappeared to." Eileen noted the wheelbarrow loaded with firewood he was pushing. It seemed he'd had a very productive morning.

"I was just letting Russell and Harry know about the pitcher of lemonade inside. There's enough for you three as well, if you're interested."

"Yes, ma'am." The younger boys started for the porch, but Eileen raised her hand, stopping all four boys.

"Before you come inside you might want to wash up. There is a water pump by the carriage house."

The boys didn't seem overly pleased with her suggestion, but they obediently turned and headed for the pump.

Instead of joining them, Mr. Tucker started unloading the wheelbarrow.

She remained where she was rather than head back inside. To make sure the boys washed up properly, she told herself.

So why did her focus seem to remain on the man working at the foot of the steps?

"By the way," he said, wiping his brow with the back of his hands, "I took your advice."

She was surprised by the unexpected comment, but at the same time felt a little touch of pleasure. "And what advice was that?"

"To plan for the worst-case outcome." He stacked another large branch on the pile.

So she *had* gotten through to him. "What did you decide?"

"When I went by Dr. Pratt's office to check on Miss Fredrick this morning, I spoke to his niece, Mrs.

Leggett, about possibly traveling to Hatcherville with us if we should need her services. She has some medical experience, so she could provide care for Miss Fredrick until she can resume her normal routines. And Mrs. Leggett is a mother herself, so she knows how to deal with children."

A surprisingly practical choice. "She sounds like an ideal candidate. I take it she said yes."

He nodded. "She did. I just hope her services won't be required."

"As do I."

He unloaded the last bit of wood and straightened. "I'll just put this wheelbarrow away, then I think I'm ready for that promised glass of lemonade." He flashed a grin. "But don't worry—I intend to wash up proper first."

He whistled as he headed for the carriage house, leaving Eileen staring after him. Being teased was an entirely new experience for her, and she wasn't sure what to make of it. On the one hand, it was a very undignified way to treat her, one she should object to. But on the other hand, when he spoke to her like that, when he gave her that look that seemed to imply a certain level of friendship, it made her feel warm and soft inside.

She had to keep reminding herself, though, that feelings were fleeting and could betray you. In the end it was respectability and prominence that mattered.

As the boys climbed up the porch steps she cautioned them to wipe their feet, then followed them inside.

And forced herself not to turn around to see what Mr. Tucker was doing.

Chapter Twelve

After the lunch table was cleared and the dishes cleaned and put away, Eileen announced it was rest time. The children were instructed to go to their rooms for an hour either to nap or amuse themselves quietly. As she had the day before, Eileen took Molly and Flossie out to the swing to be rocked before her nap. But this time she made certain Fern knew where Molly would be.

Rather than taking the opportunity to rest, Mr. Tucker slipped out to pay another visit to the clinic to check on Miss Fredrick.

He returned in time to carry a drowsing Molly up to her room.

"How is Miss Fredrick?" Eileen asked when he returned downstairs.

"There's been no change."

She noted the ever so slight droop to his shoulders. Knowing he didn't need empty reassurances, she held her peace.

He scrubbed a hand across his jaw. "I'm not sure how I'm going to tell the kids."

"Tell them that it is in God's hands, as is their own future."

"And if she dies?" The harshness in his tone hit her like a slap. "Are they to believe that was God's doing, too?"

The emotion in his voice was so raw, she wondered if he had struggled with this issue in the past. "Everyone dies, Mr. Tucker," she said gently. "These children should be well aware of that. But what you must be sure they understand is that, if she doesn't recover it doesn't mean God doesn't hear their prayers nor does it mean He doesn't care. It simply means He had something else in mind for Miss Fredrick and was ready to call her home."

He looked at her, and she watched as the tension in his jaw sloughed away. "I'll look to you to help with that discussion should the time come." Then his crooked smile returned. "You do realize that this also means we'll likely be trespassing on your hospitality a bit longer."

She lifted her chin. "On the contrary, it merely means you still do not know the end date, no more than you knew it before you checked in on the patient."

He shook his head with an exaggeratedly solemn expression that was belied by the twinkle in his eyes. "I've always heard one should be cautious when dealing with a woman who insists on having the last word."

"As you should be. Most women with that trait tend to have a quick mind and a sharp wit."

He chuckled. "I'll keep that in mind."

She let that go without comment.

"I think I'll go finish getting the carriage house set

to rights," he said. And with a wave, he turned and sauntered away.

Had they actually been flirting? It was an activity she'd once excelled in, but it had been so long...

Pushing those memories away, she turned and headed for the parlor. Time to focus on something productive, like the mending that sat in her sewing basket impatiently awaiting her attention. She would most definitely *not* be focusing on that smile of his.

Strange, though, how difficult it had become to focus on even the simplest of tasks. Surely it was due to nothing more specific than the presence of so many houseguests.

As she accidentally jabbed the needle into her thumb she acknowledged that perhaps there just might be something slightly more specific tugging at her attention.

Mr. Tucker's visit to Dr. Pratt's clinic the next day bore no better news than it had the day before. Much as they tried to keep the children busy to distract their thoughts, a thick, somber cloud seemed to settle over the entire household.

That evening, when the last of the children were settled in their beds, Eileen sought out Mr. Tucker. She found him on the front porch. But he wasn't whittling. Instead he stood near the steps with his elbows planted on the porch rail, apparently just staring out at the sky.

She hesitated, not sure whether to approach him or slip back inside. Before she could make up her mind he glanced over his shoulder and gave her a smile. "Care to join me?"

With a nod, she closed the door behind her and joined him at the rail. They stood side by side, close enough to touch if they cared to, staring out at the night sky, not speaking.

The silence drew out but it wasn't awkward or uncomfortable, in fact it felt quite…companionable. He had burned the leaves the boys raked up earlier, and the smoky scent still hung in the air. A dog barked in the distance, and she thought of Joey and his desire to have a pet of his own. Which reminded her of her own desire for a pet growing up.

No, best not to think of the past.

Time to get back to business. "There is something I need to speak to you about."

"Oh?" He turned his head toward her, keeping his elbows planted on the rail. "Is there another chore you thought of that I can take care of for you?"

"Oh, no, nothing like that." Did he think her so mercenary? She was silent a little longer. "This is not exactly my story to tell, but I felt it important you understand, not only for your own information, but also to help answer any questions the children may have."

He turned completely around this time and leaned back against the rail, folding his arms across his chest. "I'm listening."

Having those blue eyes of his focused so intently on her like that was more distracting than she wanted to let on. "It concerns Dovie. When we head for church service in the morning, she won't be joining us."

Simon frowned. "Don't tell me she's not a believer. I've heard her pray and she seems quite sincere."

"No, that's not it. I guess you could say she has

a malady of sorts that prevents her from going out amongst people."

A wrinkle furrowed his brow. "What kind of malady?"

"I don't really understand it. Ivy tried to explain it to me once. It seems Dovie gets agitated and physically ill if she tries to leave the immediate vicinity of the house. Apparently she needs to feel her room is nearby so that she can retreat to it if she feels overwhelmed."

"How unusual." He seemed more intrigued than skeptical. "So, has she always lived here with you?"

"No, she moved in this past summer. She actually lived in another town before that. But she lost her home and moved here to be closer to Ivy."

"If she can't leave the area around her home, then how did she make that trip?"

"My understanding is she took a sleeping draught and then Ivy and her husband took care of getting her here while she slept."

"That's incredible." His hand moved as if to touch her, then halted. But her own hand tingled as if realizing its loss.

"Thank you for explaining the situation." He turned back around to stare out into the dark. "You're right— the children probably *will* have questions. I'm not sure exactly what to say to them."

"You accepted the truth. Why shouldn't they?"

He lifted an eyebrow, an amused glint in his eye. "Is everything always so black-and-white for you?"

Did he think her too narrow-minded? She turned to face out into the night, as well. "Gray does exist, of course, but it's the color of shadows and fog. I find it best to stay away from it, if possible."

He didn't look her way, but she had no doubt he intended her to see the teasing smile that tugged at his lips. "An answer for everything."

As earlier, they were both silent for a while, staring out at nothing in particular. But this time it wasn't quite so comfortable. Was he as aware of her presence as she was of his?

"It's nice out here this time of evening."

His tone had been soft, but she'd been so lost in her own tangled thoughts that she barely controlled the start at the sound of his voice. Luckily he didn't seem to notice.

"The streetlamps are lit," he continued, "most everyone is in their homes, the stars are shining bright."

"One could almost imagine that the slate has been wiped clean and that tomorrow will bring a fresh beginning." As soon as she'd said the words she wished them back. Such thoughts were not meant to be shared.

But he'd already turned to look at her, a puzzled smile on his face. He brushed a stray hair from her cheek. "And what is on your slate that you wish wiped clean?" he asked softly.

That touch sent a shiver through her. For just a moment, she was tempted to tell him everything.

Then reason reasserted itself. She drew herself up and removed any hint of emotion from her face. "I believe everyone has some fault or other they'd like to rid themselves of, don't you agree?"

"I suppose. After all, only one man has ever led a perfect life."

She nodded. "Exactly. Now, if you will excuse me, I think I will retire for the night." And before he could ask her any more probing questions, she turned and went inside.

* * *

Simon watched her go. He'd thought, for just a moment, that she'd thawed toward him. But no doubt it had been the hour and the events of the day that had caused her to let down her guard. It had certainly snapped back into place quickly enough when he'd touched her. But he didn't regret the act. He'd been wanting to touch her hair all day. And it had been every bit as silky as he'd imagined. For a moment he tried to picture how it might look loose, tumbling over her shoulders.

Abruptly, he pushed away from the rail. Getting involved in this woman's business would be a mistake. His focus should be on fulfilling his obligations to the children and to Miss Fredrick.

And that meant getting them to Hatcherville as soon as possible, *not* dallying here in Turnabout. Hopefully, in no time at all this town, and this warm-below-the-surface ice queen, would be nothing more than a fond but quickly fading memory.

But as he climbed the stairs he had a feeling that the memory of this particular woman wouldn't fade quite so quickly.

The next morning was a whirlwind of activity as they worked to get all ten children ready for church. There were lost ribbons to be found, loose buttons to be reattached, shoes to be found, hair to be braided or combed just so.

By the time everyone was ready and lined up by the door, Eileen felt her hostess skills, not to mention her patience, had been tested to their very limits. But at last they were ready to make the three-and-a-half-block walk to church.

Before they could step out the front door, however, Tessa looked around with a puzzled frown. "Aren't we going to wait for Nana Dovie?"

"Miss Jacobs is not going with us," Eileen answered.

"Why? Is she sick like Gee-Gee?" Joey asked anxiously.

"No," Eileen hastily reassured him, "at least not like your Gee-Gee."

"So she *is* sick?" Tessa pressed.

Eileen cast a quick glance Mr. Tucker's way, but he was apparently leaving it to her to do the explaining. Very well. "Miss Jacobs never goes very far from this house—not to go shopping, not to visit friends, not to take walks, not even to go to church."

"Why?"

To Eileen's relief, Mr. Tucker finally decided to speak up. "Because something inside her won't let her. The same way Rose can't eat foods that touch, or Molly can't go to sleep without Flossie. Nana Dovie's heart won't let her leave this place. She can't help it, and we shouldn't think ill of her for it."

That seemed to satisfy the children. Without another word they exited the house and headed for the front walk. Eileen cast an approving glance Mr. Tucker's way, then thought better of it when she saw his self-satisfied grin.

That man didn't seem to have a humble bone in his body!

She stepped forward and took the lead with Molly and Tessa, while Mr. Tucker brought up the rear. It felt as if they were in a parade. Then she corrected herself. No, it was more like a mother duck trying to get her hatchlings safely across the lane and to the pond.

Pushing aside that unflattering image, she tried to think ahead to what they would do when they arrived. Her first thought was the realization that they would never all fit in one pew. Should they divide up the boys and girls as they had the floors, or should they put the older children together and the younger ones together? And however they did this, would Mr. Tucker expect her to oversee one of the groups?

In the end they went with the latter arrangements. The six older children sat in one pew while the four younger ones sat behind them with Eileen and Simon bookending them.

It wasn't until everyone was finally seated that Eileen breathed a sigh of relief. How had Miss Fredrick handled all of this on a daily basis, and without the assistance of Dovie and Mr. Tucker?

A moment later she began to sense something different. It took a moment for her to figure out what it was, then it hit her. There were people actually sending smiles of greeting her way.

She had so perfected the art of not meeting anyone's gaze these past two years, and not showing any outward sign of emotion of any sort, that she'd almost missed it.

It wasn't coming from everyone, of course. But there were enough that it was unmistakable. And only now, when some sense of welcome had returned, did she admit to herself how much she'd missed it.

Simon found the children surprisingly well behaved throughout the service, with minimal fidgeting on the younger ones' part.

After the service, several of the local children introduced themselves to the newcomers. If at least part of the reason was because they had been prompted by their parents, Simon had no problem with that. He let the kids tarry and visit for a while. It would be good for them to mingle with others their own age.

Mrs. Pierce stood next to him, her unapproachable ice-queen mask now firmly back in place.

Was it her choice not to mingle with her neighbors or had she been ostracized for some reason? Before he could speculate further, they were approached by a trio that included two women and an impressively large gentleman.

The man greeted Mrs. Pierce with a tip of his hat. "Good day to you."

She returned his greeting with a nod of her head. "And to you, Mr. Parker." Her expression never wavered.

Mr. Parker then extended his hand to Simon. "Hello. I'm Mitch Parker. I believe you've already met my wife, Ivy. And this is Miss Janell Whitman."

Simon acknowledged the introductions and then Mr. Parker spoke again. "Miss Whitman and I are the schoolteachers here in Turnabout. We wanted to let you know the children are welcome to attend school while you're here in town."

Simon immediately liked the idea. It would be good for the children to be around others their age on a regular basis, and it would also give them something besides their uncertain futures to focus on. Not to mention that it would give Mrs. Pierce a break from having them underfoot.

"Thank you. If it turns out we have to make an extended stay here, I might take you up on that offer."

"Just let us know when you're ready," Miss Whitman

added. "Do you know what sort of education they've had up to this point?"

"I believe Miss Fredrick taught them herself."

"Well, we can certainly work with them to see how far she's gotten with them. Are any of them eleven or older?"

"Fern is thirteen and Russell is eleven."

"Then they'll go into my class," Mitch said. "The rest, at least those six years old and older, will join Miss Whitman's class."

That would leave just Molly and Joey at home during the day. Surely that would make things easier on Mrs. Pierce. And, he had to admit, himself, as well.

Before the trio excused themselves, Mrs. Parker turned to Mrs. Pierce. "I know you have a full house, but I hope you don't mind if we make our usual visit with Nana Dovie this afternoon. I promise we'll stay out of the way."

Mrs. Pierce's demeanor thawed the tiniest bit. "Of course. Dovie will be expecting you."

"Thank you. Then we'll be by at the regular time."

As they moved away, Eileen spoke up. "Ivy is Dovie's foster daughter. She and her husband normally visit with her on Sunday afternoons."

Glad of the explanation, Simon nodded. Then he spotted Mrs. Leggett and Mrs. Pratt and excused himself to speak to them. "Is there any news?"

"My husband is sitting with her now," Mrs. Pratt said. "But I'm afraid there's been very little change." She glanced toward the children across the way. "Poor little dears—they're having a hard time of it, I imagine."

He thanked her for her concern, then smiled at the two women. "Whatever happens, I want you to know that I absolutely believe the doctor is doing everything he can. And that I appreciate all the care the three of you are giving her."

Mrs. Pratt patted his arm. "You're a good man, Mr. Tucker. The children are lucky to have you looking out for them."

Simon wished he felt as confident of that as she seemed to be.

He turned to find Mrs. Pierce standing apart from the others, a remote expression on her face, an expression that seemed aimed at no one in particular and everyone here at the same time.

It was eerie to witness, and more than anything else it made him wonder why she found it necessary to shield herself that way. Who or what in her past had done that to her?

Chapter Thirteen

When they returned to the house, Dovie had the table set and the food warmed up.

As they ate their meal, Eileen again did her best to keep a pleasant conversation going. But it was difficult when she felt herself being scrutinized by Mr. Tucker. It had started in the churchyard, his studying her as if he was trying to discover her secrets. And that was something she absolutely would not allow.

Mr. Tucker cleared his throat, and for a moment she thought he was going to address her. But instead he looked around at the children.

"I met Turnabout's schoolteachers today," he announced.

The children all paused and stared at him questioningly.

"They were kind enough to invite you all to attend school while you're here."

"What did you tell them?" Harry asked. "Are we really going to school here?"

"I told him I'd consider it. If we end up staying for

any length of time, though, I think it would be a good idea."

"Then there's no point in sending us there," Fern said firmly. "Gee-Gee is going to get better soon and we'll be on our way to Hatcherville again."

Eileen saw the small tic of emotion in Simon's face and decided to speak up and shift the focus off him. "I'm certain Miss Fredrick would agree that it's important for you to keep up with your studies."

"You don't know her," Fern said, "so you don't really know how she'd feel about it."

Simon gave her a lowered-brow look. "Mind your manners, young lady."

Fern leaned back sullenly and stared down at her plate.

"There are a lot of good reasons to enroll you," he said to the group at large. "As Mrs. Pierce pointed out, you need to keep up with your studies. It will also give you an opportunity to meet new friends."

"But we're just going to leave Turnabout eventually," Russell said. "So what good is it to make friends here?"

"Making friends is never a waste of time," Dovie said quietly.

"But—"

Simon raised a hand. "As I said, I haven't made a decision yet, but when the time comes, the decision will be mine to make and I expect you to abide by it. Is that understood?"

There was a chorus of "yes sirs" from the children, some less enthusiastic than others.

All in all, Eileen was impressed with the way Mr. Tucker had handled the situation. He'd certainly shown that he was able to use a firm hand with them when it was called for.

* * *

Simon pushed his chair back from the table. He'd eaten a bigger slice of pie than he should have but that apple and pecan filling under the golden crust had been too good to pass up.

Before he could stand, though, the door chimes sounded.

Mrs. Pierce looked up with a frown. "Now whoever could that be? It's too early for Ivy and Mitch to arrive." She stood and moved to the front hall.

While she was gone, the rest of them began clearing the table. When she returned a few moments later her gaze went right to him. Something in her expression alerted him that something wasn't quite right.

"Mr. Tucker, may I speak to you for a moment?"

"Of course."

He saw a look pass between her and Dovie, and immediately Dovie got the children busy with kitchen duty.

With a slight nod of her head, the widow indicated he should follow her into the hall.

"What is it?" he asked as soon as they were out of earshot of the children.

"Dr. Pratt is here to speak to you. He is waiting in the parlor."

There was only one reason the doctor would have come to him this afternoon. Simon steeled himself for the worst. Mrs. Pierce watched him, her expression impassive, but he thought he detected a note of sympathy lurking in her eyes. She either knew the reason for the doctor's visit or suspected the same thing he did.

Impulsively he touched her arm. "Would you mind joining us for this conversation?" He wasn't really sure why he'd asked her that, and from the momentary flicker of surprise in her eyes, she wasn't either, so he added quickly, "Whatever the news, it will likely affect our stay here, so you may want to hear what he has to say firsthand."

She nodded, her expression impassive once more. "Of course." Then she turned and led the way to the parlor.

When Simon entered the room, Dr. Pratt was standing, his coat over one arm and his hat on a chair beside him, as if he wasn't planning to stay long.

The physician stepped forward and shook Simon's hand, then wasted no further time in getting to the point. "Mr. Tucker, I'm afraid it's my sad duty to inform you that Miss Fredrick passed away a short time ago."

Simon raked his hand through his hair. He thought he'd prepared himself for this news but it hit hard just the same. While he hadn't known her long, Miss Fredrick had been a truly good woman whom he'd come to admire and respect. Even more so now that he'd had charge of the children for just a few days.

As for the children themselves, not only had they known her longer, but the woman had been a mother to them. How was he going to tell them they'd lost her? And what sort of reassurances could he offer them about their future?

They still had the house in Hatcherville, of course, and he could escort them the remainder of the way as planned. But then what?

"What sort of arrangements do you want to make for her remains?"

Simon hadn't even thought that far. "I'll contact her brother right away to see what his wishes are." Would

Wilbur Fredrick regret that he hadn't tried to get here sooner?

Dr. Pratt nodded. "In the meantime I'll contact Mr. Drummond, the undertaker, on your behalf."

Mrs. Pierce turned to him and cleared her throat delicately. "If you like, I can go through her bags to find a suitable garment to send to Mr. Drummond for her to be laid out in."

He was both surprised and touched by her offer. It was something he wouldn't have even thought about doing. "Yes, thank you." He turned back to Dr. Pratt. "If you'll excuse me, I need to figure out how to break the news to the children."

"Of course, I'll leave you to it. Again, you have my deepest sympathies. And know that Mrs. Pratt and I will keep you and the children in our prayers through the coming days." He slipped his arms into his jacket and picked up his hat. "Don't worry about showing me out. I know the way." And with that, he left the room.

When they were alone, Mrs. Pierce eyed him with obvious concern. "Are you all right?"

He was touched by her concern. Having her here made him feel less alone, more able to deal with what was to come. "I'm still trying to get my bearings," he admitted. Then he tried for a bit of levity. "Are you going to say 'I told you so'?"

She gave a faint smile. "I wouldn't do that. Especially at a time like this."

He turned serious again, rubbing the back of his neck. "Do you have any suggestions for how to break the news to the children?"

"There's nothing that will soften this news, so I believe the straightforward approach would be best. The important thing is to be ready to answer their questions—both those they ask and those they don't."

She gave him a sympathetic look. "And there will undoubtedly be tears."

He cringed. He'd much prefer dealing with outbursts than with tears.

"Remember, other than Molly and Joey, they've all been through this once before."

"I know." And for his niece and nephew it had been barely three months.

He straightened his shoulders. "I'd best go ahead and get this over with."

She gave him a look he could almost believe was approval. "Would you like to do this alone?"

"No," he said without hesitation. "In fact I'd very much like for you to be there."

Eileen stood in the doorway of the parlor, watching as the children filed in and arranged themselves on the available seating. Dovie was there, as well. Mr. Tucker, who'd called them together, remained standing, his expression solemn. She didn't envy him his upcoming task.

She found it edifying, however, that he'd wanted her there, both when facing Dr. Pratt and now. Was it just for moral support? Or had he wanted her beside him for another reason?

But she would ponder that another time. Right now the important thing was helping the children deal with the news they were about to hear.

Fern pulled Molly up on her lap and had Joey sit close beside her. From the expression on the older girl's face, Eileen could see she had a good idea what was coming. The rest of the children sat willy-nilly on the sofa and chairs. Some even sat cross-legged on the floor.

When they were finally all settled, Mr. Tucker took a deep breath, and she could almost feel him gather his strength to speak. She had to anchor her feet to the floor to keep from crossing the room and lending him the support of her presence. She would have to settle for helping him deal with the aftermath.

"The visitor who came by a little while ago was Dr. Pratt," he began without preamble. "He had some sad news to deliver. I'm afraid Miss Fredrick has passed away."

Emotions zinged around the room like beads from a broken strand. Confusion, denial, grief, anger, fear—she felt the plunk of them all against her skin.

"Does this mean we won't see Gee-Gee anymore?" Joey asked.

"I'm afraid so."

Audrey ran up and latched onto him, her lip quivering. "But, Uncle Simon, we've all been praying so hard."

He placed a hand on her head, his expression twisting a moment before he spoke. "I know you have, sweet pea, but it was time for her to go home to heaven."

As if they'd been waiting for a signal, several of the other children swarmed around him. It was as if they were drawing on his strength to give them comfort.

But whose strength could he draw on?

Seeming to read her thoughts, he cast a quick glance her way. Then, with an inhaled breath and crooked smile, he turned back to the children.

Eileen noticed that Fern hadn't moved from the sofa, but there was a new tautness about her, as if she were trying to hold every bit of emotion tightly inside herself.

"You should have let us visit her." Fern's voice was tight with accusation. "We could have at least said good-bye."

"I'm sorry, Fern. But she never woke up. She wouldn't have known you were there."

"But *I* would have known."

The words were low—almost whispered—and for just a moment Eileen could see the hurting child inside her.

Then Fern straightened, and the hard shell was back in place. "What happens to us now?"

Mr. Tucker faced her over the heads of the other children. Did Fern see his sympathy as clearly as she did?

"The house in Hatcherville is still there waiting for you all," he said. "And don't worry, no one is going to split you kids up—I won't let them. We'll find someone very nice and loving to take care of you."

"There isn't anyone else as nice as Miss Fredrick." This comment came from Lily.

"Perhaps not, but we'll do our best."

"But what if you can't find anyone?" asked Joey.

"I will," he said firmly. "I promise you—" he glanced around the room "—*all* of you, that I will find someone who will not only love you but whom you can learn to love, as well."

Eileen was surprised by the promise. She had no doubt he meant it. But did he know what he'd just committed himself to?

"For now," he continued, "a very nice lady named Mrs. Leggett has agreed to travel with us to Hatcherville and stay in the house with you until we find that special someone to care for you permanently."

The children didn't seem entirely reassured by that

news. Eileen could understand that, given all they'd
been through. In fact, she would like to know more
about this Mrs. Leggett herself. Would the woman understand these children and care for them as—

"Can't we just stay *here?*" Molly asked.

Eileen froze, unsure how to respond to that. For a
fleeting moment she wondered how it would be to—

"No, Molly, this isn't our home." Simon's words and
firm tone brought Eileen back to her senses.

Of course they couldn't stay here permanently. What
had she been thinking?

"But there's plenty of room," Molly insisted. "And
Nana Dovie and Mrs. Pierce like us." She turned to
face them, her expression reflecting a sudden doubt.
"Don't you?"

Dovie gave her a broad, reassuring smile. "Of course
we do."

Eileen chose her words carefully. "I do indeed like
you, Molly. But there is another house waiting for you,
the house your Gee-Gee purchased especially for you.
And of course you must do as your uncle Simon says,
because he only wants what is best for you."

And staying here under her roof was obviously not
what anyone would consider best for them.

Including her.

As the children headed upstairs for their afternoon
quiet time, Simon reflected that for once he was glad
Mrs. Pierce had set up routines for them to follow. In
fact, he could use some quiet time of his own right now.

Unfortunately there was still a lot to be done.

He stepped out onto the front porch, feeling the need
for fresh air and open spaces.

"So what will you do now?"

He looked over his shoulder, surprised to see Mrs. Pierce standing in the doorway. He hadn't even heard the door open. Was that sympathy in her expression?

He turned back around to study the live oak that shaded one side of her front lawn. "After the funeral I'll go on to Hatcherville with the children." The enormity of that was still sinking in. "Hopefully Mrs. Leggett is still willing to accompany me to help with the children while I look for a permanent housekeeper and caretaker for the children."

She joined him at the rail without saying anything.

Strange how today he found her reserve and quiet dignity rather soothing. "Do you know Mrs. Leggett?"

"Not well. I understand she grew up here in Turnabout, but moved away when she married her uncle's apprentice. But all of that took place before I moved here. She moved back to Turnabout recently when her husband died."

He nodded, understanding the woman's need to be around family while she adjusted to the tragedy.

"How soon will you be leaving?" Mrs. Pierce asked a moment later.

Her tone and expression gave nothing away so he couldn't tell what she was feeling. Was she merely curious? Or eager to see the last of them? "As soon after the funeral as possible."

As he said the words it hit him that in a few days he'd not only be leaving Turnabout, but he'd be leaving *her* and would likely never see her again.

And that bothered him much more than it should have, given the length and nature of their relationship. But she'd somehow insinuated herself into his world, had tickled his curiosity to unlock her secrets. He wanted to figure out why she was the way she was, why preparing for any situation and having rigid routines were so important to her, why she seemed at odds with her neighbors—folks who from all appearances were good-hearted people.

And above all, he wanted to find out how to put a permanent dent in her remote, ice-queen guise.

None of which he could pursue now.

Before either of them could say more, the front gate opened, and Ivy and Mitch stepped onto the walk. He'd forgotten that they'd mentioned coming by to visit Dovie.

As soon as the greetings were exchanged he excused himself to head over to the depot. He felt guilty for leaving Mrs. Pierce to make the explanations and deliver the news without him, but he wasn't in the mood to be around people right now.

Besides, he needed to get the telegram off to Miss Fredrick's brother right away. He supposed, if the man wanted to bury his sister back in St. Louis, it would mean making that return trip himself. Miss Fredrick deserved the escort, even in death, and it was only right for the children to attend the funeral, whether Mr. Fredrick would welcome them there or not.

Would Mrs. Leggett agree to accompany them on that trip, as well? But it was the image of Mrs. Pierce getting on that train with them rather than Mrs. Leggett that flashed through his mind.

And why that had happened was something he didn't want to explore at the moment.

Edgy and restless, Simon decided to take a walk when he left the depot. Hands jammed in his pockets, he wandered through town. Ten kids, and all of them his sole responsibility. This wasn't what he'd signed on for when he agreed to escort them to their new home. He'd asked Miss Fredrick to take Audrey and Albert in because he couldn't handle taking care of *two* kids.

And he'd made those kids promises just now, promises that he had no way of knowing if he could fulfill. What kind of man did that?

He looked up to find himself on the outskirts of town. He hadn't been out this way before. With a shrug, he continued walking, this time paying a little more attention to his surroundings.

He made a mental note of a spot he passed that looked promising for gathering more firewood. A little farther along stood a trio of persimmon trees that were heavy with fruit. He could tell that as soon as they had the first frost here, the fruit would be ready to pick. Maybe they could make an outing of it. He could bring the kids here to help him pick a bucketful or two. It would make for a tasty addition to Mrs. Pierce's pantry.

Then he remembered they wouldn't be here for first frost.

Simon halted abruptly. What was he doing? He should be back at the house before the children came downstairs.

No matter whether he wanted it or not, they were his responsibility, not that of Dovie or Mrs. Pierce.

He did an about-face and marched quickly back in the direction of town.

Eileen sat in the parlor, adjusting the hem and seams of the skirt from one of her mourning dresses. Providing the children with appropriate mourning clothes for Miss Fredrick's funeral seemed the least she could do.

Her mind, however, was on Mr. Tucker.

Where was he? He'd said he had to send a telegram, but he'd been gone for over an hour now. Ivy and Mitch had already taken their leave. The children had come downstairs a few minutes ago. They were more subdued than normal but that was to be expected. When they'd asked after Mr. Tucker and learned he was out, however, she'd seen several exchanged glances among the older children. It hadn't helped that they'd heard the blast of a train whistle soon after.

Were they worried he'd abandoned them? She was absolutely convinced that Mr. Tucker would never do such a thing, but she was irritated that he wouldn't realize that his disappearance at a time like this would affect the children in that way.

And she intended to tell him so.

Just as soon as he returned.

Chapter Fourteen

As it turned out, when Mr. Tucker returned, Eileen didn't have the heart to scold him. Though he wore his usual smile and had the same easy manner with the children, she could see the small lines around his eyes that spoke of worry or weariness, or both.

An hour or so later, Lionel showed up with a telegram for Mr. Tucker.

She watched as he read it. He clenched his jaw as tight as a bully's fist. Then he handed her the telegram without saying a word.

Eileen shifted her gaze from his face to the paper in her hand and read the terse missive.

BEST TO BURY HER THERE. PLEASE SEE
TO ARRANGEMENTS.
WILL ARRIVE TUESDAY TO ATTEND FU-
NERAL.
W. FREDRICK

When she looked up again, he was pacing.

"A surprising decision," Eileen said carefully, "but

I'm sure he has his reasons." Though she couldn't quite curb her curiosity about what those reasons might be.

His pacing didn't slow. "I'll admit that it does simplify matters for me. But it just seems wrong to make this her last resting place, a town where she has no ties and there will be no one to mourn her."

"It is her body that is being laid to rest," Eileen said gently, "not her spirit. Those who loved her don't need a headstone to remember her by."

He finally stopped pacing and met her gaze. "You're right, of course. And I don't have a right to judge—her brother *does* plan to attend the funeral after all." His expression eased. "This also means I won't have to put the kids through a return trip to St. Louis."

He nodded his head as if coming to a decision. "But whatever her brother's plans, I intend to make certain Miss Fredrick has the best funeral service I can arrange."

She believed him. "Have you ever met Mr. Fredrick?" she asked.

"No. But Sally told me about him in her letters. He apparently didn't approve of his sister taking in all the children. There were some…issues. The two of them had harsh words over it and were barely on speaking terms."

She wondered what he meant by *issues*. But she respected his reluctance to spread gossip so she let the subject lie.

"That's a shame," she said instead. "Especially since his sister went to such great lengths to build a family for these children." Then she had another thought. "Do you think he'll want to take in the children now—he is related to three of the girls, isn't he?"

"I doubt he'll want to take them in."

That wasn't really an answer. "But if he *does*, will you allow them to be split up that way?"

"I don't know that I could stop it. He is, after all, their closest relative."

"Oh."

He must have heard the concern in her voice because he gave her a reassuring smile. "As I said, that's one thing that I *don't* have to worry about—I'm sure he won't want to take them."

Eileen wasn't entirely reassured but she let the matter drop. After all, the matter was really none of her concern.

So why did she feel so personally touched by their situation?

Simon received a second telegram from Wilbur Fredrick the next morning. This one asked him to have Miss Fredrick's personal effects gathered up to be given to him when he arrived. He also wanted to make certain the funeral was scheduled for Tuesday afternoon, the day he and his wife were due to arrive.

It appeared the man didn't plan to spend more than the one night in Turnabout. Which was fine by Simon. The less the children were exposed to the man, the better.

He spoke to Mrs. Leggett again, and she assured him she was still willing to go with him to Hatcherville to take care of the children.

With Mrs. Pierce's permission, Simon invited her and her daughter over to allow them and the children to get acquainted.

All in all it was a good meeting. Mrs. Leggett was

composed but friendly. Her daughter seemed over-whelmed by the sheer number of people in the room, but she warmed to the children eventually.

As for his charges, they were polite but wary. While there were no strong bonds forged during the meeting, it was a start.

Eileen watched the ease with which Mrs. Leggett interacted with the children. It was as if they instinctively recognized her maternal qualities, something Eileen knew she lacked.

She tried to ignore the sharp jab of jealousy that thought produced, especially when Molly introduced Flossie to the woman. She'd thought she had adjusted to the fact that she would never have children of her own, but it seemed she hadn't.

Later, when she was alone, she turned to silent prayer.

Heavenly Father, I know I've been so blessed in my life and that I've done things that have let You down. Help me to focus on the good and not wallow in self-pity when I see others who have the things I want.

"Mrs. Pierce?"

Eileen looked down to see Molly standing there, looking up at her with liquid-filled, pleading eyes.

Alarmed that something might have happened to her, Eileen stooped down and mentally made note of where Simon was in case she needed him. "Yes, sweetheart? What is it?"

The little girl held out her doll and Eileen saw a tiny tear in one of her cloth arms. "Flossie has a boo-boo. Can you fix it for me like Gee-Gee used to?"

Relieved that is wasn't anything more serious, Eileen was nevertheless startled that Molly had come to her for help rather than Dovie or Mrs. Leggett. Then she smiled at the girl. "Poor Flossie. But I think I can fix her up. Do you want to help?"

Molly's expression immediately blossomed into a toothy smile, and she nodded vigorously.

Eileen straightened and held out her hand for the doll. "Then come along. Let's go fetch my sewing basket."

Rather than handing over the doll, Molly took Eileen's hand herself.

As they left the room, Eileen sent up a silent prayer of thanksgiving. Never had she had a prayer answered so quickly.

Chapter Fifteen

Tuesday morning, Simon went down to the train station to meet the Fredrickses. Though he'd never met them in person before, he recognized Wilbur Fredrick as soon as the man stepped from the train. There was a surface resemblance to his sister, but where she always wore a smile, this man looked dour. Of course, that could be the way he expressed grief, but there was something about the way the man carried himself that reminded Simon of his uncle Corbitt.

But it wasn't for him, of all people, to judge. He pasted a respectful expression on his face as he stepped up to greet them. "Mr. and Mrs. Fredrick?"

"Yes?"

He held his hand out. "I'm Simon Tucker. I'm sorry for your loss, sir. I admired your sister greatly."

"Ah, Mr. Tucker, thank you for contacting me." He gave Simon's hand a quick shake, then dropped it. "Is everything set for the funeral?"

"Yes, sir. Reverend Harper will perform a short service at the cemetery at two o'clock this afternoon."

"Excellent. Thank you again for attending to those

details," He tugged on the cuff of his jacket. "I suppose there are some bills to be settled."

"Everything has been taken care of, except for the undertaker."

Mr. Fredrick nodded without comment, then changed the subject. "If you don't mind directing us to the local hotel, my wife and I would like to rest up from our trip before the funeral."

"Of course." Simon had expected him to at least inquire about the children. But perhaps the oversight was just due to travel fatigue and grief over his sister. He reached for the bag the porter deposited beside the couple. "It's just a few blocks. Allow me to escort you there."

Mr. Fredrick made arrangements to have their other bags delivered to the hotel, and then Simon led the way away from the station. In deference to Mrs. Fredrick, who seemed rather frail, he set a slow pace.

Mr. Fredrick broke the silence first. "May I ask just what your relationship was to my sister?"

"I regret that I didn't know her well. My sister Sally was her housekeeper for a number of years. Sally passed away a few months ago and your sister took in her two children—my niece and nephew—since I was not equipped to do so myself. In return I offered to help her where I could."

"And you were traveling with them to provide escort?"

"In part. It was also my intention to move to Hatcherville myself so I could be close by, both for the sake of my sister's children and my promise to your sister."

"I see. I don't understand what Georgina was thinking, embarking on such a trip. That's very likely what did her in. That and the strain of caring for so many cast-off children over the years."

Simon did his best not to react to that statement. "I know you're tired from your travels and are still in mourning, but I need to ask—do you wish to have any involvement with any of the children who were formerly in your sister's care? I understand the three older girls are relations of yours."

The man stiffened, as if Simon had insulted him. "*Distant* relations, I assure you." He gave the ends of his vest a sharp tug. "And no, Mrs. Fredrick and I will *not* be taking them in."

That resemblance to his uncle seemed even stronger now. "I see." Obviously this man was nothing like his sister.

Mr. Fredrick cleared his throat. "I'm sure The Kirst Sisters' Orphan Asylum in St. Louis will be happy to take them in. It is one of the charities my wife and I support."

Not if he could help it. "That won't be necessary. I gave your sister my word that I'd see them safely and comfortably settled into the home in Hatcherville, and I intend to follow through with that. I'm certain I can find a good person willing to serve as caretaker for them."

Simon saw the couple exchange a look, but neither responded. Instead, Mr. Fredrick changed the subject. "Have you gathered up my sister's things?"

"The things she had with her. But many of her possessions were sent ahead to Hatcherville. I'll have those sent to you as soon as I arrive."

"Did she have any of her important papers with her?"

"I didn't go through her things. She did mention she had the deed to the property with her, along with her other important documents, but other than that I don't know."

"And where are her things at the moment?"

"Mrs. Pierce, a widow who lives here in town, has provided lodging for me and the kids. Your sister's things are there, as well."

"I would appreciate it if you would have it all sent to me at the hotel as soon as possible."

"Of course." What exactly was the man expecting to find in his sister's things? Some kind of family heirloom perhaps? But they had arrived at their destination. "Here we are, The Rose Palace Hotel."

Mr. Fredrick seemed unimpressed with the exterior of the building, but he merely held out his hand to offer Simon a handshake. "Thank you for escorting us. I will see you at the funeral, I presume."

"Yes, sir. Would you like me to swing by here on my way so I can show you the way?"

"Thank you, but that won't be necessary. I'm sure we can get directions from someone here."

There was an obvious note of dismissal in the man's tone. Simon took his cue and accepted the handshake with a promise to send over Miss Fredrick's things right away. Then he headed back to Mrs. Pierce's home.

The only word he could come up with to describe Mr. Fredrick was *officious*. He was relieved the man had no intention of getting involved in the children's lives—that wouldn't have gone well at all. He just hoped the man had enough common decency to keep his feelings about the children to himself for the short time he would be in their company.

But he'd given the self-righteous popinjay enough consideration. He needed to turn his thoughts to getting everyone ready to move on to Hatcherville. Mrs. Pierce would be glad to get her home back to herself.

As he turned in the gate he realized he was going to miss this place. In the short time they'd been here it had begun to feel like home.

Truth to tell, he was going to miss the lady of the house even more.

Would she miss him, even if just a little?

The scene at the graveyard was solemn. Mr. Fredrick and his wife stood apart from the others in town. Mrs. Fredrick was dressed entirely in black, including a black veil that covered her face and a lacy black handkerchief that she occasionally dabbed beneath her veil. Neither made any move to introduce themselves to the children or speak to Simon.

There were a surprisingly large number of townsfolk in attendance. Dr. and Mrs. Pratt, Regina Barr, the Parkers and a number of others he only knew by sight. Even Miss Ortolon, the woman who had seemed so opposed to Mrs. Pierce taking them in that first day, was present.

The children were sober, several of them tearful. Dovie and Eileen had done their best to find appropriate mourning clothes for them. Since Mrs. Pierce was herself a widow, she had a few pieces she'd adapted and Dovie had items, as well. Fern wore a skirt that had been made over to fit her. A black cape was found for both Lily and Rose. Dovie found or made black bonnets for each of the girls. For the boys, they each had a black armband to wear.

Simon felt a touch of pride in them. Though there were more than a few sniffles and tearstained cheeks, the children were, on the whole, well behaved. Mrs.

Leggett and her daughter stood with them, and the three adults arranged themselves so that each of the children had an adult close at hand.

Reverend Harper performed the service with as much solemnity and thoughtfulness as if Miss Fredrick had been a longtime member of his congregation. Simon was sure the woman would have been pleased.

Once the service was over and the crowd began to disperse, Mr. Fredrick approached him.

"There is a matter I need to discuss with you." The man didn't spare so much as a glance for the children.

"Of course." Had he changed his mind about the children?

"Perhaps you would accompany me and my wife to the hotel."

Wondering what this was all about, and more than a little concerned that he wouldn't like whatever it was, Simon turned to Mrs. Pierce. "Would you and Mrs. Leggett escort the children back to your home. Perhaps help them gather and pack their things for our departure tomorrow."

At her nod, he turned back to Mr. Fredrick and indicated the man should lead the way.

They strolled to the hotel without a word. When they arrived, Mrs. Fredrick excused herself and went upstairs to her room. Mr. Fredrick waved toward a pair of chairs in a quiet corner of the lobby.

Impatient to be done with this, Simon leaned forward as soon as he took his seat. "What can I do for you?"

"I've gone through all of my sister's things that you sent over earlier."

He certainly hadn't wasted any time. Whatever he was looking for must be pretty important.

"It was just as I figured. Unless it is among the things she sent ahead, which I very much doubt, Georgina didn't leave a will."

Simon held his tongue. *That's* what this was about? His sister's possessions?

"What that means," the man continued, "is that as her brother, I inherit all of her material possessions."

Simon hoped the man was not counting on a large inheritance. Miss Fredrick had spent most of her funds on the Hatcherville property. "I believe she had the majority of her funds transferred to the bank in Hatcherville. If you need my help in securing them for you, let me know." Not having any of Miss Fredrick's funds would make things a little tougher, but Simon wasn't particularly worried—he'd find a way to make it work.

The man dismissed Simon's offer with a wave of his hand. "I have a solicitor to handle those sorts of matters. What I wanted to make certain you understood is that the Hatcherville property now belongs to me."

Simon straightened. That was definitely something he hadn't considered. "Does that mean you'll be requiring rent money when we move in?"

"Actually, I plan to sell the property."

"Sell it?" Simon's heart sank further. Having negotiated Miss Fredrick's purchase of that same property a few short weeks ago he knew there was no way he could afford to buy it himself. "But where will the children go?"

"As I said, the good people at The Kirst Sisters' Orphan Asylum will be happy to take them in. In fact I've already discussed the matter with the Misses Kirst personally and they have said as much."

So the man had been planning this from the outset "Surely you know this isn't what your sister would want."

The man drew himself up. "Mr. Tucker, as you've said yourself, you only knew my sister for a short time. And even if what you said was true, Georgina often let her soft heart get in the way of common sense. A failing we did not share." Mr. Fredrick tugged on his lapels and stood. "Now, if you will excuse me, I need to check on my wife. We'll be departing on tomorrow's train. Good day to you."

Simon watched him leave, his mind reeling from this new setback. Without the house in Hatcherville, he had nowhere to take the children. And sending them to that orphanage Mr. Fredrick was so fond of was completely unacceptable. What now?

Eileen was working in the front flower bed when Mr. Tucker returned to the house. Truth to tell, that had just been an excuse to keep a watch out for his return. And she was glad she had. One look at his face told her something was terribly wrong.

"What's happened?"

He raked a hand through his hair, not answering her.

She needed to pull him aside before the children saw him. She waved toward the bench. "Let's sit here a minute, shall we?"

With a nod, Simon followed her up the porch steps.

She took a seat on the bench, folding her hands in her lap, but he remained standing. "Now, what happened?"

"Mr. Fredrick is claiming that, as his sister's heir, he has ownership of her property, including the Hatcherville house."

"I see." That certainly explained his agitation. "I assume he's refusing to let the children live there."

"He plans to sell the place." Simon waved a hand indignantly. "As for the children, it seems he's already talked to the owner of an orphan asylum about taking them in."

Eileen stiffened. The idea of Molly—or any of the children—relegated to a group home was unthinkable. "But that goes against everything his sister stood for."

"I agree. But that doesn't seem to bother the man." He paced the porch like a caged animal. "He believes his sister's mission was beneath her, and he has no intention of sullying his own hands with it."

"Beneath her? What could possibly make him think the care of children was beneath her? Is it because they are orphans?"

Simon shifted uncomfortably, then gave her a searching look. "I'm going to trust you with some information. But I need your word that you will treat it as confidential."

Eileen's throat tightened. From the look on his face, she wasn't certain she wanted to hear this. But she was oddly touched that he felt he could trust her. "You have my word."

"These children aren't just orphans—they are social outcasts."

"Outcasts?" She understood why that had happened to her, but— "They're only children. What could they have—"

"Not because of anything they've done," he said quickly, "but because of who their parents are."

Eileen sat back. *This* she understood.

"Fern, Rose and Lily's father died in prison. Their

mother insisted he was falsely accused, but that didn't erase the stigma."

Eileen thought of Fern's attitude, and felt she understood the girl a little better now.

"Russell, Harry and Tessa's father turned to drink after their mother died. He got killed in a bar fight." He raked a hand through his hair. "As for Molly and Joey..."

There was a long pause, and Eileen braced herself, not wanting to hear about any ugliness that might be associated with the littlest ones.

He finally continued, "There are those who think they were left on Miss Fredrick's doorstep by women who were, well, to put it delicately, less than reputable."

Eileen knew exactly what he meant. "That leaves Audrey and Andrew. Surely they are not touched by any ugliness."

Mr. Tucker winced. "My sister Sally wasn't always the best judge of character. The man she married was abusive. There were rumors that his death was not accidental but there were never any charges brought against her."

Eileen didn't say anything. She was still trying to take it all in. She definitely understood why Simon had kept this information to himself. Appearances were important, after all, and one's pedigree was a big part of that. The stains these children bore on their individual pedigrees would be difficult to overcome.

She'd grown up around people who would have shunned these children just as Mr. Fredrick had. Her stepfather had had a difficult enough time accepting her, and her only sin was having a father who came from a family of unsophisticated merchants.

But these children were already carrying the burden of being orphaned or abandoned. It wasn't fair for them to have these additional blots on their names to weigh them down. And they were innocents, after all. Just as she had been. At least in childhood.

"I hope this won't taint the way you view them."

She glanced up at his words and noticed the doubt in his expression. How long had she sat there without saying anything?

She lifted her chin and met his gaze levelly. "Who their parents are is not their fault. They should not be held responsible."

He relaxed and then grimaced. "You'd be surprised how many people feel differently."

Actually, she wouldn't be surprised at all. "Including Miss Fredrick's brother?"

"Apparently." He leaned against the railing. "Whether for that reason or mere greed, he intends to see that the children do not take up residence in that house."

"Are you certain he has the power to do that?"

"Unless I find a will among her things in Hatcherville, which I very much doubt will happen, he is her heir by default."

"Why do you think it would be so unlikely to find a will in the things she sent ahead?"

"Because she had all her important papers with her. She was quite definite about not trusting them to the freight company."

Her mind immediately began looking ahead. "What do you see as your next move?"

"We definitely can't head to Hatcherville tomorrow as planned. I suppose I should let Mrs. Leggett know I no longer require her services at least for the moment. And I should let the kids know, as well."

"What will you say to them?" She certainly didn't envy him that conversation.

"Just the bare facts, I suppose—that we're postponing our trip until some issues about the house are resolved."

"So you think there's a chance Mr. Fredrick will change his mind?"

"No. The only chance we have is if there is indeed a will amongst her things in Hatcherville, and that she worded it in a way to protect the children's interests."

"Which you don't believe will prove true."

A muscle in his jaw jumped. "I don't."

"Then what?" she pressed.

"I haven't had a chance to work that out yet." His voice fairly vibrated with his frustration, but she knew it wasn't really aimed at her.

Would he welcome a suggestion from her? "Perhaps you should talk to Adam Barr about this."

That brought a furrow to his brow. "Adam Barr?"

"You met him at church Sunday. He is Regina's husband and the manager of our local bank. He also has experience as a lawyer."

Simon stroked his chin. "I'm not sure what he could do, but I don't suppose it could hurt to talk to him. I'm willing to try anything at this point."

"He should be at his office in the bank. I'll take you there."

"You mean now?"

"Don't you think this requires immediate attention?" Considering the question moot, she added, "As soon as I speak to Dovie, we'll go."

He nodded slowly. "You're right. If nothing else, it'll help to know if I have any options I haven't figured out yet."

Eileen had to admit she wasn't exactly disappointed that Mr. Tucker and his charges wouldn't be leaving tomorrow after all. She'd gotten used to having her house filled with people. And to having Mr. Tucker to talk to.

Perhaps she could help the children deal with their grief. It had been many years since she'd lost her father, but she still remembered the overwhelming sense of loss she'd experienced. She hadn't had anyone to talk to back then.

Perhaps she could be that someone for these children.

Chapter Sixteen

Simon immediately liked Adam Barr. The man seemed to have a level head on his shoulders. He heard Simon through without interruption, then leaned back in his chair and steepled his fingers. "Do you know if Miss Fredrick formally adopted any of the children?"

"Not to my knowledge."

"And you're absolutely sure she didn't leave behind a will?"

"It's possible, but I didn't see one among the papers she had with her."

"Nevertheless we should carefully check what was sent ahead to Hatcherville. And I suggest you be the one to do the searching."

Simon had every intention of doing so. "And if a will isn't found?"

Adam spread his hands. "Then I'm afraid by default her brother inherits her entire estate. I'm sorry, but legally he is within his rights to take possession of the property and to do with it however he wishes."

Mrs. Pierce, who'd taken a seat behind him after

making the introductions, leaned forward now. "Is there nothing Mr. Tucker can do?"

Simon heard the cool confidence in her tone, but this time attributed it not to a sense of superiority but to concern.

"He can contest the claim," Adam replied, "but there's not much chance he would win."

"But would that delay Mr. Fredrick's ability to sell the house?" Mrs. Pierce pressed.

"It would. But only for as long as the case was unresolved."

Simon frowned, wondering if this was a waste of time after all. "What good will that do if he's going to eventually win the case anyway?"

"It will give you extra time to try to convince him to do the right thing," she responded calmly.

Simon dismissed that as a futile effort. "My sister put every bit of money she'd saved into that property, and now Audrey and Albert have nothing to fall back on."

Adam's gaze sharpened. "Your sister invested in this property?"

Surprised by Adam's reaction, Simon nodded his head. "Yes, and I did, too. After all, Miss Fredrick agreed to provide a home for Albert and Audrey."

"Do you have any kind of proof of that?"

Simon tried not to get his hopes up. "I have some letters from Sally that mention her investment. And I have a receipt Miss Fredrick insisted on giving me for the bit I gave her." He sat up straighter. "Why? Does that make a difference?"

"It could." Adam's demeanor had changed to that of a hound on the scent. "If we can show that you and your sister have a partial claim to the place, no matter how small, then that might be the leverage we need. It could at least give you some say into the property's disposition. It's a long shot but one worth looking into—that is if you'd like me to?"

"Absolutely. What do you need from me?"

"Do you have these letters with you? And the receipt from Miss Fredrick?"

"Yes on both counts."

"Good. Get those to me as soon as you can." Then he gave Simon a direct look. "You do understand that it may take some time to get this resolved."

"How much time?"

"Difficult to say for certain. But I'd count on anywhere from two to six weeks."

"I see." Drawing this out would make things more difficult for the children, but he didn't appear to have much choice. The one bright side was that he'd be spending more time in Mrs. Pierce's company.

"I suggest you allow me to speak to Mr. Fredrick on your behalf before he leaves town. That will put him on notice not to act too hastily in disposing of the property."

"By all means. Do you want me to go with you?"

"Yes, but just to perform the introductions. I recommend you let me do the talking." He glanced at the clock on the wall behind Simon. "Let's say five o'clock. That will give me time to look over the paperwork you have and frame my arguments."

Simon stood and extended his hand. "Thank you for your help."

"Don't thank me yet. We still have a long way to go, and in the end nothing may come of it."

Simon escorted Mrs. Pierce from the bank, feeling

more optimistic than when he'd entered. And he had Mrs. Pierce to thank for prodding him to take this step.

"It appears you and the children won't be leaving so soon after all," she said now. "In fact, it sounds like you may be stuck here until the end of the year."

He'd already given this some thought. "Don't worry. I promised I wouldn't impose on you for more than a few days, and I aim to stand by that. I'll start looking for other accommodations—"

But she raised a hand to interrupt him. "Nonsense. Of course you should stay at my place. The children are already settled in, and besides, there is nowhere else in town able to accommodate all of you comfortably. Unless you want to take over the hotel."

He felt as if a great weight had been lifted from him. "That's generous of you." Then he turned serious. "Of course some things will need to change."

"Such as?"

"We can't expect the townsfolk to supply our meals indefinitely. And we need to stop acting like visitors and begin to behave like residents."

She didn't seem as happy to hear that as he'd thought she would be. "I appreciate your intentions, but that's not necessary. The people of this town *want* to help."

"But I wouldn't feel right continuing to accept their charity." He raised a hand to halt any objections from her. "And don't worry—that doesn't mean I expect you to provide for all our meals. As I mentioned, I'm a handyman and cabinetmaker. I'll see if I can pick up some odd jobs here in town, then pay you what I can in room and board from that."

Was handyman work as far as his ambitions took him? "Perhaps Adam could find you a job at the bank."

He shrugged off her suggestion—he'd been down that road before. "Working with my hands is what I'm good at. It's how I make my living." Then he changed the subject. "I have to thank you for suggesting I speak to Adam. He seems to be a good man to have in my corner."

"If anyone can get a good outcome from this, it's Mr. Barr." She glanced sideways at him. "What will you do if you don't win your case against Mr. Fredrick?"

The woman was always trying to look ahead. "I suppose I'll have to find another place for them to live. Even if I have to build it myself."

"So you don't consider sending them to an orphanage to be an option?"

"Not as long as I have a breath in my body."

Eileen found the passion in his tone reassuring. Just the thought of the children being handed over to strangers who might not treat them kindly, or perhaps even try to split them up, squeezed something in her chest.

"Supposing you do win your case," she said. "What then? I mean, how will you go about finding someone to take Miss Fredrick's place?" She'd already decided he couldn't hire just anybody. It had to be someone who would love the children and treat them like family.

"First off, I hope when the time comes that Mrs. Leggett is still willing to help us get settled in, wherever we end up. Then I'll take out an advertisement for a permanent caretaker."

"But how will you make your selection?"

He gave her a raised-brow look, as if surprised by her tone. "Trust me, I'll interview the applicants thoroughly.

And check references carefully. It'll take a special sort of person to fill Miss Fredrick's shoes."

"You are taking a lot on yourself."

"They don't have anyone else."

"And once this paragon is found and they are settled in, do you still plan to settle nearby?"

"Of course."

Despite the fact that she would miss them, she continued to be impressed by his sense of responsibility to the children. Was it because his niece and nephew were among their number? Or would he have been this determined regardless?

She spotted Miss Whitman up ahead, stepping out of the apothecary shop. "Perhaps, since you will be extending your stay, you should get the children enrolled in school." She waved a hand to bring the schoolteacher to Mr. Tucker's attention.

Mr. Tucker nodded and stepped forward to let Miss Whitman know his intentions.

That done, they continued on their way.

"What do you plan to tell the children?" Eileen asked.

"That we've run into a bit of a snag on moving into the Hatcherville house, but that they needn't worry—I'm sticking around until we get everything worked out. And in the meantime, you have agreed to let us stay right where they are."

"It's going to be difficult for them to hear another bit of bad news."

"I think, for some of them, it might be a relief not to have to move just yet. After all, the place in Hatcherville is an unknown to them." He stopped. "There's something else I need to discuss with you before we reach your house."

"Of course." His tone had been diffident, as if he didn't think she would like what he had to say. Was there even more bad news?

"What Adam said, about my looking for a will amongst Miss Fredrick's things in Hatcherville—I think it best I take care of that right away, just so we have that question answered before this goes much further."

"I see." He was about to go off and leave her with the children. Thank goodness Dovie would be in the house to help her. "How soon do you plan to leave?"

He gave her a surprised look. Had he expected her to protest?

"Tomorrow."

Eileen tried not to wince. He *had* said as soon as possible.

"I need to collect the children's things, as well," he continued. "They can't continue with just the things they had with them on the train."

How thoughtful of him. "I'm sure they will be happy to have their belongings with them."

He gave her a relieved smile. "I truly do appreciate how generous you've been to me and the children. And I'm sure they feel the same."

His words, and the sincere tone in his voice, warmed her from the inside out.

As soon as they walked into the house the children gathered around, full of questions.

"Why did you tell us to stop packing?"

"When are we leaving for Hatcherville?"

"Where did you go?"

"Is Gee-Gee's brother still here?"

Eileen clapped her hands for attention. "Children, it's rude to all speak at one time. Quiet now, and give your uncle Simon a chance to let you know what has happened."

They quieted immediately, though they stared from her to Mr. Tucker expectantly.

With a look for her that she couldn't quite read, Mr. Tucker turned to address the children. "I'm going to explain everything and answer all your questions. But first, let's go into the parlor where we can all be comfortable."

She caught his gaze, wondering if she should join them or let him handle it alone. Apparently he understood her silent question.

"Mrs. Pierce and Dovie, if you don't mind joining us, this affects you, as well."

The children filed into the parlor and Eileen saw the apprehension in their faces. She couldn't blame them, given what news had been delivered in their last group meeting.

Mr. Tucker didn't draw things out. As soon as everyone was seated he spoke up. "I'm afraid there's been a hitch in our plans to go to Hatcherville tomorrow."

"What's a hitch?" Joey asked, wrinkling his nose.

"A delay," Simon explained. "It means we won't be heading there tomorrow as we'd planned."

"Well, I'm glad," Molly stated. "I like it here and don't want to leave."

"Well, I do," Joey said.

Eileen was taken aback by his declaration. She had expected something like that from Fern, but she'd thought Joey liked it here.

"Why is that?" Simon asked.

"Because I can't get my dog until we get to our new place."

Eileen relaxed when she heard the boy's reason. It had nothing to do with him liking or disliking being here.

"Besides, this isn't our home," Fern said firmly. "Our home is waiting for us in Hatcherville." She turned to Simon, her eyes narrowing. "Why can't we leave tomorrow?"

Eileen noted that the rest of the children wore expressions varying from worry to mere curiosity. Fern was the only one who appeared suspicious.

"Miss Fredrick's brother wants to check into the situation before we move in," Mr. Tucker explained. "It turns out the property might belong to him now."

Russell leaned forward. "But he hates us. If he owns that house, he'll never let us move in."

"I doubt he hates you, Russell," Eileen offered. "He doesn't even know you."

But Russell shook his head. "I know he does. I once heard him tell Gee-Gee that it was beneath her to take in such riffraff."

"What's riffraff?" Joey asked.

"It means he thinks we're rubbish," Fern said stiffly.

Eileen felt that insult as deeply as if it had been said of her. "Surely you misunderstood," she said quickly. "And if he *did* say such a thing, he would be quite mistaken. As your Miss Fredrick obviously believed, as well." How could anyone say such a thing in a child's hearing?

Simon wanted to do a whole lot more than give Mr. Fredrick a piece of his mind. Such pomposity and self-righteousness was inexcusable. But when it was aimed at a small child it was beyond mean-spirited. It was wounding, on par with inflicting disfiguring physical scars.

He took a deep breath, hoping to keep his tone even. "Mrs. Pierce has the right of it. Just remember how Miss Fredrick felt about you and ignore her brother's words."

"But that don't change the fact that Mr. Fredrick is gonna try to take our place from us," Russell said.

"Moving to Hatcherville is what Miss Fredrick wanted for us," Fern reiterated. "It's not right for her brother to try to keep us away."

Simon leaned forward, trying to get through to the girl. "I know, but Mr. Fredrick *is* her brother and her things belong to him now."

"Even our house?"

"That remains to be seen. But until we can untangle this mess, we'll have to stay put."

"What about all our things that were sent ahead to Hatcherville?" The girl's expression remained hard. "Does he own those, too?"

"No, of course he doesn't." Simon glanced around at each child. "Those things belong to you. It's just the ownership of the house and furnishings that we need to straighten out."

Then he smiled. "The good news is, while we're getting things all worked out, Mrs. Pierce has generously agreed to let us continue to stay right here with her."

"You mean we get to stay here?" Molly perked up at that.

Apparently the girl had formed an attachment for the place. Simon wasn't sure if that was a good thing or bad thing. "For a while. But not forever." He looked around.

"But while we're here, I'm going to enroll you in Turnabout's school so your studies don't suffer."

"Does that mean we can go to a real school just like the other kids?" Lily seemed excited by the prospect.

Predictably, Fern was not. "Gee-Gee always taught us our lessons at home."

"And I'm sure she did a fine job." Simon was careful to keep his tone conversational. "But I know she planned to send you to the town school when we moved to Hatcherville. So I think she would approve of you going to school here."

"Me, too?" Molly asked.

"No, sweet pea, you and Joey are too young to attend the town school. You'll stay here and keep the grownups company."

"Okay. And Flossie can keep you company, too."

"When do we start?" Harry asked.

"Tomorrow."

That got everyone's attention. There were lots of exchanged looks and shifting in seats. "I suggest you each go up to your room and make certain you have presentable clothes."

"But most of our things were sent ahead to Hatcherville," Rose said.

"About that. After you kids go off to school in the morning, I'll be heading to Hatcherville to make certain there aren't any important papers amongst Miss Fredrick's things. I'll gather up your belongings while I'm there and bring them back with me."

"You're leaving us? With her?" Fern's tone made it clear what she thought of *that* idea.

"You are coming back though, aren't you, Uncle Simon?" Audrey's expression looked on the verge of crumbling. Too many people she loved had disappeared from her life lately.

"Of course I'm coming back." He held his arms out and she rushed forward. "Didn't I promise I would be around whenever you need me?"

Audrey nodded as he settled her on his knee.

"And I always keep my word." That statement gave him a twinge of guilt. A more honest statement would have been he always *tried* to keep his word. "So you see, I have to come back." He tapped her nose. "And when I get back I'll have all of your clothes and other things with me."

"Like my wooden horse?"

"Exactly."

That seemed to placate her, and he let her slide from his lap and return to her seat next to Albert.

There was an immediate clamor as the children began asking him to make certain he got specific personal items for each of them.

After a moment Simon raised his hands for silence. "I promise I will get everyone's things. But I want to make something clear. I'll only be gone overnight. And while I'm gone, I expect you to treat Mrs. Pierce and Nana Dovie as if they were in charge—because they are. Is that understood?"

There was a chorus of "yes sirs" backed up by various levels of enthusiasm.

Simon stood. "Now, these two ladies and I have some things to talk over before I leave town tomorrow. Why don't you all go out in the backyard for a while? Fern and Russell, you two keep an eye on the younger ones, please."

Chapter Seventeen

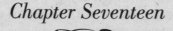

Eileen had been impressed with the way Mr. Tucker handled delivering the news to the children. He'd managed to inform and reassure them at the same time.

As soon as the children obediently trooped outside, though, he'd excused himself from the room to look for the papers Adam had asked him for, leaving her and Dovie to discuss what was in store for them over the coming days.

"He's a good man."

Eileen glanced over at Dovie, surprised by the woman's out-of-the-blue statement. "He is." She was careful to keep all inflection from her voice.

"There's not many as would so easily accept responsibility for ten young'uns that weren't his own."

Eileen agreed, but rather than saying so this time, she changed the subject. "I hope you don't mind that I told Mr. Tucker the two of us would watch over the children while he's gone."

"Glad to do it."

"I think the first thing we need to decide is what is the minimum we need to do to get the eight older children ready for school in the morning. I want to prepare a routine that takes everything into account. It wouldn't do for them to be late on their very first day." She certainly hoped Dovie was more enlightened than she on that subject.

Dovie smiled, seeming undaunted by the task before them. "There are two main things we need to focus on, and neither one of them is difficult. First is making sure they all get up on time."

"Of course." Eileen had actually already thought of that one. "With so many to get ready, I think it best to set up shifts—by bedrooms perhaps." She raised a brow. "What is the second thing?"

"Getting eight lunches prepared and packed up." Dovie waved a hand as she continued. "We don't have lunch pails, so we'll need to fix something simple that they can carry in small sacks."

Meals. Of course. She should have thought of that without having Dovie tell her. Just another indication that she was sadly lacking in motherly instincts.

But she *was* a good planner. "Then we need to come up with eight lunch sacks as well as the meals. I have some fabric scraps we can use, but I'm not sure it will be enough to make all eight." She didn't relish the idea of cutting up another of her dresses, but if that was—

"I have a few old flour sacks I been saving for next time I got a mind to make a quilt. We can use those, too," Dovie offered.

"Good. As for what we'll fill them with…" She paused, distracted by Mr. Tucker's return, then turned back to Dovie. "As you said, we should start with something simple but filling." She mentally went through the items she had on hand. "A boiled egg. Some bread.

A chunk of cheese. And I believe we still have a nice-size piece of summer sausage that we can divide up among them."

Dovie nodded. "And I can make some pecan and molasses cookies tonight that we can add as a special treat."

Mr. Tucker groaned. "You ladies are making me hungry with all this talk of food."

Dovie grinned. "Don't you worry, Mr. Tucker. I'll bake a couple of extras so you can take some on the train with you."

He gave her a boyish grin. "Thank you, ma'am." Then he sobered. "But I'd take it as a great favor if you'd call me Simon. After all, you insisted I call you Dovie. And it looks like I'm going to be here for a while."

Dovie blushed like a schoolgirl. "How can I refuse such a request from a handsome young man like yourself?"

"Good." Then he turned to Eileen. "And I'd like to extend the same offer to you, if it's not too impertinent."

Eileen froze. The use of first names between an adult man and woman was an intimate thing and not to be taken lightly. Dovie was old enough to be Mr. Tucker's mother so that was a different matter. But for her...

The last thing she needed was to be the subject of more gossip, especially now when she was starting to see signs of acceptance again. She knew from experience that one could only get away with flaunting the conventions when one's place in society was beyond reproach.

His smile faded as he shifted on his feet, and she realized she'd let the silence draw out too long.

"My apologies," he said with a smile that had a self-conscious edge. "I didn't mean—"

She cut him off before he could withdraw the offer. "Please don't take this the wrong way."

"No, of course. It was presumptuous of me to ask."

Feeling she owed him an explanation of sorts, she lifted her chin, trying to say this before her courage failed her. "My standing in the community is not the strongest." It took every bit of control she had to say that matter-of-factly, as if it was of no consequence. "So I'm sure you understand that I would want to avoid anything that would lead to fresh gossip."

Then she managed a more genuine smile. "But that said, I would be pleased to take you up on that offer when we are here at home, just among family."

The flash of surprise in his expression gave way to a look that turned her insides to warm honey. Then he gave a short bow. "I'm honored by your trust."

She felt a tremendous rush of relief when she realized he wasn't going to press her on her confession or appear to think the less of her for it.

Of course, he didn't know the details, didn't know of her culpability in her husband's death. Would he still be as friendly if he did?

Simon excused himself a few moments later to deliver his papers to Adam.

As he headed down the sidewalk, he thought about that little speech Eileen had made. She'd delivered it in her best dry-as-a-kiln manner, but he'd sensed that it had cost her dearly, not only in emotion but also in pride. Yet she had done it anyway, and for that he couldn't help but admire her.

Perhaps she was warming to him after all. That thought put a little extra bounce in his step.

He couldn't help but wonder, though, what it was that had ostracized her from her neighbors. He considered asking Adam, but immediately dismissed the notion. If she wanted him to know, she'd tell him herself.

Then he grinned, remembering how, when she made that small concession to use first names, if only in a limited capacity, she'd spoken of the house as *their* home, and she'd spoken of the group as *family*. Was that how she'd really come to think of them?

Had she even realized she'd said it?

Not that it mattered, because she *had* said it. Which meant, whether she cared to admit it or not, they were getting through to her.

Perhaps soon the ice queen would be thawed for good.

As soon as Eileen heard Simon return, she stepped out into the hallway, closing the parlor door behind her. She couldn't tell from his expression how things had gone with Mr. Fredrick, so she asked outright.

He grimaced. "Adam presented the case very convincingly, but Mr. Fredrick didn't take the news well. He intends to get his own solicitor involved and fight our claim."

Not good news, but not surprising, either.

Simon held his hat in front of him and he fidgeted with the brim as he talked. "He also wasn't happy about me going to Hatcherville tomorrow without either him or his solicitor present. But he agreed that the sooner we settle the matter of whether or not a will actually exists, the better."

"Does that mean he will accompany you to Hatcherville tomorrow?"

"No. Adam suggested a compromise—that we have the sheriff in Hatcherville accompany me as I go through all of the items. That seemed to appease the man."

Eileen was surprised that he was taking the implied lack of trust so well. "So what is the next step?"

"Adam will contact the circuit judge to schedule a date for a hearing on the matter. And Mr. Fredrick said his solicitor would be in touch."

Eileen tried to find a silver lining. "Perhaps, once Mr. Fredrick discusses this with his solicitor and sees what proof you have, he will be more willing to sit down and work out some kind of arrangement with you."

"Perhaps." His tone lacked any assurance. "But at least he won't try to sell the property before we settle this matter." He glanced around. "It's mighty quiet around here. Where is everyone?"

Eileen waved toward the parlor. "Working on lunch sacks for tomorrow."

He raised a brow. "They know how to make lunch sacks?"

She smiled, trying not to show how smug she felt. "Children can be taught almost anything if it is presented in the right way. Dovie made a simple pattern and the boys are cutting them out and then, once they are sewn together, they work on inserting the tie strings. The girls are embroidering each child's initials on their individual bags."

Which reminded her of something. "I have a question about the children."

He gave her a cautious look. "I'll be glad to answer it, if I can."

"I understand why the older children have different last names—those come from their birth families." She'd just learned their surnames when she was helping them trace the initials onto the cloth. "But why do Joey and Molly have Darling as their last names, especially if they are not siblings?"

He smiled. "It just so happens I know the answer to this one. Sally was working for Miss Fredrick when both Joey and Molly were left on her doorstep. Joey was first, and Sally said that Miss Fredrick thought long and hard about what name to give him. The first name was easy—her own father's name was Joseph, hence Joey. For the surname, though, that was trickier. She didn't want to give him her own, mainly so it wouldn't make the others feel he was more dear to her. But she did want to give him a special name so that later in life it might in some way ease the sting of knowing he'd been abandoned. She settled on Darling because every time anyone called him by his full name, he would be Joey Darling. When Molly came along, she used the same surname, for the same reason, and also so the two of them might feel the closer connection the other natural-born siblings in the house had."

"What a very thoughtful thing to have done."

Eileen's admiration for Miss Fredrick grew another notch. She would like to believe she would have been as thoughtful in selecting a name, but she doubted it. She would have been much more likely to select something practical.

And, sad to say, she wouldn't have been in that position in the first place because she very likely wouldn't have taken in such a foundling herself.

Hearing the children's laughter from the parlor, she felt embarrassed by that self-knowledge. Whose life had been the richer these past ten years—hers or Miss Fredrick's?

She knew what those in the world of her mother would say.

And she also knew they'd be quite wrong.

Simon wasn't at all surprised when Wednesday morning rolled around and all eight of the school-bound children were lined up at the front door on time to head out. They each held one of the brand-new lunch sacks filled with the items Eileen and Dovie had planned out the evening before.

There was something to be said for Eileen's insistence that schedules and routines be devised and followed. He just wished she wasn't so rigid in *everything.*

Dovie stood at the bottom of the stairs with Molly and Joey. Eileen stood at the front of the line and Simon moved in place at the end of the line, nodding at her that he was ready.

As they marched through town, their little parade elicited smiles and greetings from everyone they passed.

When they arrived in the school yard the children were still milling around waiting for the call to go inside.

Fern and Russell declared themselves old enough to fend for themselves, so Simon accompanied Eileen as she escorted the six younger children into Miss Whitman's classroom.

The introductions were quickly made and then it

was time for them to leave. Simon could tell Eileen had something on her mind as they made their exit, but he decided to wait her out.

Before she'd made it to the bottom of the schoolhouse steps, she paused and glanced over her shoulder.

"Do you think this is too soon? After the funeral, I mean?"

Simon smiled, pleased to see that she was concerned about their feelings. Had this softer side of her always been there, hidden away inside, or had the children instilled it in her?

"No, I don't." He placed a hand at her elbow, gently urging her forward. The unexpected warmth that caressed his fingers through her sleeve caught him off guard, but he did his best to ignore it. "In fact, having something new to focus on, and being around other kids their age, will keep them from dwelling too much on what they've lost."

She nodded. "Of course, you're right. But I wonder, should I check in on them at lunchtime to see how they are faring?"

Now that the steps were behind them, he really should remove his hand from her arm, but she didn't seem to mind…

"I'm sure Miss Whitman and Mr. Parker are both excellent teachers and they'll keep a close eye on the children. You should take advantage of having fewer kids underfoot to relax." He raised a hand to forestall her comment. "And before you ask, no, you don't need to be here to escort them home after school. They have strict instructions to return to your house as soon as school lets out, and Fern and Russell will see that no one takes a wrong turn. Don't worry, they're reliable."

He could tell from the momentary flash of sheepishness in her eyes that that was exactly what she'd been about to ask.

Her expression quickly resumed its customary aloof appearance. "Are you packed and ready for your trip?" She was obviously ready to change the subject.

"There's not much to pack—I'll only be gone for one night."

"The weather has been turning cooler. I hope the children have coats among their belongings that you'll be bringing back."

"I'm sure they do. St. Louis has colder winters than you do here."

The rest of the walk back to her house was spent in the same meaningless chitchat. But when they stepped up on the porch, he placed a hand lightly on her arm. "Eileen."

She turned to him, her expression wary.

"I want to thank you."

He saw surprise and relief flit across her face before she closed off again. "For what?"

"For caring about the children so much."

She seemed to soften right there in front of his eyes. Not just her expression, but all of her, as if she'd had a hard outer shell covering her that had suddenly sloughed off.

"You're quite welcome," she replied, and even her voice was softer.

The image was so real he wanted to reach out and touch her cheek. But he blinked and as quickly as it had happened, the illusion was gone and she was back to normal.

"Now, you have a train to catch and I have matters of my own to attend to," she said briskly. "If you'll get the door…"

* * *

After Simon left for the train station, Eileen looked down at Molly and Joey. She needed to find some sort of educational or enlightening activity for these two. Something that would present a challenge to their minds or social skills yet be appropriate to their ages.

Perhaps she should start with something every child loved, such as art. Learning to draw simple shapes and to color within the lines would be a good first step.

She stepped into the parlor to fetch her pencils that were stored in the small writing desk. Dovie was there, darning a pair of stockings.

When she answered the older woman's question about what she was doing, Dovie looked at her thoughtfully. "You do know that it isn't good for kids to be cooped up in the house all day, don't you?"

Eileen frowned. That wasn't the way she'd been raised. In fact the headmistress at her boarding school had taken great pains to let her young ladies know how unseemly it was to get too much sun.

Then again, she wouldn't necessarily call her upbringing ideal. And she trusted Dovie.

"But I can't just let them go outside without supervision."

"Of course not. But I believe there are a few late carrots still in the ground and some turnip tops that are ready to harvest."

Eileen nodded. Gardening could be educational. And if she could instill her love of the activity into one or both of these children, it would be something altogether satisfying.

Smiling, she set the pencils back in the desk and went

to tell the children about the change of plans, already anticipating the things she could teach them.

Later, Eileen sat in the kitchen watching Dovie teach Joey and Molly how to shell pecans for the pie she intended to make. The carrots and turnip greens they had harvested had been washed and were ready to go into the soup for tonight's supper.

Their gardening session had met with mixed success. Joey had been more interested in trying to get a look at the dog he could hear barking from another house down the block. He'd ended up pulling up an entire turnip plant rather than just the top and then had accidentally stomped on another.

Molly, on the other hand, had listened closely and asked the kind of questions that told Eileen she was truly interested in getting it right.

The current lesson on shelling pecans seemed more like playtime as Dovie showed them different techniques, made silly faces when shells went flying and pretended not to notice when they sneaked a few bites every now and then.

Eileen envied the older woman's ease around the children. She knew she would never be able to duplicate it.

The sound of the door chime brought her back to the present, and she stood. "I'll get that. The three of you look like you have your hands full."

It was probably one of the members of the Ladies Auxiliary with something for their supper meal. Simon hadn't followed through on his decision not to accept more food from the community yet.

The buzzer sounded again before she got to the door, and she frowned at the unseemly show of impatience.

When she opened the door, a breathless youth—Leo Dawson, she thought—stood there. Before she could ask him his business he blurted out, "Harry fell off a swing in the school yard and hurt himself. Miss Whitman asked me to come and tell you she sent for Doc Pratt."

Chapter Eighteen

Eileen's heart fluttered painfully for a moment as she stepped out on the porch. "You'll find Miss Jacobs in the kitchen straight down that hall." Eileen was already halfway down the stairs. "Tell her I've gone to the school and will be back as soon as I can."

With that she was off, not even bothering to fetch a hat. How badly was he hurt? Simon had trusted her to look after his charges. He hadn't been gone two hours yet, and already one of the children was hurt. Please God, let the boy be okay.

She didn't stop to exchange greetings, didn't see anyone—the streets and sidewalks could have been empty for all she knew. When she at last reached the school yard it was to see a group of children standing outside peeking in the windows and doorway.

They parted for her, and she rushed inside to find Miss Whitman and Dr. Pratt bent over a white-faced Harry.

"What's wrong? Is he going to be okay?"

"I hear he was testing the limits of the swing when he fell off," Dr. Pratt said drily. "But he'll be just fine."

Eileen's pulse slowed slightly. "Where is he hurt?"

"He bumped his forehead and sprained his wrist. We'll need to keep a brace on his wrist for the next week, but it should heal without any permanent damage."

"He's been very brave," Miss Whitman said solemnly. "He hasn't cried a bit."

Harry's chest puffed out at the praise. "I'm no crybaby." But she could tell he was in pain.

Eileen nodded, careful not to let him see how shaken she'd been. "I can see that. But I think it best if you also try to be a little less of a daredevil."

Harry's grin made no promise on that score.

Dr. Pratt closed his medical bag and looked down at his patient. "There will be no more roughhousing for you, young man, at least for the next couple of weeks. Understand?"

"Yes, sir."

"Good." Then the physician turned to Eileen. "Can I speak to you for a moment?"

Her worry returned. Was Henry more seriously injured than he appeared? She followed Dr. Pratt across the room while Miss Whitman fussed over Henry.

"I think it would be best if he goes on home now and gets some rest," Dr. Pratt said, "but he should be fine to return to school tomorrow."

"So he really is going to be okay?"

"Of course. Most boys get scrapes and sprains from time to time—it's all part of them wanting to test their own limits. Just keep an eye on him today, and keep him awake until suppertime if you can. If he appears dizzy, queasy or overly confused, send for me. Otherwise just make sure he doesn't do anything strenuous or use that left hand of his and he should recover in no time."

He gave her a searching look. "How are you doing? It can't be easy having all these children thrust on you so suddenly."

Eileen, realizing she'd been wringing her hands, straightened and gathered herself together. "I'm managing just fine, thank you, Doctor. Is there anything else I should look out for?"

"If his hand or head start hurting too much you can give him a cup of willow bark tea. You can get the powder at the apothecary shop if you don't have any yourself."

"Very well. If you'll put the fee for your services on my tab I'll settle up with you at the end of the month."

Dr. Pratt nodded, and, with another warning for Harry to take it easy, he took his leave.

Eileen escorted Harry out of the schoolroom. As soon as they stepped outside, the other children tried to press closer to get details.

Miss Whitman clapped her hands loudly. "Give them some room, children. Harry is going to be just fine, but we don't want to jostle him, now, do we."

Most of the children obeyed and parted for them to pass. But Fern stepped forward, blocking their way. "Are you okay, Harry?"

"I'm fine," Harry boasted. "It'll take more than a little fall like that to keep me down."

Eileen placed her hand on his back. "I am taking him home now so he can get some rest. You can check in on him after school."

Fern held her ground. "Maybe I should come, too,

so I can help take care of him. You're not used to taking care of hurt kids."

"I think I can handle this and you need to focus on your studies."

Fern didn't seem at all happy with that response. She lifted her head with an expression that bordered on a challenge. "I suppose with Nana Dovie there, Harry will be okay."

They stared at each other for a few minutes, but Miss Whitman and Mr. Parker called the children back to their studies so Fern finally turned and headed back to the schoolhouse.

Eileen's walk back to the house was much more dignified than her earlier rush to get to the schoolhouse had been. Not only did she adjust her steps to match Harry's, but she kept her back straight and her head high. But her thoughts were less dignified. Why did Fern dislike her so? Now that she knew a little of the girl's story, it was easier to understand why she felt she had something to prove. And as the oldest of the children, it was only natural that she would feel protective of the others.

But understanding the girl didn't make her belligerence any easier to deal with. She had to find a way to show Fern that she would not try to take her place in this family, or even that of her beloved Gee-Gee.

But that was something to ponder later. Right now she had more immediate problems. Like making sure Harry was properly cared for.

And figuring out how she would face Simon tomorrow with the news that she'd failed so spectacularly in meeting his trust to keep the children safe in his absence.

* * *

When the children returned home from school, it was as if a swarm of frisky puppies had descended on the place again. They were full of talk about the new friends they'd made, what sort of lessons they'd worked on and the games they played at recess. Eileen found herself actually enjoying the ruckus. It was too bad Simon wasn't here to see how much they'd enjoyed their first day of school.

The others made a big fuss over Harry, who was not above milking the attention for whatever he could get out of it.

At supper that night, once everyone had been served and the blessing had been said, Audrey started the conversation. "I heard some of the other kids talking about a Thanksgiving Festival. What's that?"

Eileen paused a heartbeat before responding. "Every year on Thanksgiving Day, everyone gets together to celebrate the day as a community." She used to look forward to the event, taking great pleasure in the festivities. Right up until everything changed two years ago.

"You mean like a big party?" Audrey asked.

Eileen smiled. "In a way. But it's an outdoor party."

"What all do you do there?" Harry asked. "Is there stuff to eat?"

"More food than you'd believe the schoolhouse could hold." Eileen saw she had everyone's attention and set her fork down. "Everyone brings lots of food—meats, vegetables, desserts—and it's all shared. Reverend Harper starts us off with an outdoor prayer service. Then we all eat our noon meal together. There are games and competitions for the children and some for the grown-ups, too. Lots of visiting with each other, of course. And in the afternoon there's a dance."

"Ooooh, that sounds like fun." Rose had a faraway look as if trying to picture it. "Can we go, even if we don't really live here?"

"Yes, can we?" echoed across the room.

"Everyone is welcome. Besides, you live here now, even if it's only temporary."

"I can't hardly wait," Audrey said. "When is Thanksgiving?"

"A week from tomorrow."

That brought more chatter and grins.

But not from Fern. "Do you really think it's proper for us to be thinking about going to a party when we just buried Gee-Gee yesterday?" the girl asked.

The room grew quiet as each of the other children cast guilty looks Fern's way.

"Gee-Gee was like a mother to us and we should show some respect by mourning her proper." The older girl's expression had the tight look of someone who thought they were right and everyone else was wrong.

Dovie reached over and placed a hand lightly on Fern's arm. "It's very understandable that you would think of your Gee-Gee that way, Fern. But just because we lose someone we love, doesn't mean we can't ever allow ourselves to be happy again. I'm sure your Gee-Gee wouldn't want you to miss a chance to celebrate God's blessings amongst friends and neighbors just because you miss her."

"She did encourage us to always find ways to show we were thankful," Russell said.

"I suppose." Fern stirred her soup listlessly. "But we

should think about her while we're celebrating," she said defensively.

The other children nodded solemn agreement and then the talk turned to other topics.

What sort of food would she bring to the gathering this year? Back when Thomas had still been alive and she'd been an admired member of the community, she'd taken great pride in furnishing exotic and elegantly prepared dishes. That first Thanksgiving after Thomas's death, she'd made do with a couple of pies made from pumpkins harvested from her own garden and a ham that had cost her more than she could afford, but her reception had been lukewarm. Last year, coward that she was, she hadn't even attempted to go.

But that wouldn't do for this year. There would be twelve members of her household present and that called for a much larger contribution to the meal. Could she make her funds stretch to purchase something from the butcher?

The children obviously wanted to go, and she wouldn't let her cowardice stand in their way. Besides, she knew that the folks in Turnabout would make them welcome, regardless of how they felt about her.

That evening, when she rocked the younger children on the porch swing, she missed having Simon's quiet presence nearby. How was he faring in Hatcherville? Had he found a will? If so, given how much the woman had cared for the children, surely she would have left her estate in a manner to benefit the children. Having the Hatcherville property available for the children to move into would solve most of Simon's problems.

And it would mean they would move on from here fairly quickly.

Well, she would insist they remain here through Thanksgiving at the very least. After all, the children were so excited about the upcoming community festival that it would be a shame to make them miss it.

How empty this large house would feel once they left was something she refused to contemplate.

Simon stepped off the train at the Turnabout station and felt as if he'd returned home. Strange how attached he'd gotten to the place in just a few days' time.

Though not so strange, he supposed, given how much drama had occurred since their arrival.

He made arrangements to have the trunks he'd brought back with him delivered to Mrs. Pierce's home, then headed off at a brisk walk. He was anxious to see how Eileen had fared with the children since he'd been gone. She was a capable woman, of course, and goodness knows she was up to the task of planning for just about any contingency. Still, when one had ten youngsters under one roof, it was hard to anticipate *everything* that could go wrong.

The older kids would still be at school so he'd be able to speak to her without having them all underfoot.

When he passed by the bank, he hesitated a moment. He ought to stop in and let Adam know that his search for a will had been fruitless. But he decided that could wait a little longer. The urge to check in with Eileen was too strong to ignore.

When he arrived at her house, he climbed the porch steps two at a time and entered the house without knocking.

The first person he saw was Molly.

"Hi, Uncle Simon. Did you bring our things back with you?"

"That I did, sweet pea. The man at the train depot is going to send them over just as soon as they get unloaded from the train."

"Good, 'cause I want to wear my blue dress to the Thanksgiving Festival."

"Thanksgiving Festival?" What was she talking about?

"Yes. It's like a great big party that the whoooole town goes to. And they even have dancing. And Mrs. Pierce is gonna teach me how to dance so I can dance, too."

He pictured Eileen gliding across a dance floor with his arms around her and found it a very pleasing image indeed. "Well, now, I'll bet you'll be the prettiest little sweet pea on the dance floor."

Molly giggled. Then she grabbed Flossie and began twirling about to her own humming.

Still in search of Eileen, Simon checked in the parlor and found her there with her sewing basket. It looked like one of the boys' shirts in her lap.

She glanced up and he was pleased to see a smile blossom on her pretty face. "Hello."

A heartbeat later, though, the smile was replaced by an expression he couldn't quite read. What was wrong?

"Did you have any luck?" she asked him.

"If you're asking if I found a will, I'm afraid not. I did get the children's things collected and shipped back with me, though. They'll be delivered here shortly."

The smile she gave him this time was her old reserved smile. "I know the children will be glad to have the rest of their clothing and their other belongings."

"So how did things go with the children while I was gone?" he asked, still fishing for what had put that uneasiness in her manner. "They behaved themselves, I trust."

Her hesitation told him he'd hit on the source of her discomfort. Had one of the children done something to make her uncomfortable?

"I'm afraid there was a little accident yesterday."

He stiffened, suddenly shifting his focus from worry about her to concern for the children. "What happened? Is everyone okay?"

"Harry fell off of a swing in the school yard." Her words were rushed, her expression full of self-recrimination. "He has a cut on his forehead and a sprained wrist. Dr. Pratt says he should be fine as long as he doesn't try to do too much with that hand for the next week or so."

Was that all? "So it's nothing serious."

"Nothing serious." There was a touch of outrage in her voice. "Didn't you hear me say he had a sprained wrist?"

She obviously didn't have much experience with active boys. "It'll mend."

"But you left him in my care and I didn't keep him safe."

Her feeling of responsibility was both sweet and misplaced. He crossed the room and sat on the sofa beside her, glad of the excuse to take her hand. "Eileen, this would have happened even if I had still been in town. You can't watch them all the time. Kids will take spills and have accidents. That's all part of growing up."

But her lips were set in a stubborn line. "Nevertheless, you shouldn't leave them in my care like that again."

He gave her hand a squeeze and was pleased to see a touch of pink grace her cheeks. "Come now, you're being much too hard on yourself."

Before he could say more on the subject, the door chimes sounded. No doubt it was Lionel with the trunks.

He rose to take care of the delivery, but not before he gave her hand another squeeze. "We'll speak more about this later, but know this—I would trust you with these children at any time, under any circumstances, without any reservation whatsoever."

Eileen blinked as she watched him leave the room. Had he meant that? But he didn't know—

She felt her chest constrict. It was getting harder and harder to maintain her distance. Soon, she'd have to tell him of her past failings. And she was dreading what that would do to his trust in her.

Chapter Nineteen

When the children got home from school, Simon made a big show of asking Harry about his injured hand. Just as he suspected, though, he didn't doubt the injury was still painful, the boy was much more concerned with making certain his bravado was acknowledged than with any pain it might have caused him.

"Did you find what you were looking for?" Fern asked.

"I'm afraid not."

Rose tugged on his pant leg. "Did you bring our things back with you?"

"I did. I've put the trunk with the girls' things on the second floor and the one with the boys' things on the third. You can go upstairs and unpack in a moment. But first, I have something else for all of you."

He led them into the dining room, where a small trunk sat on a chair. The lid was open, and from what Eileen could see, it appeared to contain Miss Fredrick's things.

"That's Gee-Gee's trunk," Fern said. She glanced Eileen's way as if suspicious that Eileen had been rummaging through the contents.

"I know." Simon walked over to the trunk and placed a hand on the lid. "Miss Fredrick's brother went through these things while he was here and took the items that were important to him. He wanted you children to have the rest. So you could each have something to remember her by."

Eileen knew Mr. Fredrick would not have put it so generously. It was more likely Simon had requested the items on the children's behalf. She found the fact that he'd even thought to ask for such a thing oddly endearing.

"Fern, would you like to help me lay out her things?"

With a nod the girl stepped forward. When she was done she gave Simon a dismayed look. "Gee-Gee's silver hairbrush and comb aren't here. And neither is her broach that she kept for special occasions."

"Those were probably things her brother wanted as his own mementos," Simon said calmly.

Other than a few articles of clothing, there wasn't much to be had. A carved wooden box that held sewing implements; a hat that was decorated with two silk flowers, a feather and a hatpin; a couple of lace handkerchiefs and some other odds and ends. One by one the children stepped up and selected an item.

Fern took the hatpin from the hat.

Rose, Molly and Tessa each searched through the contents of the sewing box. Rose took a small decorative pair of scissors, Tessa a brass-handled darning egg and Molly took a silver thimble.

Audrey took a lace fan that had seen better days.

And Lily took a lace handkerchief.

Harry found a magnifying glass in the sewing box and

Russell took the box itself. Joey took the feather from the hat and Albert took her wire-rimmed spectacles.

When they were finished Simon returned the few remaining items to the trunk and shut it. "Now, those things you selected are yours, to use however you like. Consider them early Christmas gifts from Miss Fredrick."

Each of the children nodded silently.

"So, upstairs with you and unpack those trunks I brought back from Hatcherville."

Once they were alone, Eileen turned to Simon. "I hadn't realized you were such a sentimental man."

He shrugged, seeming uncomfortable with that label. "I just figured they needed something of hers to hold on to."

"I would say you figured correctly." She thought of the small wooden cigar box the housekeeper had retrieved for her from her father's study after his funeral. It was the only thing she still had of his, and she wouldn't trade it for anything in the world.

Yes, Simon had done a very good thing for those children.

The next morning, as soon as the children left for school, Simon headed out to find some work. Eileen had her doubts, but when he came back at lunchtime he already had a new job well underway.

"Eldon Dempsey hired me to do some work around his farm." Simon's voice indicated he was pleased. "His roof needs some work and he's putting in some new fences. The job should take me a couple of days."

Eileen didn't know Mr. Dempsey, other than to greet him in church. He was an older man who owned a small farm outside of town. But the job sounded like simple manual labor. Didn't Simon know that he was capable of so much more?

"I met Hank Chandler over at the lumber mill when I went to pick up some supplies we needed," Simon continued. "Hank's going to let me work there part-time when I get through at the Dempsey place."

"Have you worked in a lumber mill before?" She'd only seen inside the place one time. It seemed a loud, dusty, dirty place.

"Yes. It's hard work but not as difficult as some other things I've done."

"Are you sure you wouldn't rather talk to Adam about getting a job at the bank? It would be easier work." And cleaner.

Simon grimaced. "I wouldn't be much use sitting at a desk or behind a teller window all day—I'm much happier working with my hands. Besides, I already shook hands with Hank on taking the job."

He snatched one of the biscuits Dovie had baked to go with their lunch. "I'm going to barter with Hank for some scrap lumber so I can set up a place in the carriage house for the chickens to roost."

That brought her up short. "What chickens?"

"The chickens Mr. Dempsey is going to give me in exchange for the work I'm doing for him." He pinched off a piece of the biscuit, his expression turning thoughtful. "I suppose they can just roost on the rafters until I build something more suitable, but it would be helpful to have some nesting boxes for them as soon as possible."

Eileen brought the conversation back to what she considered the salient point. "He's paying you in *chickens?*"

Simon nodded, a boyishly proud grin on his face. "It was my idea."

"But what in the world am I going to do with a flock of chickens after you are gone?"

He frowned as if she'd said something nonsensical. "You'll still want eggs to eat after we're gone, won't you? And you can sell any extra they produce to the mercantile for pin money."

That gave Eileen pause. Another source of income, however small, would be welcome. And how difficult could it be to care for chickens? "I suppose, if you want to take responsibility for getting it all set up, I won't stand in your way."

Then she had another thought. "Do you know anything about raising chickens?"

"Of course. I spent the first eleven years of my life on a farm."

Interesting. It made her want to ask him what had happened to change that, but she held her tongue.

"And I'll teach you so you can continue after we leave," he added. Then he gave her another grin. "And don't worry. When I go to work at the lumber mill, most of my pay will be in the form of cash. I'll have money to contribute to our expenses."

"Mr. Tucker, I have never asked you for payment, nor do I intend to. You and the children are my guests, not my boarders."

"I appreciate that distinction. And I gratefully accept your offer of a roof over our head. But if we're going to be here long-term, and it looks like we probably will be, I insist on contributing to the grocery bill. It's the only fair thing to do."

"Very well. But I will only take food money—nothing else."

"By the way, I've asked around about this Thanksgiving Festival the kids mentioned. It seems like that is a big deal around here."

"It's the biggest community-wide event we have. Except perhaps for the picnic and fireworks display we have on Independence Day."

"Well, we'll be long gone before July gets here, but since we'll still be around for Thanksgiving, and you just accepted my help with the food bill, you can count on me to contribute a ham or goose to the menu."

"But—"

"You and Dovie can provide the dessert." Simon was obviously not going to take no for an answer. "I'm partial to pumpkin pie, by the way, if anyone's interested."

She decided to accept his offer graciously. "Very well." Then she raised a brow. "But I make no promises as to what kind of pie we'll be bringing. I'm rather partial to buttermilk myself."

Simon watched her walk away, appreciating the added bounce in her step. No doubt about it, she was warming to him.

The next day was Saturday, which meant no school. It also meant it was laundry day. With so many people in her house, Eileen had moved laundry day to a day when there were all hands available to assist. The only person excused was Simon, who headed out for work as soon as breakfast was over.

Simon had built her some additional lines in the backyard to handle the increased volume of laundry, and he'd also come up with the idea of lining the wheelbarrow with an old sheet and using it to transport the heavy loads of laundry from the washtubs to the lines.

Eileen was very glad she had a wringer machine, but

still it took all morning to get the washing done. The clothing was washed first and then beds were stripped and dirty towels and napkins collected.

She made it clear everyone was to pitch in, boys included. Those not actively working on the laundry were put to work dragging the rugs from the various rooms in the house outside and beating them to get the dirt out.

By lunchtime everything was finally hung on the line to dry. Her helpers all looked worn-out. She figured she wasn't going to hear any objections today when it came to sending them to their rooms for quiet time after lunch.

And she was right.

Later that afternoon, when she was taking the now-dry laundry from the lines, Simon arrived riding in a small horse-drawn wagon. The children immediately abandoned their chores to crowd around him.

"Where'd you get the horse and wagon?" Russell asked.

"Can we keep it?" Albert asked.

"Hank over at the mill loaned it to me so I could get my lumber here. I'm bringing it back to him as soon as I get it all unloaded." Simon singled out the two boys who'd just spoken up. "You two want to lend me a hand with this?"

The boys enthusiastically complied, while Eileen called the others back to help her finish collecting the laundry.

A chicken coop in her carriage house. What in the world could she look forward to next?

But she was smiling as she contemplated the possibilities.

Chapter Twenty

Before the church service on Sunday morning, Simon asked permission to address the congregation.

"First off, I want to say thank you again to you folks. All of you have been extraordinarily kind to a group of strangers who landed in your midst. Most of you have probably heard that we're going to be sticking around a bit longer than we expected. Thanks to Mrs. Pierce, we have a place to stay, but I don't want to continue to trespass on your generosity, so thank you for all you've done this past week, but starting right now, you no longer need to provide us with the food for our meals."

He nodded toward a man sitting in the third pew. "Thanks to Hank Chandler there, I have a job, so I should be able to purchase food for our table myself." He spread his hands, hoping to strike a neighborly tone. "The mill is not taking up all my time, though. So if any of you have a need for a handyman, I'm available and more than happy to accept the chance to do an honest day's work."

Then, with a thank-you to Reverend Harper, he headed back down the aisle.

He received several smiles and friendly nods as he

made his way to his pew. Hopefully that would lead to a job or two. But his gaze was focused on Eileen. Seeing the light of approval there was quite gratifying.

Eileen watched him walk back to his seat and saw the positive impact his little speech had made with the folks in the congregation. Not that she'd had any doubts on that score. He was a personable man with a forthright, honest air. Who wouldn't respond to that?

And his assurance that he was ready to take responsibility for his and the kids' meals was admirable. There was no getting around it, Simon Tucker was a good man.

And perhaps, just maybe, some of his likableness was splashing over on her. Folks were actually smiling her way again. Would it last beyond his stay here?

After the service, Eileen noticed that Simon received several offers of work. Most of it was of the manual labor variety, but that didn't seem to bother him at all.

Still, if she could just steer him to something of the office or even shopkeeper variety, surely he'd be happier. After all, didn't all men have aspirations to better their lots in life?

Later that day she decided to broach the subject again.

"I know you said working with your hands is what you're good at, but I think you're selling yourself short."

His expression hardened. "I've tried working in an office before. It didn't work out."

His tone made it clear he wouldn't welcome further discussion. Had he had a bad experience? How could she convince him to give it another chance?

Monday morning dawned overcast and chilly. Simon took inventory of what rainy day protection the children had and found they were woefully lacking. Audrey and Albert each had a heavy wool cape that would repel a light rain. Russell had an oiled canvas coat that had belonged to his father. Other than Simon's own slicker, that was it.

Dovie appeared a moment later with a heavy wool cape. "Here. This is old but it'll keep the wearer dry."

"Thank you." Simon handed his own slicker to Rose and Dovie's cape to Fern. "Let's hope it doesn't rain before school lets out," he told the children, "but if you do have to walk home in the rain, you all share as best you can to help Harry, Tessa and Lily stay dry, too."

The rain held off the first part of the morning, but by ten-thirty there was a light mist in the air.

Joey had spent much of the morning on the back porch playing with his tin soldiers. But when Eileen stepped out the back door to make certain he was staying dry, he wasn't there. His toy soldiers lay in a forlorn pile, but Joey himself was nowhere to be seen. Puzzled, she stepped back into the kitchen, where Dovie was cooking and Molly was playing house with Flossie under the table.

"Did Joey come back inside?" she asked them.

"I haven't seen him." Dovie gave her a puzzled frown but didn't seem particularly worried.

"Me and Flossie didn't see him, neither," Molly called out.

"Either," Eileen corrected absently. The memory of Harry's accident was still fresh enough to make her nervous. "I certainly hope he hasn't gone out in this weather. He could get a chill."

She stepped back out on the porch and went to the top

of the steps. She called his name a couple of times, but he didn't answer. Then she noticed the door to the carriage house was open. Had he decided to play in there?

Worried about all the sharp-edged tools that were stored inside, she lifted her shawl to protect her head from the drizzle and headed for the outbuilding at a trot.

When she reached the door she pulled her shawl back to her shoulders as she waited for her eyes to adjust to the shadowy interior. But her ears were working just fine and she could hear Joey talking to someone.

"Joey, are you okay?"

"Yes ma'am. But you're scaring him."

Scaring who? She heard some scrabbling sounds and was finally able to make out the shadowy form of Joey, kneeling on the floor and bent over an animal of some sort.

Her protective instincts kicked in and she rushed to the boy's side. "What is that? Move away."

She put her hands on his shoulders, trying to urge him to move away.

But Joey didn't budge. "It's a puppy and it's hurt. We need to help him."

Eileen wasn't so sure about that. But now that her eyes had fully adjusted she could see that it was indeed a small dog. The animal was wet, dirty, and there seemed to be something wrong with its right front paw.

She'd heard once that injured animals were the most dangerous, which meant her first priority had to be to make certain Joey was safe. "Move aside," she said more firmly. "I'll take a look at him."

Joey looked at her doubtfully, then slid over to let her take his place. The animal lifted its head from the ground to stare at her, but it appeared weak and after a moment set its head back down again. The animal's gaze remained on her, though, as if waiting for her to do something.

Her heart went out to the poor thing. Joey was right—they had to help it. But how?

"I think he's hungry," Joey said. "Do you think we can give him something to eat?" He looked at Eileen earnestly. "He can have my lunch."

Eileen smiled at the boy's sincerity. "I think we can find something else for him to eat without you giving up your meal." They would need to clean the animal up, too, if they were going to see what was wrong with his paw.

She wished Simon were here; he'd know what to do. Should they keep the dog shut inside here until Simon returned?

No, if she did that Joey would insist on staying with the creature and she couldn't have that.

With a sigh, she made the only sensible decision. Slipping off her shawl, she turned to Joey. "Go on inside and ask Dovie to find our friend here something to eat and then put the big kettle of water on the stove."

"What are you going to do?" Joey's tone held an edge of suspicion.

Eileen began to gently wrap the dog in her shawl. "Something I'll very likely regret."

At his worried look, she smiled reassuringly. "Don't worry. I will take good care of him."

With a nod, Joey jumped up and raced to the house to do as she asked. Eileen slowly finished wrapping the animal, careful not to touch its injured paw, then stood with him tucked securely in her arms. The poor thing was shivering, but it looked at her trustingly.

With another sigh, Eileen pulled the animal against her chest and headed for the door. Naturally the rain chose that moment to go from a drizzle to a full-blown shower.

Simon took off his wet boots on the back porch and shook the water from his hat before entering the kitchen. He was definitely ready for a nice hot bowl of the soup Dovie had been preparing when he'd left this morning.

He stepped inside the kitchen and then halted on the threshold. What in the world—

Joey and Molly sat on the floor, and Joey had a dog on his lap that he was feeding what looked to be biscuits soaked in broth.

But more remarkable than that, Eileen sat on a chair nearby, her dress damp and covered in muddy smears, and she was attempting to dry her hair with a towel.

It was the first time he'd seen her with her hair down and she looked so completely different it left him speechless. Always before, her hair had been pinned up in a perfectly smooth, tidily arranged bun. What he saw now was a gloriously wild full mane, long wavy tresses that danced and twisted with a mind of their own. And oh, my, was that a set of bare toes peeking at him from the hem of her dress?

For a moment he couldn't even breathe.

"Uncle Simon! Look, I have my puppy!"

Joey's exuberant exclamations brought Simon's thoughts back down to earth and allowed him to collect himself before Eileen could catch him staring.

"I named him Buddy," Joey added proudly.

"That's a fine name for a dog." Simon crossed the

room and crouched down in front of the dog. "And just where did Buddy come from?"

"Joey founded him in the carriage house," Molly answered. "And Mrs. Pierce brought him inside so we could feed him and doctor him up."

Simon cut a quick look Eileen's way. *She'd* brought the animal inside? That explained the smears on her damp dress. But what could explain her change of heart?

Her cheeks warmed guiltily under his stare, and he found himself totally enchanted by this more vulnerable and feminine Eileen.

But Molly's words got through to him and he turned back to the kids. "Doctor him? What's wrong?"

"Buddy has a boo-boo on his paw," Molly said.

"We gave him a bath so we could see it better," Joey added. "But he won't let us touch it."

"I figured we'd let the poor thing eat before we give it another try," Eileen said. "He seemed practically starved to death."

"Let me have a look." Simon bent closer to study the animal's paw without touching it. There seemed to be something stuck inside the sensitive pad of his foot. Knowing what he had to do, Simon stood and looked at Eileen, trying to gauge if she was up for this.

Telling himself she would have to be, he turned to Joey. "Hand Buddy over to Mrs. Pierce, please."

Apparently recognizing the seriousness in Simon's tone, Joey stood and gave the animal to Eileen, who'd already set aside her towel.

"What are you going to do?" Joey asked.

"I'm going to remove whatever is jammed in his paw. But I'm afraid he's not going to like it."

"Will it hurt him?" Molly asked, hugging Flossie against her chest.

"Yes it will, sweet pea. But it's the only way to help him heal and get better."

He looked at the two children, who both seemed ready to cry. "Why don't you both go in the parlor until we're done here?"

Dovie stepped forward. "I think that's a good idea. And I'll go with you. Buddy probably doesn't want you to see him cry."

When they had left the room, Simon turned back to Eileen. "I need you to hold him as still as possible. From what I can see, whatever is stuck in his foot has a barb on the tip and this is not going to be very pleasant for him."

Her eyes widened. "I don't know. Perhaps Dovie would be better—"

"You're perfectly capable of doing this." Then he gave her a smile. "Besides, not only does it seem you're the one who brought Buddy into the house, but it seems you're already dressed for the part."

She glanced down at the dirt on her dress and grimaced. Then she looked up, apprehension drawing her brows down. "But what if I can't hold him still?"

"Just do the best you can." He picked up her discarded towel. "I'm going to wrap him snugly in this to make him easier to contain." He quickly put his words to action and in no time at all Buddy was securely wrapped with only his injured leg free.

Simon took a deep breath then met Eileen's gaze. "Ready?"

Her eyes were huge and apprehension fairly thrummed

from her, but she tightened her hold on the dog and gave him a nod.

Admiring her strength, he took firm hold of the animal's paw. Praying he wouldn't have to resort to his pocketknife to dig the offending item out, Simon went to work.

Buddy's yelps and howls were painful to hear, and Simon could imagine how the children in the parlor were reacting. At one point he looked up to check on Eileen and saw how white her face had turned, but she gamely held on and uttered not a word.

At last it was done, and Simon leaned back, the ugly-looking thorn in his hand. As he'd suspected, the thing had a barb on the tip and it hadn't come out without inflicting a great deal of pain on the poor dog.

Simon rubbed the animal's head, softly. "I'm sorry, Buddy. But I promise it was for your own good."

"Will his foot get better now?"

Simon looked up, surprised by the raw concern in Eileen's voice. He unwrapped Buddy and set him on the floor without taking his gaze from Eileen's. Then he gently brushed a stray tendril of that glorious hair from her cheek. "You did good. Assuming an infection doesn't set in, Buddy should be much better in a week or so."

The kitchen door opened and Joey and Molly peeked inside, with Dovie standing behind them. "Is he better now?" Joey asked fearfully.

"The thorn is out, but his paw is still going to be very tender for a while."

"Poor Buddy," Molly said as she came closer. "We're going to take real good care o' you so you can get all the way better."

"I'll get some gauze to bandage it up," Dovie said. "And I know how to make up a poultice for drawing out infection. If it works on people, I dare say it'll work on dogs, too."

Joey squatted down next to Buddy again. The boy looked up at Simon. "I can keep him, can't I?"

"Assuming he doesn't already belong to someone else, I'm okay with it. But this is Mrs. Pierce's place. She's the one you really need to ask."

Joey turned his pleading eyes on Eileen, and she gave a big sigh. "I don't suppose I could say no after we've gone to so much trouble to fix him up."

Joey let out a triumphant whoop.

But Eileen held up a hand. "However, Buddy is an outside dog, not an inside dog. You can make a place for him in the carriage house if you like."

"Yes, ma'am."

She reached over and scratched the dog behind the ears. "I suppose, though, while his foot is bandaged we really ought to keep a close eye on him. So, just until he's better, he can sleep here in the kitchen."

Joey's face lit up at that. "Yes, ma'am!"

"But just the kitchen, mind you—he's not to run loose in the rest of the house. And that's just until his paw is better."

Joey nodded.

"And you are responsible for cleaning up any messes he makes, without any fussing or foot-dragging," Simon added.

"I will. I promise," Joey said.

"Very well then," Eileen said, "I guess Buddy is part of the family now."

Simon caught her eye and didn't try to hide his amusement.

She tilted up her chin, then reached for the soiled shawl and towel. "Now I need to go clean up. You two get your uncle Simon to help you fix up a bed for Buddy over there in the corner. Then get yourselves cleaned up for lunch."

And with that she marched out of the kitchen without a backward glance.

Simon's grin widened. Who would have guessed she'd have such a soft spot for animals? It made him curious as to what other vulnerabilities she was hiding. Perhaps, now that he was going to be spending more time here, he'd have the opportunity to find out.

Then he turned to the kids. "You heard Mrs. Pierce. Let's hop to it."

Eileen twisted her hair back up in a smooth chignon, still unable to believe she'd let herself be won over by the scruffy little dog. But when he'd looked at her so trustingly, and borne his affliction so resignedly, she hadn't been able to abandon him to his fate.

So now Joey had his longed-for dog, and she had an animal invading her home. Well, she'd just have to see that Joey followed her instructions and kept the animal contained.

Of course, she was honest enough with herself to admit that the real source of her discomfort was the look Simon had given her when he first walked in. She really should have left the room to dry her hair before Simon arrived, but she hadn't wanted to leave Joey and Molly alone with the animal.

What had he thought of her disarray—hair down and

messy, clothing damp and smeared with mud, and feet bare? She'd looked a complete hoyden, she was sure.

Yet disapproval was not what she'd read in his glances. There was a warm appreciation there that had set a little pinwheel spinning crazily in her chest.

Perhaps it was best she not try to interpret just what it *had* been.

Chapter Twenty-One

Unlike the day before, Tuesday promised a day of sunshine and mild temperatures. Eileen could hear Joey and Buddy playing on the back porch and smiled at the way the boy talked to the dog as if the animal could understand him.

The other kids in the household had accepted Buddy as part of the family immediately. It hadn't mattered to any of them that he was a scruffy mutt or that he had an injury; they were all ready to make a fuss over him and claim him as their own.

And she hadn't been unaware that several scraps had been slipped to the animal as the kitchen was being cleaned up after supper. Buddy had definitely found himself a loving home.

Just as Eileen was putting the last of the breakfast dishes away, she heard the door chimes. Reflecting that she'd had more visitors in the short time since she'd taken in her houseguests than she'd had in the past two years, she hurried to see who it might be.

When she opened the door, a middle-aged man with a receding hairline stood there with his hat crushed in his beefy hands, "Good morning, ma'am. I'm Eldon Dempsey."

"Good morning, Mr. Dempsey. If you're looking for Mr. Tucker, I'm afraid he's not here. You can catch him down at the lumber mill."

"I have his chickens."

The chickens—she'd forgotten all about that. "As I said, Mr. Tucker is not in right now. Perhaps you should come back—"

"Oh, that's okay. He told me if he wasn't around, I should just put the cages in the carriage house. I only wanted to let you know I brung 'em." And with a friendly wave, he turned and moved back before she could think of something else to say.

Feeling at a loss as to what she was expected to do, Eileen tracked down Dovie in the parlor.

"Mr. Dempsey has brought the chickens."

Dovie looked up with a smile. "That's nice. It'll be good to have fresh-laid eggs again."

"What should I do?"

"I don't reckon you need to do anything until Simon comes home."

Molly popped up from the sofa where she'd been playing with Flossie. "Can I go see the chickens?"

Eileen hesitated. "Perhaps we should wait until your uncle Simon comes home."

"But—"

Dovie spoke up. "While those birds are still in their cages is a good time for you to get acquainted with them. Come along. Let's go have a look." She turned to Eileen. "You, too. You need to get used to being around them."

Eileen started to object that she had no intention of

getting acquainted with farm animals. But the protest died in her throat when she saw the determined look in Dovie's eye. Instead she meekly nodded. Perhaps she should at least look in on the fowl.

By the time they headed out the back door, they found Joey already on Mr. Dempsey's heels, asking him questions about the birds in the cages, and Mr. Dempsey was patiently answering each one.

The man dropped off four cages containing two chickens each. When he was done he tipped his hat Eileen's way. "Just tell Mr. Tucker to drop off those cages back at my place when he's done with them."

Eileen assured him she would and then he was gone.

She looked at the squawking birds and decided she didn't care to get any closer than she was now, regardless of the security of the cages. The other three, however, had no such compunction.

"Are we really going to get our very own eggs from these birds?" Joey asked.

"Sure will," Dovie answered. "Probably get the first few bright an' early tomorrow."

"Can I come get 'em?"

"I tell you what. Until you get the hang of it, why don't we come collect them together."

"Okay." Joey turned to Molly and puffed out his chest. "I'm gonna be a chicken farmer."

"I want to be a chicken farmer, too," Molly said quickly. "And so does Flossie."

"Well, now, there's a lot more to taking care of chickens than collecting their eggs."

"Like what?" Joey asked.

"Well, for the first few days I reckon your uncle Simon is going to want to keep them penned up in here so they get used to this being their new home. That means they'll have to have feed and clean water. It'll also mean everyone will have to be real careful when going into and out of the carriage house so one of the birds doesn't escape."

"I can do that," Joey said.

"Me, too," Molly echoed.

"Then, once he's ready to set them loose, someone will need to make certain they get shut up tight in the carriage house at night so owls and other critters won't get them." She gave Joey a stern look. "And that includes your dog. Buddy's going to have to be trained to protect them, not chase after them."

"Don't you worry. Buddy is going to be the best chicken watchdog there ever was."

Eileen let them continue their discussion about the chickens while she quietly slipped back inside the house.

She had given in on the matter of the dog simply because Buddy's plight had touched her heart.

The chickens, on the other hand, were not nearly so endearing. She was perfectly happy to stay away from them as long as she was able.

Wednesday morning dawned cold and overcast, and Eileen guessed they wouldn't have many more days to wait until the first frost arrived. School was out until the following Monday and the lumber mill was shut down for the same period, so everyone was home. The children were nearly vibrating with anticipation for the festival the next day and Eileen sincerely hoped it lived up to their expectations.

Simon slipped out right after breakfast to run a mysterious errand of some sort.

Eileen, Dovie and some of the girls were still working on cleaning the kitchen when he returned.

"Here you go," he said, setting a very large ham on the table with a proud expression on his face. "I told you I'd provide the main course for our contribution to the town's Thanksgiving meal."

Dovie bustled over to examine his purchase. "Now, this is a very fine ham indeed. I'll spread some molasses on it and let it bake nice and slow today. It'll be juicy and tender for tomorrow."

"You should let me do that," Eileen said. "It hardly seems fair for you to do all this work since you won't get to come with us."

"Oh, I forgot." Tessa looked suddenly stricken. "You can't leave the yard or your heart will hurt."

Eileen had noticed the seven-year-old seemed to have formed a special attachment to Dovie.

The child walked over and took Dovie's hand. "Do you want me to stay with you so you don't have to spend Thanksgiving alone?"

Dovie looked down at the little girl with an aching tenderness. "Thank you, Tessa. I think that's just about the sweetest thing anyone's ever said to me. But you need to go on to the festival with the others so you can come back and tell me all about it. Okay?"

Tessa nodded tentatively, obviously still worried about Dovie.

"Besides," Dovie added, "I won't be alone the whole time. Ivy promised to fill up a plate of all that good eatin' and bring it over so she and Mitch can take their meal with me." She winked at Tessa. "You make sure she puts a big old slice of peach cobbler on there for me."

Tessa nodded more enthusiastically this time.

"Good, I know I can count on you." Dovie straightened. "Now, you girls finish with the dishes while I find a pan big enough to bake this ham in. And you two—" she turned to Eileen and Simon "—you get to work shelling pecans for me. I plan to bake an apple pecan pie to go with this ham."

By midmorning a soft rain had started falling. That, combined with the dropping temperatures, drove everyone indoors except Joey, Audrey and Albert, who were in the carriage house playing with Buddy. Simon made certain there was a roaring fire in the parlor fireplace and most of the other children drifted in there to enjoy its warmth.

Eileen sought out Simon and found him on the front porch, carving on a flat piece of board. "What are you working on?"

He held it out to her. "What does it look like?"

It was square and had lines carved into it going both vertically and horizontally. "A chessboard?"

He smiled. "Close. A checkerboard. I thought it would be good for the kids to have something to do. I actually plan to make two of these so they won't have to wait so long for a turn."

"Perhaps you can try chess pieces for the second one?"

"I can make playing pieces to go with a checkerboard without much trouble. Chess pieces would be more difficult."

She swallowed her disappointment. "Of course."

He went back to work. "So you're a chess player?"

She drew her shawl more tightly around her. "I know the basic moves, but I haven't played much."

"How are you at checkers?" He blew the wood dust from the board.

"I've never played, but it's a child's game, isn't it?"

He gave her a sideways look before eyeing his board again. "It *is* simple enough for a child to learn, but for the serious player, there's a whole different level of complexity and strategy to be learned, as well."

She settled for a noncommittal *Hmm*.

He leaned back and gave her a look that she assumed was meant to be stern but somehow failed.

"I can see you don't believe me," he said. "I guess I'll just have to prove it to you."

Her pulse quickened in response to that look of challenge he gave her. "And how do you plan to go about doing that?"

"By teaching you to play."

"Whenever you have the game ready, I am at your disposal."

"Just give me about twenty minutes."

She glanced at the board and frowned. "But it's not even painted yet. And we can't use it while the paint is still wet."

"I don't plan to use paint."

"Then how—"

"Watch." He used his knife to start carving shallow diagonal stripes into one of the squares. When he had that one done to his satisfaction, he moved over to another, leaving an untouched square between them.

Eileen studied the affect and smiled appreciatively. The alternating grooved and smooth squares were as distinctive as the inlaid board her stepfather had had in his study. "Will you be marking the playing pieces the same way?"

"No. I'm using something much simpler." He nodded toward a pile of round discs on the porch beside his chair and she stooped down to study them.

They were surprisingly uniform in size and thickness. But they were made from two different woods, one light and one dark. A simple but effective means of differentiating the opposing pieces. And there appeared to be enough of them to use with the two boards Simon planned to make. "Clever."

He grinned. "You don't have to sound so surprised."

She smiled back at him and realized that her current position put their faces nearly level. When she inhaled, she caught the scent of sawdust and soap and outdoors—of him. The sounds of the rain and the wind and voices from the house were drowned out by her own heartbeat. Could he hear it, too?

Simon saw Eileen's eyes widen and heard the little hitch in her breathing. There was a tiny smudge just below the corner of her lush lips. She would no doubt be mortified if she knew it was there, but he found it endearing. He tightened his hold on his knife, forcing his fingers to ignore the overwhelming urge to reach over and stroke that sassy little smudge away for her. Even stronger was the urge to kiss it away.

Would she slap him if he tried?

She swayed forward slightly, and he decided it might be worth finding out….

The door opened behind them, and Eileen blinked, then stood up as if something had propelled her.

"Whatcha doing?" Lily asked.

Eileen brushed at her skirt, not making eye contact.

"Your uncle Simon was just showing me the game he's making."

"What kind of game?"

"Checkers."

"Oh, can I play?"

Simon finally looked away from Eileen and toward the little girl. He smiled at her eager expression. "I promised Mrs. Pierce I'd teach her first. But you can play afterward."

Lily looked at Eileen. "Don't you know how to play checkers already?"

Eileen shook her head.

"But even Joey knows how to play." The confused look on Lily's face was almost comical.

"Don't worry," Simon said, keeping his expression appropriately solemn. "I'm a good teacher. I'm sure she'll pick it up in no time."

Simon felt Eileen's glare without even looking at her and knew she'd definitely be playing to win when the time came. He was looking forward to it.

By the time they sat down at the dining room table with the handcrafted checkerboard between them, all of the children had heard about this being Eileen's first game of checkers. Not only were they gathered to watch, but sides were being taken, mostly along gender lines.

Simon won the first game handily and tried not to let his amusement show when Eileen's lips pinched in irritation.

She recovered quickly, though, and gave him an arch look. "I believe I have the hang of it now. Shall we try again?"

"If you insist." And he set up the board again.

He won the second game, but this time he had to make more of an effort.

"I think I really have the hang of it now." There was definitely a glint of determination in her eyes. "Shall we try once more?"

And to his surprise, she did indeed manage to win that third game.

Delighted by the flush of triumph on her face, he stood and made a short bow. "Well done. Congratulations."

She smiled graciously. "I did, after all, have a good teacher."

Before he could explore this playful side of her further, several of the children began clamoring for a turn at the game, and Eileen gave up her seat with a smile and excused herself to help Dovie in the kitchen.

As Simon moved back to the porch to begin work on a second checkerboard, he found himself whistling. Someday soon he was going to kiss that woman.

And the sooner, the better.

Chapter Twenty-Two

As they all gathered back in the parlor after lunch, Dovie turned to Eileen. "Did I hear you say there's going to be dancing at this festival tomorrow?"

Eileen nodded. "There is."

"Who provides the music?"

"There are two fiddlers in town, as well as a banjo player and a couple of harmonica players. They play in shifts or in pairs to keep the music going most of the afternoon and evening. It's not the same as having an orchestra, but it keeps the dancers twirling."

"It sounds mighty festive." Dovie turned to the children. "How many of you know how to dance?"

Her question was greeted with silence. "None of you? Well we can't have that. I'll hazard a guess that Mrs. Pierce is a fine dancer. Perhaps we can talk her into teaching some of you."

Eileen felt suddenly shy. She refused to allow herself to glance Simon's way, but she was very aware of his presence. "There's no music."

"We can sing for you," Audrey offered.

"I can do better than that." Dovie quickly left the room and shortly returned carrying a lap harp.

"What a beautiful instrument." Eileen moved closer to examine it. "How come I haven't seen it before?"

Dovie shrugged. "Haven't had a reason to pull it out until now. But I reckon I can still play us a lively tune." She settled in her chair and plucked a few notes, fiddled with the knobs, then plucked at the strings again. Finally she looked up with a grin. "Now, claim your partner, and let's see what you can do."

Eileen supposed there was no getting out of it so she stood and looked around with a smile. "Who wants to go first?"

No one stepped up.

"Perhaps they'd like to see a demonstration first." Dovie waved toward Simon. "You know how to dance, don't you? Come over here and partner with Eileen and show them how it's done."

Dovie began playing her harp and the strains of a lively jig soon filled the room. It wasn't exactly what Eileen was used to, but Simon stepped up and bowed gallantly. She curtsied and away they went with him leading her through the paces of a vigorous country dance. By the time the music died, Eileen was breathless and smiling.

Simon was a surprisingly good dancer. Not ballroom caliber perhaps, but his movements were confident and smooth. And she'd had no trouble whatsoever matching her steps to his.

"Now let's try something different," Dovie said. "Why don't you demonstrate a waltz for our young students?"

A waltz. Eileen's gaze quickly flew to Simon's, and

she found him holding out his hand, a slight challenge in his smile. Telling herself this was just a demonstration, she placed her hand in his and allowed him to step closer and place his other hand at her back. When the soft strains of the music began she followed him effortlessly, as if they'd danced together like this many times. Her gaze never left his, and the pleasure and admiration she saw reflected there was intoxicating, as if the music flowed not just around her, but through her.

Everything else fell away, and she gave herself up entirely to the music, to the feel of his hands, to the look in his eyes. Like a bit of dandelion fluff, she was floating on the wind that was the music.

When the music stopped it was as if she'd been rudely awakened from the sweetest of dreams.

She looked around, blinking as reality blanketed her again. She found Dovie watching them with a knowing grin. Merciful heavens, how much had she revealed?

Immediately she stepped away from Simon and tried to regain her mental equilibrium.

"Now," Dovie said briskly, "Eileen, why don't you work with the boys and, Simon, you can work with the girls to try to teach them a few simple steps."

Grateful for the change of focus, Eileen immediately took both of Joey's hands and tugged him to the middle of the room. They practiced for the next hour or so, meeting with mixed success. Some of the children took to it quickly, some barely managed the basics and a few dived into it enthusiastically, dancing to their own tune and quite happy to do so.

Finally Simon collapsed on the sofa, declaring himself too exhausted to continue. The rest of them took that as a cue to take a break as well, and everyone found a seat to plop down on.

Once Dovie stopped playing and the children were still, Eileen could hear the rain. If anything, it seemed to have intensified. She rose and went to one of the windows to take a look. Sure enough it was coming down in sheets, and didn't show any signs of letting up. This didn't look good for tomorrow's festival.

She felt someone come up to stand behind her and knew even before she saw his reflection in the glass that it was Simon. Their gazes met in the windowpane, and she wondered if he was remembering that lovely waltz with the same tingly, unsettled feeling she was.

Rose joined them, breaking the spell, and she edged her way between Eileen and the window. "What happens if it doesn't stop raining?" she asked glumly.

"The ground will keep getting wetter."

"Uncle Simon! You know what I mean. What happens with the festival?"

"I'm afraid the festival will be canceled," Eileen said regretfully. "There's no place in town big enough to seat everyone for the meal, and the games and the dance would all get bogged down in the mud even if we attempt to hold them."

"Maybe it'll stop before morning," Harry said hopefully.

"I hope so." Molly twirled around the room holding Flossie's hands. "I want to show everyone how I can dance."

Eileen glanced out at the downpour. The first Thanksgiving after her marriage to Thomas had been like this, and the festival had been canceled. She had partially salvaged the day by inviting two dozen of

Thomas's closest friends to spend the day with them. Thomas had been so proud of her hostessing abilities and the event had cemented her place as a social arbiter in the town.

She couldn't hope to duplicate that success, but surely there was something she could do to mitigate the disappointment the children were feeling. They'd had enough setbacks to face over the past few weeks—it was time to find something to celebrate.

She looked around, noting the grumbling and moping that was already spreading through the room. This wouldn't do at all.

"Children." She used her best authoritative tone and it captured everyone's attention. "I am disappointed in you. There are going to be troubles you have to face in this life—everyone has them. If you want to be respected rather than pitied, you must learn to handle them with grace and dignity—not whining and complaining."

From the corner of her eye she saw Simon's frown. Did he think she was being too harsh? Surely he knew these were lessons the children needed to learn.

But she wasn't without sympathy for them. "Besides, just because we can't celebrate with the whole town, that doesn't mean we can't celebrate at all."

That earned her a few hopeful glances.

"What do you mean?" Harry asked.

"Well, we still have all the food Dovie is cooking, and all of this room, and even some music—why can't we have our own festival right here? I imagine your uncle Simon could even come up with a few friendly competitions for you to take part in."

"You mean inside?" Russell didn't sound overly impressed.

"Yes, inside," Eileen answered calmly.

"But it won't be the same," Rose said.

"No, it won't." Simon sent Eileen a supportive look. "But that doesn't mean we can't make it fun."

"That's right." Dovie threw in her support for the idea. "We can have an indoor picnic."

"What's so special about eating on the floor of the parlor?"

Eileen could see their efforts were not meeting with total success, and she searched her mind for a way to get the children excited.

There was one thing that might do it...

She hesitated. The hideaway, as she called it, had once been her favorite room in the house, and Thomas had given it over to her for her private use. But she'd closed it off when she'd been forced to sell off all the lovely furnishings it had housed. Looking at it as it was now only served to remind her of all she'd lost.

But there was really no good reason, other than her pride, for her to keep it closed off and hidden. And if it would cheer up this gloomy-looking crew of kids, it might be worth opening up to serve a new purpose.

"Who said it has to be in the parlor?" she asked, arching her eyebrows.

Simon gave her a "what are you up to" look, but didn't say anything.

"Where else would we have it?" Harry asked.

"Well, there's always the *secret* room."

That immediately captured everyone's attention.

"Your castle has a secret room?" Molly asked, her

voice almost a whisper and her eyes wide. "How come we never seen it before?"

"Never *saw* it," Eileen corrected. Then she put her hands behind her back and rocked back on her heels. "Because then it wouldn't be much of a secret, would it?"

Joey, who was standing next to Dovie, turned to her. "Do *you* know about her secret room?"

Dovie shook her head, but there was a decided twinkle in her eyes. "No, but I sure am curious to find out more. What about you?"

Joey nodded vigorously.

"Will you tell us the secret?" Harry asked.

Eileen looked around, meeting each set of eyes solemnly, enjoying the sense of anticipation and excitement in the room. "I would have to know that I could trust you to keep my secret," she said, making her tone doubtful.

There were vigorous nods and choruses of "yes."

"Very well." She straightened. "The entrance to the secret room is actually right here in the parlor."

Immediately everyone began scanning the room, looking for where that entrance might be.

"Surely you've noticed the turret attached to this house when you're outside." She stepped away from the window. "Haven't you wondered where the inside of that tower is? I mean, such a room would have round walls, wouldn't it?"

"Oh." Impossibly, Molly's eyes widened more. "Please can we see it?"

Some of the quicker-witted children were focusing on the far wall, the wall that was closest to the turret. Eileen headed across the parlor in that same direction. She smiled when she heard them following close behind.

"Where is it?" asked Molly. "Do you have to say a special word for the door to appear?"

Eileen laughed. "No. You just have to look very, very carefully." She stepped up to a chair positioned in front of what to the casual observer appeared to be an ornate panel, identical to all the other ornate panels that were evenly spaced on the walls throughout the room. A closer look, however, showed that this particular panel had unobtrusive hinges on one side, and that the edges of the panel were actually seams in the wall, in fact, they were the outline of a door. She reached for one of the carved flowers and tugged. It easily pulled out to form a decorative doorknob.

And with a flick of her wrist she twisted the knob and dramatically flung open the door.

It was shadowy inside and the musty smell of disuse tickled her nose before she even entered.

Eileen stepped all the way inside and the children crowded in behind her. She crossed the room and pulled open the drapes. And turned to see the children looking around the room with expressions of awe and delight. What on earth did they see in this sadly empty space to warrant such a reaction?

She turned and studied the room herself. And for the first time, didn't see the ghosts of the beautiful furnishings that were no longer there. Instead she saw the flowered paper on the walls, the gilt work on the ceilings, the ornate scrollwork that capped the built-in shelves, the beauty of the stone hearth, the grandeur of the tall curved windows that gave the room its rounded shape. The fact that the lower half of the view from the windows was screened by holly bushes only enhanced the air of mystery.

"It's like a princess's room."

Eileen raised an amused brow at Molly's words. "A princess's very *dusty* room."

"Once we get it cleaned up, this will make a very nice place to hold our very own Thanksgiving Festival," Dovie said.

"And a wonderful bonus of having our Thanksgiving at home is that Nana Dovie can join us," Simon added.

"That's right." Tessa took Dovie's hand. "The whole family can be together."

Eileen saw the emotion in Dovie's eyes at the little girl's simple gesture and words, and felt a lump in her own throat for just a moment. She turned away and her gaze snagged on Simon's. They stared at each other for several heartbeats, and though he was across the room, the warm understanding in his gaze was like a gentle caress to her cheek.

"This room will definitely need a good cleaning before we're able to serve a meal in here."

Dovie's words brought her back to her senses and she dropped her gaze.

"We can do that," Lily said.

"I agree." Dovie put her hands on her hips. "And now is as good a time to get to it as any."

"After we clean it, can we decorate?" Tessa asked.

"I think that's a marvelous idea."

Dovie organized the cleaning, assigning the various tasks to the children according to their abilities. Before long the room was a hive of activity. Even Simon and Eileen had tasks assigned to them.

What the younger children lacked in skill and reach, they more than made up for in enthusiasm.

Eileen gave in when Joey asked if Buddy could join them "for a little while" and the animal seemed to sense the festive atmosphere.

Molly brought Flossie into the room to "help," of course, and held a running conversation with her doll about what a wonderful room it was and how the two of them could have tea parties and picnics in here over the coming days.

At one point the little girl looked over at Eileen. "You can come to our tea party, too, if you like. You can be the queen, and I shall be the princess and Flossie will be our very dear friend."

"That sounds quite lovely," Eileen responded, touched that the little girl wanted to make her a part of her make-believe adventures.

When they were finished cleaning, it was time to decorate. Dovie asked each of them to go through their things and find at least one item that they would be willing to share with everyone for the one day of Thanksgiving, and that would be their decorations.

Eileen went up to her room and looked around. At one time she had owned so *many* beautiful things. Thomas had showered her with clothing and jewelry and gewgaws. All of it was gone now. She'd had to part with everything, just to pay off the debts Thomas had left her with—not to mention purchase the simple necessities for herself.

She glanced at her trunk. No, not quite everything. There was one item, her most prized possession, the one thing she'd held on to through all those hard times.

She moved to the trunk and pulled out a tissue-wrapped package from the very bottom. She laid the package on the bed and carefully unwrapped it. The fabric spilled out, still as vibrant and beautiful as it had been the day Thomas gave it to her. The iridescent fabric of the shawl shifted between the rich blues and greens of a hummingbird's feathers with every movement. There were tiny beads sewn throughout the shawl with metallic threads, giving it even more shimmer. The fabric was supple and unbelievably soft. She could picture it hanging on the wall in the "secret" room, next to the fireplace where a tapestry had once hung.

But what if she let Dovie use it for decoration and something happened to it? Children were always having accidents and spills. She could always bring the brass candlestick by her bedside to set on the mantel, and no one would be the wiser.

But she'd know.

Eileen carefully refolded the shawl, grabbed the candlestick and headed downstairs with both items.

Chapter Twenty-Three

"Just a little higher on the left." Eileen ignored the rolling of Simon's eyes as he towered above her on the ladder. "You want it to be straight, don't you?"

"At this point, I just want it to be done." But he obligingly lifted the cord-wrapped nail a tiny bit higher.

"Stop! That's perfect."

"At last." Simon quickly hammered in the nail, as if afraid Eileen would change her mind.

As soon as she'd told him what she had in mind for the placement of her shawl, he'd gone to work rigging up a cord to hang it from using clothespins.

She turned to take the shawl from Fern, who'd offered to hold it for her. The girl was stroking it with an almost-reverent awe.

"I've never seen anything so beautiful in my life," the girl said as she reluctantly handed it over. "And you actually wore this."

Eileen smiled. "A few times—not often. My late husband and I used to throw wonderful parties for all of his friends. The house would be filled with people and lots of food. Everyone would dress up in their finest clothes and sometimes we'd even have musicians come in."

"That sounds lovely."

Eileen studied the thirteen-year-old. She was of an age where romantic notions could take over her daydreams. She hoped whoever Simon eventually found to care for the children would know how to keep the girl grounded without totally destroying her dreams.

Fern seemed to remember suddenly that she and Eileen weren't on good terms and with a short nod turned and moved to help Rose with a project she was working on.

Sighing, Eileen turned and handed the shawl up to Simon.

He gave her a sympathetic look, obviously having caught the exchange. "Give her a little more time. I think she's thawing toward you."

Hoping he was right, Eileen gave a short nod.

Then they turned their attention to hanging the shawl, and in short order it was done.

Eileen stepped back to study their handiwork and declared herself satisfied.

She looked around at the rest of the room and smiled at what a hodgepodge the group had brought into the space to decorate it.

Two other candlesticks in addition to hers stood on one end of the mantel. On the other was a large yellow-and-white stoneware vase. Who had donated that—Dovie?

Hanging from the very center of the mantel was the tired little black hat with the two red silk flowers that had been in Miss Fredrick's valise. She cast a quick glance Simon's way. How typical of him to want to include the memory of the children's foster mother in their celebration tomorrow. Then she studied the rest of the room. Scattered here and there were colorful toys, hair ribbons and pretty glass jars.

It was a far cry from the expensive furniture pieces and gilt-framed pictures and mirrors that had once graced this room. But she couldn't say that she liked it any less for all that.

"You all have done an amazing job," she said to the room in general. "The secret room has come alive again."

"It does look mighty nice," Dovie agreed. "And Simon and I came to a decision while you were upstairs."

"Oh?"

"Right after breakfast tomorrow," Simon said, "me and the boys are going to bring the dining room table in here."

Eileen wrinkled her brow. "But why?"

"Because a few of us don't think our old bones can take all the getting up and down that's involved in eating on a picnic blanket," Dovie answered.

"Then why don't we just eat in the dining room and then come in here after."

"What?" Simon put his hand to his heart, as if shocked by her suggestion. "Not have our Thanksgiving meal in the secret room? That would be tragic."

Eileen rolled her eyes, then looked around to see several of the children nodding in solemn agreement. "Very well. If you want to go to all that trouble I won't stand in your way."

"I knew you'd see reason. All right, kids, we're eating at the table in here tomorrow."

A cheer went up and then Dovie clapped her hands for attention. "It's been a long day, and we've got lots of things planned for tomorrow. Time to get cleaned up and ready for bed."

Eileen nodded. "After you're cleaned up, we'll do our story as usual—"

"Can we do it in here?" Molly asked.

"I suppose so. I'll ask your uncle Simon to help me drag in a few chairs while you're getting ready for bed." She waited for his nod before continuing. "As I was saying, we'll do our story as usual—I have a really good one for you tonight. But I'm afraid it's much too cold and wet to go out on the swing tonight. I thought perhaps instead, I could come to each of your rooms and sing a song while I tuck you in."

That plan seemed to meet with general approval, and in a few minutes they had all trooped out of the room to take care of their nightly routines.

Simon quickly brought four chairs inside the room, then stood staring at them while he stroked his chin thoughtfully. After a minute he glanced her way. "I think I'll construct three or four long benches to set along the walls in here. They won't be fancy but they'll be easy to make and it'll save having to move chairs in and out of here every time you want to use the room."

"How thoughtful. But don't feel like you have to be doing such things for me."

He smiled. "I don't mind. And it's the least I can do."

What did he mean by that?

He leaned a shoulder against the wall. "Don't think I don't know what you did this evening. It was more than generous of you to open up this room to the children. You must have had it closed off for a reason, yet when you saw how disappointed they were at the thought of missing out on the festival, you did this for them. And not only that, you're sharing your shawl, which apparently is very special to you, with the children, as well."

There was that warm-honey-in-her-veins feeling again. What this man could do to her with just a look and that crooked smile of his. "Neither the room nor the shawl was doing any good to me or anyone else locked away the way they were. It was time they saw the light of day and the joy of use again." As she said the words she realized how very true they were. Were there other things in her life, in *her,* that had been locked away for too long?

"That may be true——" he took her hands "——but there's not many as would have chosen ten orphans and their unprepared guardian to share them with."

She liked the way her hands felt in his, liked the rough calloused strength of them, the feeling that those hands would never let any harm come to her, and that, despite the work-roughened state of them, those hands knew how to be gentle, as well.

Wanting to convey her emotions, she gave his hands just the tiniest of squeezes. Immediately his gaze sharpened and she saw his focus shift to her lips. Was he going to kiss her?

Suddenly, with every fiber of her being, she wanted him to do just that. She leaned forward slightly, her gaze never leaving his face. His own gaze flew back up to her eyes and then they were searching, as if uncertain.

She gently disengaged her right hand and brazenly moved it to his cheek. What would he think of her?

He smiled then, a warm, triumphant, top-of-the-world smile. He turned his head without looking away and kissed her palm, all the while keeping his gaze locked to hers.

Eileen had never felt so shameless and so cherished at the same time. Every nerve in her body screamed at her to do something, but she didn't know what.

Finally he nudged her hand away and she didn't know whether she was glad or sad.

"Eileen."

The way he said her name set her pulse racing. "Yes."

"I'm going to kiss you proper now, if that's okay?"

Chapter Twenty-Four

Simon pulled Eileen to him, gratified when she slipped her arms around his neck to hold him close. Then he kissed her, and those enticing, full lips of hers were every bit as sweet and warm as he'd imagined. He could hold her like this forever, for as long as he could feel her heart pounding in rhythm to his.

But finally she pulled away. The reluctance with which she did it, however, was quite edifying.

"Dovie or the children…" she said, her voice shaky.

Of course. This house was too full of people. He shouldn't have put her in a position to have been embarrassed or shamed. "I'm sorry—"

She halted his words with a finger to his lips. "I'm not."

Simon smiled then and gave her shoulder a quick squeeze before putting a little distance between them. He couldn't believe he'd ever thought this woman an ice queen. She was warm and vibrant and altogether irresistible.

When she'd reached up and touched his face, it had

been the sweetest and the most unbelievably sensual gesture he'd ever experienced.

And that kiss just now, that had been absolutely amazing.

They needed to talk, to figure out what this meant. He wanted to make certain she knew how he felt, how he wanted to protect her and cherish her and be by her side always. Surely, after that kiss, she felt the same?

He led her to one of the chairs and had her sit. "Eileen, I—"

Molly padded into the room just then, cuddling Flossie and yawning widely. "Am I first?" she asked sleepily.

Simon gave Eileen's hand a squeeze, then stepped back. They would have to wait until the children were in bed to have their talk.

"You most certainly are, sweet pea," he said in answer to Molly's question. "Why don't you and Flossie come sit over here by the fire where it's warm while we wait for the others."

But later, when the children had all been tucked in and Dovie had disappeared into her own room, Eileen professed to be tired and wished him a good-night.

Simon watched her climb the stairs, confused. Surely he hadn't misread how she felt.

Was she confused by her own feelings? But she was a widow, not a blushing maiden, so he assumed it wasn't the first time she'd been kissed in such a fashion.

There had to be something else holding her back. But what?

Eileen stared at the ceiling of her bedroom calling herself a coward and a fool. She should never have let their relationship get this far. Simon wasn't the man for her, perhaps no man was.

She knew he had wanted to talk tonight, to discuss what had happened between them, but she hadn't been ready.

Because she knew, no matter how she felt about him, she couldn't let this go any further until she told him the truth about herself. And she wasn't strong enough to do that yet. Because once he knew the truth, the way he looked at her, the way he felt about her, would all change.

And she truly did not think she could bear that.

The next morning there was no opportunity for her and Simon to speak privately—she made sure of that. There was breakfast to be tended to and morning chores to be done. Buddy, who was obviously on the mend, seemed to be underfoot constantly. Twice he escaped the kitchen to wander other parts of the house and had to be tracked down.

Since it was a special day, Eileen limited the chores to what absolutely had to be done along with special preparations to be made for their own version of the Thanksgiving Festival.

As soon as breakfast was over, Simon and the older children removed the leaves from the table and carried it across the hall, through the parlor and into the secret room. There the leaves were reinstalled and then all the chairs were transported there, as well.

Simon threw himself into the preparations as enthusiastically as the children, but from time to time she caught him watching her with a seriousness that was unnerving.

Once their chores were completed, the children were allowed to play. Simon had finished his work on the second checkerboard so two games could go on at one time. Fern was overseeing the memory game Dovie had taught them with some of the younger children.

About an hour before lunch, the door chimes sounded. Wondering who would have ventured out in such nasty weather, Eileen went to the door. She opened it to see Ivy and Mitch standing there, a large hamper in hand.

"I hope we're not intruding," Ivy said as Eileen ushered them inside. "I spent the day cooking yesterday, hoping against hope the festival would be held today. I didn't want it all to go to waste, and since we'd already planned to have our meal with Nana Dovie—"

"You are more than welcome to join us," Eileen assured her. "Assuming you're willing to put up with a bit of a rambunctious celebration. We're holding our own festival."

"Oh, what fun!" Ivy loosened the ties of her shawl. "As long as you're certain we're not intruding."

Simon had joined them by this time. "Of course not. The more the merrier."

Molly tugged on Eileen's skirt. "Are they allowed to see the secret room?"

"Secret room?" Ivy's smile broadened. "How intriguing."

"I think we can trust them to keep our secret," Eileen replied solemnly. "Don't you?"

Molly nodded. "Can I show them?"

"Of course. You show them while I let Nana Dovie know they're here."

Before they could move, Buddy came scurrying by

as fast as his three good legs could carry him. He was closely followed by Joey, who was scrambling to catch him. When he saw Eileen he skidded to a halt. "He moves pretty fast for a dog only using three legs," he said proudly. Then he started off again. "Don't worry," he called over his shoulder, "I'll have him back in the kitchen in no time."

Ivy stared at Eileen, an amused expression on her face. "I see your feelings about allowing dogs in your house have undergone a change since I boarded here."

Eileen shrugged. "One must learn to adjust."

Ivy laughed outright at that, then followed Molly into the parlor.

By Eileen's estimation, the first annual Pierce household Thanksgiving Festival turned out to be a great success. By midday she'd stopped trying to keep Buddy penned in the kitchen, only warning Joey to keep a close eye on him.

There was plenty of food to go around, the games Simon devised for them to play kept everyone entertained and they even enjoyed a bit of dancing.

Eileen made certain she and Simon did not share another waltz, of course. But she did accept his hand for a reel and she even danced a round with Mitch.

All in all she decided she'd had as much fun as if they had been able to attend the community-wide event. Perhaps even more.

Before Ivy and Mitch left, Mitch helped Simon move the table and chairs back into the dining room, and Ivy helped with the dishes.

By the time the couple said goodbye it was time to get the children ready for bed. Once the last child was tucked in bed, Eileen slowly descended the stairs to where Simon waited for her, knowing this couldn't be put off any longer.

He met her at the foot of the stairs, and she could see the questions in his expression.

"Shall we sit in the parlor?" she asked.

With a nod, he followed her into the room and waited quietly while she took a seat on the sofa. He remained standing.

"There's something I have to tell you," she said without preamble.

"I'm listening."

"I suppose you've noticed that I am not the most popular of persons in this town."

"I *have* noticed that there are some folks here who treat you rather rudely."

"There is a reason for it."

He made a sharp gesture of disagreement. "There's never a good reason to be rude to a lady."

She smiled at his quick defense. "Thank you for that. But perhaps you should reserve judgment until you hear the story."

He finally moved to sit beside her. "Don't feel as if you owe me an explanation."

"But I do owe you one. And you're going to hear me out."

His brows drew down at that. But he gave a short nod and leaned back.

She took a deep breath. This wasn't going to be easy.

Simon waited, not sure he really wanted to hear whatever it was she had to say.

"I'm not originally from Turnabout. I was born and raised in Charleston, South Carolina."

So that accounted for the slight accent he heard in her voice. "Not being from around here is not a crime."

"No, that wasn't my crime. Please hear me out. I met Thomas Pierce when he made a business trip to Charleston. He became quite smitten with me, and I did nothing to dissuade him. It was something of a whirlwind courtship—we were married a mere month after we met."

He noticed she said nothing about her being smitten with Thomas. Had she cared for her husband?

"When Thomas and I moved back here, he was quite eager to spoil me. He indulged my every whim and I let him, even encouraged him."

He couldn't really picture her in that role. She was so controlled, so refined.

"What I didn't know was that eventually Thomas overextended himself. He was a partner in the town's bank and he began dipping into funds he had no right to touch in order to pay his bills—bills that he incurred to indulge me in my frivolity. And then, when it became clear the truth would be discovered, he took his own life."

Shocked, he reached over and took her hand. "I'm sorry. That must have been very difficult for you."

Her eyes registered surprise at his reaction. She gently disengaged her hands from his and resumed her story. "In the eyes of the town, I had been responsible for Thomas's ruin and his downfall. Thomas was one of their own. I was not. I was like Delilah, preying on the weakness of a good man."

His anger over what her neighbors had put her through rose yet another notch. "It seems to me," he said firmly, "that a man should be held accountable for his own actions. Your husband could have simply told you no. He could have also told you the state of his finances so that you could adjust your behavior, which I believe you would have, had you known. Instead he chose to play the indulgent benefactor and then was too cowardly to face the consequences of that choice." The blackguard had taken his own means of escape and left Eileen to face not only his debtors but also her judgmental neighbors.

Eileen studied him with something akin to wonder in her eyes. "I don't believe I've ever met another man like you." Then her expression closed off again. "But there's nothing that says I won't turn into that woman again should I ever have the opportunity. In fact there is every indication that I would."

"You're wrong. Besides, if you picked the right man to marry, he wouldn't let you."

That won him a smile. But she sobered quickly. "There's another thing."

He waited for her to continue, certain it was of as little consequence to his feelings for her as the first had been.

"More than anything else Thomas wanted a big family." She waved a hand. "If nothing else, this house is a testament to that. And I wanted to give him one. But I failed at that, as well. It appears I can't have children."

Simon felt a pang at that. He'd always wanted to have children. But then the irony of that hit him. "Look around you. I don't think having a big family will be a problem."

She drew herself up in obvious affront. "This isn't funny."

"Of course it isn't. And I'm sorry that you can't have children of your own, if that's what you want. But there are ten wonderful children right here who need you very much."

"They have you, and they have Mrs. Leggett."

"But neither of us is *you*." What was it she was so afraid of?

Her expression closed off, and she stood, drawing herself up to her full, shoulders-back height.

He got to his feet as well, bracing himself for whatever other objection she was prepared to make.

"If you must know," she said stiffly, "while I like and even admire you, I don't think we would suit well together, not as husband and wife. Our lives and our backgrounds are much too different."

Backgrounds? Did that mean what he thought it did?

But she wasn't quite done. "This doesn't change anything regarding your stay here. You and the children are more than welcome to remain for as long as you need to. And I hope we can remain friends while you are here. I merely thought it important that you understand exactly where my feelings lie."

"Oh, I think you've made that crystal clear. And don't worry, I won't be bothering you again with anything other than business concerning the children. Now if you'll excuse me, I think I'll go out on the porch for a breath of fresh air."

He couldn't believe this had happened—it was like being back in Uncle Corbitt's home once more. He'd thought she understood who he was, but apparently not. Or rather, who he was didn't measure up to her standards. He should have realized her feelings on the matter when she'd kept pressing for him to ask Adam for a job at the bank.

She wanted to remain friends—he wasn't sure that was possible. Civil was about the best he'd be able to manage.

He'd made a fool of himself. It was time he pressed for a resolution to this matter of the Hatcherville property.

He couldn't move out of here soon enough.

Eileen's shoulders slumped as she watched him leave the room. That hadn't been easy or pleasant, but it had been necessary. Much as she'd like it to be otherwise, she knew that she would end up making him unhappy if she agreed to marry him. She had only to look at the marriage between her own parents to know the truth of that. Marrying her father had ruined her mother's life and turned her into a bitter, unhappy woman. She couldn't stand the thought of doing that to Simon.

Eileen trudged up the stairs to her room. Yes, she'd absolutely done the right thing.

So why did she feel as if her heart was breaking?

Chapter Twenty-Five

To Eileen's relief, at breakfast the next morning, the kids provided most of the conversation with their re-hashing of their favorite parts of yesterday's celebration. Hopefully no one noticed the lack of any interaction between her and Simon.

Just before they finished the meal, Dovie spoke up.

"I've been thinking. Being as all of you will be here for Christmas, I thought it might be a good idea for each of us to select one person from the group to give a gift to. We can pull names out of a hat to make it fair."

This sparked a little buzz of excitement around the table and everyone generally seemed to think it was a good idea.

"To make it even more special," Dovie said, "why don't we make something handcrafted for whoever's name we get rather than going out and buying some-thing?"

"That sounds like a lovely idea," Eileen agreed. It would keep anyone from feeling inadequate due to not having money.

"But what if we don't know how to make anything?" Albert asked.

"Oh, I don't think that will be a problem." Eileen gave the boy an encouraging smile. "Use your imagination. You can draw a picture, or build something, or sew something—it'll be fun."

"What might make it even more fun is if we keep it secret from the person whose name we draw," Dovie suggested.

"Secrets are fun," Molly said. "Like the secret room."

Fern, naturally, had misgivings. "What if the matter of the Hatcherville property gets settled faster than Uncle Simon thought and we get to leave here before Christmas?"

Eileen winced at the girl's telling use of the words *get to.* "Then we will exchange gifts a little early," she said. "But I'm hoping you'll plan to be here for Christmas, regardless." She cast a quick look toward Simon, but he wasn't looking her way.

"If we're here for Christmas, can we have a tree?" Rose asked.

"I think we can work something out. You'll just need to talk your uncle Simon into cutting one down for us."

Simon did look up at that, but his gaze slid right past hers and landed on Rose with a smile. "We'll go out a couple of days before Christmas and find us a nice, full one."

Molly clapped her hands. "We can put it in the secret room and decorate it with lots of pretty things. It'll be the most beautiful Christmas room *ever.*"

Eileen thought about the elegant decorations she'd had before her fall from grace. Molly would have been

enchanted by them. "I'm afraid I don't have any decorations."

"That's okay." Dovie waved a hand, as if waving a
baton. "We can make those, too. That'll be more fun
anyway."

Thirty minutes later Eileen looked at the name she
had drawn and felt her heart sink. Fern. The girl would
never welcome any gift from her.

Of course, since it was supposed to be secret, no one
would know if she swapped names with someone. And
she was certain Fern would prefer a gift from just about
anyone else over her.

She followed Dovie into the kitchen, relieved to find
they were alone for the moment. "I have a favor to ask."

Dovie crossed her arms over her chest. "What can
I do for you?

"Would you mind trading names with me?"

Dovie gave her a surprised look. "Now, why would
you want to do that? You don't even know who I have."

"It doesn't matter. I drew Fern's name. The girl
doesn't care for me, and I think perhaps she would appreciate anything you would give her much more than
something from me."

"Nonsense." Dovie patted her hand. "Perhaps this is
your opportunity to make friends with Fern. She doesn't
really dislike you, you know. She's just hurt and confused by the blows life's landed on her, and she needs
someone to lash out at. Be patient with her."

Eileen tried again. "I'm being patient. It's just not
bearing any fruit yet."

Dovie raised a brow. "Tell me this. If one of the children came to you with a request to swap names because

they didn't get along with the person whose name they had, what would you tell them?"

Eileen winced at that, then sighed. "I would tell them that they should try to work things out." She gave in. "Very well, I'll see what I can come up with."

Eileen slowly exited the kitchen, trying to decide what kind of gift she could come up with that Fern would like.

Perhaps she could take one of the delicate lace handkerchiefs she still had and embroider Fern's initials on it for her.

She went to her trunk and threw open the lid.

There, right on top where she'd placed it last night, was that beautiful iridescent shawl.

She remembered the way Fern had looked at it, the almost-reverent way she'd stroked it.

Eileen stroked it much the same way now. It was still the most beautiful thing she'd ever owned.

Making up her mind, she shut the lid of the trunk and took the shawl to her bedside where her sewing box was stored.

Simon threw the board fresh from the saw onto the proper stack. It had been six days since Eileen had told him of her true feelings, and the sting still hadn't gone away.

So far they'd managed to remain civil, friendly even, but the tension was there, just below the surface, and he wasn't sure how much longer he could keep up the charade.

The worst part about it was he found himself still attracted to her, more fool him. He still enjoyed listening to the emotion in her voice when she recounted her nightly fairy tales to the children. Still found the little selfless things she did for the children admirable. Still found his heart touched when she did something that revealed her vulnerability.

Still ached to hold her in his arms again.

Fool! Why couldn't he just focus more on the snobbish reason she'd pushed him away?

He looked up to see Adam standing across the way watching him. When their gazes met, Adam waved him over.

Simon walked over to meet him, tugging off his work gloves as he went. What was up? Did they have some kind of decision on the case?

It was hard to tell from the expression on Adam's face if it was good news or bad.

The two men shook hands and then Adam got right to business. "Mr. Fredrick has made an offer."

This was it. "What kind of offer?"

"He's willing to refund the amount you and your sister contributed to the purchase of the property in Hatcherville. Period. He is not willing to give you any partial ownership in or access to the property itself."

A not entirely unexpected offer. If Eileen had taught him nothing else, she'd taught him to plan ahead for every contingency. "Do you think this is a fair offer?"

Adam spread his hands. "*Fair* is a relative term. I do think, however, it's the best you can hope for from Mr. Fredrick unless you want to take your chances in court."

Simon rubbed his chin while he thought about it. The kids associated the place in Hatcherville with Miss Fredrick. How would they feel about settling somewhere else?

On the other hand, there was no guarantee how it

would go if they took the case to court—he could end up with nothing. And it was unfair to the kids and to Mrs. Pierce if he let this business continue to draw out when he could put an end to it now.

With the money Mr. Fredrick was offering, he could find them another place. It wouldn't be as big as the Hatcherville property, but as long as he found something sound and with enough land for them to have a proper garden and some farm animals, he could take care of adding on to the house over time.

He met Adam's gaze. "I accept his offer."

Adam nodded, not making any sort of judgment on the decision. "I'll have the papers on my desk tomorrow morning for you to sign. The money should be wired to the bank by the end of the week."

Thanking Adam for his help, Simon went back to work feeling lighter of spirit. At last he was free to move forward again. To move out of Eileen's house.

To move out of her life.

That afternoon, when the kids got home from school, he gathered everyone together and explained the latest development.

"So there you have it," he said when he'd finished. "I'm sorry we won't be able to move into the place in Hatcherville, but this will give us the opportunity to find a new place to call home."

"Maybe we could just stay here," Molly suggested. "There's plenty of room. And Mrs. Pierce could be our mommy. And Nana Dovie can be our grandma."

Simon avoided looking Eileen's way. "But this isn't our home, sweet pea. We promised Mrs. Pierce we'd be gone right after Christmas." Perhaps even sooner.

Not satisfied with his answer, Molly turned to Eileen. "You'd like for us to stay, wouldn't you?"

Before Eileen could answer, Dovie spoke up. "There's nothing to keep you from looking for a place right here in Turnabout, is there?"

The kids perked up at that.

"Really?" Harry said. "You mean we could keep going to school here with our new friends?"

"And keep Miss Whitman for our teacher?" Rose added.

"I suppose that's one option," Simon said slowly, not sure he wanted to go that way. But the more he thought about it, the more it appealed to him. It would actually have a lot of benefits. He wouldn't need to uproot the children again, at least not entirely. Mrs. Leggett might be willing to become the permanent caretaker for the children if she didn't have to move away from Turnabout. Hank had indicated Simon could go to work at the mill permanently if he wanted. And since he wouldn't be living in this house, he really didn't have to see much of Eileen at all.

"But we wouldn't live in this house anymore," Molly lamented.

"No, but you could come visit whenever you want," Eileen said quickly. "And the secret room would always be available for you and Flossie to have tea parties in."

That cheered Molly up considerably. Simon supposed it would be up to Mrs. Leggett as to how often Molly visited here.

Assuming he found a place in Turnabout.

And assuming Mrs. Leggett would accept the job offer.

* * *

Two days later, Eileen sat in the parlor patching a pair of Albert's pants and felt ready to scream. This stiff formality between her and Simon was driving her crazy. She longed for them to go back to the friendly relationship they'd had before she'd made the horrible mistake of flirting with him and encouraging that kiss. That sweet, tender, glorious kiss.

She pricked her finger with her needle and lifted the digit to her mouth, tasting the metallic tang of blood. Feeling distracted and restless, Eileen put away her sewing and fetched her winter cape. She let Dovie know she was going for a walk, then headed out the door.

She pushed open the front gate, then hesitated. Deciding she wasn't in the mood for people, she turned away from town and headed toward the open countryside.

After five minutes of vigorous walking in the blustery air, she felt better. Perhaps, if she was persistent, she could convince Simon to at least call a truce. They didn't have to be best friends, but perhaps they could at least be honestly cordial.

How serious was he about looking for a place in Turnabout? And how did she feel about it?

The sound of an approaching wagon caught her attention and she quickly moved to the roadside. Hopefully whoever was driving would take care not to spatter mud on her.

She was pleased when she heard the vehicle slow down, then surprised when it seemed to be stopping altogether. She looked up to see Simon in a buggy.

He sat there silently watching her, and she finally

couldn't stand it so she broke the silence first. "Hello. Were you out looking for me?"

"No. I'm actually going to take a look at a place down the road that's for sale."

"Oh." She moved closer to the side of the buggy. A week ago she would have invited herself to go with him. A week ago, he would likely have invited her himself.

As if coming to some sort of decision, he gave a short nod. "Would you care to come with me? I'd value having your opinion."

Pleased by the invitation, she nodded and grabbed the side of the buggy to pull herself up. He reached for one of her hands and assisted her in. Was he finally ready to forgive her?

When she was settled he clicked his tongue and flicked the reins to set the buggy in motion. They rode along in silence for a while. She couldn't sense any softening in his attitude toward her.

She finally gathered her courage and spoke up. "I'm very sorry for causing all of this awkwardness between us."

He cut her a surprised look, but then turned back to face the road without saying anything.

She tried again. "I know this is all on my shoulders, but if there is anything I can do to fix it, I wish you'd just tell me."

Still he remained silent, his jaw tight.

"I truly value the friendship we had." Unbidden, a little sigh escaped her. "I don't have many friends," she added quietly.

He maintained his stiff demeanor for a heartbeat longer, then his shoulders relaxed. "I value our friendship, too." He gave her hand a quick squeeze. "But you have to know it can't be like it was before."

"I know." She told herself this was a start and that she should be happy to have this second chance.

"So how far is this place we're going to look at?" she asked, ready to change the subject.

"Not far. I want something that will put the kids close to school." He slowed the wagon to a stop. "In fact, I think this is it."

They were sitting in front of a ramshackle farmhouse that looked as if it would blow over with the first strong wind to come along. "Are you sure this is the right place?"

Simon gave her that familiar crooked grin that she'd missed so much these past few days. "Don't let appearances fool you. I want to check how solid the frame and foundation are. Everything else can be fixed with paint, lumber, nails and good old-fashioned sweat."

She couldn't picture any amount of work, other than tearing the whole thing down and starting from scratch, that would make this place livable.

He came around the buggy to hand her down, then started toward the house. Was he planning to go inside?

"Mr. Stringman told me there are three bedrooms upstairs and a small office downstairs that can be converted to a bedroom if I need it."

"You plan to get all of the kids into four bedrooms?"

"Three. I figure the downstairs one will be Mrs. Leggett's." He began walking around the exterior, peering closely at the walls and windows, tapping on the wood here and there. "I know it'll mean they'll have to share more than they are now," he said absently, "but it'll still be as roomy, if not a little roomier, than what they had back in St. Louis."

Smaller than this? How had they managed?

She peered through a large window into what was probably the dining room. "It will be difficult to seat everyone in there at one time for their meals."

"We can squeeze in by using benches instead of chairs until I can expand on the house. Come on, let's look inside."

She followed him inside and tried to find some positive things to say. "The big windows in the dining room are nice."

He nodded and moved toward the back of the house.

"The kitchen is a good size."

Again he merely nodded absently as he checked walls and floors.

She gave up and simply followed him from room to room. At last they headed back outside.

"It's not ideal, but it'll work," he said. "And there's plenty of room for the children to play and for us to have some animals—chickens, a milk cow, maybe even some goats or pigs. There's room for a nice garden, too."

"And what about you? Do you intend to live here with them?"

"Of course, at first anyway. I can stay in the lean-to—it's not ideal but I've slept in worse places. My priority will be to take care of the major repairs first and then to expand on some of the downstairs rooms. It won't ever be as big or fancy as your place, but it'll suit our needs just fine."

Eileen decided too ignore the *fancy* comment. He probably really hadn't meant anything by it. If this was what he truly wanted for himself and the children, than she would support his choice.

"Of course, I wouldn't want to live in that lean-to forever. I was thinking, eventually, I might build myself a little cabin on one corner of the property—far enough away to give me some breathing room, but close enough so they can easily call on me if they need anything."

It began to sink in that they would all be moving out soon. She would see them at church, of course, and maybe occasionally in the mercantile or some of the other shops around town. But it wouldn't be like now. It would be Mrs. Leggett the children would be looking for to doctor their hurts, cheer on their accomplishments and to shape their world.

"How soon do you plan to move in? Surely you don't intend to move the children here until you've made it weather-tight. We are heading into the coldest, wettest time of year, after all."

"They're a hardy group, and I'll make certain we have lots of firewood and blankets."

"But you will stay at my place at least through Christmas as we'd planned?"

"Of course." Then he smiled. "But we're getting a little ahead of ourselves, aren't we? I haven't purchased the property yet."

But he intended to. And she had no doubt at all that he would make it happen.

And then what would she do?

Chapter Twenty-Six

At supper that evening, after the blessing had been said and all the plates served, Fern cleared her throat. "Uncle Simon?"

"Yes?"

"Dora Sanders is having a party at her home to celebrate her birthday on Saturday afternoon, and she's invited me."

"And who is Dora Sanders?"

"She's Mayor Sanders's daughter," Eileen answered. "I believe she is about the same age as you are, Fern, isn't she?"

"Yes, ma'am." Fern turned back to Simon. "May I go, please?"

"When is this party?"

"Saturday at one o'clock."

"That's laundry day, isn't it?"

Eileen couldn't believe he was teasing the girl like this. "I believe, if Fern helps in the morning, the rest of us can take care of things without her in the afternoon."

He pointed his spoon Fern's way. "Does that sound like a good plan to you?"

"Yes, sir."

"Well, in that case, I don't see any reason for you not to go."

"Thank you." She turned to Eileen. "I promise to work hard as can be Saturday morning."

"I know you will." Eileen gave the girl an encouraging smile. Fern had changed over the past few days. She seemed more content, more like a schoolgirl rather than a mother hen.

Perhaps the two of them could become friends after all.

"I know why Fern wants to go to this party," Russell said.

Fern glared at him across the table. "Russell Lyles, you just hush your mouth."

But Russell only grinned wider. "It's because Kevin Grayson is gonna be there and she's sweet on him. You should see how twitterpated she acts when he's around."

Fern's face turned beet-red, and she looked ready to sink through her chair.

"Russell, that's enough." Eileen knew girls Fern's age were easily mortified, and it was too bad of her brother to take advantage of that. "You shouldn't be teasing your sister that way."

Hoping to take the focus off Fern, Eileen then turned to Dovie. "This chicken stew you cooked is delicious. Is that rosemary I taste in there?"

"It is." Dovie took Eileen's cue and turned to Joey. "I do believe Buddy is starting to put some weight on his hurt foot. He must be feeling better."

"Yes, ma'am." Joey launched into a story about the latest trick he'd taught the dog, and before long conversation around the table returned to normal.

Later that night, for the first time since Thanksgiving, Eileen joined Simon on the porch after the children had gone to bed.

"You seem unusually pensive tonight."

Simon shaved another curl of wood from the piece he was whittling. "I'm just thinking about Fern."

"Don't worry. She'll get over Russell's teasing in no time."

"It's not that."

"Then what?"

He was silent for a moment as he sliced away another curl. "Do you think Russell's right about her being interested in this Kevin Grayson kid?"

Her lips quirked up as understanding dawned. "Most likely."

"That's what I was afraid of." He sounded downright forlorn. "How do I handle things when she starts getting really serious about boys? Or worse yet, when they start getting serious about her?"

Eileen smiled. "I have a feeling you'll do just fine. And you'll have Mrs. Leggett to help you."

His only response to that was a muttered "Six girls. Six!"

A change of subject was definitely in order. "Have you decided about the Stringman place?" Eileen asked.

"Stringman is out of town, but I'll be putting in an offer when he returns on Monday."

"I see."

He must have heard something in her tone because he cut her a quick, speculative look.

She turned to look out into the night, feeling suddenly hollow inside. "When are you going to tell the children?"

"Not until I'm certain the deal will go through."

She nodded. "That's probably wise."

Then, on a totally unrelated note, she said, "We need to make this a Christmas for the kids to remember." And for her to remember, as well.

Fern was very excited about going to the party. She'd picked out a set of pretty hair ribbons as a gift for her friend and carefully wrapped it in tissue that Eileen had on hand.

Eileen had also taken the delicate lace collar from one of her own dresses and sewn it onto Fern's Sunday best. On Saturday, Fern pulled her hair back with a silver hair bow that had been her mother's, then stood back for Eileen to check her out.

"You look absolutely beautiful," Eileen declared. She wished she still had the cheval glass mirror that had once stood in her bedroom so Fern could get the full effect.

Fern looked down at her dress doubtfully. "The other girls' Sunday dresses are nicer."

Eileen pinched her lips in disapproval. "Someone will always have nicer things than you. And someone will always have things that are less nice than yours." She gave the girl's hands a squeeze. "But there's not many as will have greener eyes or rosier cheeks."

Fern did smile at that.

"Now, are you sure you don't want me to accompany you just to the front gate?"

Fern shook her head. "I know the way."

"All right. Just make sure you come straight home when the party's over."

"Yes, ma'am."

Eileen watched her go. Yes, Simon would have his hands full with his new family.

And she ached to be the one by his side to help him through every bit of it.

Chapter Twenty-Seven

Eileen walked out to the carriage house, where Simon was feeding the chickens. She rubbed her arms to ward off a sudden chill.

He glanced up at her, then immediately frowned in concern. "What's wrong?"

How could he read her so well? "It might be nothing. But I was expecting Fern to be home by now."

"You mean she's not back from that party yet?"

"No."

He set the pan of feed down. "I tell you what. You're probably right that it's nothing. But just to set your mind at ease, I'll go down to the Sanders's house and check on her." He started toward the house. "Chances are they just got to having so much fun they lost track of time."

"But Mayor Sanders and his wife wouldn't have."

"Just tell me how to get to the Sanders's home and I'll be on my way."

She decided she wasn't in the mood to sit back and wait. "I'm going with you."

He looked prepared to argue, then seemed to think better of it and nodded. She quickly stuck her head in the back door to let Dovie know where they were going, then led the way around to the front of the house. All the way to the Sanders's home she kept getting a nagging feeling that something was wrong.

Please God, let it just be my overly active imagination. But if it's not, hold her tightly in Your hands until we can find her.

They reached the Sanders's home without her having much memory of having made the walk.

Mrs. Sanders answered her knock and appeared surprised to see them. "Eileen, Mr. Tucker, what can I do for you?"

"We're looking for Fern. Is she still here?"

"Why, no. The party broke up an hour ago. But I believe Fern left before that."

Dora appeared at her mother's side. "That's right. She got real upset when she caught that fancy shawl of hers on a nail. She said she had to leave."

Fancy shawl? Fern had been wearing her black wool shawl when she left the house. "What did the shawl look like?"

"It was all shimmery-like and had lots of beading on it."

Mrs. Sanders shared a look with Eileen. "It's that fancy one you used to wear on special occasions. I just assumed you'd loaned it to her."

"Of course. Fern knows she can wear it whenever she likes. I just didn't realize she'd worn it today."

Fern had taken the shawl. Without permission.

Why hadn't the girl just asked her?

More importantly, where would she have gone?

As soon as they were out of earshot, Simon gave her

a worried look. "That was the shawl you pulled out on Thanksgiving, wasn't it?"

Eileen nodded. "Fern has run away. We have to find her."

Two hours later Fern still hadn't been found, and it would be dark soon. Eileen stood at the kitchen window, staring at nothing in particular, racking her brain for the hundredth time on where the girl might have gotten off to. Wherever it was, she prayed that it was sheltered, because it was going to be a very cold night.

Simon had been out there searching all this time. And a number of men from the town had volunteered to help. Surely Fern would be found soon.

Dovie was keeping an eye on the other children in the parlor. Ivy was there, too. Eileen hadn't been able to sit still, and she hadn't wanted her own anxiety to convey itself to the children.

Fern was an intelligent girl, she kept telling herself, full of curiosity and quick wit when she wasn't being sullen. Once she had decided to let go of some of her belligerence she'd made surprisingly good company. Just a few days ago she'd asked Eileen questions ranging from how to bake a pumpkin pie, her favorite, to where the tower rooms were on the other two floors.

Eileen stilled. Could she really be that close?

She quickly headed for the stairs, then paused with her foot on the bottom tread.

She turned and stuck her head in the parlor. All eyes immediately turned to her.

"Sorry, no news," she said. "I just need to speak to Ivy for a moment."

Ivy immediately joined her out in the hallway, her

eyes wide with worry. "What is it? Has something happened?"

Eileen shook her head, then signaled for Ivy to follow her up the stairs. "There's a possibility that she's hiding right here in the house. If I'm right, I'm going to need to go in and talk to her, but I thought someone should see that the signal is sounded so the searchers can return home."

"Of course. Do you really think she's here?"

"I'm praying really hard right now that I am right."

A moment later they were on the third floor and Eileen went straight to the little door set in the far wall. Taking a deep breath, she eased the door open. At first she didn't see anyone, and her spirits sank low enough to walk on. But then she heard a rustling noise. "Fern, sweetheart, is that you?"

Her only answer was a hiccuping sob.

Relief flooded through her as she realized that Fern was indeed here. With an unapologetically tearful smile and nod to Ivy, she ducked inside and closed the door behind her.

She slowly made her way across the low-roofed room, guided more by sound than sight as her eyes slowly adjusted to the gloom.

"Are you okay?" she asked.

A muffled "yes" drifted back to her.

"Everyone's been out looking for you. We were all very worried."

"I've done something awful."

Eileen was finally able to see the girl, and she plopped down on the floor beside her. "I doubt it's as awful as you think."

"But you don't know what I've done." The girl's voice was almost a wail.

Eileen put an arm around her shoulder and drew her close. "It doesn't matter what you've done, sweetheart. Nothing could be bad enough to make us want you out of our lives. Please don't ever run away like this again."

"I took your beautiful shawl."

"I know."

"And I ruined it."

"I doubt that it's ruined," Eileen said calmly.

Fern carefully unfolded the fabric and showed Eileen the rip. "See."

"Rips can be mended."

"But it will never look the same."

"No, I don't suppose it will."

"Aren't you even the least bit angry with me?"

"Not at all. In fact, if you don't mind, I don't know why I should."

The girl looked thoroughly confused. "What do you mean? Why should I mind?"

"I hate to spoil the surprise, but I pulled your name from the hat for Christmas. This was going to be your present."

"You're just saying that to make me feel better."

"Are you calling me a liar?"

"No. I mean—"

Eileen turned the shawl and held up a corner. "Look here, right in the very corner."

Fern studied the place Eileen indicated. Embroidered there in Eileen's most elegant script, were the words *To Fern from Eileen.*

Fern looked from the shawl to Eileen, her expression one of confusion. "But this is so beautiful. And it is special to you. Why would you give it to me? Especially after I've been so mean."

"Because it was something you wanted much more than I did. And because I know you've only been pushing me away because you're afraid I'll hurt you like others have." She stroked the girl's hair. "But I won't Fern. I promise, nothing you do can make me not like you. Anyway, you didn't ruin anything of mine. You tore a shawl that was your very own."

"But when I took it, I didn't know it was going to be mine."

"True, and that was wrong of you."

"It makes me a thief." Fern's tone was full of self-loathing.

Eileen winced, suddenly realizing what this was really about. "Perhaps. But a penitent one."

"A thief is a thief."

"Fern, look at me. You are not like your father."

The girl's head shot up in surprise. "You know about my father?"

"Yes, I've known for a while now."

"But, doesn't that make me riffraff?"

"Don't you dare ever say such a thing again. What your father did or didn't do doesn't dictate the kind of person you are. You are responsible for your own actions only, not the actions of your parents."

"But those women who visited Miss Fredrick, they quoted the Bible, saying something about the sins of the fathers being visited on their children. Doesn't that mean God is going to punish me for what my father did?"

Eileen chose her words very carefully. "First of all, the Bible also tells us not to judge others, so those women should have kept their noses out of your business unless they had something charitable to offer. And second of all, I don't claim to understand all of God's ways, but I think those verses the women were referring to have more to do with the consequences of a man's sin on his family's happiness than with how God views that man's children."

She smiled at the girl, trying to let her see the sincerity of her words. "God loves you very much and so do I. I don't want to hear any more talk of you being anything less than a beautiful child of God."

"Oh." She looked at Eileen, hope stirring in her eyes. "I'm sorry I treated you so mean before."

"I know, sweetheart."

She heard the sudden ringing of the church bells. Ivy had gotten the word out.

"But for right now, why don't we go downstairs and let all those very worried people see that you're all right. We can work out our apologies later."

With a nod, Fern got shakily to her feet. "Do you think Uncle Simon's going to be mad at me?"

Eileen smiled. "Very likely. But he's also going to be very, very glad to see that you're all safe and sound."

It just might take him a few minutes to remember that part.

Chapter Twenty-Eight

As predicted, Simon was by turns angry and relieved at Fern's safe return to the family. The girl's punishment for her actions was an extra load of chores and having to make an in-person apology to every man who'd given up his time to help in the search for her.

But Fern wasn't the only one who'd learned some hard lessons up in that turret room. Eileen had had some difficult truths driven home to her, as well. She'd tossed and turned all of Saturday night and had taken a long walk on Sunday afternoon to try to sort things out in her mind. But now she thought she had the straight of it.

And she knew what she had to do.

She only hoped she hadn't waited too long to see what had been right in front of her all along.

After the children had gone to bed, she stepped out on the porch and marched right up to Simon.

"Don't buy the Stringman place."

He looked understandably startled. "I beg your pardon."

"Don't make an offer on that house. I want the children to stay right here with me."

"With you?"

"Yes. I love them. All ten of them. I can't imagine my life without them in it now."

"Are you sure this isn't just some kind of reaction to the scare we had yesterday?"

"Absolutely, positively. I wanted them before Fern disappeared. I just didn't know it."

"You didn't—" He took a deep breath. "Do you know what you'd be letting yourself in for?"

"Not everything." She grinned at his confused expression. "I'm sure there'll be surprises every day. Things I hadn't planned for. Emergencies that will turn all my routines upside down. But I'm not afraid of that anymore. In fact, it's what I want in my life."

"Are you sure? Absolutely sure? Because these are the children's lives we're talking about. You can't say you'll do this and then renege in two months or a year. That would be unbelievably cruel."

"I'd *never* even consider doing that to them. And yes, I'm sure. And you can find yourself a place close by, so you can be near them to keep a close eye, just like you always planned."

He leaned back and studied her. "Something's changed. I can't quite put my finger on it, but you're not the same person you were before."

She smiled, happy he'd realized that. Because that would make this next part a whole lot easier. "I *have* changed. And it's because of something I realized when I was talking to Fern yesterday."

"And what was that?"

She took a deep breath. "First, there's something else I need to tell you."

"What kind of something?"

She supposed she couldn't blame him for being suspicious.

"Things about me, about how I am, and more importantly, why I am that way."

His expression flattened. "Eileen, we've been through—"

"No. Please hear me out. This is different. This is something I just learned about myself." If she had to get on her knees and beg him to listen, she would. It might be too late, but if she had to lose him she couldn't let it be because she didn't tell him this.

He was silent for a long, nerve-racking moment. But finally he scrubbed his hand across his face and gave her a weary nod. "Say your piece."

"My mother came from a very prominent, old money family," she said without further preamble. "When she was just eighteen she met a young man and fell in love with him. This young man, however, wasn't from her same social circle. He wasn't poor, but he came from a family of merchants. This didn't matter to my mother at the time. Despite my grandfather's threats to disown her, she had romantic notions and thought love would conquer all. And truth to tell I don't think she thought her father would follow through on his threats.

"So she married Arnold Beamus and moved into a comfortable home in a vastly different part of town from the area she'd grown up in. Not only did her father cut her off, but it turns out her in-laws weren't very happy with the match their son had made either, thinking she was too snobbish. She lost most of the friends she had in her old circle and had trouble making any new ones in her husband's circle. This made her very unhappy and bitter."

Simon was watching her with more interest now, and her hopes fluttered to life.

"What I remember most from those early years was how very loved I felt by my father and how very unhappy my mother was. Poppa passed away when I was five, and I missed him terribly. But my mother moved back in with her parents and seemed to want nothing more than to wipe his memory from her life. I was sent to boarding school, and eventually Mother remarried, to a man who was part of that social circle she had missed so very, very much."

She chose her next words carefully, not wanting to sound maudlin. "My stepfather didn't care for me much. On one of the rare occasions when I was home, I heard him tell my mother that breeding would out. Mother kept telling me how lucky I was to be so pretty, that it was my one saving grace. She said if I tried very hard to be just as perfect as I could, that I *might* make a successful match."

She saw the muscle in his jaw jump and wondered what he was thinking.

"Mother also told me that love was never a reason to marry—that all it had ever brought her was disappointment."

She definitely had Simon's attention now. "My dowry was not large. All the money my father had left me had been spent on those awful boarding schools I was relegated to. So I did my best to do as Mother said, to play up my looks, to make certain I was as close to perfect in every social grace I could manage, and to never, ever let myself fall in love."

She stared directly into his gaze, hoping he could read what she was feeling. "Until you kissed me."

There were tears inside her screaming to get out, but she ruthlessly held them back, not wanting to have him merely feel sympathy for her. She wanted so much more from him. "I've believed most of my life that, though I loved my father deeply, because of who he was, it made me unlovable. That my worth was based solely on outward things rather than on who I am inside."

She felt her smile waver. "And the strange thing is I didn't even realize it until I heard Fern confess those very same thoughts about herself."

Eileen took a deep breath, ready to get through this, wondering if she was making a difference in how he felt about her. "I'm sorry, Simon. I guess what I wanted to say to you is that I'm this terribly confused and mixed-up person, but I want to change. I want to be the kind of woman who can trust in the power of love. Because I do love you. And when I realized it, it scared me so badly I pushed you away. And it still scares me."

She had to fist her hands to keep from touching him. "But I no longer want to push you away."

She was done. She stood there, waiting for whatever he would do or say next.

And she didn't have long to wait.

Simon stood abruptly, nearly toppling his chair. He closed the gap between them, put a hand on either side of her face and proceeded to kiss her quite thoroughly.

Some time later, Simon released her lips, but not his hold on her. There was quite a bit of what she'd just told him that he hadn't grasped entirely yet, but that could wait for later. All that mattered right now was that she'd said she loved him.

He brushed the hair from her face, entranced by the

shimmery quality of her eyes. "And you don't mind that I enjoy working with my hands and will probably make my living that way for as long as I'm able."

She turned her head to kiss the palm of his right hand. "I love these hands," she said. "I love every scar and every callus. Because these hands make you the man you are, the man I love."

He didn't think he'd ever tire of hearing her say she loved him. "In that case, Eileen, will you do me the very great honor of consenting to marry me?"

With a blush that he found altogether irresistible, she gave him a resounding "yes," which he followed up with another kiss.

Epilogue

"Aunt Eileen, come onnnn." Molly had her hands on her hips in a pose that would have made the strictest of schoolmarms proud. "Everyone's waiting."

Eileen laughed. But then she seemed to be doing a lot of that these days. And why wouldn't she? There were so many things bringing joy into her life.

She loved that it was Christmas morning and the house was filled with children. She loved that the children now called her Aunt Eileen. She loved that she and Fern had grown so much closer.

But most of all, she loved that six days ago she had become Mrs. Simon Tucker.

"I'm coming, sweetheart. I just need to get the last cookie on this platter."

"But it's taking for*ever*."

Eileen hid her smile this time. She supposed when a group of eager children was gathered in front of the Christmas tree ready to open gifts, a few minutes *did* seem like forever.

"There." She lifted the platter with both hands and spun around. "Lead the way."

Molly did an immediate about-face and trotted from the room. As they proceeded she turned back occasionally as if checking that Eileen was keeping up. They crossed the parlor, and Eileen reflected that they'd have to rename the secret room. The recessed door was rarely closed these days, and it had become the favorite place for the family to gather.

Family. Another word that made her smile.

"Here she is," Molly announced as they stepped through the door. "At last," she added melodramatically.

"And well worth waiting for." Simon stepped forward and kissed her on the cheek. Then whispered in her ear. "Have I told you lately how much I love you, Mrs. Tucker?"

Eileen felt the warm tingle of those words all the way down to her toes. "I don't mind hearing it again," she said archly.

"Can we start *now?*"

At Joey's question, Simon let out an amused huff in her ear, then stepped back and relieved her of the platter. The look he gave her promised they would continue the discussion later.

"Since you've all been *so* patient," he said as he escorted her to one of the new benches he'd installed in the room, "I suppose we're ready."

Fern scooted over to allow Eileen to sit between herself and Molly. It gave her a good view of the large tree Simon and the children had selected two days ago. The homemade decorations were scattered on it with gloriously imperfect abandon, and she decided she'd never seen a lovelier tree.

Near the top of the tree Simon had placed Miss Fredrick's hat. Gee-Gee was a part of these children's lives, and it was only right that her spirit should be represented in their celebration.

While they waited for Simon to retrieve his Bible from the mantel, she allowed the excited chatter in the room to wash over her. Even Buddy, who had somehow become an indoor dog when she wasn't looking, was adding an occasional yip to the babble.

Simon moved to stand in the front, between them and the tree, then opened the Bible to the Christmas story. Everyone quieted as he began to read. She listened to his strong, confident voice reading of that long-ago miracle that spoke of an unfathomable grace and love, and the message resonated with her as it never had before.

When Simon finished and closed the book, he asked Russell to lead them in prayer. That was another thing she found to admire and love about her new husband, the way he was training up the children. He might not believe in routines and discipline in the same way she did, but he would do his best to see that they had a proper upbringing. And that they knew they were loved.

When Russell had finished and the amens were said, Simon gave them all a broad smile. "Shall we exchange the gifts?"

The children all scrambled to fetch the gifts they'd placed under the tree last night, and to hand them to their recipients.

There were exclamations as the children discovered who had pulled their names and then more excitement as they unwrapped the packages.

Eileen handed a small package to Fern. "Merry Christmas."

"But..." The girl looked up at her in confusion. "I thought the shawl—"

"It's not much, but I couldn't leave you with nothing to open on Christmas morning."

Fern gave her a watery smile, then very carefully unwrapped the tissue paper. Inside was a lace handkerchief with Fern's initials stitched in one corner. She stood and gave Eileen a hug. "Thank you."

"You're welcome."

Eileen felt a presence at her shoulder and turned to see Simon. He slipped an arm around her waist and led her away from the knot of children.

"I've got something for you," he said, pulling a package from his coat pocket.

"Did you pull my name?" she asked suspiciously.

He drew himself up in mock affront. "Can't a gent get a gift for his wife without pulling her name from some hat?"

She laughed at his teasing. "Forgive my indecorous question."

"As it happens, I did end up with your name, but I had to trade Dovie for it."

"You cheated! I don't know whether to be upset or flattered."

"Definitely flattered." He handed her the gift. "Now, are you going to open this?"

She accepted the package and felt a fluttering excitement, similar to what the children must have felt. When she lifted the lid on the box, she found a delicate wood carving of a star and a quarter moon.

She lifted them out and placed them in the palm of her hand, admiring the craftsmanship that had gone into their creation.

She looked up. "You made these?"

He nodded. "I know it's not anything fancy. But it's

a reminder of what you mean to me, that if I could, I would give you the moon and the stars from the heavens for your very own."

What had she ever done to deserve such a love, such a man?

"So you like it?"

Ignoring the fact that they weren't alone, Eileen wrapped her arms around his neck and gave him a quick but very satisfying kiss. "I like it very much," she said when she stepped back. "It's the finest Christmas gift I've ever received." She put a hand to his cheek. "From the finest man I've ever known."

The sudden heat in his expression brought an answering warmth to her cheeks.

Then Joey called Simon over to admire the rawhide strips that had mysteriously appeared under the tree for Buddy. With a light squeeze and wink, Simon left her side.

She watched him go, then looked at the room full of people who were enjoying this Christmas together. Her family, all of them, including Dovie and even Buddy. For a moment she stood apart, remembering how far she'd come in a few short weeks.

She'd gone from knowing she could never have children to now having ten wonderful children to love and raise as her own. From having a mother who made her feel as if she'd been a regrettable mistake, to having an older woman in her life who offered her friendship and wisdom. And she'd gone from being the widow of a husband who treated her as little more than a pretty poppet, to being the wife of one who truly loved and respected her.

She offered up a silent prayer of thanksgiving for this

blessing of a new family—one she hoped to surround herself with for a very long time.

Then Simon turned, gave her that crooked smile that always made her heart do a flip and held out his arm. With a light step and a full heart, she moved to his side and joined her forever family.

* * * * *

Karen Kirst was born and raised in East Tennessee near the Great Smoky Mountains. She's a lifelong lover of books, but it wasn't until after college that she had the grand idea to write one herself. Now she divides her time between being a wife, homeschooling mom and romance writer. Her favorite pastimes are reading, visiting tearooms and watching romantic comedies.

Visit the Author Profile page
at LoveInspired.com for more titles.

THE SHERIFF'S
CHRISTMAS TWINS

Karen Kirst

For I am convinced that neither death nor life,
neither angels nor demons, neither the present
nor the future, nor any powers, neither height
nor depth, nor anything else in all creation
will be able to separate us from the love of God
that is in Christ Jesus our Lord.
—*Romans* 8:38–39

To Teresa Bensch, sweet cousin and friend.

And to editor extraordinaire Emily Rodmell.
Your guidance makes all the difference.

Chapter One

December 1886
Gatlinburg, Tennessee

"We have a situation at the mercantile, Sheriff."

Shane Timmons set the law journal aside and reached for his gun belt.

The banker held up his hand. "You won't be needing that. This matter requires finesse, not force."

"What's happened?" His chair scraped across the uneven floor as he stood and picked up his Stetson. "Did Quinn catch a kid filching penny candy?"

"I suggest you come and see for yourself."

Unaccustomed to seeing Claude Jenkins flustered, Shane's curiosity grew as he shrugged on his coat and followed him outside into the crisp December day. Pedestrians intent on starting their holiday shopping early crowded the boardwalks. Those shopkeepers who hadn't already decorated their storefronts were draping the windows and doors in ivy and holly garlands. On the opposite side of the street, they passed a vendor hawking roasted chestnuts, calling forth memories of bitter Norfolk, Virginia, winters and a young boy's futile longing for a single bag of the toasty treat.

Shane tamped down the unpleasant memories and continued on to the mercantile. Half a dozen trunks were piled beside the entrance. Unease pulled his shoulder blades together as if connected by invisible string. His visitors weren't due for three more days. He did a quick scan of the street, relieved there was no sign of the stagecoach.

Claude held the door and waited for him to enter first. The pungent stench of paint punched him in the chest. The stove-heated air was heavy and made his eyes water. Too many minutes in here and a person could get a headache. The proprietor, Quinn Darling, hadn't mentioned plans to renovate. The first day of December and unofficial kickoff to the holiday fanfare was a terrible time to start.

His gaze swept the deserted sales counter and aisles before landing on a knot of men and women in the far corner.

"Why didn't you watch where you were going? Where are your parents?"

"I—I'm terribly sorry, ma'am," came the subdued reply. "My ma's at the café. She gave me permission to come see the new merchandise."

"This is what happens when children are allowed to roam through the town unsupervised."

Shane rounded the aisle and wove his way through the customers, stopping short at the sight of statuesque, matronly Gertrude Messinger, a longtime Gatlinburg resident and wife of one of the gristmill owners, doused in green liquid. While her upper half remained untouched, her full skirts and boots were streaked with paint. Beside her, ashen and bug-eyed, stood thirteen-year-old Eliza Smith.

"Quinn Darling," Gertrude's voice boomed with outrage. "I expect you to assign the cost of a new dress to the Smiths' account."

At that, Eliza's freckles stood out in stark contrast to her skin.

"One moment, if you will, Mr. Darling," a third person chimed in. "The fault is mine, not Eliza's."

The voice put him in mind of snow angels and piano recitals and cookies swiped from silver platters. But it couldn't belong to Allison Ashworth. She and her brother, George, wouldn't arrive until Friday. Seventy-two more hours until his past collided with his present.

He wasn't ready.

His old friend, George Ashworth, had written months ago expressing the wish to spend Christmas with him. He'd agreed, of course—it had been years since he'd seen George and longer still since he'd clapped eyes on Allison. As tempted as he'd been to deny the siblings, the memory of their father and his generosity had prevented him.

Edging two steps to his left, Shane gained a clear view of the unidentified female. His jaw sagged. Gertrude Messinger should consider herself fortunate because this woman had suffered the brunt of the mishap. The oily green mixture covered her from head to toe. Her face was a monochrome mask. Only her eyes—the color of emeralds and glittering with indignation—and lips were untouched.

Gertrude stared. "That girl was right beneath the ladder when it happened."

She put a protective hand on Eliza's shoulder. "That

may be so, but I believe it was my foot that snagged the ladder and caused the can to tip over. I offer you my sincere apology. And of course, I'll make reparations for the damage."

"Your apology doesn't change the fact I'm standing here dripping in paint!"

"See what I mean?" Claude leaned close to murmur in Shane's ear.

As a lawman, his duties ranged from unpleasant to exasperating to downright perilous. This sort of dilemma was far from typical.

Quinn held his hands out in a placating gesture. "I regret this incident ever happened, ladies. It was my hired man who left the unopened can on the ladder unattended. I'll pay for cleaning services, as well as provide enough store credit for replacement fabric and shoes, hats, ribbons. Whatever you need."

The older woman glared down her patrician nose. "This dress is beyond saving. Besides, how am I to be expected to walk the streets looking like this?" Spotting Shane, she summoned him with an imperious flick of her fingers. "It's about time you got here, Sheriff. I want this woman arrested."

Eliza and the stranger gasped in unison. Moving closer to Quinn, Shane was careful to avoid the oozing globs on the gleaming floorboards. Belatedly removing his hat, he addressed Mrs. Messinger.

"And what, exactly, am I to charge her with?"

"Public mischief."

The stranger ripped her gaze from Shane to gape at the older woman. "I am not a criminal."

"Your clumsy disregard for your surroundings is a danger to others."

"I believe that's exaggerating things a bit, Mrs. Messinger," Quinn intervened. To the other woman, he said, "What did you say your name was, ma'am?"

She shrunk back. Even with her features concealed, Shane sensed her distress. His senses sharpened. Years of dealing with those who disregarded the law had nourished his already suspicious nature. Was she hiding something?

A blob of paint dripped from her chin and splattered on the floor. "Introductions can wait, wouldn't you agree? Do you have a place where I can clean up in private?"

"My wife's seamstress shop is in the back. Nicole will provide you with something suitable to change into," Quinn offered.

Her gaze slid to Shane and then darted to the side. Definitely suspicious. When she started to move away, he clamped a hand on her arm. "You're not going anywhere until you state your name and business here."

"I see you still enjoy being difficult, Shane Timmons," she challenged, eliciting gasps from the spectators.

He released her at once. He should've heeded his initial response. Her voice had been familiar for a reason. The strands of her hair that weren't coated in paint seemed to pulse with the sun's rays. Those distinctive flaxen locks, combined with wide green eyes and crimson lips, reminded him of Christmases past. Bittersweet holidays with a temporary family that had magnified his outsider status.

"Allison. You're early."

A single, green-tinted eyebrow lifted. "After more

than a decade apart, that's the only thing you can think of to say?"

The tips of his ears burned. The crowd pressed closer, no doubt delighted by this unexpected turn of events. He hadn't divulged much about his past. Wasn't anything to boast about.

Wesley, one of the new shop assistants and most likely the reason for this debacle, appeared with a damp cloth. She thanked him with a graciousness that attested to her generosity of spirit, one of a dozen admirable traits he'd witnessed during his time at Ashworth House.

He was suddenly tongue-tied, as if he were fourteen again and being introduced to his new sister of sorts for the first time. David Ashworth had brought Shane to live with him and his children—sixteen-year-old George and twelve-year-old Allison—in their grand estate located on exclusive Peyton Avenue. While George had been cautiously welcoming, Allison had greeted him like a long-lost friend. He hadn't known what to make of the effervescent, fair-haired dynamo. Still didn't apparently.

"Um, welcome to Gatlinburg?"

This wasn't how she'd envisioned her first encounter with Shane Timmons.

Allison was supposed to be showing her former infatuation how mature and sophisticated she'd become. Shane was supposed to take one look at her and regret all those times he'd dismissed her as unworthy of his friendship. Nothing in her imaginings had prepared her for this!

A rogue drop rolled to her eyebrow, and she hurridly swiped at it, refusing to look down to inventory the damage to her person. She might be tempted to cry.

The distinguished, raven-haired store owner looked confused. "You know her?"

Another man peeked around Shane's shoulder. "You're the sheriff's first visitor. Not a single soul has come to see him in all these years."

A third person piped up. "How do you know each other?"

"Is she a special lady friend, Sheriff?"

The skin around his right eye twitched. It used to do that when he was annoyed.

"Go on about your business, folks," he instructed without taking his eyes off her. "Nothing more to see here."

Most everyone shuffled to various sections of the mercantile, only pretending to shop. Quinn led a protesting Mrs. Messinger to the shelves containing the fabric bolts and began pointing out selections. Eliza lingered.

"Th-thank you, Miss Ashworth."

"You've nothing to thank me for, Eliza." She smiled for the girl's benefit. "Hopefully the next time we meet will be under better circumstances."

Dipping her head, she rushed for the exit. Allison wished she could follow her. How ridiculous she must look! Beneath the paint, her cheeks burned with humiliation. At least that was hidden from his view.

"I wasn't expecting you until Friday," Shane accused in a strained voice. "Where's George? Clarissa and the kids? I thought you were all set to travel together."

After all this time, Allison had expected at the very least a polite welcome. Disappointment compounded her embarrassment. "Do you mind if we discuss this after I've cleaned up?" She indicated the damp cloth. "I'd like to get this off before it dries."

Shane took hold of her arm again and, keeping a more-than-was-required amount of space between them, maneuvered her between the counters and into a darkened hallway.

Unable to deny herself the pleasure, she drank in his profile. The boyish appeal she remembered was a thing of the past. His features were lean and taut, his cheekbones more defined, his jaw a line of defiance. His piercing azure eyes emitted a subtle but very real warning—don't come too close, don't try to unearth buried secrets, don't cross the line of separation he maintained between himself and the rest of the world. Framed by a light beard, even his mouth appeared hard. Sculpted and slightly fuller than many men's, Shane's was set in a perpetual frown.

He was the type of man who expected bad things to happen. Thanks to his poor excuse for a mother, he'd long ago lost the ability to look for good in the world. The hope she'd harbored that he had overcome his unfortunate beginnings flickered out.

At the end of the hallway, one door appeared to exit the building and another led to the seamstress shop. He rapped lightly before swinging it open. The woman who greeted them was everything Allison was not—statuesque, slender and in possession of the beauty that inspired men to pen sonnets. With inky black curls, flawless skin and unusual violet eyes, Nicole Darling must've had scads of men making fools of themselves in order to win her favor. Allison had long ago accepted that she didn't have that effect. Most men liked her. The problem was they saw her as a chum, not a potential wife. The handful that had been interested in her romantically over the years hadn't been able to measure up to the one who'd deemed her irrelevant.

Nicole's sincere greeting faltered when her gaze encountered Allison. Her shock was quickly masked, but it made Allison dread peering into a mirror. Shane explained what had happened and left to fetch a wagon in which to load her trunks.

Contrary to her composed demeanor, Nicole turned out to be gracious and kind. She assisted Allison out of her ruined dress and located a cleaning solution that rid her skin of most of the paint. Washing her hair would have to wait until she reached the house Shane had arranged for her and her family to rent. Nicole riffled through the racks of clothing and found a plain black skirt and matching gray-and-black-striped blouse that a customer had decided against purchasing. The skirt was several inches too short and the blouse fit her like a circus tent. Fortunately, the cape Nicole lent her covered the ill-fitting clothes. Shane was pacing the hallway by the time she was presentable. Well, as presentable as she possibly could be.

His gaze swept her up and down, his thoughts a mystery. "The wagon's this way."

Instead of heading to the mercantile's main entrance, he led her out the rear exit and down a steep flight of stairs. The deserted lane was edged by a wide, fast-moving river over mossy rocks of varying size. The opposite bank was a steep, tree-covered hill. Most of the trees were forlorn versions of themselves, their twisted branches bare, but plenty of pines and other evergreens were sprinkled throughout.

She surveyed the team of fine-looking horses hitched to the wagon. Their giant hooves stamped the winter-hardened earth and their breaths created white clouds. At the stairs' base, she took a moment to inspect the shops' rear facades and the livery beside the mercantile.

"Is this where the deliveries are made?"

He nodded and, giving her a boost onto the high seat, circled the horses and climbed up beside her. "I thought this route would be less of a hassle."

"Meaning, you'd rather no one else see us together quite yet," she retorted, old hurts rising to the surface.

He grimaced. "You've no idea what small towns are like. Every bit of news is blown out of proportion. I can guarantee half the town will have us engaged by nightfall."

Engaged to Shane Timmons? A fluttering sensation flared in her middle, one she resolutely ignored. Once upon a time, she'd been enamored with this man and desperate for his approval—something he'd never offered.

"You wouldn't have to dodge their questions if you'd simply told them about us."

"I considered it." With reins in hand, he called a sharp command and the conveyance jerked into motion. "My friends, the O'Malleys, know our history. I told them that I lived with you and George for a time."

"Do they know why?"

His lips pursed. "Only that my mother couldn't care for me."

"You mean *wouldn't.*"

His eyes turned stormy, and she regretted her words. She allowed herself to study his uncompromising jawline and the strong cords of his neck visible above his coat collar.

He turned his head slightly. "What?"

"Nothing. I'm simply adjusting to the fact that I'm actually here with you."

A vein in his temple throbbed.

"Not here *with* you," she amended. "Here in the same state. The same town, even. I wasn't sure I'd ever see you again, to be honest. You weren't planning to return to Virginia, were you?"

"There's nothing for me there."

Allison winced. One thing about Shane, he didn't mince words to spare her feelings. "Your home is there."

"Ashworth House was not my home."

Because you wouldn't let it be, she was tempted to retort.

She could still recall the moment her father had relayed the news that a young employee of his, an orphan in desperate need of assistance, was coming to live with them. While George had been resistant to the idea, Allison had seen an opportunity to help someone less fortunate. She'd been excited about having another sibling. Older and of a serious bent, George was no longer interested in her childish pursuits. But then Shane moved in and it soon became apparent that he didn't trust either of them. What Allison had never been able to fathom was why Shane had tolerated George, who did little to encourage a relationship, and yet rebuffed her attempts at friendship.

During the five years that he lived with them, she'd tried to earn his confidence, a bit of her heart breaking with each fresh rejection. He hadn't been unkind...just resolute in his indifference. Shane had tolerated her as if she were an annoying puppy begging for scraps of affection.

Shane hadn't liked her. It appeared he still didn't.

Ignoring the pinch of sadness, she resolved to make the best of her time in Tennessee. She was here for the month of December, the most exciting weeks of the entire year. She wasn't about to let a surly lawman spoil her Christmas.

Chapter Two

He hadn't meant to hurt her feelings. Shane noticed the resignation in her eyes before she averted her face. His commitment to speak the truth, a product of having lived with a drunken mother who'd thought nothing of making promises she didn't intend to keep, sometimes made things difficult for others.

He guided the horses onto a rutted lane flanked by trees. The prickly air stole beneath his collar, making him long for his office and a mountain-sized cup of hot coffee.

"Why did you come alone?" he said.

"That wasn't my plan, trust me. A problem arose in our Riverside factory the evening before our departure, and George had to postpone his journey. He insisted I come on ahead so that you wouldn't be disappointed." She said that last bit with a touch of sarcasm. "He suggested Clarissa and the children come with me, but she preferred to wait and travel with him. She didn't want to risk spending the holidays apart."

From George's missives over the years, Shane had learned that his friend had married Clarissa Smothers. Their union was marked with respect, commitment and love. He was happy for George. If he experienced a twinge of envy whenever he read about their life together, he made sure not to dwell on it.

That George had been delayed was not welcome news. He and his brood were supposed to provide a buffer. Without them, Shane had no choice but to interact with Allison. He'd be responsible for getting her settled, seeing to her comfort, entertaining her.

"Did he say when he might arrive?"

"He promised to right matters as quickly as possible and send a telegram letting us know his arrival date."

They traveled up a shallow incline. The Wattses' farm came into view, and Allison sat up straighter, her lips parting at the sight. Satisfaction raced through him. He'd always admired this particular homestead. When he'd heard the owners would be spending their holiday in another state, he'd approached them about renting it for his visitors.

Situated in the middle of a clearing, the white clapboard farmhouse with green shutters and shingled roof stood framed by forested hills that gave way to steep mountains. A fallow vegetable garden was situated on the right, a modest-sized barn behind that. The corncrib, smokehouse and toolshed had been built alongside a snake-and-rail fence.

"Oh, Shane, this is such a charming place. How many bedrooms does it have?"

"Four. George assured me that would be plenty."

"It will do nicely. The three older children will want to be together, and George Jr. will stay with his parents. Thank you for making the arrangements."

"The Wattses decided to spend this winter with their

son and his family in South Carolina. They were pleased it wouldn't be left empty."

He slowed the wagon to a halt directly in front of the house. Quickly descending, he walked to her side and helped her down, reminded again how he'd always towered over her, taller, bulkier, stronger. She'd complained about her diminutive stature and healthy figure, but compared to him, she was dainty. If he was of a mind to, he'd have no problem tossing her over his shoulder and carrying her about without working up a sweat.

From the start, Allison had evoked a powerful desire to protect and shield. A startling and unusual reaction for a boy who'd only ever looked out for himself.

As her soles reached the brown, patchy grass, her fingers tightened where they rested on his shoulders. He examined her uplifted face, taking note of her fuller lips, more pronounced cheekbones, creamy, dew-kissed skin. The years had been kind to her.

He'd recently passed his thirty-second birthday, which meant she'd soon be thirty. *Thirty.* It hardly seemed possible. In his mind, she'd remained forever seventeen—naive, optimistic, generous to a fault and completely unaware of her allure.

She took hold of his right hand and, snatching off his buckskin glove without permission, examined his palm. "I'm glad there's nothing wrong with your hand."

"Why would there be?"

"I thought you might've injured it and that was why you didn't write to me."

The arrow hit its mark. "I'm not much of a writer."

Her jutting chin challenged him. "You wrote to my brother."

"I couldn't ignore his letters."

"And yet you had no problem ignoring mine."

Her crushed velvet gloves caressed his knuckles. He frowned at the pleasurable sensation. "I didn't get any from you."

"I wrote you. Once." She released him.

"I'm sorry, Allison. I never received it."

She reached past him and retrieved her leather satchel. "It's all right. I doubt you would've answered me, anyway."

Shane stood mute as she spun, her too-large cape scraping the ground, and marched to the porch. He'd wondered if she'd changed in the intervening years since he'd seen her. Here was his answer. The old Allison wouldn't have uttered such a thing to him. She wouldn't have voiced what they both knew—he treated her differently than everyone else.

It wasn't fair. Or rational. The knowledge didn't, wouldn't, change his behavior. The reason he'd kept his distance and hadn't initiated contact with her after he left was simple—the part of him that his father's abandonment and mother's reprehensible behavior hadn't managed to blacken with disillusionment and pain, the part protected and nourished by hope, whispered lies whenever she was near.

The first lie had come the moment he met her. *Here is a girl you can trust. She wants to be your friend. Let her in.*

Thankfully, he'd recognized the untruth immediately and had taken action to thwart her efforts. More lies followed as the years passed, tempting him to relax his guard and give her a chance. He'd resisted. Better to hurt her feelings temporarily than to destroy her life with his cynicism and bitterness.

* * *

She was going to have to be more circumspect. Letting Shane know how his ongoing disregard had wounded her was not in the plan. It wouldn't be easy, but she was determined to present a friendly yet indifferent front. She could be kind without being too personal…if she really, really tried.

Allison had a good life. A loving family. Wonderful friends. Satisfying work. A supportive church. He didn't need to know that she ached for a husband and babies to love. He would never know that sometimes, when she was alone, she'd daydream about a different life, one in which he had top billing. Her favorite recurring dream featured Shane at Ashworth House, begging her forgiveness and professing his undying devotion. She especially relished the apology bit—finally hearing an explanation for his dislike would be most satisfying.

"Allison?"

She turned from the bench swing. By the look on his face, this wasn't the first time he'd called her name. "Sorry. I was woolgathering."

He waited for her to enter first. Pulling her cape panels closer together, she wandered about the room, studying photographs of the elderly couple who'd built a life here. They looked like nice, hardworking people. Their home was tidy, the furniture in good condition, handmade rugs, curtains and a quilt thrown over the sofa back providing splashes of bright color. The window views were like paintings of pastoral perfection. She could easily envision the landscape's beauty during spring, summer and autumn.

"When George told me you'd moved here, I purchased a book about Tennessee. The photographs don't do it justice."

Crouched at the fireplace, he arranged a pile of kindling. "You should see the mountains when it snows."

"Is it likely to while I'm here?"

"Hard to say." He lifted his shoulder, causing the brown duster to bunch between his shoulder blades. "The winters are unpredictable. Some years we hardly get any. Others we get snow and ice."

"I hope it does. My niece and nephews would enjoy a white Christmas."

"As would you," he observed.

"I won't deny it."

She recalled the first winter he'd spent with them. He'd been walking alone in the estate garden, as was his custom, and had come upon her making snow angels. She'd implored him to join her. He'd gone so far as to lie in the snow beside her when he'd suddenly jumped up and stormed off. It was as if he wouldn't allow himself to experience even a moment's joy.

"Promise me something. If it snows before I leave, promise you'll make snow angels with me. Just once."

He pivoted slightly in order to stare at her over his shoulder. "I'm a grown man, Allison."

"Are you immune to a little fun, Sheriff?"

He blinked at her use of his title. "Life isn't about fun. It's about duty and hard work and being a responsible citizen."

"You don't believe that." Surely he didn't.

The wood in the stacked-stone fireplace glowed orange as the flames took hold. Waving out the match, Shane discarded it. "It's not a tragedy."

Karen Kirst   321

"The tragedy is you don't recognize what you're missing."

With a noncommittal grunt, he removed his wheat-colored hat and balanced it atop the caramel-and-white-print sofa. He finger-combed his short locks into place. His hair changed with the seasons—sun-kissed blond in spring and summer and dark honey in the colder months. She hadn't seen him with a beard before. She wasn't sure she liked it. The stubble made him seem even more stern, more remote, than she remembered. One side of his coat gaped open, and the badge pinned to his dark vest glinted. Considering his profession, looking dangerous and formidable was no doubt a good thing.

"What about you?"

Allison had drifted to the dining room threshold. Gripping the doorjamb, she turned back to find he hadn't moved.

"What about me?"

"From what George tells me, you make little time for fun yourself."

Astonishment arrowed through her. "What did he say?"

"That you've been working for the company for nearly a decade. You're good at what you do, and the employees respect you. However, he's worried that between your work, charity organizations and the time you spend doting on his kids, you're neglecting your personal happiness."

"He's never indicated such a thing to me."

"Are his concerns well-founded?"

"Of course not."

He advanced toward her, stopping in the middle

of the multicolored rug. "Why aren't you married? I thought for sure one of your many admirers would've snatched you up as soon as you were of age."

She considered how to answer. Admitting that no man could hold a candle to the enigmatic, hurting young man he'd once been was out of the question.

"I could ask the same of you. You're thirty-two and still unwed."

"I'm not the marrying kind, and we both know it. You, on the other hand, were born to be a wife and mother." As soon as he'd said the words, color etched his sharp cheekbones. "You know what? Forget I asked. It's none of my business."

"It's all right." Some part of her that yet smarted from his rejection prompted her to reveal the next part. "In truth, there is someone special. His name is Trevor Langston. As soon as I return to Virginia, I'm going to accept his offer of courtship."

She'd resisted for foolish reasons. Coming face-to-face with her past had shown her that. Shane wasn't interested in any sort of relationship. Trevor, on the other hand, had been unwavering in his desire to court her.

Shane's features remained a blank mask, but the skin around his eye twitched. What was he irritated about? He didn't care about her or her life.

"Who is he?" His voice was even. Cool. Unaffected. "Would George approve?"

"My brother is aware of his interest. Trevor works with us. He's a wonderful man. Solicitous, dedicated, too smart for words…" She trailed off, realizing she was describing his assets in terms of his value as a company employee.

"I assume he's from a respectable family?"

"His family and ours have been friends for many years. We met at church, believe it or not. His sister and I have many common interests."

"Does he treat you well?"

She cocked her head to one side. "For someone who hasn't bothered to contact me in more than a decade, you're awfully curious about my romantic prospects. Why is that?"

"No particular reason. If you don't wish to discuss him, we won't."

He started up the stairs. "Come on up and choose your room so I'll know where to put your luggage."

"Wait."

His fingers flexed on the polished banister. He sighed again, something she noticed he did a lot around her. Come to think of it, he used to do it at Ashworth House, too. What about her vexed him so?

Allison went to stand at the base of the stairs, waiting for him to turn and look at her. When he did, she said, "Who his family is doesn't matter to me as much as what kind of man he is. His character. His beliefs."

A muscle jumped in his cheek. "That's nice."

"I'm not finished." Tired of skirting around the issue, she climbed the steps until she was one below him. Standing sideways, he leaned against the wall, aiming for a casual pose that didn't fool her. "You said you're not the marrying kind. Why not?"

He rolled his eyes. "I'm not discussing this right now. I've got to get you settled and swing by the mercantile for perishables since I didn't have time to stock the kitchen. There's nothing much to eat here, and it's nearly noon."

When he would've continued on upstairs, she put

a hand on his forearm. "Allowing your mother's poor decisions and ill treatment to keep you from having a family is wrong, Shane."

His eyes turned flinty. "You've been in town an hour and you're trying to tell me how to live my life? You know nothing about me save for whatever tidbits your brother's told you. So we lived under the same roof for a few years. That doesn't make you an expert on what I need, Allison Ashworth."

Chapter Three

He'd blundered. Again. George would have his hide if he knew.

The image of David Ashworth's craggy face entered his mind, and he felt ashamed. David had extended mercy to Shane when he'd least deserved it—instead of hauling him off to jail for stealing from one of his stores, David had offered him a paying job. And months later, when the older man learned that Shane's mother had died, their home had burned and Shane was sleeping in a makeshift camp at the edge of town, he'd taken him home and made him a part of his family.

Or at least he'd tried. Shane hadn't made it easy.

He threaded his fingers through his hair. "Look, I don't like talking about my past. You know that."

"I remember."

"But that doesn't excuse my rudeness, and I'm sorry. I know how much you enjoy Christmas and all the traditions that go along with it. This is your first holiday in Tennessee, and I want you to have a pleasant visit. So let's agree to leave that particular subject buried, okay?"

She didn't look happy about his request, but she eventually nodded.

The second floor was a few degrees warmer than the first, but that wasn't saying much. He stood against the long interior wall to give her room to navigate the papered hallway and examine the rooms. The color in her cheeks was heightened, due to her vexation with him or the cold, he couldn't determine.

After peeking in all the doorways, she entered the room to the immediate right of the stairs. "I'll take this one. George, Clarissa and George Jr. can be at the opposite end of the hall and the older children next to them."

"Are you still in your old bedroom at home?"

"No. Soon after their engagement, I moved to the third floor."

Hearing the wistfulness in her voice, he said, "You liked that room. You spent hours in the window seat with your books and your diary or simply observing the world from your perch."

"I did like it." An adorable pleat formed between her golden eyebrows. "But having an entire floor to myself suits me. With four children and a passel of staff members in the house, I don't get much privacy."

Removing the borrowed cape, she draped it over the carved footboard. Peering down at her ill-fitting clothes, she shook her head in disgust. Shane watched as she walked to the mirror above the bureau and inspected her disheveled, paint-flecked hair. In the reflective glass, her gaze found his.

"I made sure my arrival didn't go unnoticed, didn't I?"

"At least the color doesn't clash with your hair."

Turning, she attempted to smooth it. "It's still straight as a stick, I'm afraid."

"Curls are overrated."

He hadn't been able to figure out why a girl like Allison would be dissatisfied with her appearance. Her self-consciousness didn't make sense. Her hair was the prettiest color he'd ever seen, her countenance sweet and agreeable.

"I'll bring your trunks up and then heat some water you can use along with the cleaning solution Nicole gave you."

She thanked him with a grateful smile, making him regret his harsh words even more. George had to get here soon. Spending time with her would be a sore test of his endurance.

Pretend she's your sister.

Not a terrible idea, but he'd already tried that. It hadn't worked all those years ago. Now that they were adults, it had even less of a chance of working.

A half hour later, he was checking the foodstuffs and making a mental list of necessary supplies when Allison entered the kitchen. Dressed in her own clothes this time—a charcoal gray skirt and flattering blouse in a bold sapphire hue—she wore her hair loose. Still damp from washing, it hung in a sleek curtain to the middle of her back.

"You don't look a day over seventeen."

Her eyebrows rose a notch, and he wished the words unsaid.

Emitting a brief, disbelieving laugh, she said wryly, "I believe your memories are clouding your judgment."

He pointed out where the supplies and cooking utensils were stored, as well as the kindling for the cast iron stove. Her slight frown surprised him.

"I know it's not as large or efficient as the kitchen at Ashworth House, but it's got everything you need."

"It's not that." She'd removed her gloves in the bedroom, and her small, pale hand skimmed the pie safe's ledge. She moved to examine the stove's cook plates and water reservoir, a dubious expression on her face. "I never learned to cook."

"You don't know how to cook?"

"I've heated water for coffee before. That's the extent of my culinary skills, I'm afraid."

He should've anticipated this. Why would Allison apply herself to such basic chores when there were paid staff members to do it for her?

"You didn't think to bring one of the estate's employees to see to the task?"

"I considered it. However, it is Christmastime and they all have families. I couldn't ask anyone to spend this most special of holidays with me instead of with their loved ones."

Of course she'd consider others' comfort above her own, even if, as in this case, it was impractical.

In the silence stretching between them, her stomach growled loud enough for them both to hear. With a grimace, she pressed her hand against her middle. "Sorry. I skipped breakfast."

Shane felt as if a noose was tightening about his neck. This wasn't how this visit was supposed to go. He'd planned on being polite, yet distant, just like the old days. He and George would catch up while the women were occupied by the children. He wasn't supposed to be responsible for her every need.

"How did you plan to eat?"

"You do have restaurants here, do you not?"

"There's the Plum Café. The quality has gone down in recent months, but the fare's passable. It's closed on Sundays."

"So I'll eat cheese and bread on those days. I'm not spoiled."

"I know that."

The Ashworths had every reason to boast—success, wealth, high standing in society. A devout Christian, David had viewed his accomplishments as blessings from God and considered it his duty to use them to help others. While they hadn't lived meagerly by any means, they hadn't hoarded their wealth. David had taught his children to love Jesus first, others second and themselves last.

"Besides, the children's nanny is coming with Clarissa, and she knows her way around a kitchen. She'll take care of the meals, as well as the holiday baking."

Shane found himself with two equally problematic choices. He could take her to the café and suffer the type of scrutiny he went out of his way to avoid. Or he could stay here in this isolated kitchen with her and fix something. Dodge questions from curious townsfolk or share a private meal with Allison?

In the end, her damp hair was the deciding factor. He couldn't risk her health simply because he was uncomfortable in this quiet house that presented zero opportunities to slink off to a secluded spot like he used to do.

Inspecting the cupboard's contents, he said, "Which one sounds more appealing? Pickled peaches or sweet butter pickles?"

* * *

Allison couldn't recall the last time she'd shared a meal with a gentleman. Mealtimes were loud, boisterous affairs in her brother and sister-in-law's home. There were stories, jokes and laughter while the children were in attendance. Once the nanny whisked them upstairs or outside to the gardens for fresh air and exercise, the conversation turned to adult topics such as their family business, society news or happenings in the city.

Not that Shane Timmons fit her view of a gentleman. He was comprised of too many rough edges and dark secrets for that. He neither looked nor acted like the men of her acquaintance. Didn't smell like them, either. The sheriff smelled like long days in the saddle, strong coffee and virile man.

Having removed his outer coat before preparing lunch, he sat across from her in what must be typical lawman attire—trousers, vest and a long-sleeved, buttoned-up shirt, his sheriff's badge pinned over his heart. His light blue shirt was shot through with pencil-thin navy blue stripes. His vest was a coconut-shell brown that matched his trousers. Both pieces of apparel showcased his upper-body strength. Every time he lifted his coffee cup to his mouth, she watched the play of his biceps.

Before he'd left Norfolk, his physique had been whipcord lean. He'd packed on muscle in the ensuing years, and he looked solid enough to wrestle one of those black bears she'd read inhabited these East Tennessee forests. That, combined with his over six feet of height, made him a formidable adversary for the criminals who dared pass through his town.

"Are you warm enough?" He broke the silence for the first time since he'd said grace.

Heat from the kitchen stove permeated the adjoining dining room through the doorway. Lit candles positioned around the rectangular space added warmth to the ambience even if they didn't emit actual heat. Clouds had rolled in, obscuring the sun and making the candles necessary.

"Yes, thank you."

"I know this isn't what you'd call a substantial meal. As soon as we're done here, I'll leave you to unpack while I make a trip to the mercantile."

"It may not be typical, but it's filling. Besides, now I can say I've tried pickled peaches."

"I'm sure your friends will be impressed," he drawled, his eyes hooded.

Besides the preserved fruit, her plate boasted corn cakes, fried ham slices and sautéed onions. While simple, the food tasted delicious.

She dabbed the napkin to her mouth. "Since I'll be here the duration of the holiday season, what can I expect in the way of celebrations?"

He lowered his fork. "That's not something I pay much attention to."

"Does the town host a parade?" she prompted. "Are there parties? A tree-lighting ceremony?"

"No parade that I'm aware of. I'm sure there are parties, but I have no idea who hosts them. I'll have to put you in touch with Caroline Turner. Her mother is in charge of Gatlinburg's social events. Either one of them can help you."

Frustration warred with sadness. During his years at Ashworth House, they had done everything possible to include him in their celebrations. He'd stubbornly resisted their efforts.

Folding her hands in her lap, she studied the candlelight flickering over his rugged features. "Do you actually celebrate Christmas, or do you act like it's any other day on the calendar?"

"Apart from the commemoration of Christ's birth, December 25 is like every other day of the year." He sank against the chair, his fingers rubbing circles on the worn tabletop.

Allison wanted to ask if his view of God had changed. While Shane had believed in Him as Creator, he hadn't been able to accept His unconditional love. She struggled to find the right words, and the moment was lost.

"The weeks leading up to it are not special, magical or even particularly pleasant," he said.

"The season is about family and friends, counting your blessings and loving your neighbors."

"Charity should be year-round," he countered.

"I agree. I serve on a church committee that provides for the poor throughout the year. I've witnessed how this season magnifies their lack, however. We have to be diligent to make Christmas extra special, especially for the children."

For a split second, his mouth softened and yearning surged in the azure depths. "Where were people like you when I was a boy?"

Her breath hitched at the glimpse of unexpected vulnerability. He recovered himself all too quickly, face shuttering as he tossed his napkin atop his plate.

"I'll give you a tour of the town so you'll be comfortable navigating it on your own." Pushing to his feet, he stared down at her. "I can't ignore my duties while we wait for George to arrive."

Pricked by his words, she arched a brow. "I don't require constant supervision. I am capable of entertaining myself."

"But not cooking for yourself."

She stood and spread her arms wide. "So teach me."

His head jerked back. "You're not serious."

"We don't truly know how long my brother will be delayed," she said, sweetly. "If the café's food is as mediocre as you say it is, it would be to my benefit to learn the basics."

He put a hand out as if to ward her off. "Allison—"

Pounding on the door startled her. Unruffled, Shane pivoted and strode to pull it open without bothering to inquire who was on the other side.

"Ben."

Hovering in the doorway connecting the dining room to the living room, Allison studied the visitor. A couple of inches shorter than Shane, the attractive, auburn-haired man was broader in the chest and shoulders, his legs like tree trunks. His skin was tan and freckled from the sun, his eyes green like sea glass that sometimes washed up on Norfolk's beaches.

"Sorry to interrupt," he said with a slight grimace. "I heard you had a lady friend in town." His gaze sought out the room behind Shane, flaring when it encountered her. He nodded in greeting.

Shane turned sideways. A draft of cold air traveled through the room, ruffling her skirts. "Ben MacGregor, meet Allison Ashworth."

Swiping his hat off and pressing it against his chest, he sketched a bow. "How do you do, ma'am?"

"Fine, sir. And you?"

"I'd say my day just got brighter now that you're in it." His grin was downright roguish.

She laughed at his outrageousness.

Shane's upper lip curled. "Ben's the resident flirt. He's also my one and only deputy. Did you need something in particular?"

The deputy didn't bother denying Shane's claim, she noticed. His eyes still twinkling, he addressed his boss. "Another fight's broken out over on the Oakley spread. Figured you'd want to ride along with me." He held a gun belt aloft.

"You figured right." Taking it from him, Shane fastened the tooled-leather strip around his waist. "Sorry I can't stay and help you clean up," he told her, his head bent to his task. "I'll come later to deliver the supplies."

Her attention snagged on the menacing-looking pistol on his hip. The pearl handle was worn smooth, the barrel long and skinny.

"I've never held a gun."

Both men stared at her.

"Can I go with you?"

Shane's expression was one of disbelief. "Of course you can't go with me. Why would you ask?"

"You're a lawman now. I'd like to see how you go about upholding the law."

While Ben shifted from one foot to the other, face averted to hide a smile, Shane leveled a formidable glare at her. "Until your brother gets here, you are my responsibility, understand? It's my task to make sure you have your fun." He smirked at the reference to their earlier conversation. "And that you stay safe while doing so."

"But—"

"I mean it, Allison," Putting on his Stetson, he strode for the door. "Don't step foot outside this house until I return."

Without waiting for her response, he joined his deputy on the porch and closed the door behind him, fully expecting her to follow his dictate. Annoyed at his high-handedness—he wasn't her *actual* brother, after all—Allison wondered what would happen if she didn't.

Chapter Four

The house was quiet. Too quiet.

Shane checked the first floor. No sign of Allison. Thinking she might've decided to take a nap after her long journey, he ascended the stairs and peeked into her room. The bed was made, her trunks pushed into a neat row beneath the windows on the far wall. The other bedrooms were also empty.

Determined to unload the supplies as quickly as possible and get back to the jail, impatience jabbed at him as he bypassed the unoccupied outhouse.

Where had she gotten off to?

Intent on scanning the fields to his right, he almost walked smack into the smokehouse. Scowling, he sidestepped and stopped short. A female figure was crouched half inside the smokehouse's squat entrance.

"Allison."

She lurched. Banged her head against the wood. "Ouch!" Scrambling outside, she rubbed the sore spot. "Did you have to startle me like that?"

"I've been searching everywhere for you. You weren't in the house, the barn…" He wasn't about to admit the trepidation that had roared to life inside him. "I thought I told you to stay inside."

"You did." The baleful look she shot him transformed into a grimace. "I'm not one of your locals to boss about, however."

"What were you looking for in there?" He motioned to the smokehouse.

"Nothing. I was simply curious what was inside."

Shane removed his gloves and, stuffing them in his coat pocket, moved to her side. "Let me see."

"I'm fine."

"I'll be the judge of that," he insisted, nudging her hand aside. His fingers gentle on her scalp, he examined the spot. "It didn't break the skin."

She was very close, her round shoulder butting against his chest, the fruity fragrance clinging to her person inviting him closer. She was soft and warm and feminine, traits that were nonexistent in his world of crime and punishment.

"I told you it was nothing," she whispered, her voice off-kilter.

He took a big step back, his huff creating white puffs that hovered in the air. "You've always been a troublesome female, you know that?"

Her chin whipped up. "Excuse me?"

"You kept your father and brother hopping to keep up with your antics. I was thankfully too wise to join in."

"If I was guilty of anything back then, it was trying to be your friend."

Brushing past him in a swirl of petticoats and skirts, she marched in the direction of the house. Smoke curled from both chimneys into the gray sky above. She'd restrained her mane with a single blue ribbon, and the long ponytail bounced with the force of her steps.

He watched her for a moment before going after her, wishing for the first time in a long time that he had the kind of relationship with God that David Ashworth and his friends, the O'Malleys, had. He could sure use some divine help right then. But he'd never gotten over the feeling of abandonment that had taken root in his childhood. His pleas for his pa to come and rescue him, for his ma to truly change, for someone, *anyone*, to help make things better, had gone unanswered. Ignored. So he'd stopped asking.

Catching up to her at the corner of the house, he fell into step beside her, choosing to introduce a whole new subject. The past was a prickly maze of disappointment and confusion. Best to avoid it.

"I think you're gonna like what I brought for you."

"Oh?" She got that gleam in her eye that he didn't trust. "Did you bring me a Christmas tree? A wreath? Greenery to decorate the mantel?"

His pace slowed. "Huh?"

"I think I'd like a cluster of mistletoe, as well. Maybe two."

"What do you need all that for? You're only going to be here a few weeks."

"The most important weeks of the entire year."

"Hold on." He halted beside the wagon bed. "Why would you want mistletoe?"

Her crimson lips curved into a smile that many would find winsome. To him, it meant trouble. "You never know when an eligible suitor might pay me a visit at some point during my stay. Best to be prepared."

Shane was like an unarmed man in an ambush as

jealousy pummeled him. While she hadn't mentioned Ben specifically, an image of his deputy and Allison locked in each other's arms beneath the mistletoe wedged its way into his mind. Once there, he couldn't dislodge it.

"What about Trevor Langston?" he ground out.

"Trevor and I don't have an understanding," she said airily. "I haven't yet accepted his suit."

Going to the rear of the bed, she peered into the multiple crates. He followed, irritated that she was here one day and already getting under his skin. This wasn't supposed to happen.

"You're leaving within a month. That's hardly enough time to court."

She ignored him as she continued to catalog the contents.

"I hope you're not considering Ben. He's not the settling-down type," he went on. "Don't pin your hopes on the likes of him. I mean it, Allison."

"I'm not pinning my hopes on anyone." Rolling her eyes, she planted her hands on her hips. "I'm teasing, Mr. Lawman. The mistletoe is for decoration… and maybe George and Clarissa. The children descend into giggling fits whenever their parents smooch. It's quite entertaining."

Her nose wrinkled adorably, and suddenly he was thinking about someone other than Ben kissing her beneath the mistletoe. Someone like himself.

Having reached the limit of his patience, Shane stifled a groan and, loading his arms with heavy crates, made his way to the kitchen. It took several trips to unload everything. He didn't stay to help her unpack. Mur-

muring an excuse about work, he promised to swing by the following morning before beating a hasty retreat.

"Hurry up and get here, George," he muttered.

At the livery, Milton Warring met him at the entrance, stained fingers tugging at his scraggly beard.

"What's on your mind, Warring?"

"I've found evidence of a trespasser."

Shane climbed down and let Warring's assistant take over the rented wagon and team. When the lad was out of earshot, he said, "Show me."

The livery owner led him upstairs into the loft where mostly hay and other supplies were stored. Near the shuttered opening overlooking Main Street, he spotted an empty tin of beans and nudged it with his toe. Inside, a dirty spoon rattled. Shane bent and examined the tin and raked through the scattered straw for other clues.

"Is it possible your hired boy ate his lunch up here and forgot to clean up after himself?"

"He eats his lunch on the bench out front most days. I asked to be sure, and he denies this is his."

Shane walked the perimeter of the space, his gaze sweeping the planks. Near the ladder opening, he reached down and plucked a gold necklace from the straw. "Recognize this?"

Taking turns, they examined the locket and faded photo of a woman. "Haven't seen her before," Warring said. "You?"

"Nope." Slipping it in his pocket, Shane said, "I'll ask around. See if anyone has an idea who she might be."

He scowled. "You think he'll come back?"

"It's a lot warmer in here than it is out there. If he got away with it once, he'll try again. Unless he's moved on."

Their town saw a lot of travelers passing through on their way to or from North Carolina. Most were respectable folks. It was the disreputable few he had to worry about.

Shane put his boot on the ladder's top rung. "Ben and I'll take turns watching the place."

"Good. I want that rascal caught."

"Keep an eye out for anything else suspicious."

He left the livery and headed for his office. His deputy was warming his hands at the woodstove and looked up at his entrance.

"We have a potential problem over at Warring's." Shane related the scant details and warned him to be on alert for unfamiliar faces.

"Will do, boss." He gave a short nod. "You get Allison settled over at the Wattses' place?"

"She's Miss Ashworth to you. And I'd prefer it if you'd steer clear of her."

Folding his arms over his chest, Ben met his gaze squarely. "Because she's just here for Christmas? Or because you want her for yourself?"

When it became clear a couple of years back that he needed to hire help, he'd chosen Ben MacGregor because of his astute mind and discernment skills. They worked well together. Shane didn't approve of his deputy's flippant attitude toward women, but his personal life was none of his business.

"I don't care what you do on your own time or who you involve, as long as you uphold the reputation of this office. But I won't have you trifling with Allison's emotions."

"You didn't answer the question." From his stance

and unyielding stare, it was obvious he wasn't going to drop the matter.

"There's nothing romantic between us. Never has been. She's like a sister to me." The words sounded false, even to his ears. "I don't want to see her hurt."

"I respect you, Shane. As my boss, but also as a man. I'd be an idiot to ruin our professional relationship by doing something stupid regarding your friend."

"I'm glad you understand."

"I'm not finished." He held up a hand. "Seeing as how I'm *not* an idiot, you can rest assured that any relationship I pursue with her will be respectable."

Shane curled his hands into fists, the buckskin gloves molding to his knuckles. For the first time since they started working together, he was tempted to plant his fist in the other man's face. All because of Allison.

"If you hurt her, your career in law enforcement is over."

Ben's eyes widened a fraction. "That's not going to happen."

"See that it doesn't."

Pivoting on his heel, Shane stormed out with no idea where he was headed.

The tantalizing scents of sizzling bacon and rich-bodied coffee woke her. Snuggling deeper into the cocoon of quilts, it took several moments for Allison to remember that she was not at Ashworth House. She shot up in bed.

Pushing the tangled mass out of her eyes, she blinked at the framed needlework on the opposite wall and the mountain view through the nearest window. She inhaled again, and her stomach rumbled in anticipation.

Leaping out of bed and wincing at the cold shock to her stocking feet, she hurried to the wardrobe.

Shane must've paid someone to cook meals for her. He'd seemed reluctant to share a meal with her yesterday. No way would he commit to cooking for her the duration of her visit. Although a thoughtful gesture, it would've been nice if he'd alerted her to his plans.

She chose one of her favorite dresses, a soft but sturdy material of rich cream dotted with orange and green flowers and trimmed in green ribbon. The dress put her in mind of her beloved estate gardens in springtime. Once dressed, she brushed her hair until it shone and arranged it in a twist.

Descending the stairs, Allison noticed a sorrel horse hitched to the post out front. She entered the kitchen and the polite greeting died on her lips.

"What are you doing here?"

"Isn't it obvious?"

She crossed her arms, irrationally annoyed with him. "You of all people should know it's a bad idea to let yourself into someone else's house while they're sleeping."

Shane scooped a pile of fluffy eggs onto a plate, along with biscuits and a thick, white sauce. "Most intruders don't cook you breakfast." He held the plate out. "Have a seat. There's milk on the table. If you'd prefer coffee, the kettle's there."

Allison accepted the plate. The food smelled amazing, especially after the modest, cold supper of cheese and bread she'd had last evening. "What is the white stuff? Are those lumps in there?"

"You've never had sausage gravy?"

"I've had brown gravy."

"Biscuits and gravy is a common breakfast food here. Try it and see if you like it."

She carried her plate to the dining room. He joined her in a few moments with his own breakfast and, assuming the same chair he'd occupied the day before, picked up his fork and spiked a clump of eggs.

"Shouldn't we say grace?"

He looked startled. "You're right. I forgot. Would you mind?"

Allison nodded, unsure if he was too shy to pray aloud or if his reluctance stemmed from a lack of confidence in God's love. *Lord, please give me the courage to broach the subject. Give me the right words.*

Catching her off guard, Shane settled his fingers over hers atop the tablecloth. Her focus shattered. The heat from his hand seeped into hers. His skin was rougher than hers, his bones denser, his hold firm and sure. Allison curved her fingers inward, capturing his, returning the pressure. His breath hitched. Her own heart tumbled in her chest. This wasn't the first time they'd held hands.

That other time he'd been guiding her through the woods to safety and, although he'd scolded her for wandering off alone the entire trek home, he'd allowed her to cling to his hand, a lifeline in a dark and stormy night.

The rare moments of physical contact stood out in her mind because Shane either hadn't liked the connection or hadn't known how to handle it. Their chief cook, a boisterous, vivacious woman who'd been liberal with her affection, had hugged him just like she did everyone else. Instead of returning the embrace, he'd stood rock still, his arms imprisoned at his sides, looking as if he was being prodded with a hot poker.

When her father had occasionally given Shane a hearty pat on the back or slung an arm about his shoulder, he'd stiffened. Allison's heart had broken each time she witnessed his reaction.

Since he refused to open up about his childhood, she was left to imagine the terrible things he must've endured.

Her prayer was brief. He tugged free of her and turned his full attention to his meal. Tension prickled between them. Allison ate without speaking, her thoughts racing. He had yet to show her where he worked and lived. Did he eat alone most of the time? The thought made her sad. And unexpectedly annoyed. If only he wasn't so stubborn, so determined to remain aloof and unaffected by the people in his life.

"How do you like the gravy?" His soft query brought her attention to his implacable blue gaze.

"It's delicious." The biscuits were large and doughy and not beneficial to her waistline. "Where did you learn to cook like this?"

"In Kansas. I didn't have a lot of extra money to spend in restaurants, and I got tired of corn mush and beans real quick. The sheriff I was working for was a widower, and he'd invite me over sometimes. I commented once how I'd wished I'd learned, and the cooking lessons commenced."

"I wish I could've seen that." She smiled at the mental image of a pair of tough lawmen puttering around a kitchen.

"I'm sure you do." One corner of his mouth tipped up. It wasn't a full-fledged smile, but it was still able to make her spirits soar.

"You could pass on a few of those lessons, you know."

"Sorry. I'm not much of a teacher."

"Like you're not much of a writer?"

Over the rim of his coffee cup, he blinked at her. When he lowered it, a wrinkle tugged his brows together and the grim set of his lips returned.

"How did you fare during the night?"

Allison allowed the change in subject. She truly didn't want to travel down this road because, first, he likely wasn't going to admit his reasons for disliking her, and second, she didn't want to be the one to put that frown on his face. She wanted to make him smile and laugh. She wanted to bring him joy.

You didn't manage that before, a voice reminded her. *Nothing has changed except for the fact he's had more practice retreating into his protective shell.*

"Not terrible. There were creaks and groans that prevented me from falling asleep right away. It will take some time to get used to being alone in a big house."

"Your brother will be here before too long."

Allison didn't tell him about the idea she'd been pondering for months. While George and Clarissa were happy with the current arrangement, she'd been thinking more and more about setting up her own household, a smaller house with fewer staff in a good section of the city. Of course, that had been before she'd decided to give Trevor a fair shot at winning her heart, a decision goaded by Shane's presence and the hurtful memories he revived.

He downed the last of his coffee and stood. "Are you interested in a trip to town?"

"Certainly. What did you have in mind?"

"I was thinking I'd introduce you to the woman I

told you about… Caroline Turner. The two of you can discuss holiday stuff while I see to business."

He was pawning her off on a stranger. Allison tried not to let her disappointment show. "What kind of business?"

Striding into the kitchen, he spoke over his shoulder. "Work-related."

She swallowed the last bite and, gazing longingly at the dish of remaining biscuits, turned away and joined him by the dry sink. "Do you have to resolve another argument among neighbors?"

He took her plate and submerged it in a basin of soapy water. "No. Why?"

"My world is almost completely made up of ledgers and employee disputes and company policy. It's predictable and mundane. I'd like to see what a typical day for a sheriff is like."

"My job isn't as exciting as you might imagine. Sure, there are days when I have to break up fights or investigate crimes. But there are long stretches of inactivity that anyone would consider boring."

"At least show me the jail."

"Since the cells are unoccupied at the moment, I can do that."

"I'd like to see your home, as well."

"It's nothing special."

"Please?"

"Why is it important to you?"

"After I return to Norfolk, and George tells me what you've written in your latest letter, I'll be able to picture you in your jail or your home. Much more satisfying than a blank void."

He got a funny look on his face…like an apology.

Did he regret not contacting her? Was he about to promise to change his ways after this visit? He opened his mouth, apparently searching for the right words.

"I'll take you after lunch."

Breaking eye contact, she headed for the exit. "I'll gather my things."

Maybe seeing him in his environment wasn't the best idea. Sure, she'd be able to picture him more easily. But she'd also be able to remember being in those spaces with him. She'd wish she could return and be with him, a future that was out of the realm of possibility.

Not only would he not welcome a second visit from her, but she was determined to give a relationship with Trevor an honest try. That meant cutting all ties to her girlhood dreams.

Chapter Five

Caroline Turner was flawless.

She lived in a flawless house and wore flawless clothes that displayed her flawless figure.

Allison sat in the Turners' sumptuous parlor, sipping golden floral tea from a china cup and listening as the young woman listed Gatlinburg's holiday-themed events. She exuded quiet elegance. Her white-gold hair was scraped into a neat bun at the base of her neck. A double string of iridescent pearls complemented her off-white bodice, as did the pearl earrings at her ears. She had large, dark blue eyes, almost navy-colored, that weren't as happy as someone with a flawless life should be. Her smile wasn't happy, either. It was one a person pinned on for guests.

"We typically have a large turnout for our annual nativity unveiling." Caroline's gaze was assessing. "The sheriff doesn't attend many of our holiday functions. I wonder if that will change this year."

"He never has been one for social functions."

"While our humble festivities can't possibly measure up to what you're accustomed to, I'm certain you'd enjoy yourself."

"Norfolk has a great many events to experience, it's true. However, I'm certain I will enjoy what Gatlinburg has to offer." Allison placed her cup and saucer on the low coffee table between them. Caroline must've seen her eyeing the tray of jumble cookies, because she picked it up and extended it her direction.

"Please, have as many as you'd like."

"I shouldn't," she said, even as the scents of juicy raisins and walnuts teased her nostrils. "I've had two already."

Caroline offered her a sincere smile then, one that lit up her entire face and made her less perfect. "I find them hard to resist myself." Taking one, she sunk her teeth into it and made a little sound of appreciation. "We only have them around the holidays."

Allison returned the smile and chose a third cookie.

"I know it's bad manners to pry, but Shane hasn't spoken of you before. Or anyone else from his past, for that matter. May I ask how you know each other?"

Having already prepared a standard answer to this exact question, she said, "Shane's a close friend of my family. He worked for my father."

"I didn't realize he'd lived in Virginia." Brushing imaginary crumbs from her pleated skirts, she remarked, "I'd heard he moved here from Kansas and assumed that was his home state."

"He's always been a private person. In fact, he'd be annoyed if he knew you and I were discussing him."

"I'm afraid he's invited more scrutiny by keeping your existence a secret."

"I told him as much myself," Allison said. "He didn't appreciate it."

A husky laugh burst out of her. "I think I'm going to like you, Allison Ashworth. I'm going to relish watching you pull the rug from beneath the staid sheriff's feet."

Unsure how to respond, she was grateful when her hostess didn't probe further. Caroline returned to the topic of Christmas, specifically their custom of assembling gift baskets for the poor. Allison was keen to assist. Charitable endeavors took up much of her free time back home, holidays or no.

A half hour past the time of Shane's specified return, the teapot was drained dry and only crumbs remained on the plate. Besides remorse, Allison felt embarrassment for monopolizing Caroline's morning. When she caught her checking the mantel clock a second time, Allison went to retrieve her gloves from the carved hall stand.

"I appreciate your hospitality, Caroline. Shane must've gotten detained."

"I've enjoyed our chat. I hope I didn't make you feel as if you overstayed your welcome." Following her to the foyer where Allison fastened on her cloak, Caroline fiddled with her pearl necklace. "I'm waiting for my father to return from a trip. Today is my birthday, and he promised to be home no later than today."

There was a hint of vulnerability in the younger woman's expression, yet another crack in her sophisticated facade.

"Happy birthday. You're fortunate to have your father with you. Mine passed away many years ago, and I still miss him terribly."

"I'm sorry for your loss." The corners of Caroline's

mouth turned down. "I'm afraid my father and I don't have the best of relationships."

Allison's hand paused on the knob. "Oh?"

Pink suffused her skin. "What could I be thinking of? My manners have deserted me today. Please forgive me, Allison. You don't want to hear about my family woes." She waved a hand in dismissal. "Don't feel as if you have to leave. You're welcome to stay for lunch."

"I appreciate the invitation, but I'd actually like to explore the town a bit. Would you mind telling Shane I've gone to do a little shopping?"

"Certainly."

"I'm looking forward to seeing you again soon."

"As am I."

The cold enveloped her as she strolled in the direction of Main Street. Fortunately, she'd been blessed with a good sense of her surroundings. On the way, the clouds parted and a shaft of sunlight warmed her.

She wished she could speak to her brother. Tell him about the rented farmhouse, the quaint mountain town, her excitement about experiencing Christmas in a new place. Like Shane, she hoped George wasn't long delayed. Spending time alone with the lawman was both heady and frustrating.

Help me guard my heart, Lord, she prayed.

Caring too much for Shane Timmons had always been a problem with no solution.

"Where's that pretty little filly of yours, Sheriff?"

Striding past the barber shop on his way to the mercantile, Shane ignored the good-natured teasing. He'd brought it upon himself. If he hadn't been so flustered by the prospect of her visit, he would've seen the wisdom in letting the news travel the grapevine before her arrival. Folks wouldn't have been as shocked.

Over the years, he'd worked hard to make the Timmons name one to be respected and revered. He'd earned his current reputation as a just, honorable, hardworking man of the law, and he wasn't about to let anything tarnish it.

He'd spent too many years carrying his sloppy drunk of a mother home through the Norfolk streets, trying to ignore the vulgar taunts and insults hurled their way. In their poverty-stricken neighborhood, he'd been known as a boy no one wanted. He'd been born to poor, unwed parents. His father hadn't cared enough to stick around and his mother detested her life to the point she had to drown her sorrows in alcohol every night. His maternal grandparents had refused to acknowledge him and moved away shortly after his birth. He'd never met his father's family. Doubted they even knew of his existence.

On the boardwalk, Shane passed a pair of young men. They waited until he was several yards away before calling after him.

"Where's the paint lady? Heard she's a real looker under all that green goo."

"Hey, Sheriff, are you two courtin'?"

Not breaking his stride, he allowed their words to bounce off him. They weren't cruel like the ones he'd endured as a youth, but they called forth excruciating memories better left in the dark shadows of his mind.

Paint lady. Allison was going to love that.

The mercantile's bell jangled as he walked in. The store was bustling with activity, as it would be until after the holiday. The scents of cinnamon, cloves and oranges permeated the air. Quinn and Nicole had complimentary cups of spiced cider available during the weeks leading up to Christmas. It helped ward off the chill, especially for those folks who traveled miles to get here.

Several people glanced his way, speculation flaring as their gazes switched from him to a point in the paper goods section. Allison's flaxen hair glistened in the natural light as she tilted her head this way and that, examining a sheaf of decorative papers. If she was aware of his scrutiny, she didn't indicate it.

His neck burning at the unwanted attention his presence was drawing, he wound his way through the crowded aisles to reach her.

"I'm sorry I ran late." He pitched his voice low. "Caroline said you might be here."

"It's all right," she said, casually holding the sheaf to her chest as she lifted her emerald gaze to his. "I figure that's standard for a sheriff."

"You're not upset?"

"No." She gave him a strange look. "I've taken advantage of the free time to do some shopping."

"What are you planning on doing with those papers?"

"You'll see." With a conspiratorial wink, she started for the counter.

He followed in her wake, aware that their every word and gesture was being monitored.

"You can assist me in my project if you'd like." Her bright smile invited him to share in her enthusiasm.

"I'm not committing to anything until I know what it is you have in mind."

They reached the long, worn-smooth counter where glass displays housed everything from razors to colored-glass bowls to jewelry. She paused before the display of cakes and pies, her eyes round. He hadn't forgotten her penchant for sweets. The Ashworth cook had catered to Allison's preferences, and he and George had both benefitted.

He pointed to an apple stack cake. "These are the finest desserts you'll ever taste."

She lifted her face to his. "Better than the Oak Street Bakery?"

"Better than that."

A breath pulsed between her shiny lips. "And who is the illustrious baker?"

"Jessica O'Malley. Well, it's Jessica Parker now. She's married to a former US Marshal. She's also Nicole Darling's sister. You'll meet all the O'Malleys eventually."

"I'd like that."

"Which one would you like to sample? My treat."

She shook her head in regret. "Oh, no. I've had my quota of sugar for the day, I'm afraid." Nodding to the window through which a vendor could be seen, she said, "But I will take some roasted chestnuts."

Shane kept his expression bland. "Whatever you'd prefer."

When she'd made her purchase, he guided her out into the now sunny day, one of those rare winter days with vivid blue skies and cheerful sun reminiscent of warmer seasons. He bought her a bag of chestnuts, but declined to get one for himself.

She sampled the first bite and hummed with delight. She offered the bag to him.

"No, thanks."

"Don't you like them?"

"I wouldn't know. Never tried one."

She stopped abruptly, forcing the man behind them to sidestep quickly in order to avoid a collision. "Then how do you know you won't like them?"

How could he explain his silly aversion to something that had taunted him during this most painful of seasons? Most days he'd had to make do with stale bread and moldy cheese or a thin broth with vegetables long past their prime. Walking past restaurants, he'd smell fresh-baked bread and grilled meat and his mouth would water. He began to dread Christmas because his lack was made even harder to bear. He'd see fathers out with their sons as they carried a fat goose home to their family. He'd see kids skipping down the street sucking on stick candy. Mothers and daughters sharing sacks of chestnuts on park benches.

He hadn't longed for the food, but for the love, acceptance and security of two devoted parents. Siblings who squabbled over toys and played kickball in the yard. A clean, warm home to live in, a soft bed to sleep in every night.

A voice inside his head tried to convince him that he was no longer that ragged, defiant boy, but the feelings of inadequacy and bitterness drowned it out.

He pointed across the street. "There's the jail. Still want to see inside?"

Slowly her puzzled gaze left his to follow the line of his finger. "Very much."

With his hand nestled against the middle of her back, he guided her across the road and into the building where he spent a large portion of his time. To her, the space probably looked stark. To their left was a woodstove. Opposite the door was his desk, a scuffed relic handed down from the sheriff before him. A detailed topography map was nailed to the wall behind his chair, and the American flag hung on the right. One barred window overlooked Main Street.

Her gloved fingers trailed the desk's edge. "So this is where you keep the peace."

"Something like that."

She wandered to the first of three cells and, passing through the open metal door, pulled it closed behind her with a clang.

"What are you doing, Allison?"

Her grin was mischievous. "Go sit in your chair."

He dropped his hands to his sides. "Why?"

"Humor me."

The sight of Allison in one of his cells was a jarring one. Her loveliness had no place in a setting meant for thieves and carousers.

He dismissed thoughts of refusing. The quicker he obliged her, the sooner they could leave. Muttering beneath his breath, he circled the desk, slumped into his chair and crossed his arms. "Happy now?"

"Teach me how to shoot, and I will be."

He glared at her. "Not gonna happen."

"If I was one of your prisoners, I'd be intimidated by you."

Her tone was serious, but her eyes twinkled with a zest for life he'd always envied. "I'll never understand the way your mind works."

The main door swung open, and Claude bumbled inside, his jaw lolling when he caught sight of Allison behind bars.

Shane shot to his feet. "Claude."

"Am I interrupting something?" The banker's incredulous, gray gaze inventoried the scene.

"Shane was indulging my sense of whimsy," Allison announced. Releasing the bars to allow the door to swing wide, she exited the cell and strode to shake Claude's hand. "I don't believe we've officially met. I'm Allison Ashworth, an old friend of Shane's."

Befuddled by her charming smile, the man stood up straighter and puffed out his chest. "Claude Jenkins. I manage the bank next door."

"A pleasure to meet you, Mr. Jenkins." His hand still in her grasp, she patted it and leaned forward. "You wouldn't mind keeping this between us, would you? I've never been in a jail before, you see, and I wanted to gain a better understanding of Shane's job."

Claude nodded with enthusiasm. "Oh, I understand, Miss Ashworth. I'm aware of how sensitive to gossip our sheriff is."

Beaming, she glanced at Shane, her expression one of satisfaction. He shook his head. The woman couldn't do anything the usual way, could she? He hoped Trevor Langston knew what he was getting himself into.

"Is there anything pressing you need help with, Claude?" he said.

"No, nothing important enough to take you away from this delightful young lady." Releasing her hand with obvious reluctance, the banker grasped the door handle. "Will I see you at the church's nativity celebration on Friday evening, Miss Ashworth?"

"That's a question better directed to Shane."

Claude pinned him with a suddenly steely gaze. "You are planning on escorting her, I hope."

Shane hid a grimace. He made a point of avoiding these types of events. Singing about Christ's miraculous birth while confronted with the nativity magnified the hollowness inside him. All those church services he'd attended with the Ashworths, the sermons about eternal destination—what would he choose, heaven or hell?—would march through his mind, making peace impossible.

"If Allison wishes to attend, I'll make sure she's there."

"That's what I wanted to hear."

When he'd left, Allison turned to him with clasped hands. "What's the next stop on the grand tour? Your house?"

Chapter Six

Allison was determined not to let Shane see her nervousness. This wasn't a romantic outing. He didn't wish for her company. He'd practically been ordered to escort her.

Descending the stairs, she gave her cranberry velvet skirts a little shake to adjust the stiff crinoline beneath. The bodice was constrictive, the long sleeves snug at the wrists, but the dress was one of her favorites. Shane turned from the mantel, his luminous gaze widening as he took in her appearance.

She ran her hand along the neat French braid trailing the middle of her back. "What? Is this not appropriate? Should I change?"

"No." Stroking his whiskered jaw, he said, "You look… Christmassy."

"Christmassy?" Like an ornament on a tree?

"Nice." He cleared his throat. "You look nice."

He turned his head away, giving her a chance to admire his dark suit. The midnight black hue made him seem more imposing than usual, but it also gave him a touch of city polish. His hair was neatly combed with a few stubborn locks falling over his forehead.

She moved closer to the fireplace, where the logs smoldered. "You don't look like a sheriff tonight."

His lips curved into a smile, an actual smile, and Allison felt as if the floor beneath her feet trembled. His austere features assumed a masculine beauty that had her inching forward and desperately wanting to trace his lips with her fingertips.

Thankfully, his deep voice shattered the strange compulsion. "You're awfully preoccupied with my profession. Norfolk has an impressive police force."

She made a dismissive gesture. "It's not the same. I know Tennessee isn't exactly the untamed West, but neither is it a sprawling metropolis. There are books written about men like you."

He snorted. "My life is not a grand adventure."

"You don't see it that way because, in your mind, you're simply doing your duty. To the people you help, you are that larger-than-life hero in the pages of a book."

"I suppose we'll have to agree to disagree." Running a finger beneath his collar, he tilted his head to the clock. "We'd better get going if you want to get there before the candle lighting begins."

As he locked the door and led her into the nippy winter evening, she soaked in the vast expanse of twinkling stars. Twin lanterns hooked to either side of the wagon emitted a soft glow. "I'm sorry you were roped into taking me tonight. I know you'd rather be doing something else."

"A few hours of Christmas carols won't kill me," he drawled, assisting her up.

He climbed up on his side and, instead of taking

his seat, reached into the wagon bed and brought out a thick, multicolored quilt. Unfolding the bundle, he bent over her and tucked it about her legs and lap. His face was near enough for her to feel the brush of his cool, minty breath across her cheek.

"Thank you, Shane," she whispered, touched by his thoughtfulness.

The seat bounced a little when he lowered his large frame onto it. Seated this close beside him, she was aware of their variances in size and the fact he made her feel feminine and almost delicate.

With a nod, he issued quiet instructions to the horses. The wheels rolled over the rutted track. It was impossible not to bump into him. He shrugged off her apology. Allison glanced at his implacable profile, wishing he'd wrap his arm around her to hold her steady. Then she could snuggle into his side. But that would mean prolonged personal contact, which he didn't do. It would also indicate he felt at ease with her, that he felt affection for her, neither of which were true.

Focusing her attention on their passing surroundings—the forest on either side of the lane cloaked in mysterious shadows—she thought about her visit to his modest cabin. The one-room structure was so far removed from Ashworth House as to be laughable. Still, he took pride in his ownership. The wooden logs and chinking were in excellent condition, the puncheon floors and window glass clean of debris. What little furniture he had was of good quality. And while the single bed shoved against the wall and adorned with naught but a plain woolen blanket was a little desolate in her estimation, his home wasn't without personality.

Stacks of law journals and various periodicals had

been visible on the small table beside the russet col
ored cushioned chair. On a shelf near the fireplace,
he'd stored a collection of games—dominoes, tabletop ninepins, chess. Years ago, during the afternoon
hours after school, he and George could often be found
in the estate's library playing checkers or some other
board game. If the weather was nice, they'd engage in
a game of kickball or football outdoors. Shane had possessed more aggression than actual skill in those physical games. Sometimes she would hide in the rose arbor
and observe them, in awe of the almost frenzied energy
coming off him.

"Do you still play football?"

He glanced over at her. "Mostly on holidays or special days when folks take a break from their usual
chores."

"Who do you spend holidays with?"

"The O'Malleys."

Her curiosity about his relationship with them grew.
"You're close to them, aren't you?"

"They're the closest thing to family I've got."

She stiffened. Her hands braced on either side of her
legs, she gripped the wood to avoid bumping into him
again as the conveyance traveled around a bend and
left the woods behind.

He heaved a sigh. "I'm sorry. I didn't mean to imply
that you and your family aren't important to me."

Allison was grateful for the darkness. "There's no
reason to deny the truth." Could he detect the tiny wob-
ble in her voice? "Your life is here. Has been for a long
time."

"Your father changed the course of my life. Without
him, I'd be in jail or worse."

"He loved you as if you were his own son."

The silent accusation hung between them. Her father had given Shane a job and welcomed him into their home, but she'd seen no sign that the friendless, adrift young man ever fully lowered his guard with any of them.

He kneaded his nape for long moments. "He was the best of men."

Emotion welled up inside. Some days the grief lay dormant, like a hibernating bear, and others it roared to life, reminding her of everything her father was missing. He would've liked to have seen how well his business was flourishing under George's leadership. He would've cherished being a grandfather.

"He would be proud of you, Shane."

The faint lamplight allowed her to see his initial surprise and disbelief. Sorrow, and something akin to regret, surged in his blue eyes.

"I'd give anything to be able to talk to him again." Where his hands rested atop his thighs, his gloves stretched tight across his knuckles. "I don't remember thanking him."

Stunned by the raw admission, Allison reached over and squeezed his forearm. "My father was a wise man. He saw more than you realize."

Shane's gaze returned to the lane. When he didn't acknowledge her gesture in any way, she removed her hand.

He nodded to the cluster of buildings comprising Main Street. "Almost there."

Lamps shone in several of the windows. The white clapboard church was situated at one end of town. A golden glow lit up the night around it, allowing her a glimpse of the grand steeple soaring into the sky. Shane guided their wagon to the edge of the congested churchyard.

Their arrival didn't go unnoticed. A cluster of young men strolling past called out as Shane was helping her to the ground.

"Hey, Sheriff. Evening, paint lady."

Allison stumbled. Shane's hands curved around her waist, preventing her from plowing into him. Bracing herself against his sturdy shoulders, she gaped at the retreating group.

"Did I hear that right?"

"Um, it appears you've earned yourself a nickname."

She lifted her face to gaze up at him. He bit his lip to stop a smile.

"Paint lady?"

His heat radiated outward from where he still held her. It would be so easy to slide her hands up and around his neck…

"Could be worse."

Awareness settled across his features as his gaze roamed her face, and his fingers flexed on her waist. Yearning, intense and demanding, curled through her. *Please don't let me go*, she silently implored. *Don't pull away.*

"Here you two are. Glad to see you made it."

Claude Jenkins's intrusion brought a grimace to Shane's face. Immediately, he put her away from him and turned to acknowledge the man and his wife. Behind the couple, a handsome man with wheat-colored hair, trim mustache and goatee and a penetrating blue gaze waited to speak to them.

Claude winked at her before leading his wife away.

The stranger approached and clamped a hand on Shane's shoulder in a friendly manner, all the while studying her in the most unsettling way.

"Didn't expect to see you tonight. Is your lovely guest the reason you decided to join us ordinary revelers?"

Wearing a tolerant expression, Shane inclined his head her direction. "Josh O'Malley, meet Allison Ashworth."

"One of the esteemed O'Malleys," she quipped as he enveloped her hand in a firm shake. "Shane has spoken highly of your family."

"Unfortunately, he's given us scant information about you. I'm here to rectify that." Pulling her hand through the crook of his elbow, he winked down at her. "How about I introduce you to the rest of the clan and then you can tell us about yourself?"

"Don't trust him, Allison," Shane drawled. "He's really after dirt that he can hold over me in the future."

Josh's burst of laughter drew curious looks from passersby. "He knows me too well."

She was enjoying this exchange too much to refuse. "I'd be happy to trade stories with you. As you might imagine, Shane hasn't been forthcoming about his life here. I'm particularly interested in his professional accomplishments."

"It's a deal." Josh's eyes gleamed.

He drew her closer to the church building. Shane trailed behind them, and she sensed the weight of his attention on her. Was he worried about what she might reveal? Or did he trust her judgment?

They paused at one of several long tables to procure mugs of fragrant apple cider. Cradling the large mug, she relished the warmth seeping through her gloves. Cognizant of the curiosity she aroused in the others, Allison wondered if it was due to her being an out-of-towner or her connection to their secretive sheriff.

Josh led her to a stand of gnarled trees that resembled pitiful broomsticks. Numerous adults chatted while kids dashed after one another, shrieking and giggling. At one edge of the gathering, a beautiful brunette waved them over, a smile stretching from ear to ear.

"Allison, allow me to introduce you to the love of my life." Releasing Allison, Josh went and tugged the woman tight against his side. "My wife, Kate O'Malley."

"It's nice to meet you, Allison." Her smile was sincere. "There are quite a lot of us." She wiggled her fingers at the group of men and women, adolescents and young children. "It can be a bit overwhelming at first."

"As long as you don't expect me to remember everyone's names."

Laughing, the couple drew her deeper into the fray. Shane remained on the group's edge, engaging in conversation with a striking-looking man with raven hair and an angry scar around his eye. She learned there were three brothers—Josh, Nathan and Caleb—and their cousins, five sisters who greeted her with curiosity. The most recently married, Jessica was the only one as yet without kids.

"You're the baker, right?" Allison addressed the redhead. "Shane was bragging about your talent."

"Folks do seem to enjoy my baking."

Her husband, Grant Parker, brushed a lock of her deep-red hair behind her shoulder. "She's being modest. Jessica's desserts are highly sought after around these parts."

"My sister Jane is just as skilled." Jessica indicated her identical twin sister, who was standing a couple of yards away with a tall, distinguished fellow. "She's busy with her kids and doesn't have time to bake as much as she used to."

Allison had met only one other set of twins before, brothers in their midsixties who looked like mirror images of each other, much like Jessica and Jane. She tried to keep her fascination hidden.

"I confess to a weakness for sweets," she said. "I will no doubt prove to be a loyal customer during my stay."

The scarred man, who she'd learned was the youngest O'Malley brother, tugged a reluctant Shane to the middle of the group where she stood with Jessica and Grant.

"Interrogation time," Caleb announced with a smirk. His brown-black eyes settled on her, and she felt sure she wouldn't want him for an enemy. "Miss Ashworth, will you kindly tell us the nature of your relationship with Shane Timmons?"

Josh tapped her shoulder. "The truth, please, Miss Ashworth, not the pat answer Shane's prepped you to give."

Since Shane was standing beside her, she heard his slow exhale, sensed the flight-response of his body.

"I met Shane when I was twelve, and he was fourteen. He lived with me, my brother and father for many years."

"This was in Virginia?" Kate said.

"Yes. Norfolk. My family has lived there for generations. My father, David Ashworth, built a successful business, which he bequeathed to my brother, George."

"Allison works with George," Shane inserted. "She

oversees the hiring and termination process and ensures the employees have proper working conditions. In addition to all that, she's in charge of payroll."

"I didn't realize my brother outlined my duties for you," she said.

"George likes to talk business. You're part of that world."

"What was Shane like as an adolescent?" Caleb asked, his keen gaze studying them both. She would've liked to ask what he saw that was so interesting.

She gave Shane a sideways glance. "A lot like he is today, actually. Reserved. Determined to do everything on his own. Convinced his opinion is the only right one."

"Sounds about right." Josh snorted. "You must've been terrified."

"Allison isn't terrified of anything." Shane's sardonic reply evoked laughter from the group.

Her smile felt forced. He clearly didn't know her well. He was the one who'd intimidated her from the start, the one whose good opinion she'd craved.

"My turn." Crossing her arms, she met Caleb's stare with her own. "I want to hear about Shane the lawman."

Shane hung his head and groaned. "There's really not much to tell."

"Stop being so modest." Josh socked his arm.

"If anyone has a right to boast, it's him," Jessica said with conviction.

Shane shot Allison a *help me* look. He despised being the center of attention. Not about to miss their recounting of his exploits, she shrugged. Displeasure twisted his mouth.

"Shane's the type of man who'll help anyone without thought to his own personal comfort or safety," Josh said. "He's got a will of iron and nerves of steel."

Josh listed the ways Shane had impacted their lives. He'd once hunted and captured a criminal who'd taken Nathan captive. He'd rounded up a gang of outlaws whose female leader had almost killed Caleb and his wife, Rebecca. When a series of crimes had been committed at Quinn's store and Nicole had been attacked, Shane worked with Quinn to bring the perpetrators to justice.

Grant spoke up at the end, his expression one of earnest respect. "Not so long ago, I woke up on Jessica's property with no memory of who I was. Shane could've thrown me in jail that first day. Even after I discovered evidence that pointed to a sordid past, he believed in my innocence. Things could've gone very differently if not for him."

The adults fell silent. Allison nudged Shane. "Sounds like the contents of an adventure book to me."

He kicked up a shoulder. "It's my job. I do what's required of my position, the same as any other lawman in this nation is expected to do."

"Handsome and humble…" Jessica huffed a dramatic sigh. "If only we could convince one of the single ladies around here that he's worth the effort."

Kate shot Allison a significant look. "What about you, Allison? Are you involved with anyone?"

Her cheeks blazed with heat at the implication. "Not at the moment."

Nathan elbowed Josh. Someone let loose a low whistle.

"Isn't that convenient. Shane's not courting anyone."

"When has he ever?" Nathan's young brother-in-law, Will, observed with a hearty laugh.

Shane threw up his hands. "That's enough punishment for one night."

Threading his fingers through hers, he pushed past Josh, guiding her away from their group.

"You don't have to go," Caleb called after them. "We'll promise to behave."

He lifted a hand in acknowledgment. Still, he didn't slow his pace until they'd left his friends behind and were on the opposite side of the church near the cemetery. He dropped her hand the moment they stopped.

"It wasn't that bad, was it?" she said softly.

"They like to harass me sometimes. You presented a perfect opportunity."

"It's obvious how much they care about you. You're fortunate to have them."

After witnessing the evidence of their regard for him, she could only be happy to know he wasn't alone.

"I know." His attention shifted beyond her. "Evening, Ben."

"Howdy, boss." The rakish deputy took hold of her hand and, clasping it between his, pressed it to his heart. "You are as radiant as the North Star, Miss Ashworth. You put every other woman here to shame."

Allison didn't dare risk a glance at Shane. "You are quite inventive with your compliments, Mr. MacGregor."

"What can I say?" His grin widened. "You inspire me."

"You can release her hand now," Shane muttered.

Ben reluctantly did so. "Boss, I know how you feel about these types of shindigs. I don't mind keeping Miss Ashworth company if you'd like to skip out."

Dejection weighed heavily on her shoulders. Lowering her gaze to the grass beneath her feet, she waited for Shane to agree.

"That's mighty thoughtful of you, but Allie came with me, and I'll see to it that she gets home safe and sound."

She whipped her head up. In the semidarkness, his profile was impossible to read. He'd called her Allie just once, the day he left Virginia. On the verge of boarding the train, he'd taken her hand and told her to take care of herself.

Ben accepted his refusal with aplomb. "Understood." His green gaze slid to her. "I'll see you around, Miss Ashworth."

He sauntered off in the direction of the snack tables.

Shane scrubbed at the day's growth of beard shadowing his jaw. "I didn't think to ask your opinion. If you'd rather pass the time with him, I'll understand."

"I came here to visit you, Shane."

He stared at her for long moments. Holding out his bent arm, he said, "The reverend's getting in position, which means the program is about to start. Let's go and find us a spot."

About that time, the jangle of cowbells got everyone's attention. The reverend, a silver-haired man clad in a penguin's colors, went to stand near the church steps and waited until the crowd gathered around.

"Friends and neighbors, another year is drawing to a close," he said. "In this last month of 1886, let us reflect on God's blessings and His greatest gift to mankind, His Son, Jesus Christ." He gestured to the grouping of statues covered with burlap. "This year, I'm pleased to inform you that we have a new nativity. My thanks goes to Josh O'Malley, who carved each piece with his own two hands."

The people clapped as the reverend removed the burlap from each statue. Allison was amazed by the craftsmanship and detail of Mary, Joseph, baby Jesus and the animals.

"It's wonderful," she whispered. "I've never seen the like."

His face devoid of emotion, he nodded and sipped his cider. "Josh is a skilled carpenter. You'll have to visit his furniture store sometime."

"I'd like that."

Candles were handed out to the adults. When they were lit, the reverend's wife led the gathering in the singing of several carols. The flickering lights created a pretty glow in the darkness, and the sound of male and female voices blending together and singing about their Savior sent chills cascading over her skin. This was a humble church in a tiny mountain town, yet she'd never experienced the same awed emotion.

Beside her, Shane was peculiarly silent. His candle aloft, he stared into the distance, his focus far from here. Was he remembering some terrible moment from his past? Another sad, disappointing Christmas?

She touched his sleeve. "I'm ready to leave if you are."

He angled his head toward her, and it took a second for his gaze to clear. "Are you sure?"

Of course she wanted to stay, but she refused to be selfish when he was unhappy.

"I'm cold. I'd like to go back to the house and relax before a comforting fire."

Taking her candle, he extinguished them both and,

discarding them in a bin, led her past awaiting horses and wagons to where his was parked. As before, he cocooned her in the quilt, his movements efficient and impersonal but wreaking the same effect as the first time. She was so busy seeing to her niece's and nephews' needs that she'd forgotten what it felt like to experience a moment of cossetting herself.

"You were uncomfortable back there," she ventured. "You don't like when I question you about your past, but you didn't say I couldn't ask about your faith. Has your viewpoint altered since you left Virginia?"

He was quiet a long time. "I want to believe that the God who created all this beauty could love someone with a soul as tarnished as mine. I want to, but…"

"It's hard for you to trust." Anxious to say the right thing, she said, "No one deserves Christ's love. Or His forgiveness. But because of His compassion and mercy, He extends it to us. It's a free gift. We can't earn it."

"I've heard these same words many times." The defeat in his voice disappointed her.

Why can't you accept them as truth? "I've never stopped praying for you, Shane."

His gaze swerved to her face, his shock evident. "I don't know what to say except thank you. That you would take the time to pray for me…" He removed his hat and thrust a hand through the blond-brown strands.

"I won't stop." Her own voice grew thick. "You can count on that."

Nodding, he didn't utter another word. At the house, he set the brake and, after helping her down, started to climb the steps.

"You're coming inside?" she blurted. "I can stoke the fireplaces without your help."

He paused with one boot braced against the bottom step. It was impossible to make out his features in the porch shadows. "I thought I'd see to the task. Unless you don't want me to."

"That depends on your reasons," she said evenly. "If you're coming in because of some perceived duty, then the answer is no. I don't need to be watched after. If you're coming in because you'd like to share a cup of coffee and my company, then the answer is yes."

His long-suffering sigh originated deep in his chest, and the tenuous bond born from her confession evaporated.

"I guess I have my answer." She ascended the steps. "Good night, Sheriff."

Chapter Seven

"Allison."

Still reeling from her revelation that he featured regularly in her prayers, Shane trailed after her. He had to tread carefully because, to him, this entire visit was a necessary but not exactly welcome intrusion into his life. He hadn't invited her here. He definitely hadn't anticipated having to keep up his guard every hour of the day.

"Wait a minute." He touched her shoulder, and she whirled on him.

"I have to be honest, Shane. I hate that you see me as a burdensome child. Every time you sigh and huff and roll your eyes, I'm tempted to throttle you."

He stared at her. "I'm sorry."

He was sorry that he wasn't a different man, one who knew how to trust and love and have normal relationships. He was sorry he hadn't done a better job of hiding his unease around her.

She began to dig in her reticule, her frustration evident. He pulled the key from his pocket and held it up.

"Looking for this?"

When she went to snatch it from him, he held it out of reach. "For the record, I don't see you as a burdensome child."

"Oh?" Her chin jerked up, her hair gleaming in the night. "How *do* you see me, Shane?"

He strove for a rare moment of honesty between them. The fact that she couldn't see his face helped. "As an intelligent, caring, gorgeous woman who makes me wish I was a better man."

The admission hung between them. She didn't move or speak. He heard her swallow, noticed her moistening her lips with the tip of her tongue, could almost see her mind working to process the information.

Reminded of that charged moment in the churchyard and the weakening of his resolve, he sought refuge from the longing invading every part of him. One innocent touch from her was all it would take for him to succumb to the lies and haul her in his arms for a kiss that would likely tilt the world on end. His soul was like a parched desert that wouldn't be able to stop from soaking up every single drop of rain offered. If he unleashed this flood of attraction building between them, he feared he'd never surface again.

Because of his unsteady fingers, it took several attempts to unlock the door. Shoving it open, he strode to the fireplace. She entered at a more sedate pace, taking her time removing her cape and gloves. She crossed the living room and stopped behind him.

Please don't question me on this. Please.

"Would you like a cup of coffee?"

The tension between his shoulders blades eased. "Sure."

The flames were licking at the logs by the time she

returned. He replaced the poker in its slot and accepted the mug she held out.

He forced himself to meet her gaze. "You aren't having any?"

"It's too late in the evening for me."

He half twisted toward the mantel, touching a finger to patterned paper pinwheel stars perched there. "This was the project you thought I could help with?"

She clasped her hands together in front of her. "It's not difficult to do. Requires more patience than skill."

There were six on the mantel, all done in shades of white, green and red. She'd hung more between the stair rail rungs.

Her features softened into a fond smile. "I placed those there so they'd be on the children's level."

"Tell me about them."

She crossed her arms. "They're a lively lot, especially the boys. Danny's seven and a miniature of his father in both looks and personality." She chuckled, no doubt picturing them in her mind's eye. "Five-year-old Peter is a firecracker but he's always eager for a hug. Lydia's four. She's the most mischievous of them all."

"Let me guess, she has George wrapped around her finger."

"Without a doubt. And then there's George Jr. He's an easygoing child. He loves to snuggle and is generous with his kisses. Since he's only just turned two, he prefers to spend most of his time with Clarissa."

Unsurprisingly, she spoke of the children with great affection. "You adore them."

"I do. I've been there for each birth and watched them grow and flourish into little people with their own unique personalities."

"You should have a brood of your own."

The words cost him. He could easily picture her with a babe in her arms and one bouncing on her knee. Her children would never question whether or not they were loved.

Her smile turned wistful. "I'd like that very much."

"Does Trevor like kids?"

"I—I haven't thought to ask." She bit her bottom lip.

Wishing the question unsaid, he set his mug on the coffee table and plucked a pinecone from a bowl full of them. "What's this?"

"My meager attempt at decoration. I gathered them from the yard. If the weather's nice enough tomorrow, I plan to search for ivy or other greenery to spruce up the space."

Shane bit back a sigh. Pacing to the far corner beside the window, he said, "This would be a good spot for a tree."

Her brow furrowed. "A tree?"

"You said the children will be disappointed without one. We'll go in the morning."

"You're serious? You're going to take me to cut down a Christmas tree?"

"Yes."

"And you're going to help me set it up? Maybe even place a few ornaments on the branches?"

He found it impossible to say no in the face of her obvious delight. "If I must."

With a little squeal, she launched herself at him, her arms going around his neck. Stunned, he registered several things at once—the fruity fragrance clinging to her hair, the curve of her cheek pressed against his neck, her breath tickling the skin above his collar. The need to return her hug, to hold her close, surged within him. She was incredibly soft and warm and sweetly alluring. It took immense effort to keep his arms at his sides.

Belatedly noticing his lack of response, Allison removed herself from his person and took great care in rearranging her skirts, her chin tipped to the floor. "What time shall I be ready?"

"Ten o'clock. Dress warmly."

His heart was out of rhythm and thumping erratically against his chest. Hopefully that was her last spontaneous show of affection. Testing the boundaries of his willpower wouldn't benefit either of them.

She shouldn't have hugged him.

Every time the memory of how he'd borne her enthusiastic thank-you came to mind, she cringed with embarrassment. Riding on horseback alongside him through the mountainous terrain, all she had to do to be reminded of her foolhardy behavior was look over at his rock-hard jaw, sculpted, stern mouth and the rigid line of his broad shoulders.

He'd been quieter than usual this morning, and it was her fault.

"I stopped by the post office on my way to your place," he said, shifting in the saddle. "Still no word from George."

"When it comes to work, he can be single-minded. I wouldn't be surprised if he forgets to contact us and simply shows up here unannounced."

Shane's lips pressed more tightly together.

"You're awfully serious today," she said. "Something particular on your mind?"

Framed by the overcast day and cream-colored Stetson, his eyes looked bluer than usual "Seems I have something of a mystery on my hands."

"Oh?"

"I believe we may have a drifter problem. There's evidence someone has been spending nights in Mr. Warring's livery. This morning, Quinn got a delivery from a neighboring city. While he and the driver went inside to settle up, someone stole a box of oranges."

"A costly loss. Do you have any clues as to who it might've been?"

"None. When Quinn discovered it missing, he searched the riverside and discovered a pile of orange rinds. The culprit is headed for a massive stomachache if he eats them all in one sitting. Ben's doing the rounds today on the lookout for suspicious strangers."

"Were there any nonfood items taken?"

"I know what you're thinking," he said evenly. "Need doesn't make it okay to steal."

"Hunger can be a powerful motivation." Despite her thick green cloak, woolen scarf and fur-lined gloves, she was cold. The mountain air chilled her exposed skin. "What if he doesn't have a proper winter coat? No home to lodge in? If it's this cold during the day, wouldn't anyone caught out in the elements overnight be in danger of freezing to death?"

"Unfortunately, the danger is very real."

"What will you do if you catch him?"

He leveled his gaze at her. "My job."

"You'd put him in jail?"

"I don't always like what I'm required by law to do, but sometimes I don't have a choice. The best I could do is appeal to the business owners affected and ask for leniency. If they agreed, I'd be able to let him off with a warning."

Allison fell silent as she contemplated the difficulties of his position. Her horse navigated the increasingly hilly terrain. She had to concentrate on balancing atop his broad back.

Shane's mount pulled a little in front of hers. Shane twisted to look at her over his shoulder. "In these parts, it's common knowledge that the church is willing to help those who've fallen on hard times. My hunch is that this person is living on the wrong side of the law and doesn't want to draw attention to himself."

"Still, it's difficult to think of someone suffering like that. I've never had to go hungry, so I don't know what it's like."

"I do." A muscle ticked in his jaw. "When you're that hungry, your world narrows and finding food is all you can think about."

Her horror must've shown on her face, because he turned away. Her fingers clenched on the saddle horn as a particular memory reasserted itself. The first night Shane joined them for dinner, his eyes had nearly popped out of their sockets at the sight of the luxurious seven-course meal. Even so, he'd limited himself to scant proportions. Her father had encouraged him to help himself to as much food as he'd like, but he'd declined. It had taken months for Shane to relax enough to eat a healthy amount.

"How often did you go without?"

"It was an ongoing problem. Sometimes, I'd resort to stealing, just like our drifter."

Allison knew better than to express her dismay.

Thankfully, he was sitting forward in the saddle and couldn't see her reaction. "Did you ever get caught?"

"Once. When I was ten, the owner of the diner around the corner found me sneaking out the kitchen door that exited onto the back alleyway. I had a chicken leg and a roll. He marched me straight to jail." He looked back, saw her sagging jaw and smirked. "Don't feel too bad. The sheriff fed me a fine meal that evening."

"You were a child!"

"I broke the law."

"How long?"

"Was I in jail?" He shrugged. "Just the one night. The owner's wife found out what happened and insisted her husband show me mercy. Not only that, she made sure I had one hot meal a day for the remainder of the time I lived in that neighborhood."

"I don't envy you your job," she confessed, having trouble absorbing these rare revelations about his past. "Those instances when those who deserve punishment are the same ones in desperate need of help must wear on your soul."

"It doesn't happen as often as you might think. When we find our drifter, I'll check if he's wanted by local or federal authorities. If not, I'll make it my priority to get him the assistance he needs."

"I hope you find him soon." Before he dies from exposure.

"Me, too." Thumbing up his hat's brim, he tilted his head back to study the low, grayish-white clouds. "Looks like snow."

"The temperature has dropped significantly since last evening."

She'd woken to a frigid room. In this house, there

weren't any maids to stoke the fires and make her morning routine comfortable. For breakfast, she'd made do with coffee and a cold slice of bread smeared with blackberry preserves, all the while picturing Clarissa and the children in the estate's elegant dining room with their porridge, eggs, ham and jelly-filled pastries. After nearly a week of separation, she missed them terribly, despite the fact that she was enjoying the peace and quiet.

"How far are we from the Wattses' land?" Her hold on the saddle horn tightened as the Wattses' horse she was borrowing navigated a steep bank. She'd likely be sore tomorrow. Her outings were confined to the estate grounds and expansive city park—easy terrain compared to this.

"A couple of miles." His gaze swept her from head to toe. "You all right?"

"I'm fine."

Pointing higher up the mountain slope to where the forest thickened, he said, "We've got about a half mile of ground to cover before we start seeing the trees you'll be interested in."

By the time they reached it, Allison was grateful for a chance to dismount and stretch her legs. She was turning a slow circle, soaking in the glorious view, when Shane appeared at her side and handed her a small, squat canteen with a hand-knitted cover.

"What's this?"

"Hot cocoa." He held out two miniature cups. "Would you mind pouring while I fetch the rest of our repast?"

"Repast. That's a big word for a lawman."

He cocked a brow. "Not for a lawman who spends his free time reading."

She grinned, unwisely thrilled at being far from civilization with him. Using a fallen log as a table, she carefully poured the rich brown liquid, her mouth watering at the aroma of sweet chocolate. Shane returned with a crushed white box and a slight frown.

Peeking beneath the lid, he said, "I brought a dessert for each of us but it appears only one survived the trip in my saddlebags."

Going to stand beside him, she inspected the hefty slice of golden cake and, beside it, what looked like a pancake. "I can't believe you brought us cake." She sniffed the contents. "What kind is it?"

"Cider cake."

"You are a very wise man, Shane Timmons," she said, grinning. "You've thought of all the essentials."

"Here." He handed it to her with a slight smile. "You eat it. The cocoa is all the *repast* I need."

Taking a fork from his hand, she scooped up a large bite and held it out. "There's no reason we can't share."

Beneath the brim of his hat, his brows tugged together. "You don't have to do that."

"I can't eat this entire thing by myself. Well, I could…but I shouldn't. Come on, you know you want to." She wiggled the fork close to his lips.

His strong fingers closed over her wrist and, his gaze melding with hers, guided her hand to her own mouth. Small clouds of white formed from his exhaled breath. "Ladies first."

The pleasant blend of flavors on her tongue—cloves, an undertone of tart apple and juicy currants—couldn't distract her from his nearness and intense scrutiny. How did she get to this place? Alone with Shane on a frigid winter day, high in the mountains of East Tennessee, sharing a slice of cake?

A hushed expectancy shrouded the forest, the tranquility pierced occasionally by a hawk's cry or crack of a tree branch.

As she slowly chewed and swallowed, he studied her with unwavering focus. The shadow of a beard outlined his hard jaw and framed his mouth. He looked like a rugged backwoods hunter in his duster that hit him midcalf.

"Your turn."

Shane remained watchful while she fed him, his gaze burning into her. Her stomach fluttered. What did he see in her expression? She glanced into the box, wondering how she was going to keep her hand steady throughout this ordeal. Downfall by dessert.

Something cold and wet hit her cheek. Tilting her head, she gasped at the sight of white flakes drifting from the heavens and onto the leaf-strewn forest floor.

"It's snowing!"

"That it is." Shane didn't exude the same level of excitement. In fact, he looked a trifle concerned as he studied the sky. "We should finish up here and pick out a tree."

Allison followed him to the fallen log, where he swiftly downed the contents of his cup.

"You said it doesn't typically snow this early in the season. Do you think it will stick?"

Already a thin layer of white coated the ground. "Hard to say."

"What aren't you telling me?"

Deep grooves carved either side of his mouth. "The weather can be unpredictable and patchy. This elevation might see several feet of snow, while the center of town might get an inch." He held out a cup to her. "Drink. It'll help warm you."

"We don't have to get a tree today. We can head back right now."

Shane studied the horizon. "If we don't dally, we should be fine."

"Should be?"

"Let's just say this is the last place we want to be if the clouds decide to dump a significant load of snow on us."

388

Chapter Eight

He was questioning his decision three-quarters of an hour later. Allison had quickly made her choice, a dense Fraser fir about as tall as him, but by the time he'd gotten it cut and tied to the sled, several inches of snow coated the ground. Not a single pinch of sunlight penetrated the clouds. Fat, heavy flakes glided past them at a steady rate and gave no sign of letting up.

You were too afraid of disappointing her to heed your instincts.

Allison sat quietly on her mount, her profile solemn as she dusted the collecting snow off her sleeves.

He climbed into the saddle. "I'm going to go first so the sled will make a clear path for you. We'll take it slow and steady. You encounter any problems, speak up."

"No need to worry, Shane." Her green gaze expressed confidence. "I trust you to get us home safe."

Determined to do just that, he guided his horse between the closely spaced trees. The ground sloped downward at a gradual angle and would level out as soon as they broke free of the dense growth. Allison didn't speak, and he wondered if she was mulling over where the decorations would look best in the main floor rooms.

Minutes passed with no other sounds besides the creaking of saddles and muted slush of hooves against fresh white powder.

"There's an uneven outcrop up ahead." He pointed to where the trees thinned.

The sled bobbed and jerked as it caught on thick roots, and he worked to keep his horse calm and on task. Soon they were free of it and on flat ground. Behind him, he heard Allison cry out. He twisted around. Her horse rushed past him, its saddle empty. Seeing Allison on her back in the snow—eyes closed, body too still—sent icy fear coursing through him.

His heart threatening to burst out of his chest, Shane leaped down and scrambled to her side, dislodged snow spraying in all directions. "Allison! Can you hear me? Are you all right?"

He knelt beside her, his knees protesting the cold shock of moisture seeping through his pants. Yanking off his gloves, he gently swiped the melting flakes from her cheeks. Her skin was cool but not shockingly so. Leaning over her, he brushed a thumb lightly across her plump lower lip. "Allie, speak to me."

Her lashes fluttered open, and he was engulfed in twin pools of the deepest green.

She sucked in gulps of air. "I didn't hold on tightly enough. He shifted the opposite way of what I expected."

When she started to sit up, he put his arm around her shoulders to assist her. "Easy. Are you hurt anywhere?"

"No, merely winded from the impact." Patting the snow with her open palm, she gifted him with a weak smile. "This acted as a thin cushion. Otherwise, I'd likely be sporting some nasty bruises come tomorrow."

"You may still." Relief lessened the tightness in his chest. "Your brother would have my hide if I let anything happen to you."

He glimpsed a flash of disappointment before she dipped her head. "Right. George's good opinion is what matters." She moved to stand, and he supported her with a hand on her elbow.

"What's that supposed to mean?"

Sidestepping his hold, she straightened her bonnet and shook out her skirts, all the while avoiding his perusal. "Never mind." She finally lifted her head, her gaze going beyond his shoulder. Her lips formed an O. "Shane...where's my horse?"

Spinning, he scanned the wide open space with a sinking feeling. "I was too distracted to pay attention to him. He's got to be headed for his barn and a bucketful of oats."

"Won't he get lost?" Her worry for the welfare of the animal was obvious.

"From what I know of Martin Watts, he rides his horses out here on a regular basis. I'm confident he'll find his way home." His hands began to smart from exposure. Snagging his gloves from the ground, he plunged his fingers into the warm slots. "It does present us with a problem."

Allison looked from him to the horse and back. "We have to ride double."

Her trepidation poked his pride. "You have an issue with that?"

"I don't." She shrugged. "But I know you don't like to be touched."

He gaped at her. "And exactly how did you come by this conclusion?"

"I lived with you, remember?" Marching through the filmy curtain of snow, she laid a hand against his cheek. Despite his surprise, he couldn't help wishing her glove didn't form a barrier between his skin and hers.

What could he be thinking of? He could not *want* Allison, couldn't think of her as anything more than an old acquaintance…an adopted sister—that should smother any further thoughts of male interest in an alluring female.

Shane had trouble holding her gaze. "What are you doing?" he grated.

"Proving my point."

"I'm not going anywhere, am I? I'm not pushing your hand away."

"But it's costing you," she challenged. "When I hugged you last night, you stood there like a wooden statue."

"I'm not accustomed to spontaneous affection," he said stiffly.

Her features softened. "I'm guessing you're not accustomed to any sort, planned or spontaneous."

"It was never a part of my world."

He wasn't sure what he'd expected, but anger wasn't it. "Allison?"

Lowering her hand, she shook her head in disgust. "People like your mother shouldn't be allowed to have children if they aren't going to treasure and nurture them."

"It's in the past."

"Is it? I don't think so. Otherwise, you wouldn't insist on avoiding relationships."

"I like being alone." Now why did that statement ring false to his ears?

"I don't believe that, either." She brushed past him and went to stand beside his horse. "Do you get on first or do I?"

"Ladies first." Once she was situated, Shane hauled himself up behind her. They set out across the snowy field, and she had trouble balancing herself. He curled his left arm around her middle.

"Rest against me. You won't bob around as much."

After a short hesitation, she relaxed into his chest. A strange sense of satisfaction flooded him. It felt nice to hold her close. Better than nice. It felt wonderful. He could get used to this.

Minutes stretched into an hour. Their progress was slow, punctuated by the silence between them.

"Allison."

"Hmm?" She sounded sleepy.

He was hit with the sudden urge to nuzzle her nape, perhaps kiss her cool cheek or rest his forehead on her shoulder. His fingers automatically curved about her waist, and she turned her head so that he had a view of her profile.

"What is it?" she said, more alert this time.

"This isn't ordinary snowfall. It's heavy and piling up fast. If we continue on our current course, there's a good chance we won't make it to the Wattses'."

She considered his words. "Is it because of the tree's extra weight? Couldn't we leave the sled here and pick it up later?"

"I doubt that would make a difference. Our best option is to find shelter. There's a homestead not far from here. Fenton Blake lives there with his granddaughter, who's about eighteen years old. We could bed there for tonight and head to town in the morning."

"Will he welcome us?"

"Fenton's the sort that keeps to himself, but he won't deny hospitality to a stranger in need."

"Do what you think is best. I trust you."

Allison's confidence in him had his chest expanding with pleasure. He appreciated her calm assurance. If she'd been worried and upset about their situation, it would've made it more difficult for him to concentrate on getting them to safety.

Another hour and a half passed before he finally spotted the outline of Fenton's cabin. The peppery scent of wood smoke hung in the air, and he anticipated the heat of a roaring fire. The place where he held Allison was the only warm spot on him. The rest of him was protesting the frigid temperatures. Every few minutes, a shiver would course through her, and his arm would tighten around her, as if by holding her closer he could infuse her with some of his residual warmth.

He'd never forgive himself if she suffered because of his actions.

If not for the sting of winter air and the stiffness of her muscles, Allison would never move from this spot.

Being this close to Shane was like a dream, one she wished didn't have to end. He was solid and strong. He smelled of leather and pine and subtle spice. He held her as if he didn't mind her nearness, as if he'd do anything to keep her from falling, and it was a heady experience.

"We're here."

Her disappointment was completely unreasonable.

It was imperative they take shelter from the elements. Still, she would miss this.

Shane guided the horse almost to the cabin door. She couldn't make out the structure's details through the heavy precipitation, but it struck her as small, maybe smaller than Shane's modest abode.

Dismounting, he hollered out his presence before pounding on the door. Cold rushed in where he'd been, wrapping her in its unwelcome embrace. She pressed her hands to her numb cheeks.

Shane pounded the weathered wood a second time. "Fenton Blake? You in there? It's Sheriff Timmons."

A cry filtered through the door, and Shane fell back a step. "Did you hear that?"

"Sounds like Mr. Blake has an infant in there."

He assisted her off the horse, holding her a couple of seconds longer than necessary to ensure she was steady on her feet. His hand at her elbow, he guided her through the drifts onto the small porch. The squalling sound came again, and they stared at each other.

Shane did not appear pleased. He whacked the door with the flat of his hand. "Open up, Fenton. I—"

The rest of his words were lost as they were suddenly met by a frail, elderly man who was bouncing an angry baby on his hip.

"All your racket done woke up the babies!" he accused, his steely gray gaze pinned on Shane. When he noticed Allison on the doorstep, relief gripped his features. "You're a woman. Maybe you can get 'em to stop bawling." And he promptly deposited the infant in her arms.

Allison's soft protest was swallowed up by heart-wrenching sobs. Instinctively, she hugged the baby—a girl, she guessed—to her chest and kissed the halo of blond curls ringing her head.

Shane's astounded gaze swung from her face to the infant she was trying to soothe. His features puckered in disbelief. "Did you say *babies*?"

Fenton turned sideways and pointed a gnarled finger at a pair of matching cradles positioned at the foot of the single bed. From their vantage point, a pair of tiny fists punching the air were visible.

"Yep. A pair of 'em. Brother and sister."

"Fenton. What's going on here?" Shane demanded. "Where's Letty?"

The man's thin shoulders drooped and moisture filled his eyes. "She's dead, Sheriff."

Shane's features reflected shock. "Fenton, I'm sorry."

"Go see to your horse," he said gruffly. "Then we'll talk. You're lettin' all the heat escape."

After one last look at Allison and the baby, Shane left her alone with the unlikely trio. Once the door was closed, Fenton shuffled over to the ancient cookstove in the corner and set about making coffee.

Shifting the little girl to one hip, she managed to untie her cape and hook it on a peg. Getting her bonnet off took more fancy maneuvering.

"How old are they?" She had to raise her voice to be heard. The boy in the cradle was getting angrier by the second.

"Six months."

After stomping off most of the wet clumps of snow clinging to her boots, she advanced toward the cradle and, crouching beside it, captured one fist in her hand.

"Hey there, little fella. The one in the cradle is the boy, right?"

Fenton nodded, the lamplight shining on his dull silver hair. "His name's Charlie. The girl is Izzy, short for Isabel."

Charlie's crying ceased and tear-washed blue eyes blinked up at her. His round cherub face was bright red, his straight blond hair lank where it lay across his forehead. His nightgown bore several stains.

Izzy's fussing had grown quieter, and Allison looked down into the liquid pools of chocolate brown. The combination of light hair and dark eyes was striking. They were both pretty babies. And both in desperate need of a bath and a fresh change of clothes.

Glancing about the cabin, she saw that it wasn't spotless, but nor was it filthy. Like Shane's home, there wasn't a couch, only wooden chairs pulled around a rectangular table that had seen better days. A leaning hutch pushed against the wall beside the fireplace housed lamps and assorted tools. A rifle hung above the mantel. In the kitchen area, a couple of homemade shelves attached to the wall held dishes and cups, as well as a stack of pots. A counter where a dry sink was situated held an assortment of glass baby bottles, ceramic jugs and folded towels. A stack of nappies and infant clothing occupied the bedside stand.

How long had Fenton Blake had the full care of these infants?

Shane reentered the cabin then, his expression grim. Dusting the snow from his hat onto the porch, he hung it on the empty peg beside her things and pulled the door closed behind him. When he'd removed his duster and gloves, he cupped his hands and blew on them.

"I'll have a cup of coffee ready for ya in no time."

"Appreciate it. Thanks for letting my horse share your barn space."

Charlie figured out that she wasn't picking him up and decided to squall again. Shane winced. Well, if he wanted the noise to stop, he was going to have to help out.

Allison marched over to where he stood and held out the baby girl. "Hold Izzy so I can see to her brother."

Looking like she had lost her wits, he made no move to take her. "I've never held a baby in my life."

"It doesn't require a university education, Shane."

He transferred that dubious gaze to Izzy, who was staring at him in quiet contemplation. "Uh…"

"Don't tell me you're scared of a wee human?"

"Actually, I am."

Charlie's tirade threatened to crack the windows. Fenton was either hard of hearing or had become immune, because he continued about his business at the stove.

"Do you enjoy listening to this? Because I don't. And I'm not sure I can juggle the pair of them." Without waiting for his response, she placed Izzy against his chest and physically moved his arm up to balance her there.

"Allison," he growled in protest.

Ignoring him, she hurried to the cradle, scooped up the little boy and hugged him tight. He didn't smell as most babies should, like sunny mornings, clean sheets and Ivory soap. Her nose scrunched as the odor of curdled milk rose to greet her.

"It's all right," she soothed, lightly patting his back.

Charlie cried into her shoulder, his face buried in her

dress, and Allison's heart melted. Poor darlings. What had happened to their mother and father?

She lifted her head and intercepted Shane's intent perusal, a heavy dose of caution at the back of his eyes.

Fenton turned and, taking in the scene, set three enamel cups on the table. "You look like a natural, Sheriff. Sure you ain't held a baby before?"

Shane's frown grew more pronounced as he glanced dubiously at Izzy, who he held slightly apart from him. "I think I'd remember something like that."

The elderly man came around and took her, cocking his head to the table. "Go ahead and drink your coffee while it's hot." He glanced at Allison, who'd managed to quiet Charlie. "You the sheriff's new sweetheart?"

Shane choked on his drink, coughing and sputtering and going red in the face.

Was the thought of them romantically linked that upsetting? "We're old friends."

"What're you doing in my neck of the woods?"

Since Shane was still clearing his throat, using a chair for balance, she answered for him. "We were out searching for a Christmas tree when the weather changed. We thought we could make it home, but we miscalculated." At the questioning lift of his bushy brows, she added, "I'm staying at the Wattses' place this month."

"Allison's from Virginia," Shane rasped. "She'll be returning as soon as Christmas is over."

He said it as if Christmas was something to get through, not enjoy. She'd hoped to make this one special for him, but she was beginning to think that was an impossible task.

Chapter Nine

A part of him wished he could start the day over. If he hadn't offered to cut down a tree for Allison, a tree for a house that didn't even belong to her, he wouldn't have walked into this nightmare—a blizzard, not one but *two* babies and a grieving great-grandfather. At least, he assumed they were Fenton's granddaughter Letty's offspring.

Barely able to rip his gaze from Allison with the baby boy, he took a moment to study Fenton. He appeared slighter than last he'd seen him. His eyes were bloodshot and his age-spotted hands shook slightly. Caring for infants around the clock was a demanding task that couldn't be good for the man's health, especially considering his heart condition had worsened in recent years. The last he'd heard, the medicine Doc Owens had prescribed would help preserve Fenton's quality of life as long as he got plenty of rest. When it had been just Letty and him, she'd cooked the meals and assisted with chores. Now everything fell to him, with the added burden of the twins.

As much as Shane disliked the situation he found

himself in, he couldn't deny that the man was in dire need of assistance. Being in difficult spots was part of his job. Doing his duty for the residents of these mountains wasn't always pleasant, but he wasn't one to shirk his responsibilities.

"I hate to inconvenience you, Fenton, but do you mind if we bed down here for the night?" Shane said.

"You're welcome to share what I got. It ain't much, but the good Lord meets my needs."

"Izzy and Charlie. They're your kin?"

Quiet reigned while the older man struggled to contain his emotions. "I warned Letty not to get involved with the Whitaker clan, but she wouldn't listen. She fancied herself in love with their youngest boy. Convinced herself he loved her back. He filled her head with pretty lies. When she found out she was expecting, she didn't doubt he'd marry her."

"Clyde Whitaker is the babies' father?"

Righteous anger lit his gray gaze afire. His hold tightened around Izzy. "He might've sired them, but he ain't their pa."

Allison's expression revealed her opinion on the young man in question's behavior, one that matched his own.

"I know how the Whitakers operate. I'm not surprised Gentry didn't make his son do right by Letty."

"She was beside herself with grief. I went up there alone to try and reason with Gentry, but he blamed my granddaughter for leading Clyde astray." A vein throbbed in his forehead. "It's a wonder you didn't have to toss me in jail and throw away the key. Only the thought of Letty being left alone stopped me from doing something foolish."

Shane hadn't had a whole lot of dealings with Letitia Blake, but she'd impressed him as being a sweet young woman devoted to her only living relative.

"Has Clyde seen the twins?" Allison said.

Swaying from side to side, she smoothed Charlie's hair from his forehead. His blue eyes were watchful as he rested against her. Although she was a stranger, he seemed comfortable in her arms.

"Once. Letty took them up there when they were a month old. His pa said Clyde wasn't interested in seeing them. They turned her away."

Allison made a sound of distress. "She must've been crushed! What kind of unfeeling monsters are these people?"

Fenton's lined face reflected a mixture of anger and sorrow. "They're people in need of God's love and forgiveness, just like the rest of us. Only, they haven't acknowledged it yet."

His words pricked Shane's heart. He was in need of the same and more. How many times had he witnessed the power of prayer since making Gatlinburg his home? The O'Malleys were people with strong, abiding faith that didn't waver no matter what their circumstances. They weren't perfect, and neither were their lives, but they lived to serve God.

The O'Malleys aren't like you, an insidious voice inside his head reminded. *They're worthy of God's love. You aren't.*

"I'll pray for them," she said. "And you. I can't imagine how you've coped on your own."

"What happened to Letty?" Shane ventured.

"About a month ago, she got real sick. Coughing. Fever. Night sweats. The coughing settled in her chest, and she grew too weak to care for the babies." His eyes were wet. "I would've fetched the doctor from town, but she didn't want me traveling with Izzy and Charlie. And I couldn't leave them here with her alone for that long. It happened fast. One week, and she was gone."

Shane stared at the floor, sad for what the widower had endured. First the loss of his wife and adult daughter in a freak farm accident a decade earlier, leaving him with a young granddaughter to raise. And now having to bury Letty and assume the full responsibility for a pair of helpless, demanding infants.

"I thank God the babies didn't fall sick," Fenton went on, his voice uneven. "He protected them." He studied Allison and Shane. "And now He's brought the two of you here. You're an answer to prayer, that's what you are."

This entire situation had Shane rattled. Allison was convinced he'd be more comfortable staring down his gun's barrel at a ruthless outlaw than taking care of Charlie and Izzy. Fenton Blake's recent pronouncement had only made him more uptight. She was fairly sure he didn't wish to be the answer to this particular prayer.

"You sure you don't need some help?" Fenton lingered in the kitchen area, nursing what was probably lukewarm coffee.

"Go take a well-deserved rest," she insisted, noting the man's pallor. "Shane and I will be fine."

Sensing Shane's pointed stare, she smiled sweetly and waved Fenton away. He settled in the rocking chair by the fire with a battered, well-loved Bible.

"We'll be fine?" he whispered against her ear, sending what felt like a static electric charge zinging through her limbs. "Have you bathed a pair of squirming infants before?"

"As a matter of fact, I have." She angled her face toward his, which hovered inches from hers. Did he have to be so appealing? "Not a pair. I've bathed a baby before, and that's what we're going to do now. One at a time."

Between the cookstove and the fireplace, the small cabin was warm enough to bathe the babies without worrying about them catching cold. Fenton had assembled the soap, towels and clean changes of clothing for them. Shane had heated the water and poured it into a copper basin the twins' mother had used for such purposes. Since Izzy was preoccupied in her cradle with a handmade stuffed bear, Charlie was up first.

Balancing him on one hip, she tested the water temperature with her fingertip. "Feels good to me."

Laying him on his back on a towel spread out on the counter, she quickly divested him of his dirty gown and diaper. His halfhearted fussing ceased the instant she lowered him into the water. His eyes grew round with wonder.

She chuckled and gently lathered his arms and neck. "You like that, don't you?" she cooed.

Shane stood there with his arms at his sides, braced as if preparing to do major surgery. He'd removed his jacket and rolled the sleeves of his charcoal-gray-and-blue checked shirt up to his elbows, giving her a glimpse of fine dark hairs sprinkling his corded arms. His hair was ruffled from multiple finger-combings. A stubborn lock fanned across his forehead.

She resisted the impulse to smooth it into place. "I

need for you to hold him steady while I wash him, all right?"

His azure gaze locked on to Charlie, he placed one hand on the baby's back and another on his shoulder. "Like this?"

"Yes, sir." She smiled. George would've gotten a kick out of this.

Charlie seemed content while she washed his skin and hair. He splashed a couple of times, raining droplets on them.

Shane didn't complain, though. He was too intent on his task to utter a word. He really was adorable, she thought. Although out of his element, he was determined to do his best.

When she lifted Charlie from the bucket and laid him on the towel, his brow puckered in dismay. She bent and rained ticklish kisses on his belly. He grinned, a single tooth flashing on his bottom gum, and grabbed a fistful of her hair.

"Shane? A little help here?"

He moved close and gently disengaged the boy's chubby fingers. "He likes when you do that."

Straightening, she smoothed her hair and laughed. "Most babies do."

Shane's slight smile held a sense of discovery. "You're a natural."

"I live with four children."

He followed her to the bed, where she laid the baby and picked up a fresh gown. "Would you like to dress him?"

He folded his arms, putting his considerable muscles on display. "I'd rather watch you do it."

Her laugh was dry, husky. "Typical answer."

In no time, she had Charlie dressed and his hair combed. She held him up. "Look at you, sweet boy! What a handsome young man you are."

"Smells better, too," Shane muttered.

"I'm glad you think so." Delivering the baby into Shane's arms, she boldly tapped his whiskered chin. "Because you're going to feed him while I give Izzy a bath."

Retrieving one of the bottles Fenton had prepared, she pushed it into his hand. "Here you are. Remember to burp him."

"But I—"

Fenton snapped his Bible closed and stood up. "You can have the rocker, Sheriff. I'm going out to the smoke-house to fetch us a slab of ham for supper."

Refusing Shane's offer to go, he donned his coat and hat and slipped outside, leaving them alone with his great-grandchildren.

Shane wanted to call him back and beg him to switch jobs. He'd be much more content in the smokehouse's cold isolation than in this stuffy, crowded cabin.

The baby in his arms reached for the bottle. Allison wasn't paying either of them any mind. She was already undressing the tiny girl, talking in that sugary, cajoling tone all the while. Guess that was what mothers did to try and ward off crying fits. His own mother's face flashed in his mind.

Was it possible she'd been different in the beginning? Had she cooed and grinned and tickled him like Allison did with these two? Had she showered him with affection?

Since he'd never know the answer, he turned his

mind to the hungry boy in his charge. He sat in the rocking chair and, tucking Charlie in the crook of his arm, lowered the bottle. Charlie latched on to it, his hands overlapping Shane's as he sucked greedily.

It had been a long time since he'd felt inadequate to a task. In those early days as a deputy, he'd had to learn his job quickly or risk getting hoodwinked or shot. He'd been in the law-keeping business so long now, there wasn't much he hadn't seen or heard. This baby opened up a whole new world. Of course, Gatlinburg had its fair share of newborns and tykes toddling about, but he didn't have any personal dealings with them. He even kept his distance from his friends' kids.

Charlie's big blue eyes, the color of a clear summer day, zeroed in on Shane's face. Shane studied him in return. His blond eyebrows were thin and sparse, his eyelashes black and as long as any girl's, his cheeks like soft pillows and his miniature fingernails in need of a trim. Now that he was clean, his hair shone and cupped his head like a soft silk cap. Allison was right. He was a good-looking boy.

A boy who'd never know his mother.

For Shane not to have known his mother would've been a good thing. For Charlie and Izzy, the opposite was true. Letty had nurtured them for five months. They appeared healthy and happy. While they didn't have much in the way of material things, she'd sewn clothes and dolls, blankets and nappies for them. Shane imagined she'd loved them so much that she'd been sure their father would love them, too.

"Don't forget to burp him halfway through," Allison reminded.

Izzy was splashing about in the basin much like her

brother had done. Her chocolate hued eyes were alight with joy. Allison dropped a kiss on the baby's forehead, and Shane's chest seized with a soul-deep yearning he recognized from his boyhood. Yearning for what he had never experienced and what so many took for granted— family, a sense of belonging to someone else, of being vital to another human being's happiness.

Because he was surrounded by families, he'd insulated his heart in a thick covering of indifference. That indifference, that conviction that he was meant to be alone, made it possible for him to survive. It didn't always stop the loneliness from creeping in, but it kept him from lamenting his lot in life. He wasn't meant to have a wife and children. He was meant to fulfill a crucial role...that of town protector and upholder of the law.

His job, along with the solid reputation he'd built, gave him plenty of satisfaction.

"Shane? Did you hear me?"

"Huh?"

"Did you burp him yet?"

He glanced at the bottle, which was more than half-gone. Hurriedly setting it on the small table beside the chair, he said, "Now what?"

"Sit him up and pat his back until he releases the air buildup."

Charlie was not pleased. His face screwed up like a prune and he waved his arms around. Shane awkwardly patted his back, amazed at the feel of his tiny rib cage and spine. Shane swiped a dribble of milk from his tiny chin.

"Do it a little harder." Allison brought a towel-wrapped Izzy over and stood observing him.

"I don't want to hurt him."

"You won't."

Once again, she regarded him with utmost confidence. She was wrong to put her confidence in him. A stolen purse or an argument between neighbors? He was equipped to handle those sorts of problems. Babies hadn't figured into his training.

The door burst open, allowing a swirl of icy wind and snow inside. Fenton shoved it closed behind him and stomped his boots on the rug. He held a large ham in his hands.

"Bad news, Sheriff. Wind's picking up, and the snow's showing no sign of stopping." His gray gaze didn't look particularly worried. In fact, Shane was pretty sure the older man was pleased with the forecast, which didn't make any sense. "Looks like you may be sticking around longer than just one night."

Chapter Ten

On a thin pallet near the banked fire, Allison huddled into the quilt, unable to get warm. Cold air clung to the floorboards. The tip of her nose was cold. And her cheeks. Her ears, too. The cabin's earlier heat had waned with the onset of evening. She could make out the jut of Shane's shoulder beneath his blanket. His pallet was situated a couple of feet from hers, close enough for her to reach if she were to stretch her arm out as far as she could.

This arrangement would've felt incredibly intimate if it hadn't been for Fenton's occasional snores and the babies' soft, steady breathing.

"Shane?" she whispered. "You asleep?"

He was lying facing away from her, his head cushioned by a small pillow. "Yep."

"You are?"

Drawing in a deep breath, he shifted onto his back and rested one arm across his forehead. "What's on your mind?"

"I'm curious what your plan is."

"Plan for what exactly?" He spoke in hushed tones.

"Helping Mr. Blake and the children. You know as well as I do that he can't continue as he has been. He doesn't look healthy, in my opinion."

He rubbed both hands down his face and turned his head to look at her. His eyes gleamed in the near darkness. "He's not. His heart's weak. The medicine he takes helps manage the condition provided he takes good care of himself."

This was terrible news. The twins' mother was dead, and their sole caretaker was in poor health. "We have to do something."

"I'm not sure what the solution is. He's too far from town for someone to come out on a daily basis."

"Do you think he'd be willing to move closer?"

"A gentleman like him who's up in years? I seriously doubt it. The Blakes have inhabited this cove for generations."

Allison mulled over the problem. There had to be a solution that Fenton could live with. But what?

"I'll talk to him tomorrow," Shane said. "Maybe there's a distant relative who'd take the kids in."

She sat upright. "I can't see him allowing that. Charlie and Izzy are all he's got left."

He sat up, too. "We'll figure something out. You have my word."

"The people of Gatlinburg are fortunate to have you looking out for them, you know that?"

"Some might not agree with you," he drawled, "but I appreciate the sentiment."

She covered a yawn. "I wonder what George and Clarissa are doing right now."

"If they're smart? Sleeping. Like we should be." He

pointed over his shoulder. "No telling if those two will snooze through the night."

"You're right." Shivering, she lay down again and tugged the frayed quilt edges to her chin. "My body's exhausted, but my mind won't settle. That ever happen to you?"

He got comfortable, this time facing her. "Sometimes. When I have a vexing puzzle to solve or an elusive criminal to capture."

Allison changed her mind…being here like this, chatting with him in the stillness of the night, felt immensely personal and private.

"What keeps you up nights?" He sounded relaxed and close to drifting off to sleep. "What worries the indomitable Allison Ashworth?"

"The things that worry me would seem silly to you."

In her early twenties, she hadn't given much thought to marriage. After her father's death, she and George had assumed the daunting responsibility of running their father's business and seeing to their employees' welfare. Her free time had been devoted to charitable work or visiting with her dearest friends. There had been several men who'd shown interest in courting her and, while she'd agreed to spend time with a few of them, she hadn't allowed anything serious to develop.

She hadn't wanted to acknowledge the truth back then, but being with Shane now made it impossible to deny. Deep in the inner recesses of her heart, she'd nursed the hope that one day Shane would return to Norfolk and finally give her a chance to love him. To heal the wounds inflicted by careless parents and life's hard knocks.

"Try me," he said.

The fact that he couldn't see her expression made it easier to confess. "My mom died when I was ten," she reminded him. "I have many wonderful memories of her. I remember her as a kind, gentle, patient woman. She had this exuberant laugh that didn't match her genteel appearance. She and my father would sit and talk for hours in his study…sharing stories, playing chess, making plans for our future." Smiling to herself, she felt for the locket she kept around her neck. A gift from her father on her thirteenth birthday, it contained miniature photographs of her parents.

"Sounds nice."

"I was blessed with parents who adored each other. They didn't exclude us, however. Mother and Father were firm in their discipline. They expected us to follow their instructions. They were also generous with their affections."

"I'm sorry you lost her, especially at so young an age."

A pang of wistfulness gripped her. "It was incredibly difficult in the first few years following her death. Her absence leached much of the happiness from our lives. Our family unit had been broken, and the loss of her nearly crippled my father emotionally. He was a changed man. His faith in God was the only thing that got him through."

"Are you worried you'll lose George like you lost your parents?"

She tucked her hand beneath the pillow. "The thought crosses my mind sometimes, but I try not to dwell on it."

"What is it, then?"

"I wonder if I'll ever experience a love like my parents shared…if I'll have a deep connection with someone." She worked to keep the emotion from her voice. "I think that's why I've focused on my profession instead of romance. I'm scared of failing. I don't want to settle for less than God's best for me."

Shane was quiet a long time. "I didn't have the opportunity to meet your mother. Is it possible you remember only the good times? That maybe your memories are better than the reality?"

"I know my parents' relationship wasn't perfect. There were times when things were strained at the supper table and afterward they'd go their separate ways. But by the next day, they were smiling at each other again."

"If anyone deserves happiness, Allie, it's you."

Her heart thrummed at the rare use of her shortened name.

"But I'd hate to see you wind up alone because you've set your expectations too high."

It was her turn to be silent. She stewed over his words. *Was wanting* him *setting her expectations too high?* she was tempted to ask.

"I don't want to be alone anymore," she whispered instead. "I want to build a life with someone. I want children. Lots of them."

"How many is a lot?" He sounded more alert than before.

"I don't have an exact number in my head." Her cheeks stung. This wasn't exactly a normal conversation to be having with a man who wasn't her intended. "All I know is that I have the means to care for a whole gaggle of children and more than enough affection to go around."

"One day you'll get the family you're longing for. They'll be mighty fortunate to have you in their lives."

Emotion clogged her throat. That was the nicest thing he had ever said to her. "Thank you, Shane."

"Good night, Allison."

Shane couldn't get their late-night conversation out of his head. He sat at the kitchen table with Fenton the following afternoon, a chessboard between them. Usually he enjoyed pitting his wits against an opponent, especially if it was someone he didn't often play with. Today was different. He couldn't focus because he kept getting distracted by Allison and the babies.

On a quilt stretched across the floorboards, she sat with her legs curled beneath her and held Izzy's stuffed bear midair. Piles of pillows supported Charlie and Izzy. They were strong enough to sit up by themselves but their balance wasn't perfect. Taking turns, Allison would lean forward and lightly tap the infants on their noses, chins or chests with the bear. The simple game thrilled them.

Shane's attention switched between their bright, round faces to Allison, who looked very happy for a woman whose Christmas holiday had gone awry. What a special woman. Instead of fretting over things she couldn't change, she made the best of whatever situation she found herself in. That was a rare quality in anyone.

The bear slipped from her fingers. As she leaned forward to retrieve it, her unbound hair spilled over her shoulders, shimmering like strands of liquid sunshine. Shane very badly wanted to test its texture. Fenton had lent her Letty's hairbrush and mirror that morning, along with a dress. The design was plain. There were no ribbons or buttons or fancy beadwork, but the fabric was a rich jewel-blue tone that made Allison's creamy complexion glow with good health. She fit in these surroundings as if born for mountain life.

"Checkmate."

Fenton's triumphant announcement brought Shane's attention to the board. Bending close, he said, "I thought you were supposed to be tough to beat. Guess you got other things on your mind." He winked so that Shane had no doubt as to his meaning.

"I guess so," he admitted sheepishly. "How about another round?"

"You in the mood to get trounced a second time?" The old man's creased face lit with humor.

He kicked up his shoulder. "What else we got to do?"

Fenton lowered his voice to a conspiratorial whisper. "You could give your sweetheart a hand."

Shane rested his hands on the table. "She's a friend."

"Shame." Turning sideways in his chair, he took in the scene before him. "The man who wins her won't live to regret it."

"How do you figure?"

"You get to be my age, you see a lot. You learn to listen to this." He tapped a bent finger to his chest, indicating his heart. "She'll be a fine mama someday."

Shane didn't disagree. Allison was a natural caretaker. Nurturing was in her blood. Look at how she'd tried to enfold him in her flock the moment he arrived at Ashworth House. Any normal person would've let her. Too bad her generosity hadn't been a match for his impenetrable defenses.

"She's worried about you, you know," Shane murmured.

Fenton's brow furrowed, and he nodded, sadness stealing over his features. "It ain't been easy. There've been moments when I thought I couldn't go on. I'm not a spring chicken anymore. Feeding and diapering twins around the clock reminded me of that fact real quick. I can't let Letty down. I'm all those babies have got, but this old ticker..." Frowning, he stared at the trio on the quilt. "I worry what might happen to them if I were to suffer an episode. No one around for miles."

"I wish I could provide someone to help out. If you lived in town—"

"Stop right there, Sheriff." He held up a hand. "I know what you're about to suggest, and I ain't leavin' my land."

"I didn't figure you would."

"I'm too old to be starting over."

"You have relatives who could come and stay? Help out for a while?"

"You mean someone who'd stick around until the twins are about five years old? Nah. I hate to admit it, but what those kids need is a young, God-fearing couple who'd raise them right."

Something in his tone put Shane on alert. The way Fenton was looking at Allison, all hopeful and expectant like she was an elusive Christmas gift he'd prayed for, filled Shane with foreboding.

Izzy and Charlie's giggles lilted through the space. Over Fenton's shoulder, Shane met Allison's gaze. She smiled, a single dimple flashing, before returning her attention to the task of playing entertainer.

Shane sank against the chair back, amazed at how much he longed to be with her on the floor, to sit close beside her and join in the game. To be a part of their group.

It was the same spot where they'd conversed the night

before. He could recall the huskiness of her voice, the sweetness of her scent, the feeling that they were the only ones awake for miles. She'd opened up to him in a way no one ever had before. He'd been humbled that she'd trusted him and sorry that he'd missed out on a friendship with her.

For a moment, he'd wished her stay could be permanent. But then reason kicked in. He wasn't good enough for the likes of her, and friendship wouldn't satisfy him for long.

"What are you going to do?" Shane said at last.

The old man continued to scrutinize Allison in a way that heightened his lawman's suspicions.

"The only thing I can do. Pray and wait for the good Lord to provide an answer."

"Enjoying the peace and quiet?"

Framed by the barn stalls, Shane turned from petting one of the horses. His hat and gloves rested on a nearby hay bale. His duster was buttoned and a blue neckerchief kept his neck warm. "I needed to stretch my legs."

Allison pushed the door shut and crossed the straw-littered ground to join him. Folding her arms beneath her cape, she leaned against the stall and tilted her face up. "Admit it. The crying got to you."

"Two at once was a bit much." A slight smile graced his mouth. The growth along his jawline was heavier today.

"It wasn't long after you left that they drifted off."

After his and Fenton's second chess game, it became clear that Izzy and Charlie were ready for a nap. Allison scooped up Izzy while Fenton had taken her brother. Shane had put the board and pieces away and, mumbling an excuse about fresh air and horses, had made his escape.

"They're good babies," she said. "Especially considering they must be missing their mama."

Shane scraped a hand along his jaw. "I hadn't thought about that. They're so young…"

"Letty was their mother and primary caretaker." Pocketing her gloves, she reached out to pet the horse's face. "Did you speak to Fenton?"

"I did." Something in his tone warned her the news wasn't good.

"He won't budge from here. Can't say as I blame him. Where's he going to go? This place is all he's known. And there are no relatives in the position to give him the long-term assistance he needs."

Allison had figured as much. "What if something were to happen to him?"

Terrible ideas crowded her mind, each more dire than the next.

"Hey." He stepped closer, ducking his head to catch her gaze. "I'll figure something out. I'll send someone out here once a week to check on them. I'll even come myself if I have to."

"Once a week isn't enough." She grasped the rough edge of the stall door. "If he were to have an accident or fall ill, Izzy and Charles would starve before they were discovered."

Shane's warm hand covered hers. The gesture startled her. "Fine. I'll send someone three times a week."

She lost herself in his steady gaze. "You care what happens to them?"

"Of course, I do." He pulled away. "You think I don't

want them to be safe and cared for? That's what I want for every single resident in these mountains."

"I didn't mean to offend you." Feeling bold after their late-night interaction, she captured his hand and squeezed. "I'm simply grateful that you're willing to go out of your way to help. I know taking care of infants isn't something you're familiar with."

He nodded. "You're right about that."

"Charlie didn't have any complaints about your bottle handling skills."

Instead of answering, he gave her an arch look. He slipped his hand free and pointed to her hair.

"You, ah, have something…" Shane peered closer. "Looks like dried corn mush."

She grimaced. "Charlie can't help himself. He likes to grab fistfuls of my hair."

"I noticed. Hold still while I get it out."

Allison studied his serious countenance. His fingers were gentle as he worked the bit free. Tingles radiated across her scalp when his knuckles scraped her tender nape.

"There," he breathed huskily. "I think I got it all."

Shane proceeded to smooth her heavy mane behind her shoulder, taking his time finger-combing it so that it lay against her cloak. "It's as soft as I thought it would be."

She felt unsettled. Nervous. The strong column of his throat above the neckerchief filled her vision. "It is?"

A muscle in his jaw worked as he lowered his arm to his side. "Yeah."

His searing gaze roamed her hair and face. He would deny it if asked—and she wouldn't dream of asking—but Shane Timmons was drawn to her. The evidence was reflected in his eyes, the hungry yearning he'd be horrified to know was there for her to see.

Her elation was tempered by the knowledge that he didn't *want* to be affected by her. He wouldn't welcome these feelings, wouldn't celebrate them like she did. There was no victory in the revelation. How could there be when nothing was ever going to change between them?

Chapter Eleven

Allison's nearness, coupled with the longing in her expressive eyes, made it tough to cling to his long-held convictions. His fingers begged to sink into her silken mane a second time. Curling them into fists, he shoved them in his pockets.

His heart's pumping was fast and erratic as other thoughts bombarded him. In the deserted barn, lamps hooked on nails throughout the space gave off enough light to make it seem like evening instead of afternoon. They were alone, and she was breathtaking. Her smaller stature and form appealed to him, evoked his protective instincts and made him want to curl his arms about her waist and cradle her against his chest for hours.

He couldn't believe he'd said that out loud about her hair. The statement was of a personal nature, something he tried to avoid with her.

Allison came close and, curling her arm through his, leaned into him. With her face tilted up, he couldn't *not* look at her soft, supple lips and wonder how she'd react if he kissed her.

"Make snow angels with me."

He jerked his gaze up. "What?"

"There's no one around to see," she said diplomatically. "Besides, you owe me."

"How do you figure?"

The sparkle in her green eyes dimmed. "I haven't forgotten how you snubbed me when we were kids. A girl doesn't forget those types of things. All I wanted was your friendship."

The blood roared in his ears. He'd been so busy trying to protect himself that he hadn't cared how his behavior had impacted her.

"Allie—" His voice sounded raw.

She stopped him with a finger pressed to his lips. His throat went dry.

"I don't wish to discuss the past right now. What I want is to have a little fun, all right?"

"Fun."

"Snow angels. With you."

He didn't see the appeal of getting snow down his collar and making a fool of himself, but she was right. He did owe her.

"I let you talk me into this once before."

"You abandoned me after a minute. Stomped off muttering about little pests and foolish games."

Shane couldn't help himself. He very lightly curved his hand around her cheek, his thumb resting against the crescent below her eye. Allison held still, her lips parting.

He drew on every ounce of willpower he possessed not to kiss her.

"I was young and confused. Damaged goods. It was right that I stayed away from you."

"And now?" she whispered.

"I'm still damaged."

Her lashes drifted down. "Oh, Shane—"

"You're only here for a short while. And you're wise to the ways of the world like you weren't back then. So let's go be silly, shall we?"

Shane turned her toward the exit before he could do something unforgiveable. He grabbed his hat and gloves and pushed the door open, squinting at the white winter wonderland that greeted them.

White powder encrusted the gigantic pines and evergreens. Those trees without leaves were also coated in snow inches thick in the crooks where the branches met the trunks. Making sure the barn door was secure, he led Allison through the knee-high drifts around the barn to where the cabin wasn't visible. There was only snow and forest and the occasional cardinal to witness their antics.

He swept his arm out like a gallant knight. "Ladies first."

She grinned, her teeth as white as the sky against her red lips. She took a handful of steps into the middle of the clearing, made a complete three-hundred-sixty turn and then, with a girlish giggle, lay flat on her back and made wide arcs with her arms and legs.

"Come on!"

Shaking his head, he laid his hat atop the snow and marched over beside her. "This stays between you and me, got it?"

He could only imagine what the good folks of Gatlinburg would say about this.

"I won't tell a soul."

With a sigh, he lay on the ground, wincing at the cold sensations greeting his body. At first he felt foolish moving about like a seal bobbing on dry land. But as Allison's laughter rose toward the heavens, he started smiling, too. The powder was soft and springy. He let some of it drift between his gloved fingers.

"This is the perfect consistency for a snowman."

Allison sat up, anticipation lighting her face and making her seem like a young girl again. "I can't remember the last time I built one. Let's do it!"

Shane could've listed several reasons why staying out here wasn't a good idea. Instead, he smothered his voice of reason and let himself take part in a custom that thousands of families performed across the country each winter season. Working together, they packed and rolled and patted snow until they'd constructed an impressive-looking figure.

"See?" She surveyed their work. "This is fun, right?"

"I suppose." He shrugged, unable to resist teasing her.

They were on their knees in front of the snowman. Her hair was disheveled, her cheeks bright pink and her eyes shone like radiant gems. "You *suppose*?"

"It beats doing paperwork."

"Is that so?"

Without warning, she barreled into him, knocking him flat on his back. Shane gasped as wet snow was smushed against his face and neck. Allison bombarded him with handfuls of the stuff, the element of surprise on her side. But she was a lightweight and no match for his strength. "You're gonna regret that, woman!"

In an instant, he had her on the ground. Crouching beside her, he retaliated, dousing her with a shower of snow. She squealed and squirmed and tried to snag his hands.

"Okay, okay, I give up!" she gasped.

Leaning over, he pinned her shoulders and bent his face close. "You sure you're done?"

All of a sudden, the lightheartedness fled, replaced with a pulsing awareness between them. Her eyes were huge in her face. She was gazing at him with longing that mirrored that which was unfurling inside him. Stunned by what he saw, he scrambled to standing.

Allison had stated that she wanted to be his friend. She hadn't indicated she was interested in anything more. It was impossible.

"Here," he said gruffly, extending his hand. "Let's get you dusted off."

Averting her face, she allowed him to help her stand. "I can do it."

While she righted her cloak and brushed the moisture from her skirts' hem, he brushed the flakes from his hair and seized his hat from where he'd left it.

Where there'd been shrieks and laughter minutes before, there was strained silence. He felt bereft, of all things. Lonelier than he could recall being, which was strange considering Allison was standing right here.

"I could go for a cup of coffee," he said. "How about you?"

She met his gaze and smiled. "I could use some warming up." Turning to look at the snowman once more, she said quietly, "I wonder who's going to build snowmen with Izzy and Charlie?"

"They're six months old."

"Soon they'll be crawling. Then walking. Talking." She fell into step beside him as he started for the cabin. "Raising children isn't solely about feeding and clothing them or teaching them their letters. It's so much more than that."

He glanced at her profile. "You're worried whether or not they'll have time for frivolous things."

They stopped at the base of the cabin steps. "Fun isn't everything," she admitted. "But it is important." Cocking her head, she considered him. "Did you have fun today, Shane?"

"I'm not going to lie."

Disappointment flitted over her face.

"Today was the most fun I can remember having. Thank you, Allie."

The disappointment transformed into joy. "That makes me happier than you can imagine."

The door opened, and Fenton stared at them in concern. "You two lookin' to catch pneumonia?" he demanded. "Come on inside and warm up before the fire. I've got soup simmering on the stove."

Shane and Allison shared a smile, and he realized something had changed between them. He wasn't sure if that was a good thing, but he liked it.

Allison tickled Izzy's soft belly and waited for the drool-filled smile. Izzy didn't disappoint. Her big doe eyes shone with contentment. Bending over the mattress again, she blew gusts of air against her middle. The baby girl cackled and, using both hands, latched on to Allison's cheeks.

"Easy, sweet girl," she said, smiling as she curled her fingers over Izzy's and moved out of reach.

"Ba-ba."

Shane's pacing ceased. Holding Charlie against his shoulder, he turned and regarded them in surprise. "That sounded like a word."

"She's trying out sounds." Allison sat her up and

tugged a clean dress over Izzy's blond curls. The baby objected. Typically laid-back, Izzy didn't like having her diaper or clothing changed.

Charlie protested the lack of movement. Lightly bouncing him, Shane resumed his route from the window nearest the kitchen to the opposite wall where a wardrobe contained Fenton's clothes and personal items. Scooping Izzy into her arms, she approached the pair.

"Want to trade?"

Frowning, he shook his head. "I'm okay. I haven't worn a blister on my heel yet."

"He acts like his tummy is hurting him," she said. "Maybe he has gas."

Shane gave her a dubious look, and a bubble of laughter escaped her. Charlie decided to explore Shane's chin. His cute button nose wrinkled at the feel of his stubble.

"I think Charlie wishes you'd shave."

Ensconced in the only rocking chair, Fenton closed his Bible and observed them. "Now don't the four of you look like a picture-perfect family."

Shane appeared as startled as she felt. The observation was surprising given that his granddaughter wasn't long buried.

"The sheriff's got it in his head that he's not cut out for family life," she blurted.

Fenton raised an eyebrow. "Sometimes God has to adjust a man's thinking."

Charlie started fussing again, and Shane patted his small back. "I know how you feel, little buddy. I feel like fussing, too." He gave Allison a pointed glare.

Fenton laughed heartily. "Come sit with him. Lay him over your knees and pat his back."

Allison watched as Fenton helped Shane situate the

baby. The sight was a touching one. Shane was so careful with him. His large, tanned hand looked huge as he balanced Charlie on his lap. After a few minutes, he picked him up and held him midair.

"Like the view from there?" Smiling, Shane pulled him close so that they were nose to nose and then lifted him up again.

Charlie gurgled and sucked on his fingers.

"I think he likes that," Allison said, fascinated by this first display of playfulness toward the babies.

Shane repeated the action several times before sitting Charlie in his lap. Izzy lurched toward them, and Allison lowered her beside her brother.

"There." She nodded in satisfaction. "Now this would be a perfect image for a photograph."

He smirked. "The first peep out of them and you're coming to my rescue, right?"

"Of course." Grinning, she eased onto the nearby bed. "Do you think Ben's worried about you?"

His eyes glittered. "Ben knew I was taking you out to look for a tree."

"He did?"

"Most of the time, we keep each other informed as to our whereabouts in case of emergencies."

Something about his manner implied he had made a point to tell his deputy about their plans. While he seemed to respect Ben, he didn't appear to want him associating with Allison.

"Will he organize a search party if we're gone too long?"

Using the toe of his boot, he set the rocker to moving, his arms firmly around each baby. "Depends on how bad it is in the heart of town and if he's dealing with any problems there." He rested his head against the chair slats. "Ben and I know these mountains like the backs of our hands. He no doubt assumes I've found shelter for us."

"How long would he wait?"

"Given current conditions, I'd say a week. Why?"

She glanced at Fenton, who was at the counter washing bottles. That reminded her she should probably wash the bucket of soiled nappies and clothes—not a task she was looking forward to but one she'd willingly tackle in order to give their host a break.

Leaning forward, she lowered her voice. "When were you planning on returning to town?"

He lifted his head, his gaze alert. "It hasn't snowed in a couple of hours. If it doesn't start up again between now and tomorrow morning, we should head out then."

"I've been considering asking if he'd like me to stay awhile longer."

The rocking halted. "I've got to get back—"

"Just me."

He shot a quick glance at Fenton, who was whistling while he worked, before spearing her with a formidable stare. "Allie, I understand why you'd offer. However, this is your holiday. You're supposed to be enjoying your time away from work and responsibility. I'm sure the reason your brother sent you on ahead was because you're due a break. I admire your selflessness, but I can't let you do it."

"Let me?" Unwilling for their host to overhear, she used the rocker arm to support her weight, bringing her close to him. "I may be a guest in your town, but that doesn't mean you can dictate my actions. I've been

making my own decisions for quite some time now. I can't in good conscience abandon this precious family."

Anger sparked in his eyes. "This is my responsibility, Allison, not yours. Your life is in Virginia. What are you going to do? Play house for the rest of the month? What happens after Christmas? I'll tell you. He gets used to having you around. The kids get used to having you around. And then they lose you, just like they lost Letty."

The color drained from her face. She couldn't do that to them.

"I'll tell you what else will happen," he murmured fiercely. "You'll get even more attached than you already are. Your brother won't look too kindly on me if I send you home with a broken heart."

Chapter Twelve

"The sheriff lit outta here lookin' like he sucked on a sour apple." Fenton tossed another log on the fire. Sparks danced above the flames.

Allison sat where Shane had minutes before, taking comfort from the weight of the twins on her lap. While they were relaxed and content, she was in turmoil. She'd been certain her idea was a sound one until he'd pointed out potential pitfalls. The last thing she wanted to do was cause this family more grief. And he was right. It wasn't a long-term solution.

"Shane's accustomed to bossing people about," she said, still smarting.

Fenton scratched his head. He'd taken some time to himself earlier in the day, and his silver hair shone and his cheeks were freshly shaven. His skin was deeply tanned from a lifetime of outdoor living.

"Guess it comes natural to him after all these years of being a sheriff." Drawing a chair over, he sank onto it and rubbed his hands along his thighs. His gray eyes were wise and patient. "Whatever it is you don't see eye to eye on, just remember he wants what's best for you."

She rubbed her cheek along Izzy's springy curls. "How old was Letty when her parents passed?"

"Ten."

"That's how old I was when my mother died." She knew exactly how Letty would've felt…as if her world had been taken apart and put back together wrong. And now Letty's kids wouldn't have a chance to know her. Sadness pressed in.

"What was she like?"

He blinked rapidly and sniffled.

"If you'd rather not talk about her, I understand."

"I want to. It's not easy, ya know?"

"Even though my father's been gone for more than a decade, I still get choked up sometimes when I think about all he's missed."

Fenton cleared his throat. "My Letty was a sweet girl. Quiet. What some folks would call a dreamer." His countenance bore witness to his intense sorrow. "I wanted more for her than this secluded cove. She was smart. I thought maybe the Lord would provide a way for her to have a different life. But she got mixed up with the Whitaker boy. He didn't deserve her."

"I'm so sorry, Fenton."

While he mopped his face with a handkerchief, Allison silently prayed for God to comfort this man and to provide clear answers to his dilemma.

"Shane and I are in disagreement about my wish to stay here and help you for a week or two."

When he lifted his head, his gaze was solemn. "In the short while you've been here, I've seen how you care for my great-grandchildren. Doesn't surprise me that you'd offer. And I understand why the sheriff has reservations."

Allison couldn't discern his thoughts at all. Beyond sorrowful, he looked resigned.

"So you don't want me to stay?"

"I have a different request. Don't feel bad if you'd rather not."

"What is it?"

"You're staying at the Wattses' place?"

"Yes, that's right."

"I've got to see the doctor and purchase a few things at the mercantile. Would it be a burden if Izzy and Charlie stayed with you for a day or two? The sheriff probably wouldn't mind if I bunked with him."

"No. Not at all! I'd love that."

The request wasn't what she'd expected. She'd hoped for longer time with the twins, but she'd take what she could get. In the unlikely event they returned to town and found George and Clarissa had arrived, Shane would surely know someone who'd be willing to offer temporary boarding space.

"Are you feeling all right?" She'd noticed him pausing to catch his breath at odd times throughout the day.

"Just more tired than usual." He made a dismissive motion. "I need to see him about a fresh supply of medicine."

Allison hoped it wasn't more than he was letting on. Fenton struck her as the suffer-in-silence type.

When Shane returned to the cabin a half hour later, she left the explaining to Fenton. Shane didn't comment, simply speared her with his unreadable gaze and nodded.

Their plans made, she and Fenton spent the remainder of the evening gathering the necessary supplies. Shane disappeared outside again. She assumed he was avoiding her. There was no conversation that night. He lay with his back toward her, tension radiating off his big frame.

The following morning dawned bright and clear. Once the babies were dressed and fed and the wagon loaded, Shane guided her onto the porch.

"Do you think these will work?"

A pair of wooden crates had been altered to form seats with a slat across the top that would prevent Izzy and Charlie from toppling forward. Crouching, she patted the bunched-up blankets in the bottom.

"You made these?"

He shrugged. "Thought you might get tired holding them the entire trip."

Popping up, she hugged him, careful to keep it brief. "You're a sweetheart for thinking of them."

Color etched his cheekbones. "It was nothing."

"Are you still angry with me?"

His eyebrows shot up. "I wasn't angry, Allie."

"You were annoyed."

"I was concerned. Still am."

Basking in his warm, blue regard, she spread her hands. "I'm not staying on here, am I?"

Presenting her with his profile, he squinted into the distance. He looked like the formidable lawman this morning in his full gear, gun belt firmly about his waist, pistols visible and badge pinned over his heart. His full beard didn't detract from his appeal one iota. "I can't put my finger on it, but something doesn't sit well about Fenton's request."

"What do you mean?"

"It's not like him, that's all. Men like him don't ask to stay in town. They go in, get what they need and get out."

"He said he had to see the doctor. I'm sure he has

other business to tend to. Besides, he's got his great-grandchildren to think about now. I looked through their belongings. They don't have proper winter gear."

In the sunlight, the snow sparkled like a blanket of diamonds. "Another thing you should know—he won't look kindly upon handouts. If you're thinking of purchasing stuff for them, I suggest you broach the subject carefully."

She laid a hand on his upper arm. "Thanks for the insight. And for the seats."

He turned to her again. "You're welcome."

Allison was reminded of that charged moment between them in the snow. Being close to him was a heady experience. The feelings she'd had for him years ago couldn't hold a candle to those she was experiencing now. They weren't naive, immature kids any longer. Her reactions to him were on a whole other plane...all-consuming and difficult to fight. He was like a decadent plum pudding she shouldn't go near but couldn't stop thinking about.

Oh, if he only knew she'd compared him to a plum pudding...

He tilted his head. "You have a strange expression on your face."

"Uh, just thinking about Christmas dinner."

His brows pulled together. She was saved from further questioning by Fenton, who appeared in the doorway.

"We ready to head out?"

Shane's gaze seemed reluctant to leave her. "We are."

They reached the Wattses' property by noon. Shane's intention to make a quick escape was thwarted almost as soon as they unloaded the wagon.

Fenton pulled him aside. "I didn't expect the trip to wear me out. Allison said I could use one of the extra bedrooms. Would you mind keeping her company for a while longer? I'll be ready to head to your place once I've rested."

Shane glanced at the big white farmhouse with reluctance. He'd counted on getting Fenton settled and then going off alone to process all that had happened the last two days. He needed time and space to reclaim his former emotional distance from Allison.

He couldn't refuse the man, however. Judging by his haggard appearance, he'd benefit from a long nap. "I'll be glad to."

His gratefulness was obvious. "Sure do appreciate it, Sheriff."

Together, they crossed the yard. The Wattses' farm had received less accumulation than Blake's Cove. Still, the ground was completely covered and the buildings' roofs had about an inch of white on them. He eyed the Fraser fir propped against the porch railing.

Stifling a sigh, he grabbed the cut end and, waiting until Fenton went inside, dragged it to the living room.

"Allison?"

Passing Fenton on the stairs, she reached the bottom tread and paused.

"Are the kids asleep?" he said.

"Fenton put their cradles in my room." Dressed in the outfit she'd worn during their original outing for the tree, she'd tied her hair back with a bit of string that looked too flimsy to do the job. In spite of the past trying days, she was lovely. Maybe a little less animated than usual. "They went right to sleep."

He wasn't surprised. They'd remained awake during

the trip, observing the passing scenery with interest. The seats he'd crafted had saved Allison from having to hold them. Not that she would've minded. She wouldn't think twice about sacrificing her own comfort for theirs. That was just the sort of person she was.

"Where do you want this?" he said, jabbing a finger at the tree.

Striding to the center of the room, she turned a slow circle, tapping her chin as she considered every nook and cranny. She wandered to the wall opposite the fireplace and stood in front of the window. "This is the spot you picked out the other day, isn't it? It will serve nicely."

He set it up for her. The only reason he knew what to do was because he'd helped Josh with his last year. He'd never bothered for one for himself. Seemed a waste.

When she was satisfied that it wasn't crooked, she clasped her hands together. "It's perfect. Thank you, Shane."

Each time she thanked him with those shining eyes, he got this feeling like he was a king who'd granted her dearest wish. It was a feeling he could get used to.

That's why he asked the next question. "What are you going to decorate it with?"

"I was planning on making smaller versions of those pinwheel stars with the leftover paper." She indicated the mantel. "I can get popcorn to string later."

"Want some help?"

"You're offering to make tree ornaments with me?"

"Fenton and the kids are napping, and we've nothing else to do. Unless you'd care to challenge me in a chess game."

"That would be a short match, as you well know."

He did know. While he and George had played games, she'd been content to do needlework or simply observe their moves.

"I would enjoy having your help with the decorations, if you truly don't mind."

Cutting and pasting paper wasn't high on his list of favorite things to do. He wasn't about to tell her that, however. She'd been wonderful during their entire ordeal. This was one small way to repay her.

"Point me to the scissors," he said.

Her demeanor upbeat, she hummed a familiar Christmas tune as she brought out the supplies. They chose the dining table for their workspace.

"Let me show you how to do the first one."

Coming around to his side, Allison stood close enough that their arms brushed together, making it tough to concentrate. Crafting pinwheels wasn't what he wanted right this minute. What he wanted was to wrap his arms around her, bury his face in her hair and block out the nightmare of the past. He wanted to hold fast to her and not worry about a single thing. But the courage he employed in his job deserted him. Shane was more afraid of reaching out to Allison, of opening his heart to her, than of meting out justice to malicious criminals.

"Do you want me to make a second one?" She angled her face toward his, wholly unaware of her effect on him. Or was she? Something flickered in her eyes as they traveled his features. Was she deliberately testing his boundaries?

He dismissed the thought. Allison wasn't a calculating woman. George had indicated she had little experience with courting. The knowledge thrilled him, which was wrong for many reasons.

"Yeah. A second demonstration would bc good." Subtly putting a couple of inches between them, he did his best to focus on her instructions.

She returned to the chair opposite his, and he found he could breathe easier.

"I remember the monster tree at Ashworth House," he said. "Those ornaments weren't handmade."

He recalled that first Christmas with the Ashworths and his awe at the opulence of their decorations. To him, the ornaments had appeared to have been crafted of pure gold and expensive glass. The huge red velvet ribbons adorning the stair banisters had fascinated him. Put together, there would've been enough fabric to make a hundred fancy dresses.

"True." Her expression turned fond. "However, these days we install a smaller tree in the parlor that the children and I decorate."

"I suppose they love that tradition."

"They like to be creative, and they like to feel as if they've contributed. They're also quite fond of the frosted sugar cookies and hot cocoa that's served once our work is finished."

He could picture her there in the parlor, directing her niece and nephews in their endeavors. "Your sister-in-law hasn't made you feel unwelcome, has she?"

"Oh, no." Shaking her head vigorously, she laid her cut pieces on the tabletop in various patterns. Her hands were small and dainty and jewelry-free. "I'm fortunate in that Clarissa and I have a wonderful friendship. When she and my brother became engaged, she and I had a long talk. She told me that it wasn't her intention to move in and take over the running of things, nor did she wish for me to feel displaced or unwanted. We've worked out a system where we share the household responsibilities."

"I'm glad, Allie. Ashworth House is where you belong. I can't imagine you separate from it."

Her fingers stilled, resting flat atop her assembled pinwheel. "I won't live there forever." Her lips pressed together in dismay.

Shane realized he'd offended her. "I didn't intend to imply that you would." He gestured, the scissors still in his grip. "My memories of the estate are tied up in the past, that's all. I think of you, and all I can see is that grand house."

She slowly nodded, her gaze dropping. "While I'm content to continue on with George, I've been thinking of striking out on my own for a while."

Shane wasn't convinced she'd be happy. Imagining her all alone in an enormous house didn't make *him* happy. That wasn't her dream. "What's George's opinion?"

"I haven't told him yet." Lifting her chin, she silently dared him to keep her secret. "Besides, I don't know what the future holds. Who knows? Perhaps I will be setting up residence with Trevor in the new year."

Jealousy instantly invaded every inch of him. It was an illogical reaction. He didn't wish for her to be alone or unhappy, and yet the idea of her building a life with a stranger made him ache with regret.

"Whatever you decide," he forced himself to say, "I support you. You deserve to be happy."

Chapter Thirteen

Decorating a tree with Shane was very different from decorating one with four rambunctious children. Where the children would attack the task with haphazard gusto, he was deliberate. He studied the branches for long moments before placing each ornament.

"It doesn't have to be perfect." She softly nudged his side. "You should see our parlor tree. It may not win awards, but it's decorated with love."

The shiny ribbon dangled from his pointer finger. "I've never done this before."

Allison nodded, masking her consternation. It shouldn't come as a surprise. The estate staff had decorated the large tree in the hall, and they hadn't had a second tree then.

"Well, you're doing a fine job. I'm glad you agreed to this." She gestured toward the kitchen. "I'm only sorry I don't know how to make frosted sugar cookies."

"I don't need cookies." His steady gaze warmed her and seemingly communicated that her presence was enough to satisfy him.

Fanciful thinking, that.

He looped the pinwheel on a high branch and watched it spin and dance. They'd chosen a pretty tree, about seven feet tall with thick, full branches. Its sharp perfume competed with the smoky odor of crackling firewood.

He gestured to the coffee table. "That was my last one."

"Mine, too." Tapping her chin, she said, "It definitely needs more color. I'm thinking popcorn and cranberry strings, maybe fabric bows. And there's nothing for the top."

"Quinn stocks a small selection of Christmas merchandise. You might find a topper you like there."

She turned to him. "Will you help me finish decorating once I get more supplies?"

After a moment, he nodded in mock seriousness. "I suppose I could do that. It wasn't as tedious as I thought it would be."

"I'm relieved to hear you weren't bored," she said wryly.

"I could never be bored around you, Allie." Then, as if embarrassed at the admission, he located a broom and began sweeping up stray needles. "Did your father ever tell you how I came to work for him?"

"He didn't mention it."

Her father hadn't given them a whole lot of information about Shane's past, citing his private nature. Her father had urged them to give Shane time, probably thinking he'd share when he got ready. Only, he never did.

A sigh gusted out of him, and Allison knew it had nothing to do with her. "My mother spent most days drinking and bemoaning her lot in life. One day she got careless and, locked in the booze's haze, knocked over a lamp and started a fire. I came home to find the place burned to the ground. The police told me what happened." He stopped sweeping and rested his weight on the broom handle.

Her heart breaking for him, she forced herself to remain where she was. "I'm so sorry, Shane."

"I didn't have anywhere to go, so I spent the next couple of nights on a bench in the city park. I got tired of being hungry, so I decided to steal some items to sell on the street for profit." Memories lent him a haunted look. "I did that for a while, justifying my behavior with the thought that the folks I was stealing from had enough to spare. And then I chose one of your father's stores. The one on Federal Street." A sardonic smile twisted his mouth. "He was there for a meeting with the manager and caught me in the act."

Allison took a step closer. She could hardly believe he'd chosen to confide in her after all these years. "He must've been angry."

"He was at first. I thought he was going to march me straight to the police headquarters." He shook his head ruefully. "Instead, he took me into the store office and demanded to know why I was stealing. He chose to hear my story. And he had compassion on me."

Tears blurred her vision. "He was one of the most caring men I've ever known."

"I wish I could be like him."

The admission rocked her. Shane hadn't had the foundation she and George had enjoyed. He hadn't had anyone to love him, to instruct him in the ways of healthy relationships, to bolster his confidence. That he'd achieved as much as he had was a testament to his inner strength and determination. She liked to think her father's intervention had had a hand in that, as well.

"In many ways, you are like him," she said. "You stand for what's right. You insist on justice and fairness. You apply yourself to helping your fellow man."

He resumed his sweeping. "You're kind to say that," he said gruffly.

"It's the truth."

She wished she could make him see his own value, but she couldn't. He'd have to come to accept it for himself. She wasn't sure he ever would, and that made her sad.

Spying a stray ribbon on the floor near the coffee table, she bent and retrieved it. When she straightened, black dots danced before her eyes. She swayed.

"Allie?" The broom handle thwacked the floor. Suddenly, he was beside her, his arm around her. "What's wrong?"

Letting him support her, she closed her eyes. "I'm a trifle light-headed. Nothing serious. I probably need to eat something."

"Sit down." He guided her to the sofa, settling her in the middle and sitting right beside her. His fingers skimmed her forehead. "Are you too hot? Do you have a headache? Are you experiencing any other symptoms?"

She opened her eyes to find him hovering close, worry churning in the stormy depths. "I'm fine, honestly." She placed a hand on his chest. "I haven't slept well the last two nights. That, combined with skipping lunch, is all that's wrong."

He glanced at the mantel clock and huffed. "One-thirty already. I should've fixed our noon meal instead of messing with the tree."

"I should've paid attention to the time."

"You sure you're okay?" Beneath her palm, the muscles of his chest contracted and released.

She was tempted to explore his strength. "I'm positive. I was simply light-headed for a moment. That happens sometimes."

His gaze zeroed in on her mouth. Yearning surged there. His hand, which had come to rest on her neck, slowly slid beneath her ponytail, his thumb stroking a mesmerizing pattern beneath her ear. She decided to throw discretion to the wind.

Her pulse racing, the tattoo of her heart loud in her ears, she reached up and framed his jaw with her hand. Surprise stirred in his gaze seconds before she pulled him down to her. His sharp inhale was cut off by her lips covering his. Allison had no clue what she was doing, nor how to go about it. Shane didn't at first respond. He seemed frozen in shock. Then, with a rumble deep in his chest, he crushed her to him. He took charge of the kiss, and her toes curled inside her boots.

Her fingers clenched the fabric of his shirt, holding him hostage. Not that he protested. He delved into her hair, cradling her head, holding her fast. His lips were warm, firm and sweet. Being with him felt right, as if this was what was meant to happen all along, the two of them traveling on converging roads that took years to intersect.

When he gripped her shoulders to hold her apart from him, a sound of protest escaped.

"Shane?"

His eyes were on fire, his features hewn from granite. "You don't know what you've done, Allison."

Upset and confused, she blurted, "You mean what *we* did, don't you?"

"That cannot happen again."

Releasing his shirt, which was hopelessly wrinkled, she scooted to the couch's far edge. "Why not?"

"Why not?" He scraped a trembling hand through his hair. Shooting to his feet, he began to pace. "Because your life is in Virginia. Because you're going to marry Trevor Langston or some other man like him who knows how to be a husband and father. You're going to live in a house as grand as Ashworth House, and you're going to have enough kids to form a football team."

Allison gaped. Pushing to her feet, she intercepted him, blocking his path. "What if I don't want Trevor? What if that life isn't for me? What if... I want you?"

"No." He shook his head. Desperation flared. *"No.* You don't mean that."

She touched his arm, and he flinched. "I know what's in my heart."

"Stop, Allison." Backing away, he held up his hands. "I've said it before, and I'll say it again. I'm not the commitment type. I like my life the way it is. That won't change."

He was almost to the door when soft crying carried down the stairs. Hanging his head, he shot her a look full of turmoil. "I'll cook you a quick lunch while you see to them."

On the verge of tears, Allison brushed past him and practically bolted up the stairs. She'd made a grave error in judgment. She'd taken a risk and it had blown up in her face.

Shane left the house as soon as he had lunch prepared. Allison had assured him she'd be fine on her own and would tell Fenton he'd return for him later that afternoon. Craving privacy to deal with what had happened, he seized the chance of escape.

He wasn't accustomed to being with other people around the clock. Being cooped up in Fenton's cabin with four other humans had taken its toll. And now the kiss...

Just thinking about her softness, her innocence, made his middle drop to his boots. Allison had branded him with that kiss. He'd never get it out of his head. Not only was he going to have a difficult time not repeating it, he was going to have to watch her leave at the end of the month, knowing the next time he saw her she'd likely belong to another man.

None of this was supposed to have been an issue. He was supposed to have remained aloof, unaffected by her many attributes. This was bound to be the worst Christmas in the history of Christmases.

He decided against going to the jail. His mood was too foul for polite conversation. Taking the long route home, he was relieved when he didn't cross paths with anyone.

Shane took his time brushing down his horse and unpacking his saddlebags. Afterward, he took his rifle apart, cleaned each piece and reassembled it. His new copy of *American Jurist and Law* didn't appeal, so he returned outside to chop wood in hopes the physical activity would burn off his frustration.

Twenty minutes later, he was midswing when he heard a masculine greeting. He lowered the ax.

"Josh. What brings you here in the middle of the day?"

His friend strode past the outhouse and toolshed and into the wooded area behind his cabin. "I was manning the store when I heard someone say they saw you riding near town. Ben's been concerned. We all have."

"As you can see, we didn't freeze in the high elevations."

Lifting the ax above his head, he brought it down with enough force to slice through the wood like butter. The resulting thwack was satisfying. He tossed the pieces into the growing pile.

"Where'd you find shelter?"

"We passed a couple of nights on the Blake homestead."

"Fenton and Letty getting along all right?"

He wedged the blade in the wood and, resting his hands on his hips, regarded Josh.

"Some things have happened out at the Blakes'. Letty got mixed up with the youngest Whitaker boy. About six months ago, she gave birth to twins. A boy and a girl."

Josh's eyes widened. "I'm sure Fenton was fit to be tied."

"I'd say he was at first. Doesn't matter now because Letty's dead, and he's Izzy and Charlie's sole caretaker."

"I'm sorry to hear that." Somber now, he passed a gloved hand over his mouth. "He practically raised Letty. How's he gonna cope with two kids in his condition?"

"I don't know."

Allison had posed the same question. He didn't have answers then, and he didn't have any now.

The treetops rustled as a stiff breeze barreled down the mountains. Pulling his collar up, he grabbed the handle again. As Shane chopped, Josh moseyed over to the growing pile and toed it with his boot.

"You planning on hosting a bonfire for the entire town?"

"Nope."

His lower lip protruded as he nodded and inspected the stack over beside the barn. "That right there's enough to last one winter. Why the extra?"

"I need the exercise," he huffed.

"Right...because you're getting thick in the middle."

His dry tone sparked Shane's ire. "Why don't you go on back to the shop? Wouldn't want to miss any customers."

"You wanna know what I think?"

"Not particularly."

"I think you like Allison."

Shane sliced through another log, not bothering to answer.

"You like her a lot. Except you don't want to, and that's got you all worked up. Am I right?"

Josh sported an infuriating grin that Shane was tempted to wipe off his face.

"Go home to your wife and kids, O'Malley, and leave me be."

"Come on, Shane, I'm your friend. You have to talk to someone."

"No, I don't."

"So you're going to chop the entire forest down?" He held his hands out at his sides. "She's got, what? Three weeks left?"

"Twenty-four days."

"Tell me this. Does she fancy you, too?"

Laying aside the tool, he passed his coat sleeve across his forehead and paced to where he'd left a water bucket. He downed a dipper of ice-cold water. Josh was persistent. Even if Shane managed to get rid of him now, he wouldn't drop the subject.

"Why is it important that you know?" he said testily.

"Because I'm your friend, and I think you need someone special in your life. Allison's the first person I've seen you let get to you. That tells me she's different."

"She is different," he admitted. "Always has been."

"Then what's standing in your way?"

He waved for Josh to follow, and they made their way inside. Over coffee, Shane unloaded his entire life story. Josh didn't judge him. Didn't condemn his actions.

"I'm glad you finally told me. Took you long enough."

Cradling his mug in one hand, he stretched his arm along the top of the chair beside him. "I held off because it's not something to be proud of. I've worked hard to leave the boy I once was behind."

"You've achieved great things," he said, his gaze probing. "What I don't understand is what any of this has to do with you and Allison. I mean, what does the past have to do with the present?"

"Everything." He'd expected Josh, of all people, to understand. "I'm a product of my past."

"To a certain extent, yes. However, you're in control of how you live your life now." He tapped the table. "You know what *not* to do. I would argue that you'd make a more excellent husband and father than someone like me, who was fortunate enough to have good parents."

"That's absurd." While far from perfect, Josh and his brothers all had solid marriages and were doting fathers.

"Think about it, Shane. You were miserable as a kid.

So miserable that you'd never put another kid through that. You witnessed what a man's carelessness and neglect can do to his wife. You wouldn't dare treat a woman you loved that way."

Pushing out of the chair, he stalked to the fireplace and propped his hand against the mantel. The orange flames licked at the fat logs just as self-doubt taunted his insides. He'd been set on this solitary course for much of his life. Entertaining another way, one where he'd get to experience love and partnership, was peculiar and slightly frightening.

He knew how it felt to be let down again and again. To have his hopes dashed repeatedly. He couldn't do that to any woman, especially Allison. Couldn't do that to a helpless kid. The twins' faces popped into his mind, and his chest tightened.

"Have you never considered that God sent David Ashworth into your life for a reason?"

"What?" He twisted to meet his perusal. "Why would God do that? He didn't bother with me for the first thirteen years of my life."

Josh was aware of his struggles with his faith. Shane frequently sought excuses not to attend church services. Over the years, the reverend had reached out to him, as well as Josh's father, Sam O'Malley. Josh and his brothers had talked to him, urging him to take his relationship with Christ seriously. He hadn't listened.

Turning his chair around so that he could face Shane, he sat with one leg propped on the other. "The Scriptures tell us that it rains on the good and the bad. We all endure trials in this world, and many times we won't discover the reasons for those trials until we reach heaven. Other times, we can use the lessons we learn to bless others."

Bitterness rose up to choke him. "How is having an absentee father and drunk-out-of-her-mind mother supposed to enable me to help someone else?"

"I can't answer that," Josh said. "What I do know is that those experiences have shaped the man you are today, the same as living with David and his children did."

Shane fell silent. Not once had he viewed David's entrance into his life as anything other than chance. Eaten up with self-pity and rage, his soul starved for love and approval, he could've missed the greater picture.

"It's possible I was wrong."

"God loves the whole world. It'd be prideful to think you're the exception," Josh quietly pointed out.

Turning away, Shane stared at the flames. "I need to think."

His friend approached and laid a hand on his shoulder. "You should also read your Bible. Start with the book of John."

Then he let himself out, leaving Shane alone with a thousand unanswered questions.

Chapter Fourteen

Shane must've decided to avoid her for the remainder of the month. He'd left without saying goodbye yesterday, and she hadn't seen him since. Town business could be keeping him away, but Allison had her doubts. He'd been upset with her. Maybe even a little angry, which in turn made her miserable. Memories of being in his arms warred with the sting of his ultimate rejection. She'd basically offered him her heart on a platter, and he'd walked away.

Initiating that kiss had been a mistake. Revealing her feelings had been a mistake. Because even if he'd met her declaration with one of his own, they couldn't be together, not when his relationship with Christ was unresolved. Building a life with someone who didn't share her faith would bring trials and heartache. After her reckless behavior, she wasn't sure how she was supposed to act around him.

Just after feeding the babies their midday meal of warm milk and oatmeal flavored with cinnamon—thankfully she knew enough to manage the simple food—a rap sounded on the front door. Hope and dread surged.

God, please give me strength, she prayed desperately.

Her hand shook as she turned the knob and eased the door open. Surprise followed on the heels of disappointment. Not Shane.

"Caroline? Good afternoon."

Beneath her cream hat adorned with ruby red flowers, Caroline's hair was perfectly coifed. Her cream cloak—an impractical choice given the elements but one she could obviously afford—skimmed the toes of her polished leather boots.

"I hope I'm not interrupting anything." She looked askance at the apron Allison had found in Mrs. Watts's hutch. She'd donned it to protect her dress from the twins' mess-making skills.

"Not at all." She stepped aside. "I'm afraid I haven't yet stocked the kitchen. There isn't any cocoa or tea, but I know how to fix coffee."

"No, thank you—" She stopped short on the threshold, her delicate gloved hand pressed against her chest. "What are those?"

Closing out the cold, Allison suppressed a chuckle. Caroline was staring in comical horror at Izzy and Charlie, who were confined in the crate seats Shane had crafted for them. They were close enough to the fireplace to benefit from its warmth, but out of reach of stray sparks. Izzy clutched her bear and bounced, big eyes fastened on Caroline. Charlie's own fingers were entertainment enough for him.

Smiling, she removed the apron and draped it on the chair back. "Caroline, meet Charlie and Izzy Blake, Fenton Blake's great-grandchildren."

Astounded, she couldn't seem to tear her gaze away. "Two of them? They look the same size."

"They're the same age. Twins." Feeling mischievous, she approached the babies. "Would you like to hold one?"

"No!" She snapped her jaw shut. "I mean, no, thank you." Her lips puckered. "Why do you have them?"

"Their mother passed away nearly a month ago."

"How terrible."

"Fenton had errands here in town. They're staying with me for a couple of days."

Bending to smooth Izzy's curls and wipe a stray eyelash from Charlie's cheek, Allison struggled with the thought of having to say goodbye. She'd grown used to their toothy smiles and eager morning greetings. Every time they clutched her neck and buried their faces in her hair, trusting her to meet their needs, her heart expanded with emotion. Before meeting Izzy and Charlie, she hadn't thought it possible to form an attachment so quickly. Now she knew differently. They'd take a little piece of her heart when they returned to their cove.

It was going to be impossible not to worry about them, to wonder how Fenton was faring. She hoped Shane would make good on his promise to send frequent visitors to check on the little family.

Shaking off the maudlin thoughts, she said, "Would you like to put your cloak and gloves over here?"

"I can't stay. I came to tell you that a group of us are meeting Friday afternoon to assemble the gift baskets, if you're interested."

"I'll plan to be there. Thank you for inviting me to join in."

Considering she was a short-term visitor, it really

was thoughtful of Caroline to include her. She sensed there was more to Caroline Turner than the privileged, rich-girl persona she projected to the town. Too bad Allison wouldn't be sticking around to discover whether or not she was right.

"You did say that you were involved in Norfolk's charitable activities." Her navy blue gaze returned to the twins. "I thought you might be bored. I see now that's not the case."

"Still, I'd like to participate."

"I'll count on you." Inclining her head, Caroline bid her goodbye and returned to the buggy and hired man waiting for her beneath the giant maple tree.

She watched her leave, her mind once again drifting to Shane. Would he continue to shun her? Would that be such a bad thing?

Allison touched the tip of her finger to the paper pinwheel and watched it flutter. Her tree was beautiful but incomplete. It needed more color and texture. Shane wasn't likely to fulfill his agreement to help her finish it. Not after that ill-timed kiss and his hostile reaction.

"Is this a good spot?"

Allison turned to watch Deputy Ben MacGregor balance on a chair and hold a sprig of mistletoe to the beam between the dining and living rooms. He'd dropped by in search of Shane with Fenton in tow, whom she was beginning to suspect had mischief up his sleeve. The older man had produced the mistletoe from his coat pocket and guilted the deputy into hanging it for him.

"A little to the left." Fenton stood in the dining room observing Ben.

"I wouldn't have pegged you as a romantic, Fenton,"

she said, coming around the sofa. The sofa where she'd kissed Sheriff Shane Timmons. Her skin flushed hot, then cold.

"I'm simply following tradition." He tried to look innocent and failed.

Allison pursed her lips. He'd made several pointed remarks about her and Shane at the cabin. If he thought he could push the two of them together, he was going to be sorely disappointed.

Footsteps on the porch alerted her to another arrival. "Busy place today."

The instant she opened the door, the breath squeezed out of her lungs. She drank in Shane's rugged features, caressing them with her gaze as her fingers itched to do.

"Allison." His azure gaze wary, he spoke into the awkward silence. "I'm looking for Ben."

Using the door for support, she stepped out of his way, giving him an unobstructed view of the room. He spotted Ben first, then the mistletoe in his hand. His expression turned icy.

"Hey, Shane." Ben greeted his boss with enthusiasm. "I need to talk to you."

Shane halted on the threshold, his hands fisted at his sides. Allison could feel waves of hostility coming off him. He obviously didn't like that Ben was here. But if he didn't want her for himself, why did he care who she spent time with?

"Best place to do that would be at the office," he snapped. "Why didn't you look for me there?"

Ben belatedly noted his ire. "Oh, I did," he said, his tone flat. "I looked in the livery, the barber shop and the mercantile. When I couldn't find you, I naturally thought you might be spending time with your visitor."

Shane's nostrils flared. The two men glared at each other until Fenton ducked past the chair supporting Ben and clapped his hands together. "What do you say, Sheriff? You wanna be the first one to try out this here mistletoe? Quinn was having a sale. I'm sure Allison wouldn't mind a peck from an old friend."

Allison heard Shane's sudden intake of air. Ben averted his face to hide a smile. Mortified, she wagged a finger at the older man. "I don't mind being caught under the mistletoe with you, Mr. Blake. These two will have to find their own volunteers."

"Aw, I'm too old for such shenanigans." He waved off her suggestion, but she could tell her words tickled him.

"Where's Izzy and Charlie?" Shane directed the question to Fenton, not sparing her a second glance.

"Upstairs asleep. Allison has them in a routine already."

"Glad to hear it."

Ben gave one tap of the hammer and stepped down off the chair. "There you go, Mr. Blake."

"Fenton, remember?"

"Yes, sir. Would you like a ride back to Shane's?"

"Nothing for me to do there. I'll go after supper."

Laying the hammer on the large table, Ben strode to fetch his hat. He held the battered Stetson against his chest and cupped Allison's upper arm. Trouble twinkled in his green eyes. "I look forward to seeing you again, Miss Allison. Next time I stop by, be prepared. It's been a long time since I've caught any lady beneath the mistletoe, let alone one as irresistible as you."

With a wink, he ambled past an annoyed-looking Shane to the porch. Fenton chuckled.

Mumbling a farewell, Shane pivoted and stalked out

behind his deputy. Allison hesitated in the open doorway and overheard them talking about new evidence of their drifter. She was still there when Shane walked around his horse to climb into the saddle. He hesitated. Over the animal's broad back, he looked straight at her. Ben was talking and gesturing as he mounted up, yet Shane's gaze remained trained on her. The look was charged with emotion.

Fenton stepped up beside her, and the connection was broken. Shane bent his head so that his hat's brim blocked his face. He swung his leg up and over, fit his boots into the stirrups and nudged the animal's flank with his heel.

"Now there goes a man who could use the love of a good woman."

She didn't have to ask which man he was referring to. "He's pretty satisfied with the life he has."

"Maybe you could persuade him to see things differently."

"Me?" she squeaked, whipping her head around.

Tiny lines creased the outer corners of his eyes. "I've got eyes and ears, missy."

"You can't make someone love you, Fenton," she whispered, sorrow invading every part of her.

Sympathy mingled with understanding on his wizened face. "So it's like that, is it?"

Blinking away tears, she lowered her gaze to the rug at her feet. "I'm afraid so."

He patted her shoulder much like a caring grandfather would do. Letty was fortunate to have had him in her life. Allison wished with all her soul that her father was here to hold her. He hadn't been one to press his advice on her, but he'd willingly given it if she'd asked.

"It's plain as day he cares about you."

"He feels a responsibility for me. That's all."

He opened his mouth to respond, but no sound came out. He paled and clutched his chest.

"Fenton?" Alarmed, Allison took hold of his arm. "What's wrong?"

"Need to sit," he wheezed, fumbling for the nearest chair.

She assisted him to the sofa. "Tell me what to do. Do you need water? Medicine?"

"My satchel." Hunched forward, he pointed to the corner behind the door.

Allison brought it to him and riffled through the contents until she found a bottle. "Is this what you need?"

At his nod, she shook out a tablet and gave it to him. "I'll get water."

Unnerved, she lifted silent prayers and hurried back to his side with a cup. His color still off, Fenton sipped the liquid and, when he'd had enough, sank against the cushions and closed his eyes.

"Should I get the doctor?"

"Already seen him."

"But—"

His lids fluttered open. "No need to fret. I'll be right as rain shortly."

She felt useless, not sure what to do and wishing Shane was there. "Does this happen often?"

"Twice since Letty passed. I thank the Lord I had my medicine close at hand."

"I can't imagine how you've coped this past month."

"Prayer sustained me."

Something about his wrinkled, age-spotted hands made her want to weep. He'd endured such heartache and hardship. She hated to think of him returning to his isolated cabin.

He opened his eyes. "I've been asking God to send help. Someone who'd love my great-grandbabies as much as I do."

The hopeful glint in his eyes astonished her. "Surely you're not thinking I'm that person. Don't get me wrong, I adore Izzy and Charlie. They're precious. But I'm unwed. And my home is in Virginia."

"I didn't give God a list of attributes." His wrinkles became more pronounced with his frown. "I hate to think of them living far from me, but in my position, I can't afford to be particular. If things were different, if I was in better health, I'd never give them up. Doc told me today that I can't go on like this much longer."

Rising from the sofa, she went to the window and stared unseeing at the bleak landscape, her mind whirling with possibilities. She had resources. Position. Influence. She had the wherewithal to provide a comfortable home for them and the means to hire a nanny to assist her. She'd require a cook, of course. The twins would soon move beyond basic oatmeal. She pictured a tasteful home in her brother's neighborhood with a spacious nursery stocked with furniture and toys. A substantial garden space would do nicely, as well.

Allison's primary desire was to have a family of her own. Could this be God's way of providing one for her?

"Besides," he said in a sly tone, "I doubt you'll remain unwed for long. If Shane won't step up, there's a certain deputy who's sweet on you."

She turned around. "I can't live here, Fenton. Not with Shane nearby..."

Gatlinburg's sheriff would not be pleased in the

slightest to have her underfoot. And it would be torture for her to live so close to him, to see him on a daily basis, wanting him yet knowing he was forever out of reach.

"And Ben MacGregor is a professional flirt. If I were to express an iota of serious intent, he'd run for the hills."

From upstairs, she heard the babies stirring, babbling to themselves in their sweet, singsong voices. The idea that they could be her children, that she could love and nurture them into adulthood, filled her with a rare, tentative happiness.

"Family is the most important thing to me," she said. "I've longed to be a mother since I was a young girl. My first instinct is to seize this opportunity, but I need time to think and pray. Their future is too important."

"I understand."

"Would you mind staying in town a couple of extra days?"

He sat up and nodded, his strength slowly returning. "I ain't gonna rush you on this. The idea is new to you, whereas I've been stewin' over it since the minute you and the sheriff showed up on my doorstep."

"Please don't mention this to Shane."

"And what do I tell him is the reason for us sticking around?"

"I'll explain everything to him." The decision to become the twins' guardian was hers alone to make, but experience told her Shane would have an opinion and would feel compelled to impose it on her. "First I need to figure out how."

Chapter Fifteen

He could hear the babies bawling almost as soon as he rode up. Trying the knob and finding it locked, he pounded on the door. "Allison?"

The sound intensified. A minute later, he came face-to-face with Allison, who looked as if she'd tussled with a wild boar and lost. Dark splotches marred her cream blouse and rose-colored skirt. A hank of hair had escaped its pins and fell directly over her left eyebrow and cheek. Although her features were taut with exhaustion, he recognized her expression of determination.

"Ben's not here."

"I'm not looking for my deputy."

The red-faced baby in her arms noticed his presence and immediately lunged toward him, taking both adults by surprise. Shane caught Charlie around the ribs and, his heart lurching with something wondrous, hugged him tight. The baby's fussing ceased as he burrowed closer.

He set the small basket he'd brought inside the doorway.

"What's wrong with him?" Shane said over the crying coming from the kitchen.

Shooting him an enigmatic look, she whirled and headed for the other room. "I haven't yet ascertained the problem. It's been a rough morning."

Shane closed the door and followed her. Maybe instead of dropping Fenton off at an old acquaintance's home for a visit, he should've brought him here. When he voiced those thoughts aloud, she dismissed them, saying he could use the break.

Making soothing noises to Izzy, who was in her makeshift high chair, Allison picked her up and swiped at the tear tracks. "Shh, my darling. It's going to be okay."

Izzy's brown eyes communicated her misery.

Charlie sniffled. Resting his cheek against Shane's chest, he began to suck his thumb. "Has he done that before?"

"Done what?" She tilted her head to try and dislodge the hair so she could see clearly. Izzy latched on to it and yanked. "Ouch."

Without thinking, Shane shifted closer and gently pried Izzy's fingers loose. "That hurts, sweetheart. Can't do that."

Suddenly he had two pairs of female eyes on him. Allison's fruity scent wound about him, erecting dangerous memories of their embrace. Memories he couldn't shake, no matter how long he avoided her.

Allison looped the stray lock behind her ear and averted her gaze.

"Has Charlie sucked his thumb before?"

She looked at the boy in surprise. "I haven't seen him do it, no. It could be a new behavior or something we missed in our brief time with them."

"What should we do?" he asked, intimidated by the

massive amount of information he didn't know about infants.

"None of George's kids sucked their thumbs. The youngest has a penchant for sucking on his lower lip, and there's nothing we can do to prevent him. We should ask Fenton if this is a new behavior."

"He's left you alone with them a lot."

Her chin lifted. "It may not look like it, but I'm faring okay. They slept most of the night through." Caressing Izzy's curls, she said, "It's possible they're cutting teeth, and their gums are hurting."

"I didn't mean to imply you're not up to the challenge. You're a capable caretaker. It's just that you've had the sole responsibility since we returned to town. This is your holiday, remember?"

The kids were quiet now that they were being held. "That's right. It is my holiday, and I can spend it any way I choose." She speared him with a searching look. "Why did you come by if not to look for Ben?"

"You've had a telegram and a letter from George." *And I needed to see you.* He'd missed her in the brief time he'd stayed away...a troubling development. He wasn't supposed to get used to having her around.

He managed to get both out of his coat pocket without upsetting Charlie.

Her face lit up. "Wonderful! What does the telegram say?"

"It's addressed to you."

She shifted Izzy so she could take them. Worrying her lip as she scanned the telegram's message, her fleeting smile put him at ease. "He's set to arrive next Monday."

"Plenty of time to take part in Christmas festivities."

George's arrival would provide the remedy for Shane's current problem. Allison would be occupied by her family. Shane would no longer be obligated to keep tabs on her. The anticipated relief didn't come.

Allison's expression grew guarded, one that didn't fit the woman he knew her to be. Anxiety punched him in the gut. Whatever was on her mind was serious.

"There's something you and my brother need to know. It will be easier if I deal with you one at a time."

"Tell me."

"Fenton has asked if I would assume legal guardianship of the twins, and I'm considering it."

"What?" Shane couldn't have heard right.

Charlie shifted in his arms, and he patted his back. He had the inane thought that he shouldn't be comfortable comforting a baby, shouldn't feel as if standing in a kitchen with Allison and a set of needy infants was commonplace.

"He had an episode." Her eyes churned with disquiet. "The third one since Letty died. It scared me, Shane. The doctor warned him that his health will continue to deteriorate if he continues as he has been. He doesn't wish to give them up, but he's a practical man."

Fenton hadn't mentioned the episode or Doc Owens's diagnosis. "I understand how you feel, but you can't agree because you feel sorry for them."

"I'm not sure you do understand. You don't want a family, Shane. I do. These children need a mother, and I am willing and able to provide for them."

"You sound as if you've already made up your mind."

Lowering her gaze, she planted a kiss on Izzy's head. "I know what I want. I'm trying to be sensible, however, and consider all the ramifications. This is one of the most important decisions of my life. It will affect more than just myself." Besides the challenge in her gaze, he detected a hint of vulnerability. "I don't expect you to approve. I simply thought you should know."

Using his foot to hook the nearest chair's leg, he scooted it from beneath the table and sank into it.

"If you agree to Fenton's request, there'll be no turning back. No changing your mind."

"I know."

Charlie was starting to get antsy. Shane sat him on his knee and bounced him. The baby gnawed on his fist, trying unsuccessfully to push the whole thing inside his mouth.

"What about Trevor?"

She frowned. "What about him?"

"Could this affect your chances with him?"

"As I said before, Trevor and I don't have an understanding. I haven't yet agreed to let him come courting. Besides, if he doesn't have it in his heart to love Izzy and Charlie, then I don't want him in my life."

Shane stared out the kitchen window at the pastel blue sky. Weak sunlight did little to dispel the frigid temperatures. The thought of Allison and the twins making a home with a stranger made him ill.

"So Trevor isn't an issue. What about George? Your brother isn't going to react well. He'll throttle us both."

"It's my decision. You have nothing to do with this."

"You're wrong," he snorted. "With him in Virginia, it was my responsibility to keep you out of trouble."

The second the words left his mouth, he realized his mistake. Allison wasn't one to lose her temper often, but when she did—better duck for cover. Her entire body went rigid. Red flags appeared in her cheeks, and her eyes had a wild look about them. The only thing saving him from flying dishes was the twins' presence.

"I am an adult," she bit out. "I am perfectly capable of *staying out of trouble* with no help from you, thank you very much."

"Allie, sweetheart—" He stopped as she became more incensed.

"Sweetheart?" Advancing, she stood over him, pinning him with a fierce glare. "How dare you call me that, Shane Timmons!"

He stopped bouncing Charlie. "It was a slip—"

"You returned my kiss. You're as attracted to me as I am to you. You'd be lying if you tried to deny it. But you've decided that bachelorhood is what you want. I'm not going to try and dissuade you from that course. I *respect* your decision. As a friend, you owe me the same courtesy."

He'd never seen her so upset. He captured her wrist. "I'm sorry. I worded that wrong."

Her eyes swam with tears. "I'm not your friend, though, am I? I tried a hundred different ways to be, and you rebuffed me at every turn. Meanwhile, my brother practically ignored you, and you decided he was worthy of your time. Is it because I cared? Would you have acted differently if I'd treated your arrival in my household with disdain?"

Hurt and confusion radiated off her. His heart beat out a painful rhythm. "You know my past is complicated. I never intended to hurt you—"

Izzy whimpered. The tense atmosphere in the room likely wasn't conducive to happy babies.

Wiggling free of his hold, she edged closer to the stove. "You should go."

Anything he said right now would be wrong. "Fine." Standing, he carried the baby into the living room and situated him in one of the seats on the rug. Charlie grunted his disagreement. He waved his arms at Shane.

"Be a good boy for Allison." Patting his blond head, Shane fetched the basket he'd brought. "This is for you."

Her brows collided. "What is it?"

"Popcorn. For the tree."

"I'll repay you—"

"Consider it a late welcome-to-town gift." Striding for the door, he hesitated with his hand on the knob. He turned in time to glimpse a single tear snake down her cheek. His insides churned with guilt. "I'll go because you asked me to, but just so you know—this conversation isn't over."

"He was aimin' to poison my cattle, Sheriff!" Vernon Oakley jabbed a finger toward the man standing behind Shane. "Arrest him!"

Eddie Buchanan spat in the dirt, calmer than his neighbor and lifelong adversary. "This is the last time I'm gonna say it—I ain't done nothin' of the sort. Ought to check your facts before you go accusin' a man."

Vernon's young son—Shane guessed him to be about ten—waited inside the barn entrance, his face screwed up like a prune. The boy knew something. He just wasn't talking.

Shane's visit to Allison's place that morning seemed like a lifetime ago. Once he'd returned to town, he'd been drawn into one fiasco after another. One couple refused to pay for their meal at the Plum Café. A trio of youths who'd been playing chase on Main Street had knocked over a stand of Christmas trees for sale. The elderly widow, Mrs. Carson, who lived on the edge of town and regularly lodged complaints, insisted a mountain lion had invaded her chicken coop and what was Shane planning to do about it? The list went on. He'd eaten lunch on the go, a meager hunk of ham wedged between two slices of bread, and he hadn't gotten around to a proper supper. He was hungry and cranky and ready for this day to see its end.

Vernon's boy scuffed the ground with his boot. Dirt streaked his lean cheeks. "Pa?"

"Not now," Vernon growled, his gaze never leaving Eddie's.

Shane's thoughts turned to Allison and the twins. What would Charlie be like at this age? Would he have a kind, caring man for a father? Someone who'd teach him right from wrong, teach him to hunt and fish and what it means to be a valuable citizen of the community? Or would he have a man who ignored him...or worse?

Standing between the arguing men, Shane was too distracted to see the fist flying through the air. The blow stunned him. The force of it knocked him to the ground. He lay there a few seconds, his right eye throbbing and a headache blossoming behind his temples, pondering how he could've wound up on the Oakleys' barn floor.

Above him, the neighbors' temporary silence exploded into accusations.

"Now look what you done!"

"It wouldn't have happened if you'd left my cows alone!"

The boy crouched in front of him. "You need some help, Sheriff?"

"I can manage."

Shane levered himself up. He could feel his temper straining to be unleashed. Not once in his career had he lost focus in the middle of a volatile situation. As he dusted dirt and straw from his pant legs, the two men eyed him with a mixture of awe and trepidation.

This account was going to travel through the mountains like a hound on the hunt. For the first time, he'd allowed his personal problems to interfere with his job. He had one Allison Ashworth to thank for that. His fingers balled into fists.

"Sheriff—"

"Stop talking," he growled. "I don't want to hear another word out of either of you." To Buchanan, he said, "Get on your horse, go home and don't come back."

"Yes, sir." Hands held up in surrender, he shuffled backward until he reached the entrance. Yanking the door open, he slipped into the darkness.

"You."

Vernon retreated a step at the threat in Shane's voice. "For the sake of your family, pretend the Buchanans are on holiday until after the new year. Understand?"

His lips pressing together, he jerked a short nod.

"If you have any problems, you come to me. You do not initiate contact with your neighbor on your own."

He nodded again.

Shane switched his attention to the boy. "You got something on your mind, son?"

With a quick glance at his pa, he said, "I saw something."

"When?"

"Earlier tonight."

Sensing his unease, Shane said, "You can tell me.

Your pa wants to know the truth of what happened, don't you, Vernon?"

Looking unhappy but resigned, Vernon waved for him to continue. "Tell the sheriff what you saw, Billy."

"I was in the smokehouse when I heard someone talking. It was a voice I didn't recognize, so I came out to see who was out there. I know it wasn't Mr. Buchanan."

Vernon made a noise.

"How can you be sure?" Shane said, trying not to bring his fingers up to the tender flesh surrounding his eye. It felt swollen and bruised.

"The trespasser was short. About the same size as me."

"Did you see his face?"

"No."

"Anything else you remember?"

Billy thought a minute. "Only that his voice wasn't deep and booming like Mr. Buchanan's."

Shane settled a hand on his shoulder. "You've been a big help, young man. Thank you."

A blush stole over his skin, and he ducked his head.

"Why don't you go on back to the house while I speak to your pa."

"Yes, sir."

With one last look at Vernon, Billy hustled out of the structure. Breath-stealing air crept inside at his departure, finding its way beneath Shane's collar. The tips of his ears stung. His exposed neck prickled. All he wanted at this point was a warm fire, a hot meal and solitude. A respite from thoughts of Allison would be welcome, as well.

"You swung the first punch," he told Vernon. "Assaulting a lawman is a serious offense. You're fortunate I'm not hauling you off to jail."

He visibly swallowed. "It was an accident, Sheriff. Honest."

"Next time, get the facts before tossing out accusations. Understand?"

Vernon looked as if he wanted to argue. In the end, he thought better of it. "Yeah. I understand."

"I've reason to believe we have a drifter or two in the area. Could be your trespasser was searching for a place to pass the night. Maybe helped himself to some of your food stores."

The farmer scowled. "I'll keep a lookout. Ain't no one gonna steal from Vernon Oakley and get away with it."

Shane remembered what it meant to be so hungry he could barely think straight. A man like Vernon wouldn't understand. Or maybe he simply didn't want to. Banishing the troublesome memories, he headed for the door.

"Let me know if you have any more trouble."

Outside in the tranquil night, he mounted his horse and, using the bright configuration of stars and half-moon above, searched the fields for signs of human activity. All he saw were the indistinct shapes of Vernon's cattle. Somewhere in the distant woods, a lone owl hooted.

Riding past the house, he spotted Billy on the porch, watching. Shane lifted a hand. Billy waved and slipped inside. Through the open door, he could see Billy's ma and young brothers gathering around him.

A sensation more painful than his sore eye invaded his chest. His hard-won acceptance of a solitary life was slipping away and the prospect of going home to an empty house made him want to weep.

God, are You listening? Do You care? Josh says You do. Your Scriptures say You do.

He left the homestead behind, and darkness closed in on him.

I believe in You, God, I just have a hard time accepting that You love me. I need to believe it. I can't abide this emptiness anymore.

The stillness of the mid-December night struck him as oppressive.

A verse he'd read recently in the book of John sprung to mind. *For God so loved the world that He gave His only begotten Son, and whosoever believeth in Him should not perish but have everlasting life.*

He pondered the verse the entire ride home. He had the cabin to himself tonight. Fenton had decided to bunk at his friend's house. Probably for the best. Shane would've been terrible company. Forgetting about his need for food, he settled at the table with his Bible—a long-ago and unused gift from David Ashworth—and opened the pages. As he read, he discovered that his friend had been right. If God loved the *whole* world, and Shane was part of it, who was he to think that he alone was beyond His reach?

Chapter Sixteen

Allison's heart was a house divided—joy and hope coexisting with sorrow and disappointment. On the one hand, the prospect of becoming a mother made her giddy with excitement. The more she considered and prayed over the matter, the more convinced she was that God had brought her to Gatlinburg for this very reason. However, the bright future dangling in front of her was tempered with the knowledge that the man she loved saw her as an inconvenience. A threat, actually, to his well-laid plans.

In the picturesque, white clapboard church, female voices mingled with children's laughter and echoed off the stained-glass windows. She worked at one of several makeshift tables, grateful to be in the company of other women and to have something productive to occupy her time.

"Have you heard about Shane's mishap?"

Caroline had stationed herself across the table and was folding knitted scarves of various colors and sizes to be placed in the gift baskets.

Allison's hands stilled in the process of tying ribbons

around sacks of candy. She felt the color drain from her face. "What happened?"

"He earned himself a beauty of a shiner." Leaning over, she cupped the side of her mouth with one hand, her deep sea-colored eyes dancing with curiosity. "Shane Timmons is known for his vigilance. Something has him preoccupied."

It was plain from Caroline's manner that she thought Allison was the reason for his preoccupation. "Is he all right otherwise?"

"My guess is his pride is smarting more than anything else."

Relief unfurled in her midsection. She glanced over to the pew where the O'Malley cousins' mothers, Mary and Alice, sat entertaining Izzy and Charlie.

Her determination to maintain emotional detachment during this visit had turned into a spectacular failure. Circumstances and proximity had conspired to shatter her intentions. Allison must accept that her and Shane's paths were never going to coincide. She desired home and family. He wanted nothing to do with those things.

"Here's our chance to find out the details of what happened." Caroline's too-loud whisper interrupted her musings.

She followed the blonde's line of sight to the rear alcove. Shane had entered a step ahead of his deputy. Both men wore dusters, neckerchiefs and buckskin gloves. Deadly-looking pistols glinted at their waists. They removed their hats at the same time. While Ben smiled and chatted with young women clustered nearby, Shane fluffed his blond-brown locks, his brooding gaze scanning the crowd.

Even from this distance, his injury was visible. His

entire eye socket was ringed in ugly purple. Allison longed to soothe his discomfort, but it wasn't her place.

Turning away before he spotted her, she resumed her task. Caroline commented on her reaction, of course, and Allison recalled that she was in a small town where gossip ran rampant. If she ignored him or acted out of the ordinary, the women would wonder about the cause.

Still, that didn't mean she had to rush over and greet him with a fake smile. Five minutes passed before his heavy tread resounded down the aisle in her direction. Her stomach clenched. *Pretend you're back in the Norfolk offices*, she told herself, *and you're faced with the unenviable task of firing someone.*

Schooling her features, she lifted her head and met his gaze. Unasked questions turned his eyes a murky hue. Or maybe it was the dimming of the room as, outside, clouds passed over the sun. The stained-glass pieces lost their brilliance.

"Afternoon, Caroline." He inclined his head. "Allison."

"Good afternoon, Sheriff," Caroline greeted with a catlike smile. "Are you and Ben here to take the first batch of deliveries?"

"Yes, ma'am."

He glanced at the babies. "How did the twins fare last night?"

"Fine." She forced her tone to remain light. Carefree. Let him think she was no longer affected by their heated exchange. "Thank you for asking."

His mouth turned down. Up close, his cheekbone looked red and slightly swollen. His eye was bloodshot, and the crescent of skin beneath the lower lid was yellow. It was extremely difficult not to stare, not to give in to the instinct to caress the ravaged skin.

He's not yours to nurture, she reminded herself.

His knuckles whitened about his hat's crown as the atmosphere between them grew thick.

Caroline intervened. "Would you mind taking Allison along with you? I'm sure she'd enjoy the experience."

Allison wanted to kick the conniving blonde beneath the table.

After some hesitation, he nodded. "It's not very exciting."

"I beg to differ, Sheriff. Our Virginia friend here is deeply involved in charitable work. I know she'll get a thrill seeing firsthand those families who benefit from our church members' generosity."

"Sorry." Allison shrugged. "I can't leave the twins."

"Don't worry about them." Caroline made a dismissive gesture and, coming around the table, physically manipulated Allison in Shane's direction. "They're in good hands with Mary and Alice."

Ben walked up, taking a position beside his boss. "Hello, Caroline."

"Ben."

"Allison, how are you?" He raked her with his sparkling gaze. "Might I say that outfit is most becoming on you? Before now, I never realized that the combination of blue and silver could put a man in mind of merry holidays."

The skin around Shane's eye began to twitch.

Caroline uttered a sound of disgust. "You need to lay off the honey, Deputy. There is such a thing as playing it up too sweet."

Ben lifted his hands in an innocent gesture. "I'm completely sincere."

Allison summoned a smile. "I appreciate the sentiment, Ben. Thank you."

Shane spoke up. "Caroline, will you point us to the baskets ready to be distributed?"

"Certainly."

While he and Ben loaded the baskets in the wagons outside, Allison spoke with Mary and Alice, who reassured her that they were happy to watch over Izzy and Charlie. Long before she was ready, Shane was handing her up into the wagon and settling onto the seat beside her. Since Ben was heading in the opposite direction, he strode to the other wagon.

Shane took the reins in hand. "Warm enough?"

"Yes, thanks." Like before, he'd rustled up a quilt from the rear. This time, he left it to her to wrap it about herself. "How many homes will we be visiting?"

"Ten."

Uncomfortable silence fell between them as he guided the team along the wooded lane leading away from town. She studied his profile. "Is it as painful as it looks?"

Beneath his brim, his expression remained unchanged. "I was wondering how long it would take for you to mention it. I won't lie. It smarts."

"What happened exactly?"

"Remember the neighbors with the long-standing feud?"

"The Buchanans and the…"

"Oakleys. I was trying to sort through an argument and wound up standing in the wrong spot."

Troubled, Allison observed the passing landscape.

Caroline's words had taken root, but putting voice to those questions wasn't something she was willing to do. If she was the reason he'd lost control of the situation, she didn't want to know.

Shane guided the wagon onto a narrow, overgrown path. The terrain was uneven, the mountain face jutting sharply above them. Naked trees clung to the rocky soil. A bushy-tailed squirrel darted across the path, reaching safety with seconds to spare. When they approached the dilapidated homestead, a woman peeked out a dirty window.

Allison chose to remain in the wagon. Some of the more reclusive families were wary of strangers.

After a quick exchange with the woman of the house—there was no sign of her husband—Shane returned and maneuvered the wagon around.

"Mrs. McGuire was very appreciative. I could tell she was curious about you." Shooting her a side glance, he said wryly, "Ben was right. You look like a Montgomery Ward catalog advertisement."

She touched the matching royal blue bonnet trimmed in silver ribbon. "I wear this every year around the holidays. I'm not so vain as to insist on wearing an outfit only once. I get plenty of use out of my wardrobe."

Spreading her hands on her lap, she studied the gloves she'd ordered on a whim. Crafted of heather-gray leather, they were overlaid with intricate black lace and adorned with a single silver button at her wrists. "I suppose these are a bit impractical."

He arched a brow. "You suppose?"

Enjoying this return to lighthearted banter, she launched into accounts of her life in Norfolk. She told him about the friendships she'd forged at her church. He wasn't surprised to hear that she was part of a singing group, remarking that her singing could be heard up and down the halls of Ashworth House on a regular basis.

Shane was an attentive listener. The conversation turned to her profession, and she found herself pouring out her frustrations. He had such a calm approach that he balanced out her more passionate nature. Why couldn't he see how good they were together?

Before she could grow morose, Shane's posture changed, his fingers curling about the reins.

"What is it?"

He pointed to the house that was fourth on their list. "Fire."

It was unfortunate that Allison had to see this aspect of his job. She was a strong woman, though, and he couldn't completely shield her from the harsh realities of life.

After a quick survey of the burned-out shell of what had once been a large, dogtrot-style cabin, he returned to the wagon. Allison had gotten out and was pacing along the length of it, her polished black boots flashing with each flare of her ruffled skirts.

"We have to return to town."

She halted, her troubled gaze sliding to what was left of the structure. "Were there victims?"

"I didn't see any evidence of any." That didn't mean he wouldn't.

The tension left her. "That's a relief. But where do you think the owners could be?"

"The man who lives here, Harold Douglas, is a widower in his late fifties. It's possible he's out of town."

In the woods, birds called to one another, some singing cheery tunes that struck him as out of place on this dreary winter day.

"How long ago did this happen?" she said.

"Can't say for sure. The ashes are cold." He'd found something strange in the barn. "There aren't any animals around."

Rubbing her gloved hands together, she cupped them and blew. "Someone would've had to have released them."

Gesturing to the wagon, he took hold of her elbow and assisted her up. "Could've been a neighbor, but it's unlikely that person wouldn't have ridden to town to alert us."

He settled beside her and ordered the horses into motion.

"Wouldn't the smoke have been visible in town?"

"Depends on the wind patterns. Whether or not it happened at night. When it rains at this elevation, sometimes thick mist cloaks the peaks."

"That's why they're called Smoky Mountains."

"Another fact from your research?"

"Yes. What happens now?"

"I'll gather a group of men to help me dismantle the debris. First, I'll need to comb through it for clues."

Her exclamation startled him. "Shane! Look!" Balancing herself against his shoulder, she leaned close. "There. In the trees. I saw something."

Pulling hard on the reins, he brought the wagon to a rumbling halt. The horses bobbed their heads. "What is it?"

"I don't know. I saw movement. Someone was watching us."

"Stay here."

"Be careful."

His pistol at the ready, he entered the winter-deadened forest, dry leaves crunching beneath his boots. He could be dealing with a curious trespasser or one with more sinister motives. At this point, there was no way to know if that fire had been an accident or set deliberately. Muscles bunched with tension, he kept his finger on the trigger as he repeatedly scanned his surroundings.

Somewhere off to his left, a twig snapped. He whirled. The sound of pattering feet met his ears, and he gave chase. The runner was quick. Agile. When he topped a rise, he caught a glimpse of his prey. Brown cap. Thin. Younger than he'd expected.

"Hey!" he yelled. "I just wanna talk."

The young man didn't slow, didn't look back.

Many minutes passed before Shane admitted defeat, bracing his arm against a tree trunk and panting hard. After one last inspection of the woods, he retraced his steps, on the lookout for anything the trespasser might've dropped in his haste.

He reached the lane where Allison waited and, as always happened when he looked at her, his heart kicked against his ribs. The destruction of Harold Douglas's home wasn't his only dilemma. The widower's whereabouts and the identity of the trespasser were problems, sure, but ones he had a chance at solving. As for the feelings Allison evoked in him, he wasn't sure there was a solution.

Chapter Seventeen

"I've made my decision."

Deep in her heart, Allison had known all along what her ultimate course would be. There would be obstacles, of course, and those who'd disapprove of her choice. None of that mattered.

Standing on the threshold, Fenton's weathered features became guarded. "Well, let's hear it."

Charlie bounced in her arms and babbled at his great-grandfather.

"I was just about to put them down for a nap," she said.

"I'll give you a hand."

Removing his hat and coat, he hooked them on pegs and readjusted his suspenders. Scooping Izzy into his arms, he followed Allison upstairs and helped change the babies' diapers and dress them in sleeping gowns. When the twins had quieted in their cradles, she and Fenton went to the kitchen.

She heated the water, and Fenton pulled a golden canister from the shelf. "Would you like tea?"

"Yes, thank you."

Once the sugar and milk were on the table, they sat across from each other.

Allison set her spoon aside and smiled, aware that this moment was a huge turning point in her life. "My answer is yes. There's nothing I'd like more than to be Izzy and Charlie's mother."

His wariness melted, and his gray eyes glistened with moisture. "I hoped you'd agree. I had a feeling you would. The way you've taken to those babies…" Blinking fast, he peered down into his mug and seemed to struggle with his emotion.

Overwhelmed, Allison battled her own tears. Fenton adored his great-grandchildren. While this was a moment of celebration for her, it was one of unbearable sadness for him.

"I know Virginia sounds far away, but it's not a terrible distance." She covered his hand with hers. "I'd like for you to come and visit as often as you're able. I'd arrange for comfortable travel for you. You could even spend the winters there if you're so inclined."

He shook his head sadly. "I ain't never been out of these mountains."

"I think you'd like Norfolk. It's a beautiful place. There's the Elizabeth River or the Chesapeake Bay for fishing. Beaches to explore. Woods for hunting. Izzy and Charlie will be exposed to museums and musicals, plays and festivals. They'll have my niece and nephews for playmates."

"Sounds nice." His brows pulled together. "I'll give it some thought."

"And of course we'll visit you, too. We'll make multiple trips," she promised, wondering how she would cope with being forced to see Shane again and again.

No matter. She'd do anything to ease the pain of this separation.

"There is one thing you have to do before you leave."

A tiny arrow of unease winged through her.

"I want you to go out to the Whitakers' place and get their consent. You can take the sheriff as a witness."

"I thought they already made their stance clear. They didn't want to claim them."

"That's what they said a couple of months ago."

"Then why?" Worry eclipsed her joy. What if they refused her simply out of meanness? What little she'd heard about their family wasn't good. They could destroy her dream before she got a chance to live it.

"I'm looking out for you, missy. Save you trouble down the road," he said. "Don't you wanna leave here with a clear conscience?"

"Yes. Of course."

But she couldn't help wondering if, by doing what Fenton suggested, she'd be making a terrible mistake.

Allison was nursing a cup of coffee and wishing she knew how to prepare biscuits and gravy when someone knocked on the kitchen door. A frisson of unease skated across her skin. The sun had yet to crest the mountaintops. Who'd be paying her a visit in the dark, early-morning hours?

Approaching the door, she pressed her ear to the wood. "Who's there?"

"Allie, it's me."

Shane? Opening the door, she shivered as cold air washed over her.

"Can we talk?" he said. His features were stamped with exhaustion, and the bruises around his eye were more mottled. At least the swelling in his cheek had receded.

She quickly admitted him, grateful she'd taken the time to dress and brush her hair.

"Has something happened? Is Fenton okay?"

"He's fine. He was still asleep when I left." Standing in the middle of the kitchen, he removed his hat and finger-combed his hair. "I'm sorry for flustering you. I probably should've waited to come, but I couldn't sleep and I wanted to share some news with you."

"About the fire? Did you find Mr. Douglas?"

Moving to the stove, she readied coffee for him and held it out. His gloved fingers brushed hers as he took it with a murmured thanks.

"No. We cleaned the burn site yesterday and there was no sign of him." He took a long sip. "The neighbors didn't have any helpful information except to say Douglas had had some family visiting a while back."

"And the person we saw in the woods?"

He shook his head. "No idea who it could've been." Pulling out a chair, he said, "Do you mind if we sit?"

Allison resumed her seat and wrapped her hands around her cup. Nervousness fluttered in her middle. He looked serious. There were tired lines on his face, but his azure gaze was bright.

"Do you remember the Bible your father gave to me?"

"He gave it to you for your sixteenth birthday."

"I've been reading it."

Astonished, Allison stammered, "Y-you have?"

He'd struggled with his faith ever since she'd known him. Through the years, whenever she'd thought of him—which had been a daily event, his presence was stamped on Ashworth House—she'd talked to God about him, asking for protection first and also for his heart to be open to the truth.

"I went to Josh's last night. We prayed. Well, I prayed. He guided me." A spurt of joy transformed his austere face. "I've finally accepted that God loves me. That Jesus died for me. For the first time in my life, I know what peace feels like. Peace about where I'm headed once I leave this world, that is."

That's it. That's what was different about him. He exuded a calmness, an inner confidence that had nothing to do with his abilities and everything to do with his understanding of God's affection.

"Oh, Shane. I'm so very happy to hear that." How desperately she wished to hug him! "My father would be dancing a jig right now."

Laughter rumbled deep in his chest. "I'm not sure I can see David doing that, but I reckon he'd be as pleased as punch." Shifting in his seat, he grew serious once more. "I always thought God had abandoned me, like my pa. Now I can see how He used David to change the direction of my life. He extended not only mercy and forgiveness, but unconditional love. I just wish I hadn't been so stubborn."

Allison dared to give his hand a quick squeeze. "You were young. You'd experienced hard things."

"What's funny is I still have problems. The difference is I know I'm not alone."

She offered up a silent prayer of thanksgiving. "This is the single most important decision a person can make. You don't know how long I've prayed for this. My brother, too."

He ducked his head. "That means a lot."

Her heart was light with Shane's news. Knowing what a private man he was made the fact that he'd shared such a personal decision with her that much more special.

"I'm really, really happy you told me."

"Even if I disrupted your morning?" He smiled.

"You didn't disrupt it. You made my entire day brighter."

His gaze grew more intense, and she averted hers. The longing to hold him took root. She got up and carried her cup to the dry sink, her back to him.

"I'm eager to share my news with George."

"He'll be thrilled."

The scrape of the chair against the floor was followed by his slow tread to her side. His fingers brushed her spine, and she jumped.

"I think you have news of your own to share."

Turning, she found him watching her with expectation. "Did Fenton say something to you?"

"He didn't have to."

She squared her shoulders. "You're right. I spoke with him yesterday."

"You're going to be the twins' mother." His expression revealed nothing of his thoughts.

"Yes."

"I can't say as I'm surprised."

"You don't approve."

His forehead creased. "I didn't say that."

Chest cramping with disappointment, she made to move past him.

"Allie." Blocking her retreat, he gripped her shoulders and waited until she lifted her gaze to speak. "You're the most nurturing person I've ever known.

You've got a heart made for loving. If anyone can give those children the home and security they need, it's you."

She bit down hard on her lip and commanded herself not to cry. He couldn't know how much his approval meant to her.

"You honestly think I'll make a good mother?"

His hands slid over the curve of her shoulders to her upper arms. "The best."

Between his announcement and her news, the room seemed charged with emotion. How she yearned to walk into his arms and remain there. But he didn't want that.

Stepping out of his hold, she hugged her midsection. For an instant, he looked bereft. Then he swung away, picked up his hat and went to the door.

"I'd better get to work. Thanks for the coffee."

She stayed on the opposite side of the room, wishing he could stay and hoping that didn't show on her face. "Have a good day, Shane."

Cold settled in his bones. Shane readjusted his neckerchief in an effort to cover as much exposed skin as possible. The mid-December night was lit only by a half-moon suspended in the inky sky. Every now and then, wisps of clouds passed in front of it. Positioned near the post office entrance, a dense cloak of shadows concealed him.

Come on, he silently bid the drifter. *Show yourself.*

Quinn had come to the jail that morning, having discovered more empty tins—peaches, cherries and the like—as well as a discarded container of chocolate creams in the alley between the livery and mercantile.

He and the other store owners were anxious to find the perpetrator.

Determined to catch the man and put an end to the filching, Shane had decided to take the first shift of surveillance. If the drifter didn't show tonight, he and Ben would take turns keeping watch until he was apprehended.

While his body remained motionless, his muscles begging for his soft mattress, his mind refused to rest. He replayed the scene in the Wattses' kitchen, returning again to Allison's reaction to his news. He dared not examine the reason she was the first person he'd wanted to tell. Or why he'd been so impatient to see her.

Allison was going to be a mother. Fenton's subdued, contemplative mood the day before had clued him in that something had changed. Shane felt sorry for the man. He'd had to say goodbye to everyone he'd ever loved. And while he was certain Allison would do everything she could to involve Fenton in the twins' lives, the fact remained that they would soon be living hundreds of miles away. Shane had to admit he'd miss them, too.

And Allie. You'll miss her most of all.

He gritted his teeth and attempted to lock the melancholy away. Allison's dream was coming true and he was determined to be happy for her.

With effort, he turned his thoughts to the Douglas mystery. Josh and Shane had combed through the ashes looking for clues. There wasn't any evidence pointing to an act of arson. It appeared the fire started in the kitchen. In addition to the cookstove, there'd been a small stone fireplace. Sparks could've hit a rug or discarded newspaper. The presence of a trespasser bothered Shane, though. In his perusal of his favorite law journal, he'd learned that sometimes a criminal returned to the scene to see for himself the destruction he'd wrought. The idea made his gut clench with distaste. No matter how long he did this job, he'd never grow accustomed to the evil some folks visited upon others.

The wind shifted, suffusing the air where he stood with the twang of pine and holly berry garlands wrapped about the posts and windows. Movement registered in his peripheral vision. Furtive movements like that of a frightened rabbit.

Shane focused on the alley between the mercantile and livery. The slight figure that crept onto the boardwalk and peered into the store windows was too small to be a full-grown man. Not bothering to unsheath his weapon, he strode silently across the deserted street. He was mere steps away from the boardwalk when the boy's head whipped up. A squeak shredded the night. He took off toward the livery. Smothering a groan, Shane gave chase.

He pursued him around the livery's far side and down toward the river. No doubt the kid aimed to lose him in the woods. Shane had too many unhappy business owners to let that happen.

He pushed himself faster and, snaking out a hand, managed to grab hold of the boy's collar.

"Gotcha."

"Let me go!"

He tried to wriggle out of his jacket in a bid for freedom. Shane clamped down on his shoulders—wincing at the evidence of thin bones beneath—and held him in place.

"Listen to me," he barked, using his firm, don't-mess-with-the-sheriff voice. "I'm not going to hurt you, but you have to cooperate. Understand?"

"Why should I believe you?" he scoffed.

"Because I'm the sheriff. It's my job to see to it that everyone in this town obeys the law, including myself."

"You ain't takin' me to jail?"

In the absence of light, Shane couldn't decide if this was the same kid he'd chased out at the Douglas farm. Mixed in with the kid's anger over getting nabbed was a heavy dose of fear. Memories bombarded him, stirring a well of compassion. There was no telling what events had led him to stealing food and sleeping in a stable. Shane intended to find out before this night was over.

"My office is inside the jail, so in order to discuss this matter like men, we'll have to go there."

Keeping tight hold of his shoulder, Shane marched him inside the jailhouse and, closing the door, jabbed a finger at one of the chairs before his desk. "Sit."

The boy's eyes were mostly obscured by his cap. The rest of his face was coated with grime. Peeking from beneath his cap was straggly hair of an indiscriminate color. Instead of sitting down, he folded his arms over his chest and glared at the floor.

"What's your name, son?"

Shane winced again. He'd had the same exact question directed at him once upon a time. And just like this boy, he hadn't been inclined to answer.

Without really thinking about it, Shane offered up a prayer for assistance in sorting through this mystery. Despite the circumstances, he felt a glorious peace suffuse him. He wasn't working alone anymore.

Resting his weight on the desk's edge, he said, "Listen, I know you don't trust me. My name's Shane Timmons, by the way. I've been the sheriff here for a long while."

The boy scuffed his boot along the floor.

"I'd like to call you something other than 'boy.'"

His head jerked up, caramel-hued eyes flashing. "I'm not—" He clamped his lips together and fisted his hands.

"You're not what?"

"I'm not talkin' to you."

Shane tamped down a wave of frustration. "I can't help you if you won't at least tell me why you're out on the streets at this time of night."

He tried several times to get the boy to cooperate. When a loud rumble met his questions, Shane decided they could wait.

"Come on, then." Striding to the nearest cell, he held the barred door open and fished his key ring from his belt. "This here'll be your bedroom for the night."

His eyes got huge. Fear surged. "You're lockin' me up?"

"I don't trust you to wait here while I go fetch us some grub. This way I know you'll stay put."

He looked from Shane to the cell and back.

"The quicker you do as I say, the quicker we get to eat."

Swallowing hard, he shuffled inside. Turning the cell door lock was one of the hardest things Shane had ever done. Allison would wallop him good when she got wind of this. But what other choice did he have?

"Sit tight. I'll be back as soon as I can."

Hurrying home, Shane snagged the loaf of bread he'd bought yesterday, along with three boiled eggs, a jar of pickled okra and a cheese wedge. On his way out the door, his gaze fell on the tabletop pin game. The boy could use it to entertain himself if he couldn't sleep. When he reentered the jail, his unlikely prisoner was in the same exact spot he'd left him in.

There was no denying his deep suspicion as he peered at Shane.

"It's not a hot meal, but it'll do. Help yourself to as much as you want." Shane placed the basket on the cot beside him.

"Ain't got no money."

His throat grew thick. "It's free."

Leaving the cell door open, Shane busied himself sweeping the floor that didn't need to be swept and straightening desk drawers that didn't need straightening. He'd assumed their drifter was an adult man, perhaps someone who'd fallen on hard times, someone without family to take him in. Maybe even someone trying to avoid the law. Not once had he considered they were dealing with a youth. Judging by his leanness and disheveled appearance, he'd been fending for himself for a while.

Shane snuck a peek at the cell. The kid held an egg in one hand and a hunk of bread in the other and was stuffing large bites of both into his mouth as fast as he could.

Well, he'd caught his drifter. What was he supposed to do now?

Chapter Eighteen

"I need your help."

Allison struggled to mask her surprise. Standing in the entryway between the kitchen and dining room, she studied the pitiful figure sitting rigidly on the couch.

"*He's* your drifter?" she whispered.

Turning to look at Shane, she found him standing far too close. The doorframe pressed into the spot between her shoulder blades, and she had nowhere to go.

"Looks that way. I haven't gotten much information out of him." His liquid blue gaze soaked her in. "I thought you'd have a better chance of success."

Seated in his high chair, Charlie whacked it and started spouting gibberish. Izzy joined in. Shane's attention slid to them, and he smiled. If he could see his reflection right now, he'd be stunned. There was no denying the unabashed affection in his expression. Whether he admitted it or not, he cared about the babies.

Her babies. That bubbly feeling of joy overtook her again.

Tilting her head in the direction of the living room, she said, "Has he had breakfast?"

He nodded. "I fetched us both plates from the café."

"You left him unattended in your home?"

"I couldn't do that."

"Then where…" She gasped, drawing the boy's attention. Leaning closer, she hissed, "Shane Timmons, please tell me you didn't lock up that poor child!"

His hands settled on her shoulders, startling her. They were warm and heavy. "I didn't have a choice."

His mouth hovered close. A day's growth of beard darkened his jaw, and she had the urge to explore the short bristles.

Focus, Allison. "What exactly do you expect me to do?"

His fingers tightened a fraction before falling away. A sigh gusted out of him. "You're good with people, kids especially. See if you can pry anything out of him. A name would be a good start."

"I'll give it my best effort."

"Thank you, Allie."

"While I'm doing that, you have to finish feeding the twins."

A furrow appeared between his brows. She studied his profile as he took in the messy kitchen scene. He was so dear, his handsome face etched upon her mind and heart. Soon George and his brood would descend upon them, and these precious moments of privacy would be nothing but a memory. The days would fly past, Christmas would come and go and it would be time to leave Gatlinburg.

While she eagerly anticipated setting up her new life with the twins, the prospect of not seeing Shane on a regular basis made her ache. She wasn't sure how she was supposed to cope with going back to hearing snippets about him from her brother.

Settling in the chair between the siblings, he picked up a bowl of oatmeal and shot her a long-suffering look. "Go on, then."

Pinning on a smile, Allison went into the living room. "Hello there. My name's Allison Ashworth."

Arms crossed tightly about his middle, the boy shrugged. "Sheriff already tol' me."

His pants were about an inch too short and nearly worn through in the knees. The thin jacket wasn't at all appropriate for winter.

Her heart squeezed painfully at the evidence of neglect and dire need. "Shane's worried about you, you know. His job is to help people. He can't do that if you refuse to talk to him."

He shrugged again.

"It would be nice to know your name."

A long pause. "If I tell ya, can I leave?" Beneath the hat, caramel-colored eyes snuck a peek at her.

"Where would you go?" she said gently. "Do you have relatives close by?"

"No family." When he finally lifted his head, he seemed fascinated with her ruby earbobs and the locket about her neck. "The name's Mattie."

Ah, progress. "Nice to meet you, Mattie."

"Are you rich?"

She couldn't help it. She laughed out loud. "That's not considered a polite question, young man."

"Why not?"

"I'll explain another time." Watching as he scratched his head, she said, "How about we chat later? You'll feel much better once you've had a bath." Smell better, too.

Popping up from the cushion, he held his hands up. "No!"

His vehemence confused her. "I promise you'll have complete privacy."

"The thing is…" His panicked gaze cast about the room for a handy escape.

"What's bothering you, Mattie?"

"M-Mattie's just a nickname. M-my full name is Matilda Rose Douglas."

Allison's jaw sagged. Beneath all that grime and the bad haircut was a girl?

"How old are you?"

"Eleven."

Tall for her age, she was extremely thin. They'd have to do something about that, Allison decided, even if she had to personally see to it.

"Well, Miss Matilda Rose, the sheriff sure is in for a surprise, is he not?"

Allison was hiding something. A smile had played about her mouth as he'd brought in pails of water to be heated on the stove and remained there until she shooed him out of the kitchen and ordered him upstairs. He could hear their muted voices but couldn't make out the words. Light streamed through her bedroom windows and shifted into patterns on the polished wood boards. It felt as if he were invading her privacy. At Ashworth House, she'd invited him to explore the dizzying array of toys and curiosities in her childhood room, but he'd resisted. He hadn't wanted to be drawn into her world.

The baby in his arms batted his shoulder. Glancing into her big brown eyes, he said, "This time I didn't have another option, did I, Izzy?"

Allison hadn't been in town two full weeks and she'd already made this house, this town, her own.

Izzy pressed her lips together and blew. She batted his shoulder again and uttered a string of unintelligible sounds. Hiking her higher, he smoothed a stray blond curl from her soft brow.

"You're a sweetheart, you know that?" he murmured.

He'd miss all of her major achievements—crawling, walking, talking. He wouldn't be the recipient of her drawings, her hugs, her kisses. He wouldn't be the one toting her about on his shoulders, swinging her in a wide circle as she laughed, buying her china dolls and miniature tea sets.

Someone else would do all that. Someone like Trevor Langston.

Sadness gripped him. Jealousy, too. He was jealous of a man he'd never met.

Forgive me, Lord.

Allison would make a wonderful mother, of that he had not a single doubt. Nurturing came natural to her. Generous with her affection, she held enough love in her heart for a hundred orphans.

What about a lonely sheriff who ached for a family to call his own but was too scared to admit it? Could she love a man like that?

Shane ceased his route about the room. Where had those thoughts come from? Love had nothing to do with their relationship. At best, what they had was a tenuous friendship. That kiss wasn't his doing, after all. *She* kissed *him.* It was only natural that he'd responded.

Light footsteps along the hall brought him out of his troubled musings. Propped into a seated position on the rug at the foot of the bed, Charlie waved his bear around.

Allison appeared in the doorway, her smile anticipatory in nature. What was so amusing?

"Sheriff Timmons, I'd like for you to meet Matilda Rose Douglas."

At Allison's urging, the child stepped into the room. It took several moments for the name to register and for him to absorb the change in appearance.

"You're wearing a dress."

From the looks of it, a brand-new dress of evergreen, paisley material with rose ribbons, the same one Allison had purchased in town last week. She'd been collecting items to take to her friends in Norfolk. This particular gift had been intended for a close friend's daughter.

Allison touched the sleeve. "Isn't it beautiful?"

Hearing the warning in her tone, he grunted in agreement.

"Your name's Matilda?"

She stood straighter, her hands clasped tightly at her waist. "No one calls me that anymore."

Now that it was washed and combed, he could see that her hair was a honey-brown hue. Cut even with her earlobes, a matching ribbon had been wound about her head and tied beneath the strands. Now that her face was squeaky clean, he could see the feminine curve of her cheek, the girlish set to her mouth.

It hit him then that he'd locked up a little girl. His hold tightened on Izzy, who protested by squirming.

"How old are you?"

"Eleven."

His head dipped. A moment later, he felt Allison's

hand curving about his biceps. "Don't be so hard on yourself," she murmured. "You couldn't have known."

Transferring Izzy into Allison's arms, he scraped both hands down his face. His eyes felt gritty from lack of sleep. He'd tried to snooze in his hard desk chair last night, but the kid had tossed and turned and whimpered in the cell, making Shane wonder what nightmares were haunting him. *Her.* Matilda.

"That was you I was chasing through the woods, wasn't it? Are you kin to Harold Douglas?"

Her upper lip curled in a manner too old for her years. "I don't claim him."

He saw far too much of himself in her. "But you are related."

Her attention on the twins, she said, "He's my uncle. My ma died when we were livin' in North Carolina. Pa said his brother would be happy for us to stay with him for a while."

Her brow knitted, and Shane heard what she didn't say. Her father must've been wrong.

Retrieving the locket he'd been keeping on his person since discovering it in the livery, he held it on his open palm. "Is this yours?"

With a soft cry, she rushed and scooped it up, prying the sides open to stare at the tiny photograph. "Momma!" Her lower lip trembled. "I thought I'd lost this forever."

"I found it at the livery."

When she didn't volunteer information, Allison spoke. "Matilda, where is your father?"

"Dead."

He sought out Allison's gaze. Sympathy radiated from her. Like she had wanted to do for him all those years ago, no doubt her first instinct was to rush in and fix things. Only, some things couldn't be rushed.

"What happened?" he said quietly.

"He and Uncle Harold were cuttin' down a tree. It fell the wrong way."

"I'm sorry, Matilda."

She appeared to be weighing his words, probably trying to decide if he was trustworthy. He had many more questions he wanted answered, but he sensed it would be better not to overwhelm her.

"Do you still have that popcorn I bought?" he asked Allison.

Her brows rose in question. "I do."

"I don't have to be at the jail until later. Why don't I pop a batch? We can string some for the tree."

Allison studied him for long moments, that familiar pleat between her brows. "Good idea. Matilda, would you mind helping me string it?"

The girl looked dumbfounded. "Me?" She tugged at the stiff collar. "I ain't never done nothin' like that."

Allison's smile was gentle. "I'll show you how."

Hope brightened her eyes. Shane waited, breath suspended. Would she seize on to it? Or, like he had done, would she crush it?

"O-okay, I guess."

"Wonderful." Allison beamed. "Shane, I'll join you after I get these two down for a nap."

"You don't need a hand?"

"No, I'll be fine." Her manner portrayed confidence.

Ushering Matilda into the hall, he closed the bedroom door. "You ever tasted fresh-popped corn?"

She shook her head, her eyes full of mystery.

Descending the stairs, he said over his shoulder, "I'll make a big batch so that we'll have plenty to sample."

When they reached the kitchen, Matilda said, "Are you and Allison hitched?"

He had a tough time not gaping at her. "No." He held up his left hand to show the bare finger. "We've known each other a long time, that's all."

Of course, it was more complicated than he'd made it sound.

She adjusted and readjusted the ribbon headband. "Oh. So she's a widow."

"No." Shane tossed wood into the stove box. He was beginning to wish he was upstairs with the twins. At least they couldn't pepper him with questions he wasn't quite sure how to answer. "Allison is Charlie and Izzy's caretaker. Their mother recently passed."

Shadows passed over her face. He gathered the supplies and explained the steps to making popcorn. Matilda didn't speak. It was possible she was entertaining the same thoughts as him. The chief one being what was he going to do about her?

Chapter Nineteen

Funny how some wishes came true, only in a skewed way—not bad, necessarily, just different than one envisioned. As a girl, Allison had daydreamed about taking part in Christmas traditions with Shane. Caroling. Decorating cookies. Wrapping presents for the charity baskets.

Not once had she imagined a scene such as this one—a comfortable living room in a rented house with Shane instructing a mystery of a girl who it seemed had no one in the world to care for her. A girl whose haunted eyes and defiant attitude reminded Allison of the young boy her father had brought to live with them so many years ago.

Seated on the sofa stringing popcorn, Allison observed the pair from beneath lowered lashes. Matilda had started out with her. An attentive student, she'd followed Allison's instructions with surprising precision. But her focus had repeatedly slipped to the sheriff, who was tying strips of red, green and gold fabric to the branch tips. Matilda appeared to be simultaneously in awe of and intrigued by him. It hadn't taken much urging to get her to join him by the tree.

Allison was touched by his incredible patience with Matilda. Watching the tough, unflappable sheriff gently guide the wisp of a girl in a timeless tradition filled her with bittersweet longing. *You have the babies*, she scolded herself. *Isn't that enough? Must you want to add these two to your brood?*

Ordering herself to be satisfied with what God had granted her, she began to hum a familiar carol.

"A shame the Wattses don't have a piano." Shane smiled over at her.

She lowered the needle. "You never enjoyed my singing."

"Wrong." Tying the fabric into a bow on one of the high branches, he glanced over his uplifted arm. "I used to sit and listen to you for hours."

Crouched on the opposite side of the tree, Matilda stopped what she was doing, her manner watchful.

"I would've remembered that."

He planted his hands on his lean hips. "You wouldn't because I didn't allow you to see me."

Shock shimmered through her. "I don't believe you."

One dark brow arched, and his expression shouted a warning. "Why would I lie, Allison?"

She thought back to those afternoons in the music room where she'd practiced for hours on end. The idea that he'd witnessed every moment without her knowing made her angry. He'd led her to think he couldn't stand to breathe the same air as she. "Why would you spy on me?"

"I wasn't spying. Exactly." Conflicted emotions passed over his face. "I—"

"Stop!" Rushing beside the coffee table, Matilda flung her arms out wide. "Don't argue!"

Shane's arms dropped to his sides, and he took a half step forward. "There's no cause to be upset, Matilda. We're not arguing." His gaze punched Allison's. "We're…discussing the past."

Setting the nearly completed string aside, Allison rose. "There is a difference, sweetheart. Shane and I are friends, which means we sometimes have issues to work through."

Matilda shifted her weight from one foot to the other, obviously unsure if she should believe them.

"Remember I told you we've known each other a long time?" Shane said.

She nodded and slowly lowered her arms.

"We met when I was fourteen, and she was twelve."

Her eyes got round. "*I'm* almost twelve."

A lopsided smile curved his lips. "You see? Allie and I have known each other half our lives."

She grazed Matilda's sleeve with her fingers. "When you care about someone, you do everything possible to avoid hurting them."

Bowing her head, the girl fiddled with the locket around her neck. Fine strands of honey-hued hair whispered across her cheek.

Shane crouched in front of her. "How long ago did your pa die?"

"Sixty-two days. I've kept count in a ledger I found."

Allison's heart twisted with sympathy.

"And afterward, did you stay with your uncle?"

Matilda nodded.

He cleared his throat. "Did he hurt you?"

"He threatened to." Her small hands twisted in her skirt. "Mostly he yelled and threw things. He didn't ask to be saddled with his brother's kid, he said."

A vein in Shane's temple throbbed.

"I was happy when he left and didn't come back."

Shane exchanged a glance with Allison.

"When was that?" he said.

"About a month ago. He said he was ridin' over to Cades Cove to see to a business matter."

"How did the fire start, Matilda?"

"I didn't set it," she exclaimed, wrapping her thin arms about her middle. "Honest!"

"I wasn't implying you did. I'd just like to know what happened."

Allison listened as she haltingly recounted the events. It had been early, shortly after dawn, and she'd been in the barn milking cows, trying to carry on as if her uncle had never left. If he returned and found that she'd shirked her duties, he'd yell again and possibly make good his threats to punish her. When a stray dog happened by, she'd followed him into the fields and spent a good while making friends with him. By the time she returned, the cabin had been engulfed in flames. Frightened, she'd bolted into the woods.

Remembered terror turned her eyes dark. "I didn't know what to do."

Shane looked grim. "There was nothing you could do."

Allison could well imagine the girl's distress. After losing her father, her one trusted caregiver, she'd been in an unfamiliar town with a man who hadn't made her feel safe. Then to be left alone and homeless in the world…no wonder she hadn't approached any of the locals for help. She couldn't have known if she'd wind up in a worse situation than before.

"You like animals, huh?" Shane said, stroking the bristles along his jaw in a contemplative gesture.

Matilda didn't blink at the change in subject. "Cats are my favorite. I like dogs, too. And foxes."

"Do you like cows?"

She shrugged. "I like 'em more than chickens."

Hiding a smile, Allison wondered at the reason for his questions.

"They're much better than chickens," he agreed. "Did you make friends with any of the cows on the farms close to town?"

Understanding lit in her gaze. "You wanna know if it was me that boy saw that night, don't ya?"

"His name is Billy Oakley, and I think his pa, Vernon, would rest easier if he knew who'd been on his property."

She stared at the floor. "Will I get in trouble?"

"No, Matilda." His gaze locked with Allison's. "Allie and I want to help you."

"I was just passin' through. I didn't see any harm in pettin' them." Her features were strained. "Are you takin' me back to jail?"

"No. You're not going there again." He awkwardly patted her hand. "Unless it's to visit me, of course."

"Where will I go?" Her voice quivered.

Shane's gaze centered on Allison again and, at his unspoken question, she nodded.

"For tonight, you'll stay here with Miss Allison. We've got time to figure out what happens after that."

"Uncle Harold will thrash me if he comes back and sees his cabin's gone."

"Try not to worry, sweetheart," Allison said. "Shane and I will make sure you're safe. For now, we have a tree to finish decorating. The twins won't sleep for much longer. What do you say?"

The girl looked at both adults. "Okay."

They resumed their task. Allison attempted to lighten the mood by regaling Matilda with tales of her childhood escapades. Shane remained quiet. When they were satisfied every visible branch was properly adorned, he instructed the girl to remain in the living room and led Allison into the kitchen.

"What's on your mind, Sheriff?"

"Thanks for letting her stay."

He stood so close. Did he realize he was breaching her space?

"Of course. She's a sweet girl. I hate that she's had to endure such trials."

"I'm going to send out a search party. We need to locate Harold as quickly as possible."

"You're not going to make her go back to that monster, are you?"

"He's her guardian, Allie."

"A rotten one. It's your job to protect the innocent, remember?" Glaring, she tapped his badge.

His fingers closed over hers, warm and work-roughened, and despite her anger, she reacted to his touch as usual.

"I don't want her with him any more than you do."

"Then why would you let him have her?"

"I didn't say I was." His thumb grazed her knuckles. "Let's focus on locating him first. Then I'll work on finding Matilda a more suitable living situation."

Allison tugged on her hand. Shane let go and sunk his hands in his pockets.

"A word of advice. Don't go entertaining wild ideas."

She bristled. "What are you talking about?"

"I know how you think. I'd guess you're already furnishing a bedroom for her in your future home."

He was wrong. "*If* that were true, why would you care?"

"Taking on six-month-old twins by yourself is one thing. Add a confused, hurting girl like Matilda, and you'd be in over your head."

"Your confidence is reassuring," she sniped, stung by his utter lack of faith in her decision-making skills and potential as a mother. She wasn't rash. She'd just met the girl.

"Sometimes, Allie, I want to…" Huffing out his exasperation, he thrust his fingers in his hair.

Jamming her fists into her hips, she jerked up her chin. "Spit it out, Sheriff. You want to what?"

Shane erased the distance between them. Her heart stuttered. One of his hands found a home in the curve of her neck, fingers splayed wide, thumb pressing her jaw upward. The other settled heavily on her shoulder. His heat registered through her blouse.

His dear face was inches from hers, his eyes a blazing inferno, his uneven breathing loud in the room.

"You should think about what you're doing, Shane Timmons."

Allison wanted his kiss with a physical ache, but she'd tasted its destruction once already and wasn't prepared to do so again.

He didn't respond. Didn't move. He appeared locked in an internal war.

She reached up and covered his hand with her own. Her lids slid shut. Drawing on the pain of past rejection, she curled her fingers beneath his and tugged them down.

"*This* isn't what you truly want." The words scraped at her throat like razor blades.

Allison opened her eyes in time to see him bow his head in defeat. Moving away before her willpower crumbled and she threw herself into his arms, she was at the dining room entrance when his gruff voice stopped her.

"I'm staying here tonight."

She whirled. It hurt to look at him. "What? No."

His jaw worked. "Fenton can sleep in one of the spare rooms upstairs. I'll sleep on the couch."

"No."

"Yes."

"Why?"

"Because I remember what it feels like to be alone, scared and at the mercy of others. I don't trust her not to run."

Sleep refused to come. His body begged for rest, but his mind wouldn't succumb. The fact that his legs were about six inches too long for the sofa didn't help matters. Instead of lying on his back as he was accustomed, he had to lie on his side, his legs curled into the cushions. Add to that the knowledge that Allison was at the top of the stairs, and he didn't stand a chance.

What had he been thinking? He couldn't explain what had overcome him, couldn't fathom what it was that always flared between them like a lit match to a pile of hay. One minute he'd been worried for her, concerned her big, malleable heart was leading her into trouble, and the next his mind had been empty save for the need to hold her.

He couldn't wait for George to arrive. George would bring with him distraction and a hefty dose of common sense. No way would Shane be tempted to act like a sixteen-year-old boy with Allison's older brother around. Of course, his presence meant the end of their relative privacy. Her company was going to be in high demand, what with her sister-in-law and niece and nephews added to an already full house.

Above him, a floorboard creaked. Faint whimpering followed. Shane pushed the quilt aside and sat up. He couldn't distinguish which room the sound was coming from. A doorknob clicked. The mournful sobs grew more distinct. *Charlie.* He'd gotten fussy after supper. Allison's soft shushing and murmurs reached him as she padded up and down the long upstairs hallway.

Without giving his decision too much thought, he snapped his suspenders into place and climbed the stairs. The treads beneath his stocking feet were cold. He gripped the smooth banister near the top and stepped into the darkness.

"Allie?"

Her stride faltered. "I thought you'd be snoring by now," she whispered.

"Unfortunately, no. What's the matter?"

"He feels warm to the touch. I think he's cutting a tooth."

The prospect of a fever sent rivulets of apprehension through him. "I'll fetch a lamp."

He went to the kitchen and lit one. By the time he returned, she'd resumed her circuitous trek, the baby snuggled to her chest. Her hair formed a straight curtain of pale gold down to the middle of her back. She'd donned a Christmas-red housecoat, complete with white ruffles at the collar, wrists and hem. She looked like a Christmas package.

His attention transferred to the baby. Until this moment, he hadn't taken note of how the twins' hair color matched hers. No one would think to question their parentage. They'd assume they were her natural children.

"Fevers are dangerous," he said, setting the lamp beside the wall. "Should I fetch the doc?"

The flickering light reflected in her large green eyes. "George's kids developed slight fevers when they were teething. It's nothing to be too concerned over."

The need to hold the boy overtook him. He held out his arms. "Let me."

The baby came to him without complaint, his pudgy fingers fisting in Shane's collar. Charlie's fine hair tickled his cheek. Shane began to walk along the hall, passing Fenton's closed door first and then Matilda's. Was she comfortable in the warm bed? Or was she wide awake, alert to her unfamiliar surroundings?

Allison leaned against the railing, crossed her arms and silently watched his progression.

After a couple of turns, he worked up the nerve to speak what was on his mind. "I apologize for earlier. I jumped to conclusions. Despite evidence to the contrary, I do trust your judgment."

Her expression was unreadable. "Apology accepted."

He continued walking, and Charlie drooled on his shirt. When he came near again, she murmured, "What are her options? If Harold consents to give her up, I mean."

Moving beside her, he spoke in hushed tones so as not to be overheard if the little girl was awake in her room. "Possibly find a local family to take her in."

The corners of her mouth turned down. "But not as a means to get free labor, right? You'd find a family who wants her to be an important part of their lives?

Maybe a couple who hasn't been able to have children on their own."

"I'll do my best."

Allison angled toward him. "I don't like the sound of that. I want you to promise me, Shane."

"I can't do that. Trust me, I will do everything in my power to find her a good home."

"Why don't you take her in?"

His chin met his chest. "*Me?* What do I know about adolescent girls?"

Preposterous. How could she suggest it?

"You can relate to her in a way few others can. You understand how she feels and what she requires to feel safe." Her gaze implored him to see things her way. "You can give her security, guidance and love—the kind of childhood you never had."

He shook his head, actively rejecting her reasoning. Failure loomed like a crouching mountain lion ready to pounce and devour him. He knew how to be a lawman: how to manage disputes, investigate arson and murders, track outlaws and effect daring rescues. Home life, family relationships, *love*…those weren't part of his language. Never had been.

Despair invaded him. "I'm not like you, Allison. I don't have what it takes to be a family man."

She opened her mouth to argue, so he handed a sleepy Charlie to her.

"There's no use trying to change me, Allie. You'll have to accept that some things are simply not meant to be."

Chapter Twenty

"George!" Allison squealed and threw her arms about his neck. His familiar shaving soap suffused her senses. She didn't care that Main Street was bustling with shoppers and holiday deliveries and that Shane was looking on, awaiting his turn to greet her brother. "I'm so happy you're here at last," she breathed into his itchy plaid scarf.

Laughing his hearty laugh, George pulled back, his expression slightly quizzical. "You act as if it's been a year since you've seen me."

"Believe me, it feels like an entire year has passed since I arrived."

He gave her an odd look.

Dressed in a bulky wool coat and smart gray bowler hat, he looked the same as always—his round, boyish face with lively bluish-gray eyes like their father's and thinning brown hair. Perhaps her great relief at seeing him had to do with the emotional ups and downs of the past weeks. He represented home and normalcy.

Shane chose that moment to step forward, gloved

hand outstretched and a welcoming smile on his face. "George Ashworth. It's been too long."

Allison edged out of their way. George gripped Shane's hand, pumped it several times and pulled him in for a brief hug. Around them, people stared and whispered on their walk along the boardwalk.

"I can't express how wonderful it is to see you, old friend." Glancing about at the festooned storefronts and the majestic mountain peaks towering over the town, he said, "You've chosen a right beautiful place to settle, I see."

"It is at that."

"What happened to your eye?"

"Got in the middle of an altercation between neighbors." He shrugged.

George gestured to Allison. "She give you any trouble?"

Shane's smile slipped. Not looking at her, he quipped, "No more than I expected."

George's thick brows crinkled. "What have you been up to, sister?"

Suddenly, explaining the huge life change she was about to undertake struck her as a daunting task. In her mind's playing out of events, George's reaction to her news had gone smoothly. Leaving the twins at home with Fenton had been a wise choice. It would give her time to sort through her speech and gather the courage to deliver it.

Instead of answering him, Allison peered around him at the stagecoach. "George, where's Clarissa and the children?"

He smoothed his mustache. "I'm afraid they aren't coming. George Jr. came down with a cough and fever earlier in the week. She didn't want to risk traveling with him."

Allison masked her disappointment. "Of course. I would've made the same decision."

He patted her arm. "I'm sorry, but I can't stay for Christmas. I'll be here through the week, and then I'll have to return home."

"Not staying for Christmas?"

"The kids would be devastated if I wasn't there to see them open their presents," he said.

She shifted her gaze to the narrow alleyway beside the post office, where a pair of young lads were petting a calico cat. "Yes, I know."

"Will you be returning with me?"

She sensed the immediate shift in Shane's posture, the intensity of his full focus on her. What did he want her answer to be? Was he ready to bid her goodbye? Or was there a small part of him that wished she'd stay?

"I'll have to give the matter some thought," she demurred.

One week. She wasn't prepared to leave that soon. She'd counted on attending the Christmas Eve pageant. And now with Matilda in their lives—the search party hadn't yet located Harold Douglas—she'd started planning a lavish Christmas morning breakfast complete with gifts for the orphaned girl. And what about Fenton? She'd developed a deep well of affection for the older man. Taking the twins away sooner than planned wouldn't be fair.

Then there was the one piece of unfinished business to tend to—paying the Whitakers a visit. She'd wrestled with Fenton's request, unsure if she should fulfill it. They'd already decided to cut Izzy and Charlie from their lives. What good would it do for her to revisit the issue?

Pushing the troubling thoughts from her mind, she linked arms with George as they followed Shane to the wagon. "I know what we'll do. We'll host a party. You'll have the opportunity to meet Shane's friends and a few of the acquaintances I've made."

George considered the idea. "What do you say, Shane?"

Stowing her brother's single trunk in the wagon bed, Shane turned, his breath creating a fog in the crisp air. "I say let Allison have her party. She usually gets whatever she sets her mind to, anyway."

Her brother looked at them both as if working out a puzzle. Uh-oh. While he didn't usually intrude into her personal affairs, she wasn't sure how he'd react if he knew what had transpired between her and Shane.

"Oh, don't mind him," she said airily. "He's playing the part of the grumpy lawman today."

Shane stalked past them both and climbed into the wagon, leaving George to assist her. Unfortunately, she wound up sandwiched between the two and, because of their size, there wasn't an inch of free space on the narrow seat.

Hands folded tightly in her lap, she remained silent as they caught up, talking over her as if she was invisible. Not that she truly minded. Her mind was a whirlwind of unrest. Between the torturous closeness of Shane— she registered his every movement, smushed as she was against his shoulder, thigh and knee—the worry over the Whitakers and imparting her news to George, she was anxious to the point of being nauseated.

George appreciated the beauty of the Wattses' homestead as much as she did. Seeing the farmhouse and surrounding fields and mountains through his eyes, Allison acknowledged how much she'd miss this place. She would've taken great pleasure in seeing spring transform the land. And later, summer yielding its bounty. Perhaps when she brought the twins to see Fenton, she could pay the Wattses a visit.

Guiding the team to a halt alongside the porch, Shane set the brake and quickly disembarked. He strode to the rear and, untethering his horse, secured the animal to the hitching post.

He'd been distant the past few days. When he wasn't out doing his job, he divided his time between Fenton and the children. A couple of times she'd caught him staring, but she hadn't been able to decipher his thoughts. And she wasn't inclined to ask. Not after his stinging rebuke.

Before ascending the steps, Allison informed George that there were some people inside she'd like him to meet. At his unspoken question, she said, "I'll explain everything later."

After introductions, Fenton greeted George with a toothy smile. "So you're Allison's brother. She's had nothing but high praise for you."

George shook his hand. "That's a relief." He chuckled. "Between living with me and working in the same building, she's bound to get tired of me."

Shane strode past them, George's trunk wedged on his shoulder as he carried it upstairs.

George spotted Matilda, who was seated on the rug between the twins. The girl had formed a quick bond with the twins and took great pride in helping Allison and Fenton with them.

"And who might this beautiful young lady be?" Walking over, he bent to her level.

Her honey-brown eyes were huge. Watchful. "I'm Matilda Rose Douglas."

"A pretty name to match its owner." He nodded sagely. "I have a little girl at home, but she's a lot younger than you." He switched his attention to the infants. "And who are these fine-looking babies? Your brother and sister?"

"No," she said solemnly. After giving their names, she said, "Miss Allison is their guardian."

George was silent a beat. Then, twisting slightly, he looked at her with a world of inquiry in his eyes. Allison twisted her fingers into knots. She felt like such a coward all of a sudden.

Fenton stepped forward. "Izzy and Charlie are my great-grandchildren. Their ma recently passed, and your sister has been helping me care for them."

"I see." His gaze promised this wasn't the end of the conversation.

Shane returned to the living room. Fenton pointed to the mistletoe not far from where he stood. "Still got all its berries, Sheriff. Something's wrong if you need an old man to remind you to take advantage of the moment."

Color climbed up his neck. "I don't need any reminders, thank you," he gritted.

George went over and clapped him on the back. "That's one thing I failed to ask you about. Are there any romantic prospects on the horizon? Perhaps some pretty mountain filly who's caught your eye?"

Allison's midsection tightened further. She backed

toward the door. "I—I believe I forgot something in the wagon. I'll return in a moment."

Sagging against the closed door, she relished the bracing air washing over her. The distant chatter of birds greeted her, as did the lowing of cattle. In Norfolk, she'd be greeted with the blowing of ships' horns, seagulls' crying and horses' hooves clattering against the cobblestones.

She descended the steps and wandered away from the house with no particular direction in mind. A quarter of an hour later, George found her in the barn.

"Allison? What are you doing out here?"

Stroking the horse's strong neck one last time, she faced him, silently offering up a request for divine strength. His stocky frame outlined by the entrance, he gave the small structure's interior a cursory inspection before returning his gaze to her.

"What are you hiding from, my dear?" he said.

"You."

"Excuse me?" He tugged on his earlobe. "I'm quite certain I must have clogged ears."

She took a deep breath. "A lot has happened since I arrived. Amazing, wondrous things. I couldn't have predicted any of it."

Serious now, he came closer. "You've piqued my curiosity. What sort of things?"

"I need for you to listen with an open mind."

"Go on."

"I always thought I'd get married young. I thought..." She pressed a hand to her throat as her voice grew scratchy. "I assumed by the time I reached thirty that I'd have four or five children and more on the way. As it turns out, I was wrong."

He tilted his head to the side as their father had done, which made her even more emotional. "There's time enough for children, Allison. You just have to give some poor fellow a chance at winning you."

"I don't need a husband in order to have children."

He let that sink in. "What Matilda said was true, then? About the twins?"

"It's not official, of course. I have to visit a lawyer when I return to Norfolk. However, Fenton has asked me to adopt them, and I agreed."

Allison held her breath as he paced the straw-covered ground. At one point, he removed his hat and smoothed his hand over his balding head.

"Aren't you going to say something?" she demanded.

Halting, he said, "I'm trying to figure out what Father's response would've been."

"Father took in Shane, didn't he? He taught us to act out the Bible's teachings. He said that authentic love was more than mere words, remember?"

"He was a widower when he took Shane in."

"Why is that important?"

"He'd experienced marriage and had decided he didn't wish to remarry. What if, by taking them in, your prospects become limited?"

"You sound like Shane. I didn't mention it, but I've been considering setting up my own residence for quite some time. Long before I came here."

"You're not happy at the estate? Have we done something?"

"No!" Going to him, she clutched his arms. "George, I've adored sharing a home with you and your family. Can't you understand how important it is to me to have one of my own?"

His eyes searched hers. "You'll be a fine mother to those kids." His voice was noticeably gruff.

With an exclamation of relief, she threw her arms around his neck and kissed his smooth cheek. "Thank you."

"For what?"

She released him. "For believing in me."

A throat cleared behind them, and Shane entered. "Sorry for interrupting. Fenton sent me to tell you he has potato soup and cornbread ready if either of you are hungry."

George patted his stomach. "I could eat. What about you, sis?"

"Not just yet." Her emotions were still running high.

When George started for the door, she hung back, intending to remain in the barn alone. She was surprised to hear Shane say he'd be along later. He'd been avoiding her for days. What could he possibly want?

Shane waited until he was sure George was gone. "You told him of your intentions?"

"I did."

Allison's wary expression reminded him of how folks who were distrustful of the law regarded him. He missed her shining eyes. Her bright smile. This was proof he hadn't a clue what he was doing when it came to relationships. He'd pushed her away again, like he had countless times in their youth, and it felt both familiar and wrong.

Having the siblings here together had unleashed memories of the past, memories he'd fought to keep contained, not only because they reminded him of the desperate-to-protect-himself boy he'd once been but because of all those times he'd hurt Allison. She'd been such a sweet, pure-hearted girl. Her only crime had been attempting to be his friend.

The expression she was wearing now took him back to those days, and he was amazed that David hadn't banished him for his bad behavior. The mere idea of anyone making Matilda sad, or Izzy or Charlie, made his blood boil.

He advanced and, instead of taking her hand like he was tempted to, turned to pet the horse. "He's not angry?"

"Not at all. He didn't say as much, but I know he has reservations."

"George loves you and wants nothing but good for you."

Shane paused in stroking the soft mane. *He* wanted Allison to be happy. In the deepest parts of him, he acknowledged that he'd do anything, sacrifice anything, to ensure her safety and well-being. That didn't mean he loved her, though. Did it?

He had no experience with love, so he questioned his ability to recognize it.

Behind him, her measured footsteps carried her toward the entrance. She was leaving already?

He quickly turned, relieved to see her resting her arms on the milk cow's stall. Presented with her profile, he soaked it in, gaze lingering on her pert nose and soft crimson lips. The Christmas-red, fur-lined half-cape matched the red-and-white ribbon choker about her neck. The creamy softness of her skin was imprinted on his memory.

"I'm blessed to have a brother like George. He's given me opportunities not available to many women.

When I expressed interest in working for the company, he could've laughed it off as a ridiculous notion. Instead, he taught me the various aspects of the business and suggested positions he thought might be a good fit." She angled her face in his direction. "He respects my judgment in our professional environment. I shouldn't be surprised then that he does so regarding my personal life."

"I'm happy for you, Allie."

Not crossing to her and taking her in his arms cost him.

"Are you truly?"

He straightened but kept a tight grip on the stall slats. That she'd question him on this cut deep. "I've given you the impression I don't care about you." He sucked in a ragged breath, his hold on the slats weakening along with his willpower. Words weren't his strong suit. "I'm sorry about that." He let go. Took three steps her direction. Never in his existence had he felt this intense pull to another person, this craving for connection. He'd gone his whole life without affection. Now he couldn't seem to get enough. "Despite what you might think, I want your dreams to become reality."

"Thank you for saying that."

"I mean every word."

She lifted her chin. "I haven't told George what happened between us, nor do I plan to."

"Are you hinting I should do the same?"

A dry laugh escaped her. "I'm confident you won't breathe a word to him. I'm telling you so you won't worry that I'm spilling secrets."

"I agree he doesn't need to know."

"Especially considering nothing will come of it."

Shane schooled his features. What if he wanted something to come of it?

Closing his eyes, he pinched the bridge of his nose. *No. You can't think like that.*

Think about what's best for Allison...and that's not you.

"I'm going inside," she said quietly.

"Good idea." Opening his eyes, he followed her through the double-wide door.

The sight of his deputy galloping along the lane put him on alert.

"Are you expecting Ben?" Allison shot him a sideways glance.

"No." He strode to intercept him. "What's happened?" he called.

"Tommy Marsh and his buddies were messing around and accidentally set the Christmas tree alight." Ben's jaw was set in hard lines as he reined in his horse. "Whole thing went up in flames. The churchyard's full of squalling kids and mamas bent on retribution."

Beside him, Allison gasped. "How horrible! And so close to Christmas."

Scowling, Ben shoved tangled auburn strands out of his eyes. "The townsfolk worked hard on the decorations. Wasn't an easy tree to set up, much less arrange all those ribbons and hand-painted ornaments on it."

Shane turned to Allison. "I've got to sort this out. Tell George I'll see him later?"

"Of course."

After instructing Ben to wait for him, Shane took her elbow and guided her toward the house. "Now that George is here, there's no need for me to occupy your sofa any longer."

While he'd missed his soft bed, he found it comforting to be near Allison and the kids. He could protect them. Not that they needed protecting. It just felt good to be close in case they did need him.

Her eyes churning with anxiety, she said, "I think the chances of Matilda running away have lessened, don't you? She's relaxed around the both of us. She treats Fenton like a stand-in grandfather, and she adores Izzy and Charlie."

Instead of reassuring him, her words caused uneasiness to settle between his ribs. A bond was quickly forming between Allison and Matilda. They were both bound to be hurt.

He wished the search party would send word of their findings.

"I agree. I think she feels safe here." On impulse, he pulled her close for a hug. As the scent of her wrapped around him, he reminded himself to keep it brief. And friend-like.

"What was that for?" she said, astounded.

"A thank-you for allowing her to stay longer and for making her feel welcome."

Not giving her a chance to respond, he hauled himself into the saddle and urged his horse into motion. When he reached Ben, the younger man was staring at him with open curiosity. Shane had forgotten all about the deputy's presence. That's how muddled Allison had him.

"Not a word, MacGregor," he warned. "Not one word."

Chapter Twenty-One

There were days when he gained great satisfaction from his job. This wasn't one of them.

The Christmas tree mishap had dampened the town's holiday spirit. When he'd reached the church, the crowd had immediately surrounded him five and six people deep on all sides. He hadn't even had room to dismount. They wanted Tommy and his friends to suffer for their carelessness.

The men were fit to be tied. He couldn't blame them. Chopping down a tree that large, dragging it here and then erecting it had amounted to several days' work. The women were outraged, not so much for themselves, but for the children. Their tearstained faces still remained in his mind.

Christmas was eleven days away.

Thankfully, Reverend Munroe and his wife had assumed the job of consoling the crowd. Jessica Parker, having heard the news, passed out free cookies to every single child there. Quinn and Nicole brought complimentary cups of apple cider. By the time it had been decided to put up a new tree, with Tommy and his friends charged with helping to make a new batch of decorations, the high emotions had waned and hope restored.

Shane tossed his pencil on his desk and rubbed his pounding forehead. He eyed the dark sky through the window and prayed for no more complaints that night.

A figure passed by.

"Keep walking," he muttered.

The knob twisted. He prayed for forbearance. *Please God, I'm not sure I can maintain a civil attitude. I'm exhausted from too many sleepless nights, and I haven't eaten since breakfast.*

When the door scraped open and Fenton walked in, Shane nudged his chair and stood up. "Fenton." Rounding the desk, he searched for signs of physical distress. "Is everything all right?"

His color looked good, and he didn't seem as exhausted as he had at the cabin. "Fine and dandy." He lifted a basket. "Allison was worried you hadn't had a chance to eat. She asked George to deliver this, but I volunteered to do it since I'm bunking with you once again."

Pleasure at her thoughtfulness filled him. Taking his burden, Shane placed it on the desk and began to unpack the contents. "I sure do appreciate you bringing it by," he said. "I was beginning to get as churlish as a bear coming out of hibernation."

Fenton chose a chair to ease his frame into. "Nice, ain't it? Having a beautiful woman worry over ya?"

Snagging a slice of cornbread, he bit off a hefty portion and chewed. "You can stop the matchmaking, old man."

His teeth flashed white against his sun-branded skin. "You don't have to be alone the whole of your life, ya know. You got a ready-made family ripe for the pickin'. Allison cares about you. She deserves a man who'll take good care of her."

Shane finished off the slice and folded his arms. "I'm not the right man for the job."

The truth hurt. Mere weeks ago, he'd been content with his lot. Now he yearned for a petite, blond-haired spitfire to be part of his life. Allison had unleashed hopes he had no means of fulfilling.

Fenton studied him with his perceptive gaze. "You'd keep her from making fool decisions, I know that."

Shane replaced the plate he had started to lift out. "What fool decisions?"

"She's intending on leaving Gatlinburg without squaring things with the Whitakers. I'd hate to see her heart broken if they found out afterward and decided to act out of spite."

His appetite vanished. Fenton had a point. The Whitakers might not claim the twins, but there was a chance they'd cry foul if they got wind someone else wanted them.

"I'll talk to her."

Fenton slapped his knee. "If she'll listen to anybody, it's you."

Long after the old man had gone, his parting words lingered. Why would Allison listen to him? Was his opinion that important to her?

Lost in thought on his way home, he didn't hear anyone approaching until the last moment. A big hand came down on his shoulder. Shane whirled and reached for his pistol.

"Hold on," the shadowed figure exclaimed. "It's me. Ben."

The tension left his body. "What were you thinking?" he demanded, annoyed with himself for having lost awareness of his surroundings. As a lawman, he was considered a target by some. He'd learned early to always be on guard.

"I called your name several times," Ben said with a hint of exasperation.

He eyed his deputy's scruffy appearance and dirt-streaked boots. "Did you just get back? Where are the others? More importantly, where's Douglas?"

"About twenty minutes ago. As for the rest of the search party, they're at the reverend's arranging for a coffin."

"Harold Douglas is dead?" While he'd briefly considered the possibility, he'd expected to find Douglas holed up with a friend, delaying his return to Gatlinburg and the responsibility of his niece's care.

"We found him about a mile outside of Cades Cove." Ben's breath formed white puffs in the frigid air. "Couldn't find any signs that he hadn't died of natural causes. Snow's on the ground. Could've been exposure. Or maybe his heart gave out."

"Thanks for taking charge of this."

His deputy's expression reflected surprise. "It's my job to help you. What will happen to the girl?"

"That's a very good question." One he didn't have the answer to.

Shane rode out to the Wattses' farm the following morning. Understandably, the news of her uncle's death didn't sadden Matilda. She was worried, however, that she was going to be shipped off to a foundling home. He'd assured both her and Allison that no arrangements would be made without her knowledge. Before he left, Allison reminded him of his promise to find the best home possible.

With her words ringing in his ears, he'd gone to the reverend for recommendations and then spent the day visiting those folks with potential. He'd dismissed a few outright. The ones he saw promise in went on his list of candidates. The weight of his decision rode heavy on his mind. Matilda's future depended on him, and he refused to rush the process. She deserved to be in a place she felt safe and cherished.

That evening, he was locking up the jail when Josh hailed him. "You busy?"

"Nope. Heading home. What's on your mind?"

"I heard about Harold Douglas."

"News like that doesn't take long to spread." He gestured to the lane. "Walk with me?"

"What will you do about his property?"

"Try to sell it. Any money we get will be kept in trust for Matilda."

"Maybe one of the neighbors will be interested."

"Maybe."

Josh's lantern light bounced along the uneven track. Around them, the forest gave the impression of being asleep. Stars winked above them. It was going to be a frigid night, likely below freezing. He hoped the Wattses' upstairs would remain warm enough. Infants were susceptible to illness. And Matilda was skin and bones. At the cabin, Shane tended the fire while Josh drifted around the room. "I thought Fenton was staying with you."

"He's been a bit of a nomad. Since George arrived,

he's been staying in one of the guest bedrooms. It's a sight more comfortable than this place."

"He's probably happy to spend time with the twins, considering."

Josh's initial surprise at Allison's decision had turned into support. More times than Shane could count, his friend had expressed his admiration for her, along with not-so-subtle hints.

"A shame she can't find a local man to settle down with," Josh said now. "Fenton wouldn't have to be separated from his great-grandchildren. If only I had another brother. Or a friend who isn't yet wed…"

A spark shot out and landed on Shane's wrist. Jerking, he rubbed at the sore spot. "Give it up, O'Malley," he growled.

Huffing an exaggerated sigh, he moved to stand beside the mantel. "You need some holiday cheer in here."

He turned to regard him, brows raised. "Have you ever known me to care about sentimental stuff?"

His blue gaze was searching. "I thought maybe this year would be different."

"It's been a long day. State your business so I can get to sleep."

No doubt sensing his impatience, Josh got serious. "I came to see if you've found a home for Matilda yet."

Shane removed his gloves and hat. "I've a few people in mind. Why?"

"Have you considered Megan and Lucian? They've got the space and the desire for lots of kids."

Crossing the room, he shucked his duster and hooked it on a peg. Josh's cousin Megan hadn't been able to have kids the natural way. She and her husband had adopted a little girl from New Orleans. They'd also taken in older siblings who'd needed a home. The couple treated those kids as if they were their own flesh and blood. Matilda would be loved.

For some unknown reason, he held back. "I'll think about it."

Josh observed him for several beats. He opened his mouth, then closed it again. He went to the door. "Sleep on it."

"Josh?"

"Yeah?"

"Thanks for thinking of her. It's just—" He kneaded the tight muscles along the ridge of his shoulder, his tired mind scrambling for the right words.

"You don't have to say anything." Josh smiled. "Get some rest, friend."

He exhaled. "Tell Kate and the kids hello for me."

"Done."

Josh slipped into the night. Shane watched his bobbing light until it was no longer visible. Allison's suggestion that he take in Matilda refused to leave him in peace. The idea was ludicrous. He was a bachelor with zero experience with kids. If that wasn't enough reason, his profession as town sheriff sealed it. He worked odd hours and dealt with sticky situations. There was no guarantee he'd make it home each night. He couldn't do that to a kid.

Seeking His heavenly Father's wisdom, he uttered a prayer for direction.

Matilda needs a home, Lord. I want her to have a good one. Please help me make the right decision.

"You're coming with me."

A disbelieving laugh burst out of Allison at Shane's

proclamation seconds after she opened her door. "Let's try this again, shall we? You knock. I greet you. You address me as you would a law abiding citizen."

In the face of her lightheartedness, Shane found himself grinning at her. "I suppose I could do that." He dipped his head and glanced at her through his eyelashes. "Miss Allison Ashworth, I'd like for you to come riding with me."

"Riding? In this cold?" She peered past him to the gray sky. "Are you aiming to get us stranded a second time?"

"It's not gonna snow."

Her green eyes twinkled with merriment. "Ah, so you fancy yourself a weather predictor now?"

"I'll saddle your horse for you."

Tugging her lower lip between her teeth, she pondered his request. They hadn't exactly been on the best of terms recently. No doubt she was suspicious of his motives.

She had a right to be.

Chatter punctuated with an occasional infant's shriek filtered out onto the porch. The living room was empty. Everyone was probably congregated in the kitchen. He would've liked to see the kids, but this errand was too important to delay.

"What? You don't trust George and Fenton to keep a proper eye on them?" Shifting his weight, he said, "Or are you not inclined to ride alongside a lawman?"

She waved a hand to indicate her skirt and blouse. "I'll go change into something warmer while you ready my horse."

Pivoting, he spoke over his shoulder. "Ten minutes, Allie."

Her annoyed huff was followed by the snap of the door in its frame. Before the day was out, he was going to be on the receiving end of far more than that. A pity he hadn't thought to bring a piece of cake along to sweeten her mood once it soured.

This is for her own good, he reminded himself.

They set out at a leisurely pace. She asked if he'd resolved the tree situation, and he asked after George and her day. If not for the hard knot of anxiety in the pit of his stomach, he might've enjoyed himself. Allison was good company. Intelligent, witty, observant. As they traversed the hilly terrain, he related the details of a particularly intriguing criminal case he'd read about. Listening attentively, she provided insights that hadn't occurred to him. He could discuss almost anything with her, which put her in elite company. There were less than a handful of people on this earth he could say that about.

Allison shifted in the saddle to inspect their surroundings. "This looks familiar. Where are we headed exactly?"

Shane met her gaze head-on. "The Whitakers' homestead."

He braced himself as first confusion crossed her face, then understanding and finally full-blown anger. Yanking on the reins, she urged her horse to a stop. Shane followed suit.

"I thought you wanted to spend time with me." Her forehead creased and mouth pulled into a frown. The real hurt he witnessed had him sliding to the ground.

He rested a hand on the saddle cantle. The other he curved around her wrist. "I did, Allie. I do."

"No, you wanted to trick me into doing something

I'm not prepared to do." She tried to wiggle free, but he held on.

"I'm sorry I hurt you. Please, hear me out."

Ceasing her struggling, she stared straight ahead, her lips a tight line and bright flags of color high in her cheeks.

He disliked upsetting her. He much preferred making her smile. "It'd be easier if we could talk face-to-face. If I release you, will you give me a chance to explain?" Instead of galloping off into parts unknown, he added silently.

"You can talk," she said stiffly. "Then I'm returning to the house. Where you go doesn't really matter."

He released her and stepped back, half expecting her to dig her heels into the horse's flank. Still not looking at him, she gracefully dismounted. She stood sideways to the way he was standing, her arms huddled about her midsection.

Clenching his fists, he battled the urge to wrap her in his arms. No question how that would go. He liked his nose the way it was currently situated on his face.

"I didn't tell you earlier because I knew you wouldn't budge from the house," he said quietly. "I thought… if I got you out here, you'd be more willing to listen."

"You manipulated me."

"You have a right to be angry. But I know how people like Gentry Whitaker and his clan operate. They're petty and closed-minded. They're miserable and want everyone around them to be, too."

"Then why risk it?" she demanded, glaring at him. "Why should I allow them to decide Izzy and Charlie's future? Fenton is their blood relative, too. He's been with them since their birth. The Whitakers have seen them once!"

"They'll find out. Sooner or later, one of them will come to town, and someone will take great pleasure in informing them that a well-to-do lady from Virginia has taken custody of their kin. Even though they've had nothing to do with the twins, they'll view it as an outsider getting one over on them," he said. "Besides, Fenton wants you to do this."

Allison buried her face in her hands. "What if they forbid me to take them? What then?" Her words were mumbled, but her desperation came through loud and clear.

Taking hold of her upper arms, he gently urged her toward him. "I'll hire a lawyer. We'll fight this together."

She lifted her head. Her misery struck him like a physical blow. After praying the whole night through for a positive outcome, Shane was pretty sure God was tired of hearing about this. He prayed again, anyway. *Please let the Whitakers do what's right by those babies.*

"I'm not family. They are."

"Think about it, sweetheart." He rubbed his hands lightly up and down the length of her arms. "As things stand now, a judge would look favorably on you. The Whitakers have proved their apathy. If you flee the state, then Clyde Whitaker will be portrayed as a wronged father desperate to have his children returned."

She took a shuddering breath and moved away, forcing him to drop his arms.

"The choice is yours," he said, wishing she'd let him comfort her. "We can ride back the way we came. Or we can continue on."

* * *

Shane was right.

Allison knew it deep down in her soul, where hurt and anger couldn't drown out sound reasoning. Trepidation wrapped its tentacles around her, suffocating the bright hope inside. *You have to fight it*, she silently scolded herself. *God put you in Izzy and Charlie's lives for a reason. He has a plan. It may not turn out to be the plan you want, but He knows what's best.*

Resuming her place on the horse's broad back, she urged him onward. Knowing Shane would follow, she didn't bother looking back.

Even though his intentions were good, she couldn't help but feel wounded by the fact he'd misled her. He hadn't wanted to simply *be* with her. Not like she yearned to be with him…every minute of every day.

Wake up, Allison. He's never going to want that.

She should be grateful he was willing to help her in this, especially since he hadn't initially approved of her plan. After half an hour of letting her take the lead, Shane edged his horse alongside hers. He pointed out a wisp of smoke curling through the crooked treetops.

"We're almost there."

Allison's tummy flipped on itself. Unable to speak, she nodded.

As they drew closer, she began to notice the discarded tools half-buried in dirt and leaves and rusted farm equipment that looked as if it hadn't been used in decades. The chicken coop was a mess of twisted wire. One good, stiff wind could topple the open stable. Was this family too destitute to do repairs? Or did they simply not take pride in their ownership?

They came around to the ramshackle cabin's front

side. Allison heard the click of a rifle. Beside her, Shane stiffened as a grizzly bear of a man loped off the porch, his gun leveled at them.

"What brings you all the way out here, Sheriff?" His upper lip curled in contempt.

"Afternoon, Gentry." Shane positioned his horse slightly in front of hers. "The lady and I have business to discuss with you and your son."

He flicked a careless glance her way. The flatness of his eyes sent cold dread through her.

"She ain't expectin', is she?"

His crude manner sparked her temper. How dare he insinuate such a thing!

Splayed against his thigh, Shane's fingers curled into a tight fist. Before she knew what was happening, he had his weapon drawn.

"Watch your mouth, Whitaker." His voice dripped with venom.

Allison shivered at this rare glimpse of Shane's ruthless side.

Inch by inch, Gentry lowered his rifle. "Last time a female came 'round here lookin' for Clyde, she claimed he'd ruined her."

"You're talking about Letitia Blake, I presume." Shane kept his pistol trained on the man. "She's the reason we're here."

Snorting, he scratched his nose. "She send you? I done told her and her grandpa that we don't want anything to do with those brats."

Allison found herself hoping Shane's finger would slip on the trigger. Hateful, hateful man.

"Letitia Blake is dead."

The news didn't evoke sorrow or regret. Gentry's

mouth twisted, but he remained silent. Did he possess a heart?

Taking his time holstering his pistol, Shane drawled, "Since the twins are without a mother, you don't mind if Miss Ashworth here takes them in permanently?"

Surprise registered on his face. His eyes narrowed as he took renewed interest in her. Allison returned his gaze and tried not to let her distaste show.

Spitting a stream of tobacco juice on the ground, he said, "Don't matter to me."

She blinked. It was that easy? He was willing to hand over his grandchildren to a total stranger?

Shane pulled a piece of paper from his duster pocket. "Mind putting that in writing?"

"Can't do that."

The tension radiating from Shane had his horse prancing to the side. Soothing the animal with a soft command, Shane leveled an impatient stare at Gentry. "Why not?"

"Clyde's the one who has the final say."

"And where is Clyde?"

"No idea." His crooked-tooth grin bore the stamp of meanness. "He took off over a week ago. But I'll be sure to tell him you stopped by when I see him."

Chapter Twenty-Two

"Telling you not to worry won't help, will it?"

Allison followed Shane out of the barn, her mood as bleak as the winter day. Somewhere along the way, she'd lost her holiday spirit. She'd let her problems eclipse the wonder of Christ's birth and the celebration of family and friends.

"You're worried, too," she responded, looking over at him. "I can see it."

His brows lifted. "A sheriff doesn't worry."

"Underneath that badge, Shane Timmons, you're human like the rest of us."

"Thought I was doing a good job of hiding it," he muttered, tugging his Stetson lower. "I haven't had much interaction with Clyde," he said. "Not knowing what to expect from him bothers me."

"Not knowing when he'll return bothers me."

They reached the back stoop and the door leading to the kitchen. Shane reached for the knob but didn't turn it. His deep blue gaze roamed her features. "Guess this means you aren't leaving with George."

"I have no choice but to stay, do I?"

His nearness made her head swim. She didn't have to touch him to know how the light scruff along his jaw would feel beneath her fingertips. They itched to explore the hard planes of his face and smooth texture of his beautiful mouth.

He visibly swallowed. Releasing the knob, he edged closer. "You still angry with me, Allie?"

"No."

"Not even a little?"

"Maybe a little," she conceded. "But I understand your reasons."

During the quiet trek home, her thoughts had turned to Shane's position in the community and the demands placed upon him. He regularly dealt with unsavory characters and challenging situations. When he wasn't risking his life to protect others, he was seeking to solve mysteries or having to restore peace after instances such as a torched Christmas tree.

Placing her hand on his chest, she said softly, "You spend so much of your time fixing other people's problems. Who do you turn to for help? Who listens when you need to talk?"

A furrow appeared between his brows. Undefinable emotion surged in his eyes. "You're the first person to ask me that."

"It upsets me to think of you shouldering your burdens alone."

He'd been alone for most of his life. He deserved companionship. More than that, he deserved to experience the give and take of a loving relationship. Allison would give anything to fulfill that role.

Having stuffed his gloves in his pocket while in the barn, he now lifted a bare hand to her cheek. The sensation of his warm, work-roughened hand gingerly scraping across her skin as he curved a stray tendril behind her ear sent a shiver of longing through her. If he tried to kiss her, she wouldn't have the strength to heed common sense.

"I have Josh and his brothers," he murmured.

"But they have wives and children. Haven't you ever wondered what it would be like to have that for yourself?"

His gaze lifted from her mouth to delve into hers. "Allie, I—"

The door swung open, startling them both. George stood there, his expression turning speculative as he took in Shane's proximity to her. "I thought I heard voices out here."

Pretending nothing was amiss, Allison walked past him into the house. "How is everything?"

George scooted closer to the stove to give Shane room to enter. "Izzy and Charlie are napping. Matilda and Fenton are in the living room playing their third round of checkers."

Untying her bonnet ribbons, she removed it and set it on a chair. "Did they eat their mashed potatoes?"

He nodded. "And guzzled their milk." To Shane, he said, "Did you enjoy your ride?"

Shane's hat landed on the tabletop. His blond-streaked hair bore the indentation of the hat. He ran his fingers through it. "It wasn't exactly a pleasure outing." He addressed Allison. "Do you want to explain or shall I?"

"Go ahead."

She listened as he relayed the events to George. When he had finished, George folded his arms over his chest and stroked his mustache in a contemplative gesture. "Sounds like a tricky business." He turned to her. "I'm assuming you're going to stay until it's resolved."

"You understand, don't you?"

"Of course. Stay as long as you have to. I'll situate things at the office."

Relief rushed through her. "Thank you, George."

Matilda entered the dining room and paused on the kitchen's threshold, her big brown eyes fastened on Shane.

He gifted her with a smile. "Hello, Matilda. Who won the game?"

She twisted her fingers together. "Me."

"Good job."

"I think Mr. Blake let me win," she said solemnly.

George made an excuse to slip away, leaving the three of them alone.

Shane pulled out a chair first for Allison, then for the girl. He waved her over. "You sure about that? He hasn't been inclined to let me win."

When they were all seated, Matilda traced invisible shapes on the polished wood. "You're an adult," she mumbled. "I'm just a kid."

"Did you enjoy playing with him?" Allison asked.

"Sure."

"Then that's all that matters." She smiled.

Shane nodded his agreement. "I have a little more time before I need to get back to the office. How about you and I play a game?"

"You don't really want to," she blurted, unhappiness etched onto her features. "You're just putting up with me because there's no one else to do it!"

Scraping her chair back, she raced for the door.

"Matilda!" Allison exclaimed, stunned at her outburst and uncertain how to make things better. She
started to rise.

Shane stopped her with a hand on her shoulder. "It's
okay. I'll talk to her."

"I'll accompany you if you want."

His chin was set at a determined angle. "Josh said
something not long ago that's beginning to make sense.
He said that God might've allowed me to go through
what I did so that I could help someone else."

The similarities between his childhood and hers were
clear. "Matilda," she said.

"Yep." He strode for the door. "Pray for me?"

"You have my prayers, Shane. Always."

He found her out at the fence line using a young
dogwood tree as her refuge. "Awful cold to be out here
without a coat."

She didn't acknowledge his presence. Her chin
dipped low, her short hair fanned over her nose and
cheeks. He hoped she wasn't crying. Slipping off his
duster, he draped it around her shoulders. The hem
dragged the ground.

"There. That should keep you warm. Just don't try
and walk in it."

Slowly, she lifted her head. In place of tears, he saw
apprehension and a hint of suspicion. The man who'd
had charge of her had placed that mistrust there.

"You haven't found anyone willing to take me in
yet, have you?"

"I'll be honest with you, Matilda. I've spoken to several couples, and two of them are excited to meet you."

Her jaw went slack.

"The Murrays are in their midfifties. Their kids have all married and moved out of the house, and they're open to the possibility of raising another." Stepping over to the snake-and-rail fence, he rested his hand on the highest post and gazed out at the green fields with brown patches where the grass had withered. "The Johnsons are in their early forties. They've always wanted children but haven't been blessed with any. I believe you'd be well-treated in either home."

Matilda didn't speak, probably trying to accept what she'd been so sure couldn't possibly be true.

"There's a third family, friends of mine actually, who have several adopted children. I haven't yet talked to them, but I'm planning on it. The thing is, this isn't a decision that should be rushed. I want the very best for you."

Holding the sides of his duster together, she shuffled closer. "Can I tell you a secret?"

"Shoot."

"I like living with Miss Allison and the babies. I always thought I'd like a younger brother or sister. With them, I could have both."

Shane closed his eyes for a brief moment. He'd expected this might happen. "Allison doesn't live here. Her home is in Virginia. When she leaves, she'll take Izzy and Charlie with her."

Her pointed chin jutted. "I don't mind. I'm sure I'd like it there." A hint of desperation stole into her eyes. "I can help Miss Allison. I'd do anything she asked."

"Matilda, it's not as easy or straightforward as you think. I—"

"She'd stay if you married her." She seized his hand,

stunning him into silence. "Then I could live with you, too."

His heart cracked down the middle. She couldn't know that the idea had crossed his mind. More than once. Risking his happiness, he could do...but theirs? Four people he cared deeply about? It wouldn't be right.

Shane searched his brain for an appropriate response and came up short. What could he say that wouldn't devastate her?

"Allison's life is in Virginia. Mine's here. I'm sorry, Matilda."

Blinking rapidly, she released his hand and, shrugging out of his duster, thrust it at him.

She pivoted and started marching across the yard.

"We'll figure this out," he called after her. But by then, she was running for the house, and he wasn't sure if she'd heard him.

"Are you enjoying the party?" Allison sidled up to George, who'd slipped away from a group of men near the bonfire and was heading for the house.

He smiled down at her, his mustache curving above his mouth. "It's a nice party. Thank you, sis."

They meandered to the corner closest to the kitchen stoop. Since the house wasn't spacious enough to hold everyone, guests drifted between the inside, close to the food and drink, and the rear yard, where a huge bonfire chased away the night's chill. On the other side of the fire, a group of fiddle and guitar players performed a lilting Christmas melody. Every once in a while, one of them would bring out a harmonica.

Closer to the barn, youngsters jumped rope and engaged in games of hide-and-seek. Most of the adults gathered in clusters to converse, mugs of apple cider or coffee aiding the fire in warming them.

"Gatlinburg has a strong sense of community, doesn't it?" he said. "And the townsfolk admire Shane. He's come so far since those early days. Father would be amazed at what he's accomplished."

"More importantly, he'd rejoice that Shane has finally accepted that God loves him."

Allison was thrilled to see the change in his way of thinking, to hear him speak of spiritual matters and pray with confidence.

Searching the crowd for what seemed the hundredth time, she said, "He's still not here."

"You know he's not all that interested in parties."

"He promised he'd come." The night was nearly half-over. She plucked at the wrists of her cranberry-colored dress.

"Maybe he got held up. His job keeps him busy, I'm sure."

"I hope he hasn't stumbled into trouble. You should hear some of the tales the O'Malleys related to me. He faces danger so often that I worry it's become commonplace. He can't ever truly let his guard down."

George turned to face her. The dancing flames cast flickering shadows over his round face. "You're still in love with him, aren't you?"

Allison gasped. "Why would you say such a thing?"

"You've been smitten since the moment you laid eyes on him. I suspected he was the reason you dodged interested suitors, but I wasn't entirely sure. That's why I insisted on you coming ahead without me. I thought spending time with him would cure you of your infatuation. I had hoped you'd return to Norfolk having put

Shane Timmons out of your head." He blew out a long breath. "I see now that I was wrong."

Her mouth worked but no sound came out. There was no use denying it.

"How does he feel about you?" George asked gently.

Chafing her arms, she shook her head and gazed at her boots. "I'm not sure. Whatever he feels isn't strong enough for him to take a chance on us." Despair invaded her. "Shane has no plans to marry."

George enveloped her in a hug. "I'm sorry, Allie," he murmured against her hair. "I truly am."

"It's not your fault." Willing away the tears, she wiggled free. She didn't want to arouse the others' curiosity. "I'll have to deal with my dashed hopes later. Right now, I have a party to host."

"Let's go inside and check on the children, shall we?"

"Last time I saw them, they were being entertained by Caleb's young sister-in-law, Amy, and Megan's daughter, Lillian."

The warmth inside welcomed them as laughter and a jumble of conversations carried through the house. Allison smiled at the people circled around the dining table. They had a lot to choose from among platters of meats, assorted vegetables, homemade breads and a variety of pies, cookies and cakes.

When she reached the doorway, Caroline noticed and waved from a spot near the fireplace. Sophisticated in a dress of midnight blue overlaid with silver netting, the blonde was in deep conversation with twin sisters Jessica Parker and Jane Leighton. Allison started to join them but was waylaid by a tap on her shoulder.

Turning around, she was surprised to see the handsome deputy. "Ben, I had no idea you'd arrived."

Did that mean Shane was here, too? Cutting off the questions before they could form on her lips, she pasted on what she hoped was a serene smile. "I'm glad you could make it. Have you eaten yet?"

"Not yet." Green eyes dancing, his wavy auburn locks tamed into submission, he grinned. "I apologize for arriving late. I have a demanding boss."

Behind her, the main door scraped open. Her skin prickled, and she knew without looking who had entered. Her pulse sped up. Would he come and speak to her right away? Would he avoid her? They hadn't been alone since that charged moment on the stoop. She'd replayed the moment in her mind many times, trying to guess what he'd been about to say.

Ben bent closer, mischief stamping his features. "Did you happen to notice where we're standing, Miss Allison?"

Her heart skipped a beat. The mistletoe. It had been up there for so long she'd forgotten about it. "Uh, I don't believe anyone expects us to observe tradition."

"What's the fun in that?" he exclaimed softly. "Besides, I can't ignore the chance to make the good sheriff squirm."

"Look!" a youthful voice rang out. "They're underneath the mistletoe."

"Don't just stand there, MacGregor. Kiss the woman!"

Male laughter assaulted her ears. Hot color flooded her cheeks. Ben kissing her in front of Shane was the worst of nightmares come true.

Well and truly caught, Allison froze as Ben lowered his head.

Chapter Twenty-Three

White-hot jealousy seared him. His vision clouded as his deputy took hold of Allison's hand and bent to kiss her.

I can't watch this.

Not caring who saw him leave or what significance they attached to it, he spun and pushed outside. Descending the steps, he strode for his horse waiting with others beneath a copse of trees farther down the lane.

"Shane."

"I've decided not to stay, George," he tossed over his shoulder, not slowing his pace.

The hasty footsteps behind him didn't falter. When he reached his mount, he pivoted. Dark shadows obscured his friend's features.

"That must've been the shortest attendance on record. Didn't take you long to decide you weren't having fun."

"Figured out I wasn't in the mood to socialize."

All he could picture was Ben's satisfied grin seconds before he swooped toward Allison. His gut churned with the need to march back inside and rip them apart.

George stroked the horse between his ears. "He didn't kiss her. Not a real kiss, anyway. It was more like a brotherly peck on the cheek."

Brotherly? Not likely.

Shane wished he could make out the other man's expression. It didn't signify, he supposed. George wasn't stupid. Even if he hadn't discovered them on the stoop, he knew his sister better than anyone.

"Allison's free to do as she pleases." Just not in front of him. It hurt too much.

"She's in love with you, you know."

Shane's heart squeezed into a painful mass. Scraping a weary hand over his jaw, he shook his head. "You're wrong."

"Then tell me why she lost her joy once you left town. Tell me why she's turned down suitor after suitor—good men who would've treasured her. Tell me why she was crushed each time I got a letter from you, and you didn't have a word to spare for her. Did you know that sometimes I find her revisiting your favorite spots in the house? The look on her face…" He trailed off.

"No. It can't be true." Shane took a few halting paces away. He could hardly breathe for all the waves of emotion pummeling him.

"Why not?" he said patiently. "You were able to accept that God, who knows you better than you know yourself, loves you. Why is it so impossible to believe my sister would?"

Whirling back, he sliced the air with his hand. "I don't deserve her! I wouldn't know the first thing about making her happy. I'd wind up disappointing her, and that would destroy the both of us." He slapped his fist into his opposite palm. "You should've warned her.

Should've insisted she accept another man's suit years ago."

"You think I could simply *command* her to stop caring about you?" he said, incredulous. "Love isn't something you control."

Oh, he didn't have to be told that. His love for Allison was so much a part of him there'd be no rooting it out. He wasn't sure where he ended and it began. Perhaps that's why it had taken him so long to recognize his feelings for what they were.

"I've been married a long while," he continued. "It's not about making the other person happy. It's about putting their needs above your own. It's a partnership. I love my wife in a romantic sense, but she's also my best friend. There's no one else I'd rather have at my side through good times and in bad."

What his friend described sounded perfect and exactly what he wished he could have with Allie.

Shane thrust his foot in the stirrup and, grabbing hold of the saddle horn, hauled himself up. "I need time."

George moved out of the way. "Think about what I said."

With a wave, he left the yard and entered the deserted lane. His thoughts a chaotic mess, he took his time getting home. The quiet cabin that had been his refuge until she arrived now struck him as forlorn. Desolate. Pitiful.

He could easily picture Allie in the cushioned chair, the babies in her lap. And Matilda sitting on the rug at her feet, playing with a doll.

Calling himself a fool for allowing such thoughts to taunt him, he removed his duster, suit coat and vest and went to the kitchen to fix himself coffee. He preferred peace and quiet, he reminded himself. He had enough trouble at work. What did he want with soiled nappies and milk bottles and drooling, teething babies, not to mention an eleven-year-old girl who'd soon be interested in boys?

Settling into the chair, he chose the periodical on top of the stack and tried to lose himself in his reading. An hour passed and he hadn't progressed beyond the first article. He was riffling listlessly through the pages when a rap on the door startled him. Fishing out his pocket watch, he frowned at the clock face. Visitors at this time of night meant there was trouble somewhere.

Please let it be anyone except Ben. Shane was pretty sure he wouldn't manage to be civil.

Tugging the door open as he was snapping his suspenders in place, he couldn't mask his surprise. "Allie. What are you doing here?"

"I came to see if you were all right."

Resplendent in a white-trimmed cranberry cloak that swirled around her fitted dress of the same hue, she was too beautiful for words. Her deep green eyes and ruby-red lips complemented her milky skin. Her blond hair was parted along one side and pulled into a thick, shining twist. George's words pounded inside his head. *She loves you.*

Shane searched her countenance, peered into her eyes for proof. How was he supposed to believe she loved him if she didn't tell him herself?

What good would come of it, anyway?

She took in his informal attire and stocking feet. "I know it's late. I would've come earlier but I had to wait until the guests left and Izzy and Charlie were asleep."

A tentative smile graced her mouth. "They won't allow anyone else besides me to put them in bed now."

He glanced past her to the lone horse. "You shouldn't be out alone at night."

"George accompanied me as far as Main Street. He's waiting for me at the jail."

"With Ben?"

Her features tensed. "Are you going to invite me in, Shane?"

Gesturing for her to enter, he leaned against the closed door as she stopped in the middle of the room and completed a slow circle. This wasn't the first time she'd been here, but a lot had happened since that initial visit. The lateness of the hour created a sense of seclusion, as if the entire town slumbered and only he and Allison were awake.

"Why did you really come, Allie? Your brother could've told you I simply decided not to stick around."

Lowering her hood, she tugged off her gloves and stuffed them into her cloak pocket. "I know the reason you didn't stay. I wanted to be certain you weren't planning to punish Ben in some awful way."

The sight of them together flashed in his mind, and the ire he hadn't managed to fully quell built to a new high. Deliberately shoving his hands deep in his pockets, he prowled to where she was standing. She lifted her chin, fully meeting his gaze.

"You're worried about my deputy, are you?" His voice was deceptively soft.

"We *were* standing beneath the mistletoe," she pointed out. Her nonchalant manner grated.

"He didn't have to enjoy himself quite so much," he

gritted, aware such sentiment was more suited to an adolescent than a full-grown man.

She lifted a single eyebrow. "He was trying to get a rise out of you. Looks like he succeeded."

"Like I told your brother, you're free to kiss anyone you please."

"You don't mean that."

Shane's pulse skittered, sped up. "In fact, I do."

"Be honest, Shane. You left because you wanted to be the one beneath that mistletoe with me."

She was right and wrong. He did want to be there with her...just not with an audience. The fact that they were completely alone right now, with no chance of interruption by Fenton or an inquisitive young girl, tested Shane's determination to avoid hurting her further. All he had to do was lower his head a couple of inches...

The blood rushed in his ears. Surely she could hear his heart whacking against his chest cavity. He slipped his hands free of his pockets. So close.

She licked her lips, lending them a high shine. He swallowed a groan.

Remember what's best for her, Timmons. Can you afford to throw common sense out the window?

Shane gathered the willpower slipping away and, turning his back to her, stalked to the door.

"Go home, Allie." He jerked the door open and, not looking at her, sucked in the biting air. "George has two days left. Go Christmas shopping. Wrap presents and drink hot cocoa. Forget about the upheaval of the past few weeks, if only for a little while."

She didn't move at first. Just when his self-control was starting to splinter into tiny pieces, she barreled past him into the moonlit night. Once in the saddle, her face hidden by the cloak's hood, she said, "You're welcome to see George off on Monday, but I'd appreciate it if you'd keep your visits to the Wattses' at a minimum. Official business only."

Shane stepped off the stoop. "Allie—"

Her horse leaped into motion, leaving him alone with a heap of regrets and low-burning resentment for the parents who'd bequeathed him this legacy.

"Have a safe trip." Allison hugged him even more tightly than she had one week ago.

"Keep us informed of your plans," George said against the scarf wound about her neck. "Clarissa and I will be praying morning, noon and night."

Releasing him, she smiled at the phrase her father had often said.

His brows pulled together. "Have you found alternate lodging in case your stay extends past the new year?"

She prayed that wouldn't happen. "One option is to stay with Megan and Lucian Beaumont. Or rent a place in town."

Out of the corner of her eye, she noted the tall, commanding figure striding their way. Clutching her brother's arm, she pecked his cheek and lifted her skirts. "I'll see you soon. Give Clarissa and the kids a kiss for me!"

Acknowledging his slightly baffled farewell with an uplifted hand, she made her way to the crowded boardwalk and hurried in the opposite direction. She hadn't seen Shane in two days and wasn't prepared to see him now. Allison had come to the painful conclusion that there was no use spending time together because, sooner or later, their brief moments of harmony always ended. Being at odds with him made her miserable. More miserable than being near him, wanting him and knowing he would never be hers.

Nearing the post office, she noticed an unfamiliar man staring at her with peculiar intensity. She glanced away. When she looked that way again, he was gone.

Continuing on to the Wattses' homestead, the exercise helping to dispel her edginess, she let her mind drift to Norfolk and potential neighborhoods she should consider. Shane would not be pleased to know she was imagining a bedroom for Matilda done up in the little girl's favorite colors—yellow and white. With occasional rocks crunching beneath her boot soles, she jerked her chin up even though he wasn't around to see.

"It's my life," she announced to the vacant lane. Throwing out her arms, she startled a pair of pretty deep-blue and brown birds. "He has no say in what I do."

The instant the words left her mouth, she experienced misgivings. In the twins' case, that was so, she supposed. But Shane was in charge of finding Matilda a permanent home. She had huge doubts he'd agree to let her take Matilda in. He'd assume she couldn't provide enough love and attention for a third child. Well, he was wrong. Just like he was wrong about his potential as a spouse and father.

Allison didn't hear the stranger's approach. One minute she was walking along, lost in thought, and the next he loomed large in her path.

She stopped short, a cry slipping through her parted lips. "Who are you?"

It was the middle of the day. Surely he didn't have evil intentions…but they were alone here, nothing but trees and wildlife around for miles.

Beneath his battered hat, his hazel eyes burned with anger and some other emotion she couldn't pinpoint. "The father of the babies you stole."

Her stomach dropped to her toes. "Clyde Whitaker?"

He was young. She should've expected it, knowing Letty's age, but he was fresh-faced, clean-shaven and handsome in a mountain-man sort of way. Far different from his unkempt father.

"I've been watching you. Waiting for a chance to get you alone."

Unease lodged in her chest. "That was you at the post office."

"I wanna see my kids," he scraped out. Feet planted wide, he towered over her.

Nodding, she managed, "Of course. Come to the house anytime." Scooting to the right, she made to walk past him. "They're likely napping, but you could wait with Fenton—"

He seized her arm. "I want to see them without any nosy onlookers, understand?"

Annoyance sparked inside. "That may be difficult, considering Fenton is their great-grandfather and he's practically raised them."

Clyde scowled and lifted his fingers from her flesh. "Meet me at the old Lowell gristmill tomorrow afternoon. It's not far from the Wattses' place. A mile at most." He gave her the directions. "Three o'clock."

"Why would I do that?"

Anguish surged in his gaze. For a moment, his hard attitude slipped, and she glimpsed a vulnerable young man wrestling with grief. Then he clenched his fists. "Because, Miss Ashworth, in the eyes of the law, those are my kids. Not yours."

She stiffened. His implication was clear. "Can you give them the life they deserve? One that Letty would approve of?"

His mouth tightened. "If you don't let me see them—alone—you won't be leaving Tennessee with them. Not without a fight. Is that what you want for them?"

"No," she whispered.

"Lowell's gristmill," he repeated. "And make sure your good friend the sheriff stays home, you hear?"

Pivoting, he loped toward the woods.

Allison didn't linger to watch him disappear. Upset, she hurried home, needing to see the twins and reassure herself they were okay. Fenton and Matilda looked up in surprise when she burst through the door.

He lumbered up from the sofa. "Everything all right?"

"Yes." Affecting nonchalance, she deliberately smoothed the folds of her dress. "Everything is peachy. I, uh, was in need of a bit of exercise." Pointing to the stairs, she said, "The twins asleep?"

Matilda nodded, her gaze bouncing from Allison to Fenton. "I looked in on them five minutes ago."

Allison rubbed her hands together. "Thank you, Matilda. You're a devoted helper."

Avoiding Fenton's narrowed gaze, she drifted to the stairs. "Well, I think I'll go and rest a bit, as well."

She tiptoed into the bedroom she shared with the twins and spent several minutes soaking in their sweet, innocent faces relaxed in sleep. Clyde's threat still rang in her ears. If she didn't do as he wished, he was going to take them away. It was a risk she wasn't willing to take.

Chapter Twenty-Four

Three days until Christmas. In a normal year, Allison would be shopping for last-minute gifts and preparing for her trio's annual church performance of assorted carols. The level of excitement in the house would be palpable. The children weren't the only ones impatient for December 25 to arrive. The estate staff looked forward to the presents she and Clarissa chose for them—unique and specific to each person—and spending Christmas Day with their families.

A pang of homesickness hit her. Dismissing it, she finished bundling Izzy and Charlie into their gear and carried them to the living room below.

Fenton reentered the house, his hat low over his eyes and coat collar pulled up to shield his neck. *He could use a new scarf*, she thought inanely. *A useful Christmas gift.*

"Sure you don't want me to keep 'em here?"

"They've been cooped up too long." She fastened her green cloak's buttons with shaky fingers. Perspiration dampened her nape. "The sun's shining, and it's warmer today than it has been. A change of scenery will do them good."

"I don't mind manning the wagon for ya."

"I've driven plenty of buggies around Norfolk's busy streets. I can handle these mountain lanes."

Matilda descended the stairs. In spite of Allison's anxiety, she registered the girl's healthy color and the slight difference in the fullness of her cheeks. Regular meals were doing wonders for her. While her physical condition was improving, the uncertainty of her future meant her emotional state remained fragile. As soon as Allison had handled Clyde—*if* she managed that— she would speak to Shane. Enough delaying. Matilda needed a solution.

"Can I go with you?" She slid the locket between her two fingers back and forth on its chain.

Aware of the mantel clock's ticking, Allison went to her and squeezed her shoulder. "Not this time, sweetie." Seeing the crestfallen look Matilda tried to hide, she said, "I have an idea. Why don't you and I go to town one afternoon before Christmas?" Bending at the waist, she whispered, "We'll pick out something special for Fenton."

Interest leaped to life. "And for the sheriff?"

Straightening, she nodded. "Sure."

She tied her bonnet's strings into a neat bow and scooped Charlie into her arms.

Countless times in the hours since their isolated encounter, she'd considered seeking out Shane. But Clyde had insisted she come alone. No telling how he'd react if she flouted his wishes.

"Would you mind bringing Izzy outside?"

Fenton complied, following her into the yard and

placing Izzy in one of the makeshift cradles, long boxes made comfy with a nest of blankets. Allison situated Charlie, leaning down to give him a quick kiss on his velvet-soft cheek. Her throat was so thick she could hardly breathe. What if Clyde decided he wanted them for himself?

In those brief moments in his presence, she'd sensed there was goodness in him not present in his father. Working on a daily basis with people from all sorts of backgrounds had helped her develop discernment. She had to trust he simply wished to see that his children were all right.

Besides, there had to be something redeemable in him if Letty had loved him. She'd sought him out before and after the twins' birth. No way would the young mother have done that if she'd feared for her or her children's safety.

Pulse racing, she rounded the bed and, lodging her boot atop the wheel, climbed onto the seat and gathered the reins.

Fenton bid her goodbye. Matilda emerged from the house and latched on to a porch post. Allison waved and managed a tight smile.

The babies were quiet as the wagon rolled along the lane. Their stomachs full of warm milk and grits, they would likely drift to sleep before she reached the appointed meeting spot.

It wasn't long before the abandoned, overgrown gristmill came into view. At the sight of the lone figure pacing a line into the grass, she started to whip the horses around and flee. Instead, she eased them to a stop and waited.

Muscle jumping in his jaw, Clyde strode forward, hazel gaze wary. "You alone?"

She jerked a nod.

He craned his neck toward the bed. "Are they with you?"

"Yes."

When he started that way, she scrambled down and blocked his path.

Shame dawned in his green-brown gaze. "You don't trust me. I understand. But I promise I'm not a threat to you or my children. They're my flesh and blood. I'd never hurt them. I simply need to see them. Just once."

Convinced his earnestness was sincere, Allison stepped aside.

He walked to the rear of the bed. She followed on his heels and was afforded an unobstructed view of the raw emotion passing over Clyde's attractive features. His throat convulsed. Gingerly lifting a still-awake Charlie from his makeshift crib, he tucked him against his chest and peered intently into his face.

"Hey, little man. You look like your momma, you know that?" His voice cracked and, burying his face in Charlie's wispy hair, he exhaled a shuddery breath.

Allison's anxiety diminished. In fact, she felt as if she were intruding on a personal moment between father and son.

"He's a good baby," she said unnecessarily. "They both are."

Clyde's eyes were wet when he lifted his head. Reaching out, he fingered one of Izzy's curls. She blinked up at him.

His large, tanned hand anchored Charlie against his

chest. Continuing to caress Izzy's hair, he scraped out, "I should've been there for her. For them."

Allison was quiet. A hawk soared in a circular pattern overhead, its cry shrill. "Why weren't you?"

His features hardened. He started to put Charlie back in his bed. When the baby fussed, Clyde shot her an uneasy glance. "I wanna hold my daughter."

"Give Charlie to me." He passed his son awkwardly to her and picked up Izzy. Still too young to be wary of strangers, the infant swatted his cheek with her chubby hand and let loose a stream of gibberish. A rumble of laughter shook his chest. "You take after your momma, don't ya, little one?"

Allison's heart was torn. Anyone could see the man had regrets, and his fascination with his offspring was undeniable. But what did that mean for her and the twins' future? No matter what Shane said, if Clyde truly wanted to raise his children, no judge would deny him that.

"They look healthy," he said, looking to her for confirmation.

Shifting Charlie onto her other shoulder, she nodded. "They are."

"You probably won't believe me, but I loved Letty. I wanted to marry her."

"Based on your behavior, it is difficult to believe."

His expression could only be described as tormented. "We had no place to go. Her grandpa despised me. And my parents...they never approved of her. They insisted she was trying to trap me. I should've stood up to my pa. If I had a chance to do it over again, I would," he said fiercely.

Allison reminded herself of his youth. He and Letty

had been engaged in a forbidden relationship. Without family support and the means to sustain themselves in the face of an unplanned pregnancy, their options must've seemed nonexistent.

He hugged his daughter closer. "I should've tried harder to convince her to run off with me."

"You were willing to leave your home?" Shock punched through her. She'd assumed he shared his father's views.

"Wasn't sure how I'd earn enough to support a family, but I knew I wanted to be with her. But she wouldn't leave her grandpa." Unhappiness tugged at his mouth. "I got angry. I accused her of not loving me enough. We argued, and I told her to leave me alone."

Hurting for a girl she'd never met, Allison said, "What about when she came to see you after the birth? You refused to even meet the twins."

"What?" Astonishment mingled with denial. "No. She didn't do that."

"Fenton told me. He has no reason to lie," she said gently.

Shaking his head, he put Izzy in her bed and stalked into the field. Ripping off his hat, he put it over his face and suddenly his shoulders were quaking. Tears welled in Allison's eyes. She faced the other direction to give him privacy. Gentry was behind this. He had to be.

Charlie plucked at the cluster of blossoms on her bonnet. Dislodging his fingers, she put his hand to her lips and kissed his fingers. He smiled and babbled. Her heart fissured. There was so much more to this story than she'd imagined. The players were flawed, three-dimensional humans with real feelings. Both Clyde and Letty had made mistakes. Neither were blameless.

Clyde wasn't the evil blackguard she'd made him out to be.

Many minutes passed before his muted sobs ceased. When he returned to the wagon, he refused to meet her gaze. His skin was mottled.

"I've got matters to tend to at home." His hands balled into fists. "Once that's settled, I'll come to the Wattses'. You and I have decisions to make."

Momentous, painful decisions. Allison desperately wanted to ask him exactly what he intended to do. She refrained. This wasn't the time.

She prayed he'd visit her soon, because she wasn't sure how long she could wait and wonder and imagine the worst without losing her mind.

"You're gonna wear a hole in the floor." Pausing in his Bible reading, one finger marking his spot on the page, Fenton shot Shane a resigned glance.

Matilda sat cross-legged at the foot of the tree, playing with a set of paper cutout dolls she'd crafted from Allison's decorative paper scraps. He'd known something was amiss the moment she entered his office. Matilda didn't like the jail and wouldn't have come unless something big was troubling her. If she hadn't gone outside and seen the wagon turn in the opposite direction of town, he wouldn't have known to be concerned.

He crossed to the window for probably the fiftieth time. "If she's not home in ten minutes, I'm going to ride through these mountains and knock on every single door until I find her."

Starting with the Whitakers. His well-honed instincts told him Gentry or Clyde had something to do with her prolonged absence. What other reason would she have had to mislead Fenton and Matilda?

Staring out at the desolate landscape, he worked to contain the fear eroding his composure. Panic was there beneath the fear, waiting for him to weaken. He'd dealt with thieves, kidnappers and murderers. He'd even come close to meeting his Maker a time or two. None of that compared to what he was experiencing now. This past hour had been the longest of his life. If anything happened to her—

He bowed his head, his fingers digging into the windowsill. *I love her, God. So much that it hurts to look at her sometimes. I beg You to preserve her life. Keep her safe. Keep the twins from harm.*

Pivoting, he strode for his duster and Stetson. "I can't wait around any longer."

"How do you know where to start?"

"Gentry's will be my first stop." Anything was better than staying here and allowing his mind to catalog every single scenario.

"Maybe you should take your deputy with you."

"No time."

Temperatures in the high forties swirled around him as he pulled open the door. A blue jay fluttered into flight, taking refuge in the maple's high branches. The indistinct jingle of harnesses stopped him in his tracks. Squinting down the lane, he waited, heart hammering out an impatient rhythm. *Please be her. Please—*

At long last, the team and wagon came into view. Calling the news to Fenton, he bounded into the yard, his gaze pinned to the woman whose well-being meant more to him than his own life.

Beneath her bonnet's brim, Allison's features were

drawn and pale. The evidence of her tears tightened his gut. She looked extremely fragile, an unusual sight that filled him with foreboding. As soon as she guided the team to a stop, he inspected the wagon's rear space, his shoulders loosening at the sight of the sleeping infants.

Helping her down, he asked Fenton and Matilda to carry the children inside. "Allison and I are going for a short stroll," he murmured to the older man. "We'll be inside in a few minutes."

"Take all the time you need." Fenton's concerned gray gaze tracked Allison, who hadn't uttered a single word.

Wrapping his arm protectively around her waist, he guided her to the side of the house.

"I know you're angry with me." She turned toward him, eyes shimmering with emotion. "I can't bear it right this minute, Shane—"

"Shh." Urging her against him, he traced her quivering lips with his finger. "Sweetheart, angry is the last thing I'm feeling."

He brushed her inviting mouth with his and exhaled soul-deep relief. Allie was safe and sound in his arms. *Safe.* That's all he could focus on for several long moments. Then he registered her arms snaking around his neck, her fingers knocking his hat to the ground and whispering through his hair, the extraordinary sweetness of her kiss as she wriggled closer.

Joy exploded in his chest. What he felt for her was unlike anything he'd ever known…innocent and hopeful and noble. This love made him forget, if only for a little while, the nightmares dominating his past.

He skimmed her spine in search of the stray tendrils along her nape. If he had his way, he'd untie the ribbons beneath her chin and expose her flaxen hair to his exploration. But it was cold. And he needed to find out what had transpired to upset her so.

Trailing his fingers beneath her ears, over the ribbons and along her cheekbones, he registered her shiver as he eased the kiss to lingering, featherlight sweeps against her lips.

She murmured his name before lifting her head. Her happy gaze was tempered with a hint of perplexity. Wasn't hard to guess that she was searching for an indication from him that this embrace was significant, that it meant he had forever on his mind.

The joy he'd experienced minutes before fizzled out like firecrackers' ashes flickering to the earth.

That he loved her didn't matter. Didn't cancel out his lacking formative years. What mattered was that he *would* fail her. He had no doubt of that.

Sliding his hands along her sleeves, he gently disengaged her arms and, bringing her hands to his mouth, kissed each one in turn.

"Tell me what happened, Allison," he urged. "Where did you go? Why didn't you come to me for help?"

Chapter Twenty-Five

The resignation in Shane's hooded eyes was unexpected. After the tender kiss they'd shared, it was the last thing she wished to see. Disappointment spiraled through her. Nothing had changed.

"What happened?" she repeated dully, the brief spurt of happiness fading. She curled her arms about her middle. "Clyde Whitaker happened."

His gaze sharpened. "He approached you?"

"Yesterday. On my way home from seeing George off."

Biting out an exclamation, he edged closer. "He didn't harm you, did he?" His worried gaze swept the length of her.

"He's not like his father. We were mistaken, Shane. Fenton was wrong about him." Turning toward the mountains, she relived Clyde's emotional outburst. She told him everything that had transpired at the abandoned gristmill. "He loved Letty and planned to marry her. They argued, and Gentry used that to drive them apart."

She found it difficult to fathom how any father could willingly hurt his child.

"Does he…" He remained behind her. "Does he intend to raise them?"

"I don't know." Her voice sounded small and vulnerable, bruised like her heart.

He urged her around to face him. The evidence of his turmoil deepened her worry. "I'll help in any way I can, Allie."

A fresh onslaught of tears clogged her throat. The situation was impossible. *Nothing is impossible with God, remember?*

I trust You, Father, but I see my dreams slipping away. Izzy and Charlie. Shane. Will I be returning to Virginia the same as I left? Alone?

"What are you thinking?" he said.

"Why did you kiss me?" she blurted.

His lids flared before a shutter descended, closing her out. Shaking his head, he bent to retrieve his hat.

"I know you, Shane Timmons." She refused to let him retreat. Getting into his space, she declared, "You wouldn't have crossed that line if you didn't care about me."

"Our relationship is the last thing you should be worrying about."

"You admit we have one?"

"We're friends." Flicking a stray blade of grass from the crown, he put his hat on and speared her with an enigmatic gaze. "You're right. I do care. Very much."

Hope sprung to life. She reached out to him. "Shane."

"It's not enough." He flinched away, and she caught a glimpse of his misery. "No matter what happens with the twins, you're going home to Norfolk," he bit out.

"I could stay here." Desperation forced the words from her lips.

Visibly agitated, he flung his arms wide. "I can't be the man you want me to be, Allison. Why can't you get that into your head?"

She wrapped her arms around his strong body. "You already are," she exclaimed against his chest. "You simply can't see it. Your view of yourself is warped. Please let go of the past."

Beneath her cheek, his heart raced. His muscles twitched. When his arms came around her, she thought he was relenting. But he set her apart from him.

"I'm never going to marry you." His chest heaved. "Do you hear me?"

Aching clear down to her soul, she bit down hard on her lip to keep from crying. She nodded.

"I want to hear you say the words." His fingers tightened on her shoulders. "Say it, Allie."

Her vision blurred. Why was he bent on torturing them both? "Y-you won't m-marry me."

Shane's features twisted. He bowed his head in defeat. Releasing her, he turned and left without another word, and her heart broke for the second time that day.

On Christmas Eve, Allison woke before dawn with a vague headache that had persisted for days. She'd lain in her bed the night before, staring at the rafters and yearning for a few hours of blissful, mind-numbing sleep. What she hadn't counted on was reality invading her dreams. While Shane had dominated them, Clyde had made an appearance, too. Both men had been upset with her, and she'd woken with a heavy spirit.

Pulling on her housecoat, she padded over to the

cradles and, crouching down, listened for the reassuring sounds of their breathing. It was too dark to make out their faces, and she didn't want to light a lamp and risk disturbing them. Uncertainty her constant companion, she pressed her face into her hands and prayed yet again for answers. Clyde hadn't come that first day. Or the next. Yesterday she'd been convinced he'd appear.

Matilda and the children had picked up on her distress, despite her efforts to maintain a calm front. Matilda had retreated into subdued silence, and Izzy and Charlie had been fussy and refused to take their afternoon nap.

Drifting to the window, she pulled the curtain aside and soaked in the star-studded expanse. Was Shane warm in his bed, oblivious to the world around him? Was he, like her, having trouble sleeping? Or was he out there in the night somewhere, doing what lawmen do?

He'd left almost immediately after their excruciating exchange, stopping only to instruct Fenton to fetch him if Clyde showed up. What he was supposed to do if Clyde demanded she return his children, she didn't know.

The predawn hours were marked with tranquility. So when her peripheral vision registered movement, she clapped her hand over her mouth. Beneath the lone maple near the porch, a figure separated from the shadows. A single flame flared, and she recognized Clyde's youthful features.

Struggling into the first outfit her fingers encountered in the wardrobe, she tiptoed down the stairs and tugged her boots on, not bothering to lace them. Slipping outside, she winced as cold enveloped her. Allison marched across the yard.

"What do you think you're doing?" she whisper-shouted.

The flame had gone out, but she saw his body stiffen. "I, uh…"

"This is hardly appropriate." Folding her arms across her chest, she glared at him even though he wouldn't see the proof of her ire. She didn't have a younger sibling, but in that moment, she understood what it might be like to be a big sister. "Lurking around someone else's residence in the wee morning hours could get you shot!"

"No one was supposed to see me."

"Well, I did. You're fortunate I didn't scream the house down." Belatedly noticing the bundle at the tree's base, she softened her tone. "What's going on, Clyde?"

"I wanted to be near them," he admitted.

"You've been spying on me?"

He bristled. "They are *my* children."

Without her cloak, Allison was already chilled. The tips of her ears stung. "Let's go inside. I'll fix coffee."

After a long beat of silence, he nodded and gathered his belongings. Trying to be as quiet as possible, she led him through to the kitchen and lit several lamps before turning her attention to the stove. He paced behind her.

The kettle warming and cups set out, she said, "Why don't you have a seat?"

Another hesitation, and he sank into one of the chairs. Placing his hat on the one beside him, he smoothed his wavy, sandy blond hair. His eyes were the exact hue as Charlie's. Had he noticed how much his son favored him?

Joining him, she folded her hands in her lap. "I've been wondering what's been keeping you. Did you sort things with your father?"

Sliding his hands along his thighs, his upper lip curled. "There ain't no sorting things with him."

"I'm sorry to hear that." She noticed his ears and nose were bright pink, as were his cheeks. "Did you spend the night out there?"

"Not the whole night."

She raised an eyebrow.

He shrugged. "I've been here the past three evenings. Got here shortly after sunset and left after the last light went out in the house."

"What was different about tonight?"

"I don't know." Lashes sweeping down, he studied a spot on the floor. Odd how she couldn't find any of her initial dislike. Shane would probably think her naive, but she couldn't help it. She was sorry he'd endured heartache and had no chance to rectify past mistakes. Letty was gone. He had to live with his choices for the rest of his life.

Allison readied their coffee, thankful she at least knew how to do that much. Seated once again, Clyde accepted his with a grave nod.

His gaze met hers across the table. "You're from Virginia?"

"Yes. Norfolk."

"Guess you got a fancy house."

"It's true that I have the financial means to provide Izzy and Charlie with a comfortable life."

"I've been dirt poor my whole life," he mused, work-worn hands molded around the cup. "Don't see that changing."

"In my mind, love, guidance and emotional security are of far greater value."

Clyde studied her with open curiosity. "Why do you want to be their mother?"

"They've become precious to me." Allison had difficulty forming the right words, knowing he would weigh them, dissect her reasons. He hadn't made a decision yet, that much was obvious. "I've wanted a family... children...for many years. I've never been married, you see, so when I met those sweet babies in desperate need of a mother, I began to imagine myself in that role. As the days passed, they formed an attachment to me and I to them."

Blinking away the gathering tears, she angled her face away and plucked at the ends of her sleeves. Beyond the glass, dawn crept across the blue-black sky. Her entire body felt on edge, nerves stretched to their breaking point.

"Tell me about your life in Virginia."

Allison told him about her parents and George, her childhood and about Shane entering their world. She told him about her church, her friends, her charity work. She talked about her niece and nephews, too, hoping he'd see what a good life Izzy and Charlie could have.

Clyde quietly sipped his coffee, and she longed to read his mind.

"Letty would want her babies to grow up in a good home."

Her pulse skipped. Meeting his gaze once more, she soaked in his sorrow and the wish for a different outcome.

"You can provide that for them," he said gruffly. "But I can't let you take them away. I need to be a part of their life. For their momma's sake, I gotta be sure they're okay."

Her throat started to close up. "What are you saying?"

"You can raise them if you stay here."

Allison rose and, blindly dumping her mug's contents in the discard pail, gripped the counter's edge.

"You have a problem with that?"

"Not me." She envisioned Shane's reaction. How could they possibly coexist in this small town without making each other miserable? "I like Gatlinburg. I've made friends here."

"It's the sheriff, ain't it?" The chair legs scraped against the wood. He joined her at the counter. "I've seen you together. You don't think he'd like it if you stuck around?"

Unwilling to discuss Shane with him, she said, "If I stay, what role do you intend to play in their lives?"

"You wouldn't have to worry I'd take 'em back someday. I'll sign papers." His eyes darkened to midnight. Scraping his hand along his jaw, he said, "I can't give them the kind of life they deserve. Trust me, they don't want the Whitaker legacy. I just wanna know them, and I want them to know me."

"If someday I met someone I wished to marry, you'd have no say in my choice." While that was not likely, she had to make it clear he couldn't control her life.

His nostrils flared. "As long as the man you choose treats my kids right, I'm fine with that."

Allison touched his sleeve. "Spend the day with us."

"Huh?"

"I need time to consider everything. Besides, today is Christmas Eve. Do you have special plans?"

Anticipation flashed over his features. "What about Fenton?"

"He's a good man, Clyde. Give him a chance to get to know you."

He looked doubtful. "All right. I'll stay."

He'd rather be anywhere else but here.

The merry atmosphere inside the church clashed with his black mood. Adults talked and laughed together along the wooden pews. Near the front, Megan was attempting to corral the rambunctious children, while Lucian and their older kids were busy arranging the pageant props.

He'd never attended the Christmas Eve service before, and he wouldn't be here now if not for the reverend and Claude's insistence. What he wanted to do was hole up in his cabin and hibernate the whole winter long. If only he could sleep for months and wake up free of this constant, all-consuming pain and desolation, not to mention the burning anger he felt for himself, his faceless, coward of a father and his pathetic excuse for a mother.

He'd done the unthinkable. Instead of keeping his distance, he'd fallen in love with Allison. And, just as he'd feared, he'd wounded her. The memory of their last kiss and the destruction afterward kept him up nights. He was so sleep-deprived, he walked around town in a fog, his eyes gritty, his head pounding and his chest one huge, numb hole.

His gaze lit on the rough-hewn cradle filled with straw. This year, Christ's birth held a special significance. Jesus hadn't come to earth for everyone else *except* him. Shane was included in the ones He loved and wanted for His own.

I'm sorry, Lord. I realize my attitude isn't what it

should be. Help me focus on You and Your priceless gift. And I beg You, please prevent me from hurting Allison further.

"Good-sized crowd tonight." Ben had moseyed over to the far right corner where Shane stood alone, trying to blend in with the shadows. Sconces lining the space's outer walls provided the only light. "I don't see Allison, though. She is coming, isn't she?"

Readjusting his gun belt to set lower on his hips, he bit out, "I have no idea."

Ben's hearty chuckle sparked Shane's annoyance. "This has been a satisfying holiday season, I must say."

He ran a finger around the inside of his shirt collar. His suit coat wouldn't sit right on his shoulders. His waistband felt awry. Shane was uncomfortable in his own skin.

"Aren't you going to ask why?" His deputy had dressed up for the service, his unruly hair tamed into submission.

"Nope."

Shane focused once more on the rear alcove to his left, unwillingly searching for Allison. Would she show? Or would she stay away because she dreaded seeing him? He'd feel even guiltier if he caused her to miss the highlight of the season.

"I haven't had the opportunity to see you like this before." His green eyes danced. "For a while there, I suspected you weren't quite human. You were so controlled. So perfect. Then Allison Ashworth came to town, and suddenly you developed normal emotions. Glad to see you're like the rest of us common folk."

"Perfect? Me?"

Serious now, he said, "You're the finest lawman I've ever known."

"I'm only the second one you've worked with."

"No need to compare you to anyone else. I aspire to reach your standards. If I do, I know I've done my best for the folks of this town."

Shane looked out over the crowd, not really seeing any one individual as he processed his deputy's praise. He hadn't known Ben saw him as someone to model himself after.

"You do a fine job," he said gruffly. "Proud to work with ya."

Ben's wide grin reappeared. "I appreciate that, boss."

Unused to doling out praise, he pushed off the wall and gestured to the exit. "I'm going to take a walk around outside."

"I'll keep an eye on things in here."

Shane strode to the alcove. Rounding the corner, he almost collided with Allison, who had Izzy in her arms.

"Sorry," he rushed out, steadying her with a hand at her elbow. Her light, tantalizing scent washed over him, making him ache clear down to his boot soles. Her hair was a shining braid-halo about her head, and she was wearing that cranberry outfit that made him think of snowy mornings and hot cocoa and marital bliss. "Wasn't watching where I was going..." He trailed off as his gaze intercepted the young man behind her. "Allison?"

"Clyde's here at my request," she said stiffly. "Be nice."

Clyde met Shane's glower with an unflinching perusal of his own. He looked too natural carrying Charlie. Didn't they look like the proper family?

"Let's find a seat, shall we?" Allison directed over

her shoulder. Her wide green eyes swerved to him. "Would you mind, Sheriff?"

He realized he was blocking their way and had caused a line to form behind them. Stung by her distant manner, he edged back. *You brought this on yourself, Timmons.*

They walked past him. A small, mitten-encased hand slipped into his. Matilda smiled tentatively up at him. "It's Christmas Eve, Sheriff."

"That it is." He tapped her nose. "You must be getting anxious to open your gifts."

"There are four with my name on them!" Her eyes shone.

Allison had bought her another dress, he noted. This one was crafted of floaty, pristine white fabric and accented with a bright red sash about her waist. Her short hair had been combed to a high shine and adorned with a matching ribbon. She was flourishing in Allison's household.

"Any guesses what they might be?"

Her brow wrinkled. "I'm not sure. Maybe a new scarf or hat. Miss Allison likes pretty things."

His gaze involuntarily slid to the last pew nearest them. She and Clyde were engaged in what looked to be a serious discussion. Concern warred with the need to act. But she didn't seem to require his interference. Her lovely countenance exuded determination.

"Sheriff?"

"Hmm?"

"Know what I want most for Christmas?"

The hope in Matilda's eyes socked him in the gut. He'd failed her, just like he'd failed Allison. He'd allowed his worries over Allison and the twins to eclipse this little girl's very real and urgent need.

Tugging her aside, he crouched to her level. "I think I have an idea."

"I want to live with Allison and the twins."

Lord, give me wisdom. Gingerly smoothing a hank of hair behind her ear, he strove to reason with her. "Sweetheart, we've talked about this before."

She bounced with excitement. "Miss Allison's not going back to Virginia. She's gonna live right here. Mr. Whitaker asked her to stay in town, and she said yes."

His breath froze in his lungs. "Are you certain?"

"I overheard them talking this afternoon. Isn't it wonderful?"

Chapter Twenty-Six

Surely Matilda had misheard. As the congregation's voices lifted to the rafters in a reverent rendition of "Silent Night," Shane wasn't singing. His attention was on Allison and Clyde. Standing side by side, the babies in their arms, they appeared at ease in each other's company. A telling clue. They must've come to an agreement. Could it be marriage?

A roar of protest built inside him. He thrust his fingers through his hair, tugging at the ends. Allison was meant to marry for love. But if Clyde had issued an ultimatum, she wouldn't hesitate. She'd do it for Izzy and Charlie.

Shucking his suit jacket, he draped it over the hard-backed chair shoved against the back wall. It was roasting in the church's confines. He could find relief outside, but something kept him here. A penchant for torment, he supposed.

On Allison's other side, Matilda sang along, occasionally twisting around to look at him. Fenton was on the end, dapper in his black pants, white shirt and a bow tie that had to be a gift from Allison. Like Shane, the old man wasn't singing, but he looked content for someone who eschewed town life.

That was Allison's doing. The woman possessed an incredible ability to draw others in, to care and nurture and offer her whole self without asking for anything in return. In a few short weeks, she'd created a ragtag family, one he'd give anything to be a part of. *He* was supposed to be by her side, supporting her, loving her. Not Clyde. Not some faceless Norfolk businessman. Him.

The song ended, and the people resumed their seats. Clyde murmured something, and Allison smiled.

That smile pierced Shane's heart. How was he supposed to stand by and watch her hand her life and love over to another man? And if Matilda was mistaken, and Allison was planning to leave Tennessee, how could he survive her absence? Everything in him rebelled. He couldn't go back to his former way of living. Couldn't face that bleak existence.

He loved her. More than that, he needed her in his life. But after everything that had happened between them, would Allison be willing to give him a chance to show her how he felt?

Megan directed the children to take their places. As scores of other children had before them, they portrayed Mary and Joseph's welcoming of the Christ child, events that changed the course of mankind. His thoughts shifted to Jesus's purpose, His plan and, ultimately, His forgiveness.

Shane's father and mother had acted despicably. They hadn't sought forgiveness from their only child. But by withholding it, the only person he was harming was himself. What had a lifetime of resentment gained him? Fear and bitterness, that's what. The good people of

Gatlinburg thought he was courageous, when, in fact, he was afraid of a lot of things. Not the usual things, like outlaws and violence, but things common to everyone—love, family, relationships.

I need Your help, Father. I want to let go of the past, but I can't do it alone.

He was still pacing and praying when the program ended. Those in attendance started gathering their things, and he noticed Matilda had fallen asleep. Threading through those already making their way to the exit, he greeted Fenton and, ignoring Clyde, sought Allison's gaze.

The moment she saw him, her features grew guarded. Sadness filled him. He could only blame himself.

"Want me to carry her to the wagon?"

Shifting Izzy to her other shoulder, she glanced at the sleeping girl. "Yes, please."

While she and Clyde took the lead, Shane hung back with Fenton. Matilda was a slight weight in his arms.

He sensed Fenton's perusal as they traversed the grassy churchyard. "What's on your mind, son?"

His gaze glued to the couple yards ahead of them, he said, "Why didn't you send for me when Whitaker showed up?"

"He was there when I went down for breakfast this morning. She had it handled."

"She doesn't need me," he murmured without thinking.

"Allison is a strong woman, that's true. She can do a lot of things on her own. Still needs you, though."

Shane was accustomed to helping people in tangible ways—rebuilding after a fire, searching for lost possessions, getting injured folks to the doctor. While he was confident in his abilities as a lawman, this thing with Allison was different. He didn't know how to go about being one half of a relationship, whether it be as a suitor or fiancé or husband.

"Are they getting married?"

"Is that why you're walking around like a coonhound without his mate?" His eyes reflected amused shock. "The boy's nine years younger than her."

"He's a man, not a boy, and you know it. Plenty old enough to marry."

His amusement faded, and Shane knew he was thinking of his granddaughter. "As far as I know, he's given her permission to raise the twins. But she has to live here. I ain't heard no talk of marriage."

Shane fell silent as they neared the wagon, waiting until the babies were situated before settling Matilda in the back. Allison thanked him but offered nothing more.

Shane touched her arm. "We need to talk."

"You're right, we do. About Matilda's future."

"Among other things," he said. "Can I come over tomorrow?"

She hesitated. "Tomorrow's Christmas."

That she didn't wish to spend her most favorite day with him hurt. "The day after, then."

Her eyes went soft. "Do you have someone to spend Christmas with?"

"The O'Malleys."

"Good. I'm glad you won't be alone." Sincerity rang from her voice. "Good night, Shane."

Watching her climb onto the seat and ride off with her makeshift family, he felt like the loneliest man in the world.

"Merry Christmas, Allie."

* * *

"Thanks for including me, Allison."

Midafternoon on Christmas Day, hat in hand, Clyde's gaze swept the room a final time. The woolen scarf she'd given him—yet another gift meant for a friend in Norfolk and needed here instead—was wound about his neck. His humble surprise and gratitude over the simple gesture had brought tears to her eyes. He hadn't received much in the way of kindness in his home, she'd surmised. The decision to stay in Gatlinburg was the right one. Clyde's affection for his children was undeniable. After spending the past two days in his company, she had no doubt the twins would benefit from knowing their father.

After he'd gone, she began to pick up discarded ribbons and strips of plain brown wrapping paper. The twins were asleep upstairs, worn out after a full day of being entertained by Clyde and Matilda. Matilda was in her room, likely enjoying the book Allison had bought her. While her reading proficiency needed improving, she seemed content to pore over the many drawings until Allison or Fenton had time to read the story to her.

Allison paused before the tree and fingered a popcorn strand, remembering the brief bursts of happiness she'd experienced with Shane. Making snow angels. Crafting paper ornaments. Sharing dessert and cocoa on a deserted mountainside.

They could have tons more moments together, if only...

She lowered her hand, despondency dimming the joy of the day. Allison had played the *if only* game most of her life, ever since a fourteen-year-old boy had arrived and stolen her heart. It had to stop. She had to accept what was and forget dreaming about a reality that wasn't going to materialize.

God had granted her dearest wish—a family of her own. That Shane wasn't included caused her great sorrow. It was something she was going to have learn to live with. Perhaps someday in the distant future she'd be able to walk down Main Street and greet him without her heart splintering into pieces.

Taking the stack of paper and ribbons into the dining room, she deposited everything in the corner and turned to the table laden with leftovers. Without Fenton, they would've feasted on bread and cheese for Christmas dinner.

Through the windows, she heard male voices. Thinking Clyde had lingered to speak to Fenton, she didn't bother to investigate. She had carried a stack of dishes into the kitchen when she heard a rap on the main door.

Hurrying through to the living room, she swung it open. "Did you forget something?"

"Hi, Allie." His husky voice washed over like warm caramel.

"Shane."

His tall frame filled her vision. Dressed more formally than usual, he had on his cream-colored Stetson, camel-hued suit coat and a navy vest and shirt that molded to his broad chest.

"I know you preferred that I wait until tomorrow, but I have gifts to deliver." He indicated the bulging pillowcase thrown over his shoulder.

"The shops aren't open today."

His mouth curved into a tentative smile. "I did my shopping early."

Flustered, she retreated. He entered, his gaze lingering but a moment before sliding away. His presence seemed to shrink the room as he lined the paper-wrapped gifts on the coffee table. She studied his sun-tanned, capable-looking hands and wished she could latch on and not let go.

She smoothed her hair and hoped there weren't bits of mashed potatoes in the strands. "Izzy and Charlie are asleep, but I can get Matilda for you. Fenton's in the barn."

"How about I go and get him while you find Matilda?"

There was an earnestness about him that threw her off-kilter. Allison couldn't pinpoint what exactly was different. His mouth was softer, the lines of tension that usually bracketed it gone, and his eyes were brighter.

She gave her head a little shake. *You're being fanciful. Perhaps he's merely had a good day visiting with his friends. It is Christmas, after all. No doubt it's one of the most relaxing days of the year for a lawman. Folks were busy feasting and celebrating.*

"All right. I'll meet you back here."

With a half grin, he nodded and let himself out. Why was he so lighthearted all of the sudden?

When Matilda saw Shane, she threw herself in his arms. "Merry Christmas, Sheriff!"

His face relaxed further into full-blown affection. Ruffling her hair, he murmured, "Merry Christmas, Matilda."

Allison fought off the emotions threatening to overwhelm her. Shane handed out the gifts. Matilda didn't hesitate to tear into hers. Fenton sat on the sofa, watching with obvious pleasure. Like the other adults, he'd grown fond of the little girl.

"Look what I got!" she exclaimed, showing off her

assortment of peppermint sticks, hair ribbons and a set of marbles and jacks.

When he came to stand before Allison, he shot her a mock grimace. "What do you get the woman who has everything?"

Not everything, she wanted to protest. Opening the box, she gasped at the delicate garnet brooch nestled in creamy fabric.

"Do you like it?" he said, a furrow between his brows. "I couldn't decide between one that matched your eyes and this one. The red color put me in mind of Christmas, and I know how much you adore this time of year."

"It's exquisite." She removed it to get a closer look. "I'll treasure it. Thank you, Shane."

With a grave nod, he slipped his hands in his pockets, watching closely as she pinned it to her bodice.

"How does it look?"

"Perfect." But he wasn't looking at the jewelry. He was looking at *her*.

"Oh, I almost forgot." Allison brushed past him and retrieved those packages remaining beneath the tree. "These are for you," she told him.

Matilda crowded close as he opened them. He seemed pleased by the gifts—new gloves and a shaving set—and touched that they'd thought of him.

When he saw what was inside the box from her, his smile widened in surprise. "These are great, Allie."

"When I saw your journal collection, I sent George a letter and asked him to bring the latest editions."

She'd also tasked her brother with choosing a leather wallet for Shane and engraving his initials on it. He took his time inspecting it, his blunt fingers running along the smooth leather. His azure gaze brushed hers. "Thank you."

"I'll pass your thanks on to George. He picked it out."

"I have another gift for you, but I'm afraid I left it at home." He spoke with his gaze downcast, his long lashes obscuring her view.

"Another one? The brooch is more than enough." And no doubt had cost him many weeks' earnings.

Neatly laying his gifts aside, he stood and addressed her, the teeniest bit of stiffness entering his tone. "Will you come with me to get it?"

"Now?"

"Yes. Please."

"I don't know...the twins will wake up soon—"

"I'll see to Izzy and Charlie." Fenton waved off her objection. "You don't wanna disappoint the sheriff on a day like today, do you?"

Having no choice but to agree, she went to gather her bonnet and cloak. Shane had her horse saddled by the time she went outside. He exuded a familiar tension, and she wondered at his strange mood. Perhaps this was a mistake. Spending time alone with him would only serve to intensify her misery.

She wouldn't address the matter today, but tomorrow they would have a serious discussion about how they would navigate life together in this small town.

The ride to his house was blessedly brief. Shane wasn't inclined to converse, and he seemed lost in a world she couldn't access. In the blustery December afternoon, his cabin struck her as isolated and sad.

The inside was unchanged. No decorations, not a single piece of greenery to denote the season. She tried to ignore the melancholy that arrowed through her.

Standing uncertainly in the middle of the chilly room, she waited as he tossed his gloves and hat on his bed. "Um, make yourself comfortable. You can hang your bonnet here." He indicated a single hook by the door. "Your cloak, too, if you'd like."

As she removed her bonnet and gloves, Shane went to the single hutch in the corner and riffled through the contents. Finally, he closed the cabinet doors and turned to her. She couldn't see what he held in his hand.

His chest expanded in a ragged sigh. "I'm not sure how to do this." Beneath his tan, he looked pale. "I don't know what to say. Or how to say it."

"You're making me nervous, Shane."

"Right. Sorry." Hurrying over, he took her hand and guided her to the lone cushioned chair. "How about you have a seat."

Bewildered, she sat and arranged her skirts and waited.

"I knew you were special the moment I met you. We were both very young, but I was drawn to you. In my dark, miserable world, you represented joy and light." He began to pace, gesturing as he spoke. "I did everything I could think of to push you away. And I succeeded."

"That didn't stop me from caring."

"I know," he said softly, his eyes in turmoil. "I regret every moment of pain I've ever caused you."

She bowed her head. Was this an elaborate attempt at an apology? "I think I should go."

"No!" His vehemence brought her gaze up. "Please stay, Allie. Hear me out."

Lips pressed together, she nodded and told herself

that all she needed to do was stay strong for the next few minutes and then make her escape.

His throat worked. "When I learned you were coming, I arrogantly thought I'd do what I'd done in the past. It worked then. Surely it would work again." His mouth curved into a self-deprecating smile. "I've been a first-rate idiot. It's a wonder you've put up with me."

Allison wanted to tell him none of that mattered. That the pain was worth it if it meant they could be together. More than anything, she wanted to tell him she loved him.

She didn't dare.

"Many others would've given up. They would've told me off. Refused to spare me a moment of their time." He went on his knees before her, drawing a gasp. "But not you. You're an amazing woman, Allie. I've never met anyone who could hold a candle to you."

Shane's gaze warm with ardent admiration, he took her hand and pressed something hard and cold into her palm. "I know I'm confusing you. Maybe this will explain my feelings."

Allison's breath caught. The plain gold circle was polished to a high shine. Not a single nick or scratch marred its surface. "It's a wedding band."

"Quinn wasn't thrilled that I interrupted his breakfast this morning, but when I explained my reasons, he graciously opened the store so I could pick this out."

Hope unfurled in her chest, but she needed to be sure. Needed to hear him voice his intentions. "This is the gift you couldn't wait to give me?"

"This has to be the worst marriage proposal in history." With a groan, he bent his head, his forehead resting against her knee.

She gingerly smoothed his hair, relishing the blondish-brown strands' silken softness. "Talk to me, Shane."

Straightening, he stared deep into her eyes, hiding nothing of what he was feeling. "It's hard to put this into words, but here it goes... I know that I admire your compassion and determination. I adore your smile. Your laughter makes my petty problems fade into the background, and your zest for life makes me realize I've been far too serious for too long. I need to learn to have fun, and you can teach me that." Reaching out, he reverently traced her cheek. "I know that I don't want to live another day without you. I want you to be my wife."

Her eyes filled with tears. "I never thought I'd hear you say those words."

He cupped her cheek. "Ah, sweetheart, I forgot to say the most important ones. I love you, Allison. I've loved you for a while... I just didn't know how to recognize it. If you'll let me, I'll spend the rest of our lives making up for the tears I've caused you. I'll spend my days finding ways to make you smile. What do you say?"

"I love you. I think I've loved you since that first day. But I have to be sure this is what you want. You won't be taking on a wife, but an entire family. Izzy and Charlie. Matilda. Life with us won't be easy. It'll be messy and demanding. I have to know you won't shut me out again. I couldn't take that."

His expression turned grave. "I don't know how to be a husband or father, but with God's help and yours, I'll give it everything I have. I'll need you to be honest with me and tell me if you sense that I'm withdrawing. I'm not adept at expressing my feelings, as you've seen, but I give you my solemn promise that I won't shut you out again."

Overwhelmed, feeling as if a lifetime of impossible wishes were being granted her, she laid her hand against his cheek. "Surely this is a dream."

"If you say yes, it'll be a dream come true."

"Yes! Yes, I'll marry you."

"Yes?" His clear blue eyes lit with happiness, and his smile dispersed any lingering doubts. "Can I kiss you now?"

At her nod, he framed her face and kissed her with a tenderness that made her heart sing. The past no longer lingered between them. There were no questions, no reservations. Shane *loved* her. Holding him closer, she basked in his affection, amazed that he was hers.

He raised his head far sooner than she wanted. Grinning lazily, he made up for that by brushing sweet kisses along her cheek, temple and forehead.

"You're right," he murmured, his breath fanning her eyebrows. "This does feel like a dream."

"I always thought I'd have a spring wedding," she mused.

Lifting her hand, he kissed her knuckles. "I'd wait a lifetime for you, Allie."

"I've waited for you since I was twelve. Spring seems very far off." She brushed a stray lock of hair off his forehead. "Do you think we could find a place to live by February?"

"Sweetheart, if that's all that's holding us up, I'll find a place before the new year."

"I like the way you think." Allison laughed and pulled him close again.

Epilogue

One year later

Shane let himself into the farmhouse, sacks of roasted chestnuts warming his pockets. He hung up his Stetson and shrugged out of his coat. The place was quiet. It shouldn't be at this time of day, not with eighteen-month-old twins and a gregarious twelve-year-old around.

"Hello? Where is everybody?" he called, unfastening his gun belt. "I've got a treat to share."

The patter of little feet echoed along the upstairs hallway.

"Sheriff's home!" Matilda assisted her siblings down the stairs, her face bright with excitement. After a year of living with them, she still called him by his title. She treated him as if he were her pa, though, and that made him happy.

Giving her long braid a gentle tug, he chucked her chin. "How was your day?"

"Allison taught me how to make gingerbread," she announced proudly, eyes dancing.

"Did she now? I thought I smelled molasses when I walked in."

Not satisfied with the basics Fenton had passed on in the early days of their marriage, his wife had appealed to the O'Malley women for further instruction. He had zero complaints about her cooking skills these days.

"Papa." Izzy and Charlie tugged on his pant legs, impatient for their daily greeting. One by one, he swung them up for hugs and sloppy kisses. Their giggles tickled his ears.

He'd never tire of this...being these kids' father and Allison's husband. Not every day was picture-perfect, but whose life was? Their home—the cozy white farmhouse with green trim in the shadow of the Smoky Mountains, the house where he'd fallen in love with Allie and the one he'd purchased from the Wattses—was marked with love and understanding and patience.

Fenton was a treasured part of their family and a regular visitor. His health had stabilized since he'd started getting more rest. The farmhand that Shane had hired went a long way in easing Fenton's burdens.

Clyde's visits were far less frequent. Unable to reconcile with his father, he'd worked odd jobs across the state of North Carolina, unable or unwilling to settle down. He'd kept his word, though. He'd given his permission for Shane and Allison to adopt the twins and was content to be known as a favorite, albeit distant, uncle.

Glancing toward the dining room, he wondered what was keeping Allison. It was her habit to welcome him along with the kids, and he was eager to see her.

"I got something for you." He placed the sacks in her hands.

"Chestnuts!" She inhaled deeply. "Thanks, Sheriff."

The twins crowded her in efforts to peer inside.

"Can I share with them?"

"Of course. You'll have to shell them, though. And make sure the children stay seated while they eat. No running around."

"Yes, sir."

He leaned down to ruffle Izzy's wild curls and tap Charlie on his button nose before they joined Matilda at the coffee table.

Whistling a favorite Christmas carol, he laid his sheriff's badge on the side table and walked to the foot of the stairs. "Allie?"

"I think she's in the kitchen," Matilda told him.

Passing the dining table decorated with a red-and-ivory cloth and topped with greenery and candles in shining holders, he entered the sweet-smelling kitchen. Trays of gingerbread men covered the work surface in the middle of the room. His wife was at the other counter drying dishes.

"Hello, beautiful." Putting a hand on her shoulder, he bent to kiss her cheek. The wetness there surprised him. "Hey." Tipping her chin up, he inspected her tearstained features with concern. She'd been distracted the past few weeks, which was unlike her. "What's the matter?" Another thought hit him. "George and Clarissa are still coming next month, right?"

"As far as I know, they are."

He exhaled. Allison was looking forward to seeing her family, especially her niece and nephews.

"Then why are you crying?"

"Don't mind me." Averting her face, she reached for a spoon to dry. "How was your day?" She dashed the moisture away, not meeting his gaze.

"Other than the fact Ben has broken another young lady's heart, and my lunch was interrupted by her tirade, it was rather uneventful."

"Hmm."

Shane's gaze widened. Allison shared his opinion about his deputy's disregard for the local ladies' finer feelings, and normally she would've demanded more information.

Gently taking the towel and spoon from her hands and laying them aside, he said, "Let's sit." Guiding her to the small table, he sat and pulled her down beside him, curving his arm around her shoulders. "Talk to me, Allie."

"I can't."

Something inside him froze. "You haven't had a problem telling me what's on your mind before." This past year of marriage had taught him so much. Together, they'd worked hard to be open and honest with each other. He trusted his wife as he'd trusted no one else.

"I'm afraid you're not going to be pleased with what I have to tell you." When she finally turned her face up to his, her green eyes shimmered and her lips trembled. "Our house is full. Our days are busy. The twins are into everything and only going to need more attention in the coming year. Matilda will need help with school reports and navigating friendships—"

"Allie." Cupping her cheek, he peered deep in her eyes. "I love you. I like that our life is messy and chaotic, because it means I'm not across town, alone in that cabin where the quiet was deafening. I chose this life with you, remember?"

The love she held for him surged in her eyes, and as always, it humbled him. Each and every day, he thanked God for giving him a second chance with this woman.

He'd been blessed with what he'd always wanted—a family of his own.

"I love you, too. I—I don't know if you're ready, though… I mean, I know we talked about more kids, but—"

"More kids?" His heartbeat hammered in his ears.

Her gaze wide and hopeful, she bit her lower lip and nodded. "I've been tired lately. And sick to my stomach. I went to see the doctor today. He told me that I'm about eight weeks along."

Easing back, he examined her middle, stunned that his and Allie's baby was nestled there. "You don't look any different."

Her laugh was shaky. "That's all you have to say?"

Framing her face with his hands, he kissed her for long moments, emotion rising up within him. His eyes grew wet as he gently rubbed her middle. "This baby is as precious to me as you are."

Happiness wreathed her face. "Truly? You're fine with this?"

"Oh, sweetheart, I'm not fine. I'm awestruck. Over the moon. Pleased as punch." Kissing her again, he whispered, "And very, very blessed."

Circling her arms around his neck, Allison smiled, at last free of worry. "Wouldn't it be funny if we had twins?"

He shot her a look of mock horror. "If that's the case, Fenton is moving in with us."

She laughed, and Shane joined her. He was confident that whatever the future might bring, they'd walk through it together.

* * * * *

SPECIAL EXCERPT FROM

LOVE INSPIRED

INSPIRATIONAL ROMANCE

When a therapy dog trainer must work with her
high school crush, can she focus on her mission
instead of her heart?

Read on for a sneak preview of
Their Unbreakable Bond *by Deb Kastner.*

"Are you okay?" Stone asked, tightening his hold around her waist and gripping one of her hands.

"I— Yes." She didn't have time to explain to Stone why this had nothing to do with her sore ankle, nor why avalanches were her worst nightmare and that was the real reason why she'd suddenly swayed in his arms.

Not when there was work to be done. There were people in Holden Springs who needed help, and she knew she should be there.

Tugger whined and pressed against her leg as he'd been taught to do as a therapy dog. He could tell her heart rate had increased and her pulse was pounding in her ears, even if she didn't show it in her expression, although there was probably that, too. The dog was responding to cues most humans couldn't see, and Felicity reached out and absently ran a hand between Tugger's ears to steady her insides.

"Have they set up a temporary disaster shelter yet?" she asked.

"Yes. At Holden High School," her sister said. "They're using the cafeteria and the gym, I think. I'd go myself except I have clients in the middle of service dog training back at the center. Do you mind taking Tugger and heading out there?"

Felicity did mind. More than anyone would ever know, because she never talked about it, not even to her siblings. But now was not the time to give in to those feelings. She could cry into her pillow later when she was alone and the people of Holden Springs were safe.

"I'll take Tugger." She nodded. "And Dandy, too," she said, referring to a young black Labrador retriever who was part of the therapy dog program.

"I can tag along, if there's anything I can do to assist," Stone said. "That way you'll have an extra person for the dogs."

Felicity was going to decline, but Ruby spoke up first. "Thank you, Stone. They need all the help they can get. From what I hear, there are a lot of families who were suddenly evacuated from their homes."

"It's settled, then," Stone said. "I'm going with you."

Felicity didn't feel settled. The last thing she needed was Stone alongside her. It would distract her from her real work.

She sighed deeply.

A bruised ankle.

Stone's unnerving presence.

And now an avalanche.

Could things get any worse?

Don't miss
Their Unbreakable Bond *by Deb Kastner,*
available January 2022 wherever
Love Inspired books and ebooks are sold.

LoveInspired.com

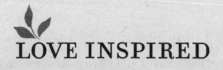

LOVE INSPIRED

Stories to uplift and inspire

Fall in love with Love Inspired—inspirational and uplifting stories of faith and hope. Find strength and comfort in the bonds of friendship and community. Revel in the warmth of possibility and the promise of new beginnings.

Sign up for the Love Inspired newsletter at **LoveInspired.com** to be the first to find out about upcoming titles, special promotions and exclusive content.

CONNECT WITH US AT:

 Facebook.com/LoveInspiredBooks

Twitter.com/LoveInspiredBks